VOICES ON THE WIND

Evelyn Anthony

ARROW BOOKS

Arrow Books Limited
62–65 Chandos Place, London WC2N 4NW

An imprint of Century Hutchinson Ltd

London Melbourne Sydney Auckland
Johannesburg and agencies throughout
the world

First published by Hutchinson 1985

Arrow edition 1986

Printed and bound in Great Britain by
Anchor Brendon Limited, Tiptree, Essex

ISBN 0 09 945830 6

To my dear friends,
Derrick and Hella, with love

1

They were making the descent on London; he looked briefly out of the window at the familiar landmarks: the wide silver ribbon of the Thames, with the neat suburban houses red-roofed in the sunshine as they approached Heathrow. He thought of England as a patchwork quilt. Small, cultivated squares of colour. Even the vast sprawl of Greater London had a pattern seen from above. He didn't think England was a beautiful country. It was an island which tried to be a continent, boasting of its variety in landscape and native architecture. There was no true sweep and grandeur about it. Everything was on a tiny scale. He didn't admire the miniature. He didn't like the people any better than their country. He checked the time; the flight was on schedule. He had allowed two hours to reach the little Sussex village. Just about lunchtime. She would be at home. She never went away for weekends. For the last two years she had spent most of her time alone. The groundwork had been thorough, but it hadn't given him a mental picture. The photographs were taken long ago. The face had a ghostly quality, like the snaps of dead heroes, their caps at a jaunty angle. He couldn't imagine what she would be like. He passed through customs, picked up his hired car and set out for Amdale village. A little English gem, the Shell guide book described it. He drove

7

within the speed limit, still on schedule. It wouldn't do to be stopped by the police for speeding. He turned down the gentle slope leading to the T-junction, and he could see the spire of Amdale church, beckoning above the trees. It was just after twelve o'clock.

When the telephone rang at nine thirty she knew it was her daughter, Dorothy. The excuse for cancelling the visit was quite genuine. She was so sorry but the children had been asked to go sailing and she didn't like to disappoint them. She was sure her mother understood and she promised they'd all come on their next half-term. Katharine Alfurd listened to the brisk voice until it paused, and then said, yes of course, quite right not to drag the boys down for a boring lunch when they could sail instead. No, no, she'd got masses of things to do – she hadn't got round to preparing any food. It didn't matter in the least. Give them all her love, and yes, dear, see you soon. It was very childish to mind. Ridiculous to have that sting behind the eyes as if she might be idiot enough to cry. But she had been looking forward to seeing her grandsons.

It was a beautiful day, that was something. She could do some gardening. A waste to watch television when the weather was so lovely. She was sick of most of the programmes. She made breakfast, fed her little Jack Russell terrier, talked to it and promised a nice long walk. It sat and looked at her, eyes bright and full of love, the stump of tail beating a tattoo on the floor. Her husband had given her the puppy six months before he died. Perhaps he knew she would be lonely. He hadn't been very fond of his daughter, even when she was quite small.

A bossy little prig, he said to Katharine once, when Dorothy was grown up, and he'd been especially irritated by her. God knows where she gets it from – certainly not from you, darling. Nor from him, she thought, remembering the incident that morning. A changeling child, planted by some malicious fairy, to perplex the parents. Criticizing Dorothy

8

made her feel guilty. Her husband had wanted a boy; she had wanted one too. No doubt that had been conveyed to Dorothy. You never knew how much children sensed subconsciously. She had an expression of patient disapproval when she came to the cottage. Katharine could see the sharp appraisal of how she was looking after the house and keeping the garden tidy. She was horrified because the terrier slept in Katharine's bed and snuggled into the armchair. She lectured her mother about smoking too much, and became quite agitated over the gins and tonics. But going down to the village pub was what upset her most. Katharine was going over in her mind the scene when they were last together.

'Mother,' the voice was shrill in her memory, 'Mother, you've got to realize that you're letting yourself down in the village. You can't go and sit in the bar and bore people to death with all that stuff about the war. Don't you realize nobody cares? They only laugh at you – What would Daddy say?'

I don't know, Katharine imagined the answer, because he never wanted me to talk about it either. She didn't remember what she'd really said to that.

'Don't tell me you talk to strangers? I suppose you buy them drinks?' What a rasping voice, filling the little kitchen and ringing in the ears.

She'd been proud of her answer to that. 'No, as a matter of fact, they buy drinks for me.' It had been a nasty quarrel, followed by a long letter from Dorothy apologizing and then resuming the lecture. Katharine read it, was thankful for the effort to make peace, and ignored what was said. Of course, it was sensible; most people would agree that she shouldn't spend her time and her limited money on haunting the bar in her local pub, looking for someone to talk to. It was dangerous, her daughter pointed out, and that made Katharine laugh. I know more about danger than you'll ever know. And even now, I can take care of myself. One doesn't forget lessons learned like that. She washed up the china and the dog's bowl, dusted the sitting room, picked out the faded flowers from the vase on top of the television set, looked at her watch. The garden was small, a perfect size for the retired couple. Very nice trees and shrubs, a patch of easily mown lawn, and a small border that kept her busy. But not busy enough. She called the terrier. It bounded after her. It was a comic little dog, like Toby in the Punch and Judy show. Children didn't look at such things now. It had always made her laugh. And she had never lost her capacity to see the funny side of herself. It was a great help in adversity. A great help now, when loneliness and boredom were the enemy and the guns had been silent for forty years. She said out loud in the sunny garden, 'Well, Kate, no grandchildren today, but no Dorothy either. So to hell with the weeds. Polly, we'll take ourselves down to the Bear for a little lunch. There might be someone interesting in today – you never know.'

She took trouble to do her hair and put on lipstick. Age had no damned compensations, whatever people said. Luckily she had kept her figure. The Irish skin and colouring didn't fade with the years. She checked her money, counted out some cigarettes, slipped the lead on the terrier. They allowed Polly into the bar. Kate knew it was because they were sorry for her. Her husband had been born in Amdale. Not in the cottage but in the old Georgian house on the edge of the green. People from London lived there now. She and Robert had never met them. She locked up, pandering to her daughter in her mind, and despising herself for doing it. But these days you never knew. . . . She set off down the village street, Polly trotting gaily at her side. The man who had flown in from Paris watched her go.

The lounge bar was empty when she came in. It was early, of course; she wouldn't have to sit there for long before someone turned up. She smiled at the man polishing glasses.

'Good morning, Jim.'

'Morning, Mrs Alfurd. What can I get you – the usual?'

'Yes, please.' She settled on a stool, the terrier at her feet. The bright smile didn't deceive Jim. She looked miserable.

10

Behind her back he tipped an extra measure into the gin and tonic. He hadn't been in the village long, but his governor said she had been a smashing looking woman when she first came to live at Amdale. The Colonel was very popular. No money, like a lot of people. After his death she went a bit eccentric. Started talking a lot of nonsense about herself, buttonholing complete strangers when the locals wouldn't listen any more. Always a lady, though; just a bit over the edge being alone. But she did drive the customers away. You could lose her on a crowded Saturday with a lot of passing trade, but she was a right pain if there were only a few people and she could get her hooks into someone. Kate lit a cigarette, sipped the drink. Damn Dorothy for not bringing the little boys. They were such fun and she'd made a special pudding and bought a lot of food she couldn't possibly eat.

The man saw her through the window, and pushed the door open. He moved quietly, never letting a door slam, not advertising his arrival in a room. He came up beside her and slid on to the next stool. He felt her look at him.

'Good morning.'

He turned, smiled and said, 'Good morning.' There was no sign of Jim; he had gone through to customers in the other bar.

Looking at her face to face the old photographs made sense. The snap of a girl with short hair and the unbecoming Service cap. A picture taken on a scorching August day when she sat in the sun's glare on the beach, bare-legged and laughing. The photograph had been torn across, and stuck together. She must have been beautiful, with that skin and those blue-green eyes.

'It's a lovely day,' she said. 'Are you staying in the village?'

He shook his head. Jim came in and he ordered a glass of wine.

'No, Madame. It's very charming. Do you live here?'

'Just down the road.' She lit another cigarette, offered one to him. He hated the brand, but he took it and thanked her. She gave a little sigh and relaxed. He was a nice man, quite

11

young. And French. What a coincidence, to find a compatriot on a morning when she was feeling particularly low.

'You're from Paris?'

He looked surprised. 'Yes; how did you know?'

Kate laughed. 'Well, you're obviously French and I just guessed. I'm very good at accents, I've got a natural ear. But French is no problem for me. I was born and brought up there. Although I'm English.'

'How interesting. When did you leave France?'

Kate finished her drink. It tasted rather strong, and she was feeling confident. Not the lonely old bore that everyone avoided, gassing on about herself. At last she had met someone who would really be interested. She took courage and called out, 'I'll have another, Jim.' Then she turned round to the stranger. 'My family came to England in 1940. Mother was French, so we all talked French at home. My name is Kate Alfurd.'

'Paul Roulier,' he said. 'Please, let me buy that. Do you go back to France often?'

'Not since 1947,' she said.

'What a pity. You should make a visit.'

'Do you know Nice?'

'Yes, very well. I worked there for three years.'

'I wouldn't recognize it,' she said. 'But then I was there in funny circumstances.' It was easy to launch out with strangers, but she found the Frenchman inhibiting. Nobody believed her; there were times when she had begun to listen to herself and doubt. Her daughter never talked about it, as if it was something that embarrassed her, and Robert, her husband, had kept his part a secret from their closest friends. If this man thinks I'm lying or making it up, she thought, I won't have any real identity left. Maybe I shouldn't take the chance. Maybe I should go home.

He saw the hesitation. He said in French, 'Madame Alfurd, I would be so interested to hear about it. I would like some lunch. Please will you join me?'

12

As if it were a challenge she replied. Her French was faultless, the accent slightly provincial. 'That's very kind of you, Monsieur Roulier. The smoked trout is excellent, I always have that on a Saturday here. And if you are really interested in my story, I'd be delighted to tell you.' The beautiful smile appeared again. He couldn't help being attracted by it. 'I'm afraid I've bored everyone to tears for miles around. I hope I won't bore you.'

He took her to a corner table; it was standing on an uneven floor. The wobble maddened him. He put a piece of folded paper under the shorter leg.

'If they're bored by you, they must be very stupid,' he said. He had very light blue eyes; a rare smile that seldom reached them. There was something that she felt akin to, although the age difference was at least twenty years. 'Please tell me about the time you were in Nice. Why was it "funny", as you said in English?'

Kate said simply, 'Because I went back in 1944. I worked for the Resistance. You know the Nazi war criminal, Eilenburg, they extradited from Chile last month?'

He nodded. 'I've read about him. The "Butcher of Marseilles". There's been a furore in France about the trial.'

Kate said, 'I knew him too. Can you believe that?'

'Why shouldn't I believe it?' Several couples had come into the bar. There was a level of noise and some laughter, but they didn't hear it. His concentration upon her was so intense she wasn't aware of anyone else being there. She leaned back, and suddenly she looked tired and near her age.

'Because nobody else does,' she said. 'Nobody believes a word or gives a damn. They think I'm dotty because I live alone since my husband died. But it's true; I worked with the Dulac network until the Gestapo broke it up. I worked as radio operator for Jean Dulac. I know what happened and I know what Eilenburg did. But he wasn't the worst. The real criminals have never been touched. There's some of us left

13

who'd like to see them dragged out to stand in the dock with him. And they weren't Germans.'

Somebody told a motorist's joke and there was a loud burst of laughter like gunfire. The little terrier barked in response. 'I know that,' Paul Roulier said. 'That's why I've come to England. To talk to you, Madame Alfurd. Will you help us find them?'

At the door of her cottage, Paul Roulier had said, 'Of course, you need to think about it. But I have to know soon, Madame. There isn't much time.'

How can silence be so loud, she thought, picking up the little dog, holding it on her lap like a shield. I can hear my own heart beating. God, what have I done with his telephone number – she searched her bag in a panic, only to find it neatly written on a business card, the name of a modest London hotel inked in above.

'Will you help us find them?' No more than that; no attempt to persuade her afterwards, just the short walk back to her front door and the cool handshake. 'I have to know soon. There isn't much time.' SS Standartenführer Christian Eilenburg was in the prison hospital in Marseilles. The evidence was being gathered for a trial that was already tearing France to pieces before it opened. His crimes would be punished, but what about the others – so many sins had been hidden, the sinners protected. She sat on, chain-smoking, the dog asleep. For a long time she used to see their faces, when she closed her eyes and tried to sleep. Her companions in arms who were also her friends. Judy, who fell in love and paid a dreadful price . . . Fred . . . Ma Mère, who was too old to be in it . . . Janot her son . . . Jean Dulac. She had spoken his name that day to the strange Frenchman. He was so real in her mind's eye she could have touched him. Dynamic, inspiring, a born leader who was a hero to men and women. 'A great man,' Katharine Alfurd said aloud. 'They put a statue up in the market square after the war. I heard about it, but I didn't want to see it. Nobody must mention your clay feet, my darling, because at the end you redeemed all those terrible mistakes you made.' She stood up, confronting the memories suppressed for so long. 'I loved you so much. I loved you, but I couldn't save you, because you wouldn't listen. You just laughed and kissed me and it was too late then. But there was you, Pierrot. You saved my life and I tried to get you hanged for it –'

Forty years ago. She had married, soon after the war, had a child, settled down to a normal life. Which meant that she had given in, because she knew she couldn't win. Her husband had persuaded her that it was hopeless to continue. Pointless to torture herself over what was past. She could remember the night very clearly. They were nestled close together in bed, talking as they often did after making love. It was always a vulnerable time for her. 'Give up, my darling. There's nothing you can do, and there isn't any proof. Put it out of your mind once and for all, and for God's sake let's be happy. Let the dead rest in peace.' That was the moment when she finally accepted defeat. Judy; Fred; Janot; Ma Mère. Jean Dulac, her lover, whom she had never really stopped loving. And Philippe Derain, who was Pierrot. That was why she couldn't stop talking about it now, telling perfect strangers who thought she was making it up. Because she was guilty and the dead were not at rest. In the night's silence she heard their voices on the wind.

She had never mentioned her wartime life, nor had Robert Alfurd. When he died it was as if she was released from a vow of silence she didn't know she'd taken. Naturally, nobody believed her. Now Christian Eilenburg was in the spotlight. Forty years ago had become Now. Fate, or God, if you believed in Him, had given her a second chance to put those ghosts to rest. The terrier ran to the garden door and looked expectant. 'Yes, Polly dear, we'll have our walk. As soon as I've done this.'

She was put through to Roulier's room, and he answered as if he had been waiting for the call. 'This is Katharine Alfurd. You'd better come down and see me. Yes, tomorrow would be fine.' She hung up. A sentence floated into her mind; it had no connection with the brief conversation. The candle of the wicked shall be put out. From the Old Testament. Of course, it was a coded message, broadcast from London. There had been a group of them crouched round the forbidden radio on the top floor of a deserted factory. She remembered the excitement when the message was repeated. How they embraced each other in their joy. The candle of the wicked. . . .

'You bastard,' she said quietly. 'Whoever you are, you'll pay for that.'

Paul Roulier put through a call to Paris. His exchange was short. 'I made contact and I'm going there tomorrow. It may take some days but I'm confident it's going to work.'

They had moved him to the prison hospital. His blood pressure was already low after the long flight from Chile. A few days after the first examinations had begun, Christian Eilenburg had a heart attack. When he recovered, he merely smiled. He accepted the pills and submitted to the tests, and all the time his eyes mocked them. Wouldn't it be ironic if he died, just when he was in their hands and they were preparing him for sacrifice? He could cheat them at the last, by dying before the trial. How frustrating for his enemies, how bitter for the people crying for revenge. And how convenient for others, who were cursing the Chilean Government that had given him up. After they had felt safe for so many years. They must be praying for him to die. A week after the attack, the senior police doctor examined him.

'You've improved,' he said. 'The reading is only slightly below average. You'll live, Eilenburg, and I'm going to make sure that you do.'

The prisoner glanced up at him. 'My heart is strong,' he said. 'It won't give out again. Doctor, how old are you?'

'Thirty-three.' The answer was curt. He didn't want to talk to the man. Treating him was bad enough.

'Why should you care whether I get to a court or not? You weren't even born till the war was over.'

'I care about what you did,' the answer snapped back at him. 'You and the others who got away. And I'm not a Jew, if that's what you think. I'm French!'

Eilenburg smiled. His false teeth had been taken away when he was ill. The mouth was a toothless slit, the eyes bright and still clear blue.

'Then you should kill me before I get a chance to give evidence,' he murmured. 'A lot of Frenchmen would be grateful. And Frenchwomen.' He turned his head and shut his eyes. The doctor stood and looked down at him. Then he walked out. The old man tilted his head and saw him go under his eyelids. He knew the type. They were the trouble-makers, the self-styled patriots. How his indignation burned, that young man – how they had all burned with that righteous fire, when they planted bombs that blew up other men of the same age, who also had fire in their hearts for their country. Or ambushed them and slit their throats; set them up for women to poison with a glass of wine. He knew the type, and he had treated them as they deserved. He made martyrs of them, and they didn't see the justice of it. He sighed. He felt tired; probably because of the tranquillizers he was given. Rest, Standartenführer Eilenburg. Sleep, Standartenführer Eilenburg. Grow strong so that we can stand you up in the dock and sentence you to life imprisonment, or death, if we can get the law amended.

They might regret it, he thought, and the little smile twitched round his mouth. They might wish they'd let him die before they let him speak. Even left him to end his days in Chile, and take the truth to the grave with him. So now, he was going to conserve his strength for the trial. He would turn French justice into Christian Eilenburg's vindication. He would not be tried alone.

Ten minutes' drive from Paul Roulier's London hotel, two men were dining together in a house in Montpelier Square.

17

It was a tall, elegant Georgian house, far too big for one man living alone. It was a family house, needing children on the nursery floor that overlooked the square. The man who lived there had inherited when his father died after the war. He scarcely remembered his mother; she'd seen very little of her only son and died long before he left preparatory school. There had never been a woman in his life. He lived in solitary state, looked after by a couple who'd worked for him for over thirty years. In his spare time, before he retired, he'd covered a set of Chippendale chairs with exquisite *petit point* needle-work. He was old now, and out to grass, as he said; he had time to start on a small carpet.

The dining room was lit by candles; the silver shone; he enjoyed good food and took pride in his cellar of fine wines. As the two men talked, a film of cigar smoke drifted up to the moulded ceiling. The host had a rich, rather theatrical voice, more suited to a Shakespearean actor than a retired colonel.

'What a pity about Eilenburg. You'd think someone in Paris would have had the sense to put a stop to it.'

'I thought they had,' his guest remarked. He had a summer cold, and his voice was croaky. He shouldn't have accepted the cigar.

'Obviously not, old chap. He got better.' The port came in the Colonel's direction. He saw a few drops spill on to the polished table. He leaned over and dabbed at them with his napkin. He loved his 'things' as he called them. He dusted the good china himself, and made his own mixture of bees-wax and turps to preserve the furniture.

'It'll be years before he comes to trial,' his guest said, 'you know what the French bureaucracy is like. Some kind of deal will be arranged, I'm sure. Too many important people have too much to lose if he is allowed to give evidence. They won't let it happen. So there's no need for us to worry.'

'I don't worry,' the Colonel said. 'It would be much easier to block any investigations now than it was after the war. And just supposing things got out – would you really mind, after all these years? I'm damned if I would!'

18

'That's not the official view,' the younger man reminded him. 'They don't want the past raked up.'

'Then why don't they do something about it? We would have done. I think this is a very good port. Sixty-two was a great year.'

The Colonel's white hair gleamed in the candlelight. His friend smiled and shook his head. He hadn't changed. He had never hesitated to sanction murder. He was incredible in those days. He really could get people to die for him as well as kill. 'It is good,' he agreed, finishing the port. 'You certainly do yourself well. Food was first class.'

'Morag's a competent cook,' his host agreed. The previous subject had been abandoned. They wouldn't mention it again. 'She's improved; I sent the old dear on a course two years ago. Ten days in Paris. She loved it, and she came back full of enthusiasm. The English can never really make good sauces, but her pastry was like a feather. *Mille-feuilles* that melted in the mouth, too.'

'Bit extravagant, wasn't it?' His friend said this with a smile.

'Why not? I've nobody to leave money to; not like you, old chap, with your nice family. How is my godson Richard, by the way?'

They talked about innocent topics like a young man's career at the Bar, and the vagaries of a certain daughter-in-law, until it was time to break up their evening together. The host snuffed his candles carefully, not spilling any wax. He didn't clear anything away. Morag's husband, who had been his batman till he retired, cleaned up in the morning. He locked the front door, checked the safety catches on the windows at ground-floor level, and went up to bed. He had enjoyed his dinner. He liked his old friends, and that particular colleague had been his closest associate. Brilliant chap. Mind like a Chinese puzzle. Married a nice girl. The Colonel spent weekends with them during the summer. But he didn't mind staying in London; he loved his house and his hobbies and became restless if he stayed away too long.

He felt relaxed and contented. At three o'clock in the morning he woke with a fit of palpitation. He had remembered Katharine Alfurd.

It was a very long time since Katharine had cooked for anybody. Dorothy insisted on doing it when she came over. She apologized to Paul, 'It was a scratchy lunch, I'm afraid. I've been so occupied since yesterday, getting things in order. How do you like your coffee? I haven't had time to make notes or get any papers together. I've only got some letters and they're personal. I'd like to begin at the very beginning if you don't mind.'

Paul said, 'Please, that's what I want.'

She liked the Frenchman. Silly for a woman of her age to warm to a man so much younger, but there it was. He could be my son, she thought, and took comfort from that. 'I may be a bit long-winded,' she said. 'If you can't follow it, just stop me and say so.'

She lit a cigarette. 'It started after I'd been in the Wrens for two months. I got this letter right out of the blue, asking me if I'd go for an interview in London. My qualifications suggested I might be suitable for a special job. I couldn't make head or tail of it; I didn't have any qualifications. I was nineteen and all I could do was cook quite nicely and speak French. The letter was signed by a Colonel James Reed. Naturally I was intrigued. And I wasn't enjoying scrubbing the passages as a punishment for losing some item of kit – God knows what, I can't remember. So I put in a request for leave to go to London. We were at Portsmouth Barracks. The permission was given so easily I should have suspected something. I took the train to Waterloo and then arrived half an hour early in Baker Street. I went into a local Lyons tea shop and had a cup of tea and a bun. And you know, suddenly, when it was time for the appointment, I started feeling nervous.'

Paul said slowly, 'You had no idea what they wanted?'

'Not a clue,' Kate replied. 'It was an office building and a

20

woman in civilian clothes took me up three flights of stairs and I was shown into a room on the top floor. There were two men sitting there, one behind a desk. I saw the red tabs and the rank badges and I nearly had a fit. One of them got up and held out his hand; I'd forgotten to salute.

'I'm Colonel Reed,' he said. 'How nice of you to come.'

2

'Miss Fitzgerald,' the Colonel said, 'we want you to think this over very carefully. You must not make up your mind without realizing the risks involved. And they're very serious. You're a bit younger than we like, but unfortunately we're in desperate need of people with your special qualification.'

Bilingual in French. Able to speak and write and even think like a Frenchwoman. She had blushed when the Captain started a conversation in rapid colloquial French, but she answered without hesitation, slipping back into her second language. The Colonel was watching her closely. A very striking looking girl, with Irish colouring so seldom found among the native Irish. Dark hair, the rose-bud complexion, beautiful green-blue eyes.

As she talked she lost her identity; he was fascinated to see her shrug and use her hands. She became French as she spoke. But only nineteen. Very, very young. How long would she last? He put the question out of his mind. There were obstacles to overcome before he need worry about her life-span in Occupied France.

'Very good,' the young Captain said. 'Very good indeed.'

They were being friendly, trying to make her feel at ease. She felt the senior officer exerting pressure on her. Don't rush into a decision. Think what may happen to you. You're really too young for this sort of thing. But we're so desperate and you have something so valuable to give. . . . There was a subtle contradiction there, and for all her innocence she sensed it. He wants me to say 'yes'. That's all he cares about. The warnings and the rest are just dressing. They were waiting for her to say something.

'I think I'd like to go,' she said. 'But I do need to know a bit more about it.'

'You can't know very much more,' the Colonel said. 'You may refuse when you've thought it over, or you may fail to pass your training course. But I think Captain Alfurd could give you a few details. Sketch in a little more for you.'

He had a fine voice; it reminded her of a famous actor. Very penetrating eyes, and a neat brush moustache under that big nose. She had scarcely noticed the other man, the Captain who spoke perfect French. The Colonel blotted out other people when he talked.

'Alfurd,' he said. 'Can you spare Miss Fitzgerald a few minutes and brief her?'

They hadn't used her surname, or treated her as a ranker in the Women's Services. It was all conducted on friendly, civilian terms. Which made saying 'no' more difficult. The Colonel got up, ending the interview. She pulled herself together and saluted; then shook hands with him. He had looked tall when she came into the room. Standing, he was quite short. He smiled and the deep-set eyes were kind.

'Thank you for coming to see me,' he said. 'Captain Alfurd will look after you now.' They went downstairs, the Captain leading the way. On the second landing he paused. He looked at his watch. She waited, feeling awkward.

'It's nearly one o'clock,' he said. 'Why don't I take you round the corner and we can have some lunch. Much easier to talk than in my office.' He had gone on down the stairs without waiting for her answer. She caught up with him in the hall. He turned and she had time to look at him properly. He grinned, and she liked him for that. Very fair, rather

23

washy grey eyes, young – uniform made him better-looking. It improved most men.

'Let's go then,' he said.

'All right; as a matter of fact, I'm starving.'

Round the corner was a small private hotel. Kate went into the cloakroom and combed her hair. It was short and curly, and stayed neat under the Wrens cap. She hated herself in the dark, ill-cut uniform. The officers looked terrific, but she didn't expect to rise out of the ranks. He ordered them a drink. She said gin and tonic, which she wasn't used to, but it sounded better. At home they always drank wine. She hadn't any head for spirits. He asked her about herself. She described her first weeks at Portsmouth and made him laugh. She began to feel at ease with him. Over the table she said, 'Tell me, Captain Alfurd, how did you know I was brought up in Paris?'

'Because I was sent a copy of your file. Anybody with links in Occupied Europe or bilinguals are referred to us. We don't always follow them up, but you seemed particularly promising.'

'Why?' She had a way of asking direct questions, and meeting the eye till she got an answer. Not a fool, he judged, and not lacking in courage either.

'Because you were a girl, educated, right family background. Described as willing and cheerful in your report. Nice photograph too.'

'How much can you tell me?' Another direct one.

'Not much, I'm afraid. If you accept the Colonel's offer and join us, you'll go through a period of training. Six months. You'll have to pass certain tests, satisfy your instructors, and the officer in charge that you're the right material, mentally and physically, for this type of job. All I can tell you is that obviously you'll have to operate somewhere French-speaking and you won't have a nice time if you get caught by the Gestapo.'

'Can't you tell me what kind of work?'

He shook his head. 'No. The senior course officer will

decide what you're suited for. Courier, wireless operator – that kind of job.'

She frowned. 'I wouldn't have to kill anybody?'

'I wouldn't think so.' He made the question sound silly. He was smiling slightly, almost teasing, when he said, 'Do you think you could?'

Kate laughed out loud. 'I can't swat a fly,' she said. He laughed too. She might surprise herself one day.

'The main thing,' he said, 'is to be sure you want to get involved. On the good side, you'll work with some tremendous people, but you'll have no contact with anyone outside. You'll have to dedicate yourself completely to the job. You'll be yelled at and pushed to your physical limit, and then beyond that. You've got to be very fit if you go over; and very careful about details. I don't have to tell you about discretion. That's number one. You don't mention anything even to your own family. And that's not as easy as it sounds. Am I putting you off?'

She shook her head. 'No, not a bit. The good side sounds very good. And the bad side I can probably guess.'

He was serious at once. 'The bad side,' he said, 'is that you won't come back. And that's really all I can tell you. Except to say that personally I hope you'll join our organization. I think you'd be a great asset.' He changed the mood. 'I can't bear to think of you spending the rest of the war scrubbing passages in Pompey.'

She thanked him for lunch; it was meagre and the vegetables were watery and stale. She wasn't hungry though; excitement was knotting her stomach as she said goodbye to him, and queued for the bus on her way back to Waterloo station.

She didn't need time to think about it. Take a week, the young officer encouraged. Unless of course you're absolutely set on it. Then give me a ring. She took the card with the telephone number scribbled on it. SOE. The Special Operations Executive. She had never heard of it, but then why should she? Discretion was Number One. Secrecy, adven-

25

ture, danger! A little lurch of the knotted muscles then. But useful, really useful. Not just a conscript wasting her time doing menial routine jobs that a thousand other girls could do far better. They'd thought she was particularly promising. That was nice, to be told that. And she wasn't scared by what he'd called the bad side. If things went wrong and she got caught . . . she shrugged, sitting in the crowded, smoky train. That was part of the risk. If she was killed, so were people every time there was an air raid. I don't need a week, Kate said to herself. I don't even need twenty-four hours, but I'll wait till Wednesday to make it look as if I've taken their advice. Pity I can't tell the family. Never mind. They'd only worry. She wedged herself into the corner so she could watch the countryside speed by. Her thoughts were far away.

The Colonel was in his office when Captain Alfurd came back. He knocked on the door and came in.

'How'd you get on, Robert?' The Colonel looked up briefly.

'I took her to lunch, Sir.'

'I thought you might. Well?'

'I think she'll join,' Alfurd said. 'And I think she'll be good, too.'

'Let's hope you're right. Now, Simpson wants us to go over to Whitehall at four o'clock. He's mounting a presentation for Winston.'

He bent over his desk again. The girl was forgotten.

The Fitzgeralds were an affectionate family. When Kate arrived at the house, her mother rushed to meet her. 'Kate, Kate, darling!' She was a small, rather plump woman, pretty as a bird in her youth, with sparkling brown eyes. They brimmed with tears as she embraced her daughter. She spoke with a strong Parisian accent. 'How are you? You look tired. Come in, I've been waiting all day for you to come. I'll make tea, and your Papa will be home soon. He was so excited to hear about your leave.'

It was wonderful to be home, Kate thought, looking round

at the familiar furniture, recognizing her mother's needle-work on two new cushions; all the security of a happy family enveloped her like sunshine, although it was raining and dismal outside.

'Maman,' she said, hugging her, and broke into French. 'Maman, let me go upstairs and take off this ugly uniform and put on some of my own clothes! I won't be a minute – Oh, it's so lovely to see you and be at home!'

Her bedroom was the same as the day she left it. Photographs of her parents and her brother; snapshots of their old home in Paris. The teddy bear nightdress-case propped on the pillow, exactly as it had been since she was ten years old and given it for Christmas. She ran to the wardrobe, to the chest of drawers, pulling out her clothes. Minutes later the Wrens uniform was draped over the back of a chair, and Kate hurried down to find her mother.

'I've got fat,' she announced. 'This skirt is really tight! It's all that awful stodge we get to eat – bread and potatoes and caterpillar cabbage – Oh, Maman, what have you got in the oven?'

Her mother laughed. 'Something special. Not stodge, my darling. There's your father, I can see by Mimi's face; she knows when he's walking up the street, that dog!'

The little terrier bounded out to the front door, and Kate ran to meet her father. They were very similar in looks. Born in County Wexford, he'd been educated in England and gone to Cambridge to read law. Opportunities were poor at home, and the professional classes sent their sons overseas. For thirty years he had worked with the same Anglo-French banking company, and married Denise in Paris, where they made their home. Both their son and daughter had been born there and the family was more French than anything else.

'Kate.' He hugged her, held her out to look at her. 'You're looking well. Very well, just my little Kate again.'

There was a special bottle of wine opened for the dinner conjured out of rations like a miracle. They talked and laughed and interrupted each other, and after dinner, the questions began.

'Tell me,' her father said, 'how did you get this job? And why do you have to change services?'

'Because they want interpreters in the WAAF, and as soon as someone realized I was bilingual, they thought I'd be better employed speaking French than scrubbing bloody floors – sorry, Daddy, that slipped out. Don't you think pale blue will suit me better than that navy serge?' She laughed and they joined in. She hated lying to them. More questions, forcing her to elaborate. 'Six months' training . . . why six months, Maman – I don't know. No not training, really, just going to courses and learning to type and use some short-hand. Then maybe some lovely cushy job in the Air Ministry! Just think, I'd be able to get home at weekends. . . .' She saw the joy on their faces.

'We're thrilled for you,' her mother said.

They talked about her elder brother, David; he was taking a gunnery course at Manobeir. She was given his last letter to read. It was funny and individual, just like him. They had got on well as children; having a brother made Kate more of a tomboy. That night, lying in the comfort of her own bed, nursing the luxury of a hot-water bottle, Kate thrust the memories of her childhood aside. It was no good slipping back mentally, when she had made the decision. Lying to the people she loved had been both difficult and shaming. But that was part of the price she must pay every day of her life from now on. She didn't belong to herself or her family any more. It was a chilling thought, and for a moment the niggle of fear stabbed like a pain. Of course, she wanted to tell her parents, to ask for their support, even to share her excitement and, yes, fear again, with them. But it wasn't possible or kind. They'd worry themselves to death. Her father knew the situation in France better than most. Her mother fretted over David in the safety of Wales. Besides, wasn't she taking too much for granted – how did she know she'd even pass the rigorous tests ahead? Scotland was going to sort out the candidates, she'd been told, seeing the Colonel on her way through London. A lot of people got injured or gave up. Only the fit and the courageous got past that initial stage. She had no guarantee. She fell asleep thinking about it, and didn't wake till lunchtime.

It was a bright day outside. Her father worked in a reserved occupation in London; she spent a happy day with her mother, helping her in the house, drinking cups of tea and gossiping. The mood of childishness had passed. She was a woman, with another woman, who was a loved friend and companion as well as a mother. Denise Fitzgerald saw the change in her daughter, and thought it was sad and wonderful how quickly that change had come about. Still so very young, but with a confidence that hadn't been there when she left for Portsmouth, only a few months before, red-eyed and uncertain of what was waiting for her.

'Kate,' she said, 'is there a young man?'

Kate was surprised. 'Good Lord, no. What makes you ask that?'

Denise Fitzgerald shrugged. 'Nothing. You seem so grown up. I wondered if you had fallen in love. I'm being silly, take no notice.'

'I haven't even met a man, Maman,' Kate said. 'I told you, I've been marching up and down the parade ground and scrubbing floors as a punishment, and putting on weight because all we do is eat and scrounge off each other. I haven't been off with a sailor, I promise you!' She laughed and kissed her mother. 'Maybe I've had to grow up in a hurry,' she said. 'What are we going to have for dinner? I'm starving.'

The week went by too quickly; she avoided telling more lies by busying herself and refusing to think about it. Every night she helped her father check the blackout when he came off the smelly, stuffy train from Victoria. Three times the sirens wailed and they went down to the Anderson shelter in the garden, but no bombs fell. They went for walks with the terrier, Mimi; she started making herself a blouse with a remnant her mother had saved up, and refused to wonder when she'd finish it. Already, the crisp east wind was stinging her in the face, warning that winter was coming, and the leaves were deep on the ground. It was comforting to be with them, but by the end of the week she was ready to go. She said goodbye to them at the local station early on Saturday afternoon. She had a travel warrant to get her to London and from London overnight to Scotland. She would be met, her instructions said, at Lossiemouth.

The loch was like a sheet of dirty steel on that October day. Massed clouds overhead gave it their own sombre colour. There was no shift of wind to move them. They lowered over the water and the house close by the edge of it like God the Father's frown. It was a place built to withstand the weather, with thick walls and deep-set windows. A high hedge separated it from a second house, humbler in origin, built of the same heavy stone, with a low sloping roof. There was room for twelve students to be housed in both buildings, four instructors, two senior officers and a commandant, apart from domestic staff.

It was an isolated place, part of a group of similar centres in the Highlands, chosen for their locations in bleak countryside. In the depth of winter they were cut off by snow. A Major in the Scots Guards and a Captain in the Royal Corps of Signals were walking by the side of the loch. The house, with its big domestic annexe, belonged to the Major's grandfather.

'Bloody shame about Harris,' the Major said. 'He was shaping up well.'

The Captain shrugged. 'Too cocky, that was his trouble. He's the "I'm out for a gong" type and we don't want those. I'm not sorry he's out.'

Major McKay didn't answer. Arthur Taft took dislikes to people and there was nothing to be done about it. The trainee they were discussing had antagonized him from the start. Personally McKay regretted losing him. He had courage and an aggressive spirit, and even Taft had to admit that if he had got through the physical training, he would have made an excellent pupil for the sabotage section. He had tried an over-ambitious descent in the rope-climbing two days before, hit an outcrop and cracked his shin bone in three places.

McKay and Taft had been senior selection officers at Loch Gary for eighteen months. They had a good team; four top instructors, experts in their fields. They concentrated on the French Section, known as F. Their students were all destined for the SOE operation in France if they survived the final selection course. Activity in F Section had been building up steadily in the last year. Some of their pupils, as McKay called them, had already distinguished themselves establishing resistance groups all over France. A number had been captured and were dead.

He wondered sometimes whether Taft worried about them as much as he did. It would be difficult to judge. He never referred to anyone after they left. He was a dour, surly man, devoid of charm. McKay had nothing in common with him but a determination to pick the very best out of the men and women and not let anyone doubtful slip through. They often disagreed until the last moment.

'Well,' McKay said at last. 'We'll have the new ones by tonight. Derain, Le Brun, Hunter, Sansom, Gunn and Fitzgerald. Let's hope we'll find one of them turns out useful.'

'Fitzgerald's only a kid,' Taft said snappily. 'Bloody ridiculous sending someone of that age.'

'That's what I said,' McKay agreed. 'But the boys in Baker Street hand-picked this candidate for some reason. I made no impression at all.'

'Must have lost a few then,' Taft grunted. 'But that's not our responsibility. We send them out of here able to look after themselves, fit as fleas and raring to go. What gets buggered up in Hampshire is another matter. Getting cold out here.' He hunched his body up against a sudden squall of wind that tore at the loch water, lashing and whipping at it in a fury. The rain spat down on them.

'Christ, what a climate,' Taft muttered.

McKay ignored the remark. 'Michaelson is the conducting officer; this is his fourth group in three months. I hope he's in a better state than last time.'

Taft turned away from the sheeting rain, his head sunk down into his shoulders like a turtle. He surprised McKay by saying something in defence of Captain Michaelson.

'He looked at the end of his tether last time,' he said. 'Living with them day and bloody night without a break for weeks on end. He shouldn't be back so soon. Typical Baker Street.'

There was a running war between Taft and the senior officers in F Section. The last time Captain Michaelson had spent five weeks with a group of six trainees on the loch, Taft hadn't found a good word to say for him.

'Let's turn back,' McKay suggested. He looked at his watch. 'Hickey and his lot will be back in half an hour. The new lot should get here around seven if the train's on time.'

The storm was passing and, as the clouds cleared, a brilliant patch of sky was reflected like a sapphire in the loch. Taft hated the place; McKay had grown up there and he loved it above anywhere else in the world.

Katharine was so stiff she ached when she got up and pulled her baggage off the rack above her head. The train hissed at the platform, sounding like a punctured tyre. Doors were opening and banging shut and the guard was shouting 'Lossiemouth, Lossiemouth'. The station's name had been blacked out.

She heaved her bag on to the platform, shoved the door shut and got her ticket ready. She felt creased and grubby after the endless journey. Her smart new WAAF officer's uniform had been slept in and it looked like it. She went through the barrier and waited outside. Five other people stood about, kitbags at their feet. Four men and a woman. Two in army uniform, two in RAF. The woman wore a smart khaki uniform. Kate recognized it. The First Aid Nursing Yeomanry. FANY. The Americans choked on that one. An officer with three pips on his overcoat was walking towards them. Kate didn't hesitate; she joined the group. She saw him frown and wondered what she had done wrong.

'I'm Captain Michaelson,' he said. He shook hands with the men first, the army nurse and finally with her.

'I'm Flight Officer Fitz–' she started, hoping to please, and smiling in her most friendly way.

'I know who you are,' he snapped. 'There's a bus picking us up. It should be here by now.' It rounded the corner and pulled up. 'Get in please,' he said. He followed last and sat in the front beside the army driver. The girl had slipped on to the bench seat beside Kate.

'Charming manners,' she whispered. 'I'm Judy. No last names.'

'Thanks for telling me,' Kate murmured. 'Nobody else did. I'm Kate. I'd love a cigarette. Do you want one?'

'Thanks. What a journey! Did you sleep?'

'On and off; more off than on. It's going to be pretty cold up here.'

'Don't you know Scotland?' She had a pleasant voice, with a trace of accent.

'No,' Kate answered. 'We live in Surrey. There's going to be a storm.'

'It'll pass,' the girl called Judy said. 'You get sudden squalls of rain and wind, then they blow over and it can be beautiful.'

There was a tap on Kate's shoulder and she looked round. Three rings on the sleeve; the Squadron Leader had a very strong accent.

'I should put those out,' he said quietly. He nodded towards the silent figure up in the front. 'He doesn't like to smoke when travelling.'

'Thanks,' Kate whispered. What pale eyes, she noticed. A French face, under the British cap. Fine-featured, an aquiline nose; a narrow-lipped mouth that was smiling at her. And the ice-grey eyes with flecks of green in them.

'Did he come up on the train?' she asked.

'Probably.' He shrugged.

'Do you know him?' she asked again.

'Only by reputation,' he whispered back. 'I'm Philippe.'

'Judy.'

'Kate.'

Both girls trod out their cigarettes under their seats. From his position by the driver, Captain Michaelson saw them do it in the driving mirror. He heard a subdued giggle. Christ, how he hated dealing with the women. The tough, butch types were different, but when it came to girls like these two. . . . He had bitten the head off the youngest one. All bright smiles and puppy friendliness at the station. Giving her rank and real name. And the preliminary Selection Panel had passed her. Easy for them. Not looking beyond the eager candidate, intent on giving the right answers to their loaded questions. He couldn't get Lisette out of his mind, that was the trouble. He kept seeing her in every woman.

He realized that he had clenched his hands to stop them shaking. It took the best part of two hours before they reached the Loch and the darkness was not even lit by a star. A biting wind tore at them as they stepped out of the bus; Kate shivered, glanced round quickly and heaved her bag up. The mass of the house loomed up at them, blacker than the sky. Inside the transformation was dramatic. Lights, a big fire burning in the hallway, a fine carved stair that led out of the hall. A group of people standing by the fire, in khaki and air-force blue, looking at the new arrivals. All men, Kate noticed. The dour young officer who'd travelled with them directed them up the stairs.

'I'll show you your rooms; have a clean up and come down in fifteen minutes. We'll have a drink and I'll introduce you to the others. We have dinner at eight thirty tonight. Make yourselves at home.'

Kate's room was next to the girl called Judy. It was

pleasantly warm. Shabby, but with a comfortable bed and a good light to read by. Plain, solid Victorian furniture, and rubbed chintz. A large coloured print of a child holding two kittens faced the bed. Years ago, she thought, this was a child's bedroom. Now it's mine. God, I wish I could just stretch out and go to sleep. I'm so tired I'm not even hungry. And I don't fancy spending the next six weeks with that Captain Snappit breathing down my neck. There was a knock on the door. Judy looked in.

'Are you ready? I thought we'd go down together.'

Kate jumped up, feeling guilty. 'I haven't even combed my hair.'

The older girl said quietly, 'I'd hurry up then. I'll wait for you, but it doesn't do to be late.' She waited while Kate fumbled in her holdall for lipstick and quickly combed her hair. She's quite beautiful, she thought, but she doesn't know it. Michaelson is going to give her hell. It would be interesting to see how the girl coped. There was a lot of the schoolgirl about her, and an independent gleam that Captain Michaelson would do his best to extinguish. If he succeeded, she was out. Judy looked at her watch.

'I'm going down,' she said.

'Wait for me!' Kate threw the holdall into a corner and hurried after her. 'It's only a minute or two after he said,' she protested.

'It's still late,' Judy answered. 'It'll count against you.' They were almost at the door of the staircase and the man called Philippe was already by the fire, talking to the others.

'How do you know?' Kate demanded.

'Because I've been here before,' Judy answered.

Captain Michaelson advanced on them. 'Come and meet the rest of the group,' he said.

Kate hardly listened to the names. Six men, all different, roughly the same age, all shaking hands and answering to names like Raoul and Jean and Bernard, which sounded unconvincing. Some with accents, others completely English; one with a distinct Welsh lilt. She felt shy and excited.

Someone gave her a gin and tonic and lit a cigarette for her. The conversation was forced. Questions about her journey; over hearty laughter about the state of the trains. She wanted to join up with Judy, but she was talking to Michaelson. She had been there before, so she would know the form.

'Hallo.' She found Philippe beside her. The young soldier she'd been talking to moved away.

'You look anxious,' he said. The amazing translucent eyes smiled at her. She found them disconcerting, and wanted to look away. 'You needn't worry,' he said. 'You'll find everyone here helpful and friendly. They're not encouraged to say too much when they first meet you. And I gather one of their best men has retired injured, so there's a little cloud over them all tonight.'

'You sound as if you've been here before too,' Kate answered. 'Judy has, she told me. I thought one only had to train once.'

'For me it's a refresher; for Judy,' he shrugged, 'I don't know. I don't know anything about her. Or about you. Except you are very new.'

'I'm *new*,' she agreed, 'and I wish I wasn't. How did this person get injured?'

'He had an accident rock-climbing,' Philippe answered. 'They lost a girl two weeks ago. She put her foot in a rabbit hole and broke her ankle when they were out on an exercise. So you'll have to be careful not to hurt yourself.'

He was being kind and reassuring. She wished she liked him. 'I'm pretty tough,' she said. 'My PT instructor said so.'

'I'm sure he did,' was the answer, 'but I think you'll find this quite a lot harder than parade-ground PT. Would you like another drink? The first evening is relaxed, but they don't serve alcohol normally. Just now and again.'

'That won't worry me,' Kate said. 'I don't drink anything except wine.' She pulled a face. 'I don't even like gin.'

'Then you'll have wine tonight,' Philippe smiled. 'Always on the first night, there is wine for dinner. There is the gong.

Come, I'll show you where we go.' He guided her by a light touch on her arm. A gong. It was like something out of a Hollywood film. This imposing house with its evidence of class and privilege, but going back a very long time. The confident shabbiness of generations. The dining room was like a school refectory. One long table, orderlies in white coats to serve the food, an atmosphere like a school. The food was generous; quantities of vegetables and luxuries like fresh bread and butter. The wine was thin and sour, but she was thankful for it.

She didn't try to talk; she found herself seated next to Captain Michaelson, who hardly spoke to her at all, and the strange men on either side were polite but disinterested. The new girl had nothing to contribute. They seemed preoccupied and exclusive. She felt miserable, which Michaelson noticed. Homesick on the first night, he thought. Nobody was making a fuss of her, though she was the best-looking girl they'd seen in a long time at Loch Gary. And she hadn't flirted with Philippe, who had given her the opportunity. That was a good sign anyway. He wasn't sorry for her. She had no right to expect his sympathy, if she felt like a lost soul, and wanted to turn round and go straight back to her Portsmouth Barracks and forget it all. She had only herself to blame for coming to Loch Gary, and for getting involved in the Service. Women shouldn't be allowed, he protested silently, and again his hands trembled, remembering Lisette. Women shouldn't be sent over. . . . By Christ, he was going to lean on this girl. And he'd see the instructors did the same. She'd hate his guts for it, but she might just live to thank him. Unlike Lisette, whom he'd sent out to her death only eight months ago.

Kate had never been so cold in her life. Her hands and feet were numb, a vicious wind whipped at her face, and the summit of the rock loomed overhead, slippery and smooth. It was the third rock-climbing exercise that her group had been set and the most difficult. Michaelson had supervised their preliminary training, under a grim-faced PT instructor; stiff and sore, Kate remembered Philippe's warning the first day. 'Don't try too hard, let your body get accustomed, or you'll hurt yourself.' She hadn't listened, determined to prove herself, and found out just what good advice that was. She hated heights, but never said a word. They climbed a modest outcrop and she felt more confident. And Michaelson watched her, silent when she did well and scathing about the least mistake. The evenings became more relaxed; people formed friendships, hoping they might end in the same team, but not knowing. The group who had been there when Kate arrived dispersed ten days later. No one knew who had passed or failed. The next morning they weren't there. That was all. No questions were asked, no explanations offered. The discipline was accepted without demur because the penalty for breaking it was a taxi ride to Lossiemouth and a rail voucher out. After the rock-climb, there would be twenty-four hours' rest, Michaelson had announced the night before. They would begin with a survival course in open country the following day. Next to Kate the airman muttered, 'Christ,' and pulled a face. 'What's he trying to do, kill us off?'

'You made a comment?' The chilly stare passed over Kate for once. The young man grinned; he was always cheerful, and Kate liked him. His name was Fred and he came from the Midlands.

'Just a silent prayer, Sir.'

Michaelson said, 'Next time, keep it more silent.'

The night before the climb Kate couldn't sleep. The second climb had been a miserable ordeal, undertaken in sheets of icy rain, and she was trembling with fright and exhaustion when she reached the top. The instructor was there first, assessing each of them as they arrived and she felt he paid special attention to her.

'Lovely view,' he said, inviting them to stand up and take a look. She didn't linger to admire it; there was no view in the driving rainstorm and he knew it.

'Don't like heights?' The question was sharp.

'Not much,' she said.

'Didn't think you did. You won't fancy going up Corrib's Peak. Right, take ten minutes' breather and down we go.'

Corrib's Peak. Everyone knew it was a major test and failing it meant ultimate failure on the course. Courage, fitness, agility and determination were the qualities needed. Philippe was not among the team. He tried to help her, giving advice on the finer points of the climb. He knew it well and there was nothing to worry about. He seemed to sense her fear. Concentration was the secret, to channel the mind in the direction of the next hand and toe hold, so that it couldn't take a mental peep below. Regular breathing helped the supply of oxygen to the muscles and regulated the heartbeat. It also controlled the nervous impulses. She was grateful to him, wondering why he took so much trouble with her. He was a detached man, set apart from them by his field experience. The instructors treated him with respect and Michaelson talked to him as an equal. Even so, it was obvious that they didn't like each other.

There were two very senior officers from F Section, who came and went from group to group. A charming Scotsman who introduced himself as Major McKay and a sour, abrasive Englishman called Taft. These two, Judy told her, were the final judges of who left to go on the second stage and who returned to their original units.

The morning of the climb came, and they set out just after daybreak. Corrib's Peak! She didn't look up when they arrived at the bottom. She held fast to the Frenchman's advice, shuttering her mind against the pictures her imagination painted. They started up, roped together, five of them, with Judy in the middle and Fred behind Kate. He managed to make a joke as they started. There was no rain, only the bitter wind. Kate went on; hand hold, toe hold, hand hold, toe hold, inching up, following the back view of the one above her, numbed and beginning to ache with tiredness. Keeping her eyes fixed on the next place to grasp and heave upwards. She was not going to be sick. She was not going to listen to the devil at her ear that urged her to look down and see how far she'd come. She was going to get to the top, without slipping, or shouting up to the others to give her a minute to rest, or actually just losing hold and swinging out from that rope like a puppet on a string. . . . If you fail this, you might as well pack up and go home. Everyone knew that. She wasn't going to fail. She didn't realize when a hand reached down to haul her up; she clung on with her dead fingers and heaved and toed her way the last few feet to the plateau. She sat and gasped for breath and suddenly a sense of sheer well-being came over her. Adrenalin poured into her bloodstream and she wasn't tired or nauseated any more. She'd done it. She'd made the climb and Corrib's Peak was conquered. She saw Judy, who called out, 'Well done!'

'You too,' was Kate's reply.

The instructor crouched beside her. 'Like to see the view?'

She started to get up and he put a hand on her shoulder. 'Only a joke, Miss. You did well. Have a rest and a smoke anyone who wants.'

After a pause Kate said, 'Where's Fred?'

'Down the bottom,' came the answer. 'Didn't like it. Cut his line and stayed below.'

'Oh, poor Fred, what a shame.'

There was a celebration that night. Philippe was the first to congratulate her.

'It was thanks to you,' she said. 'I couldn't have done it without all your advice.'

He smiled and for a moment the pale eyes reflected it. 'You were a little frightened, I thought. Yes?'

Kate said, 'I was absolutely terrified. I was having nightmares about going up there. Any height makes me sick.'

'Then you must be specially pleased,' he answered. She looked past him to Michaelson. He was sitting next to Judy. He hadn't said a word to her, but she had heard him praise the others.

'It doesn't matter how hard I try,' she said. 'I can't do

right with him. He ignored me tonight. You'd think I'd chickened out, like poor Fred. I ought to go and talk to him, he looks so down. He'll be sent home, won't he?'

'Maybe, maybe not. He has other skills. Not everyone has to have a head for heights,' Philippe answered. 'Don't let the Captain worry you. He knows you did well.'

A party developed that went on way past midnight. Drinks were served after dinner and she settled down to comfort Fred.

'I couldn't bloody do it,' he complained. 'I thought it'd be just a piece of cake. But I got frozen up, Katie.' He called her Katie, but no one else did. 'Christ, I could've fallen and broken my bloody neck if I'd gone on. Well, I'd better start packing my gear for the morning trip to Lossiemouth.'

While the party went on in the hall downstairs Michaelson was in conference with the senior officers, McKay and Taft. They were discussing Fred.

'He should go,' Michaelson insisted. 'He's a good chap, but he showed a total loss of nerve today.'

McKay and Taft looked at each other. They echoed Philippe's comment. 'He's got other skills, remember. They say he was one of the best safe men in the Midlands. You'll get people who'll get themselves up Corrib, but they won't be able to open a German strong-room. I think you should forget about this morning, Michaelson.'

'Then why did the others have to do it? Because if they're pushed, and they have to use the escape route to Spain, they might *have* to make a climb like that! Or are you saying that Fred Gunn's expendable, if things go wrong?'

Taft said acidly, 'They're all expendable and you know it. We train them, we equip them, and we send them out. What happens after that is not our business.'

'Well,' Michaelson got up. 'I'm glad you can look at it like that.'

'That's how you should look at it too,' McKay said quietly. 'The Fitzgerald girl did well today.'

'Yes,' Michaelson said. 'Unfortunately she did. But

there's a way to go yet. I'll say good night. They're having a bit of fun downstairs. I'll tell Gunn he's staying on. No point in spoiling his evening.'

When he had gone McKay lit a cigarette. The dour Taft didn't smoke. 'He's got a real down on that girl; we'd better keep an eye on her.'

'He should pack it in,' Taft remarked. 'He's got a thing about women after Lisette. Personally I think we should put in a word with F Section and get him posted out of here.'

'I agree with you,' McKay said. 'But not till he's seen this lot through the first part of their course. You can't upset them in the middle by changing. Then he goes. Now, nightcap?'

'Good idea,' Taft said. They gave themselves a generous helping of the precious whisky before they each went to their rooms.

Fred was the hero of the survival course. They were taken out on to the moors, given a meagre basic ration and a compass and told to report back to the main house by four p.m. the following day. They were sixty miles deep into wild countryside, without radio linkage or any knowledge of the terrain. They steered by compass. As if on signal, a tremendous storm broke. The sky blackened as if it was night. Rain swept like scythes, soaking through their waterproof clothes, blinding in its velocity. Thunder exploded and the lightning streaked viciously through inky clouds. There wasn't an inch of shelter on the moors. Then to everyone's surprise it was Fred, the urban dweller, who took command. He huddled them in groups of three, facing inwards against the wind, holding the tarpaulin over themselves as a shield. Their bodies helped to keep the supplies dry and to maintain some kind of warmth. He kept their spirits up by joking.

'Bloody Walt Disney couldn't do better than this lot – next thing we'll see the Wicked Queen! How's Snow White doing in the corner?' That was to Judy, who was shivering with cold and flinching at the thunderclaps.

'I'm okay. Sadistic bastards, they *knew* the weather was going to do this!'

'I'll bet they did,' Fred shouted, above the yelling of the storm. 'Warming their backsides by the fire and thinking of us!'

When the storm slackened, they began to walk, encouraged by Fred, who set a brisk pace. It would help to dry off, he said. If the clouds lifted, he might get a setting. But the general direction they should take was north east. How did he know, they demanded. Because he'd taken a fix when they left, and that was the rough compass reading. Come on, step it out, he roared, imitating their instructor's buzz-saw voice. At intervals they stopped, rested, used some of their rations. But they walked throughout the night, guided by brief glimpses of the stars through broken clouds. Judy and Gerard, a young Frenchman, paired off, supporting each other. He had a severely blistered foot and she was chilled and exhausted. Kate had no partner. She was soaked and shivering, but otherwise in good heart.

How funny about the little airman. The rock had defeated him, but the vile terrain and blistering cold and darkness didn't worry him at all. It was good to see the comradeship between the weaker and the strong. Judy and Gerard with his raw, bleeding heel . . . Fred helping another man, who'd complained of a feverish cold before they started out. He'd be lucky to escape pneumonia by the time they got back.

And get back they did, at exactly twenty-two minutes before four o'clock the next afternoon. Judy was in bed for three days, running a temperature. Fred's companion got pleurisy and was taken to hospital. He didn't return to the course. Kate and Fred suffered no ill effects. She could see that Michaelson was disappointed when she came down to breakfast the next morning.

'Ladies and gentlemen,' Michaelson announced. 'You've been here two and a half months. We've lost one of you through illness. Another redeemed himself after making a fair mess of an exercise. . . .' Fred turned to Kate and grinned. 'The rest have done well in some areas of training and badly or fairly in others. We're coming now to the last two weeks of this particular course, and I'm going to hand you over to Mr Finch. Mr Finch will teach all of you the basic principles of unarmed combat, and from there he will show you how to switch from defence to attack. Some of you – Philippe and Judy – have done this before, so you can occupy yourselves by assessing the others and helping Mr Finch with demonstrations. If you feel you need smartening up, he'll put you into a class. I must warn those of you who have no experience of this, that you can get hurt.'

'He's looking straight at me,' Kate murmured.

'Miss Fitzgerald, if you have any comment to make, why don't you let us all have the benefit? I'm sure we will all learn something.'

A month ago, Kate thought, I would have sunk through the floor. But not now. I've had enough of your bullying. 'I said you were looking straight at me, Captain.'

'How very presumptuous of you.' There was complete silence. Michaelson let it continue and then said abruptly, 'Now, perhaps we can get on.'

Kate stepped forward, brushing aside Judy's restraining hand on her arm. 'Captain Michaelson, if you don't think I'm suitable for this course, I wish you'd say so.'

She was surprised to see a red colour creep into his face.

'I will, at the right time. Which isn't in the middle of my briefing. If you have anything to say, then come and see me in my office at six o'clock.'

'Thank you,' Kate answered. 'I'll be glad to.' She turned and went back to her group. She saw a very odd expression on Philippe's face.

Mr Finch appeared later that morning. He was small and slight and unprepossessing, with a broad Yorkshire accent. Track-suited, wearing gym shoes, they were lined up in a row. He looked them over carefully, taking his time. He nodded to Philippe and frowned when he saw Judy. He actually snorted when he came to Fred, who looked painfully skinny out of uniform.

'I'm here,' he announced, 'to teach you how to take care of yourselves. And so as I can do it, I'm not going to take care of you, if you see my meaning. Now, let's play a little game, ladies and gents. Let's imagine we're in a dark street with houses either side and nobody about. Right? Right. You, Sir, Mr Gerard, is it? Right, you're walking down this street, minding your own business and someone's laying for you. . . . Right? Right, come along then, walk past me – you don't see me 'cos I'm hidden in a doorway, right? Right.' The young Frenchman walked past the instructor. Finch moved up and threw an arm lock on him.

'What do you do now, eh? How do you break this hold – come on, come on, don't be bashful – I'm a German, right? Making an arrest.'

Gerard, a rather taciturn man, who prided himself on his fitness, made a quick and violent movement. Finch changed his stance and threw him very hard indeed on to the stone floor. 'I can see you've got a lot to learn, Sir, but never mind. I'm here to teach you, right? Anyone else want to try?'

Nobody volunteered. Satisfied, Finch nodded. 'Right,' he repeated yet again. 'We'll start with the basics. Mr Philippe, will you step forward and show the ladies and gents how it's done?'

After a hot bath, Kate lay on her bed, lit a cigarette and closed her eyes. She'd learned a lot by watching. Finch had taught her a few simple rules, and she felt she'd mastered them. How to break a stranglehold; how to knee an attacker without knocking him in the thigh instead of the crutch. It was done gently and slowly as part of a general demonstration of technique. She felt he was only waiting for an opportunity to throw someone like the unfortunate Gerard. Judy knocked on the door and came in. 'The bathroom's free,' she said. 'I've had mine.'

Kate held out the cigarettes. Judy took one and sat on the edge of the bed. She looked tired, Kate thought, and on edge.

'Got a light?' She mimicked the maddening voice that had gone through their heads all afternoon.

'Right? Right! I thought if he said it again I'd go mad and start screaming!'

'He's a nasty little brute,' Judy murmured. 'I remember him from my first time. He used a hold on me that nearly broke my bloody arm. He's a right little sadist. You watch out for him.'

'I will,' Kate said. 'And talking of sadists, I'm going to have it out with Michaelson tonight.'

'You made quite a stir this morning.' Judy puffed rapidly at the cigarette.

There's something the matter with her, Kate decided. Maybe it's this little horror, Finch. I'll ask her later. 'I suppose it was a silly thing to do,' she admitted, 'but I've had enough of him picking on me for everything. Do you realize he's never said a single word of encouragement from the moment I got here? All he's done is snipe at me, made me feel a perfect fool whenever possible, and try to undermine my confidence. I'm going to ask him why.'

Judy said slowly, 'He never gives explanations. He has picked on you, Kate, it's been very noticeable. But he doesn't exactly like me either. Trouble is, he can't flunk me, because I'm only on a refresher course. But he'd like to. I think the whole thing has got on top of him. Ever noticed his hands? He shakes like a leaf. My God, it's nearly six – you'll be late.'

'Oh no, I won't,' Kate promised her. 'I'm going to be outside that damned door at exactly 1800 hours! Wish me luck. The way I feel I may get thrown out on my ear.'

'Come in.' Michaelson was sitting at his desk. There were a lot of stubs in the ashtray in front of him. He scowled at her. Kate walked over to the desk and said, 'I won't keep you long, Captain.'

'You won't indeed,' he said. 'I'm very busy.'

'And very rude.'

He jerked upright, stared at her, and was about to say

46

something. Kate didn't flinch or look away. Suddenly he made a gesture; it was almost despairing.

'I'm sorry. It's a waste of time your coming here, but you might as well say your piece and get it over.'

'It's not a very long piece,' she said quietly. 'Just one question really. What have you got against me?'

'Against you? You in particular? You must be a very conceited young woman to ask a question like that.'

'If I'm conceited,' Kate answered, 'it's no thanks to you. I've never done anything right, so far as you're concerned. So why haven't you chucked me out?'

He leaned back in his chair, tipping it slightly. He made his expression as unpleasant as possible. 'You'll know that at the end of the course.'

'I want to know the reason; I'll take my chance on the result. You've taken a personal dislike to me, Captain Michaelson, and you've done your best to make my life hell since I came here. Either you stop it and give me a fair chance with the rest of the group, or . . .'

'Or you walk out,' he finished for her. 'I don't know how we'll win the war without you!' He lit a cigarette; she saw that he could hardly hold the lighter steady long enough to light it.

'I'm not walking out,' she said quietly. 'I wasn't going to say that. That was wishful thinking on your part. I'm going to get through and go to Europe and unless I make a mess of it, you're not going to bully me out of the chance.'

'Bully you?' The chair came back on its feet with a bump. He pushed it away and got up. He walked a few paces and then turned round to face her. 'Bully? My God, you bloody silly little idiot, you don't know what bullying means.'

Kate didn't answer. The sight of those trembling hands kept her quiet. There were lines of deep strain on a face that should have been young.

'Sit down,' he said. 'You smoke, don't you – here, have a cigarette, help yourself.' He tossed the lighter to her. 'You say I've given you hell. Well, that's my job. To make life tough and difficult so we can weed out the people who won't last the pace when they go overseas. But not tough and difficult enough! They send in girls like you, puffed up with a lot of nonsense about damaging the Germans in Europe and helping our gallant Allies to resist – did they give you all that cock-and-bull at the interview? Yes, of course they did. Told you you mustn't rush into it, oulined all the risks; not too many gory details, of course, and then said you were indispensable . . . but you must think it over very carefully and ring up some charming army chap – did he take you out to lunch by any chance? By God he did, I can see by your face! What a lot of shits they are!'

'I don't know what you're talking about,' Kate said slowly. 'It happened, but not like you put it. I do think I've got an important job to do. And why do you help them, if you think it's nonsense and they're playing some kind of dirty trick on people like me?'

He didn't answer her directly. 'It's not the men I mind.' He was speaking low, as if he was talking to himself. 'Men can take care of themselves. You can train them to be tough, to kill. To die fighting, or take the L pill. But it's madness for women! Criminal bloody madness to pretend they're men and send them out there!' He sat on the edge of the desk. 'You're very sure of yourself; you think it's going to be a bit of an adventure. I saw your attitude the first morning when you stepped off the train. I said to myself then, Oh Christ! You wouldn't listen to me, I suppose? All right, I haven't been nice to you or fair, but just try and listen to me this once. You're no coward, and you're far from stupid. I'd say that in some ways you're better equipped for this sort of thing than most of the girls I've trained here. But that doesn't make you remotely suitable to go into Europe and take on the most highly trained and ruthless counter-Intelligence service in the world. And that's what this is all about. Not tramping over the moors or climbing rocks, or having Finch throw you about and getting a few bruises. I'm talking about the Gestapo!' He grabbed another cigarette. Kate held the lighter for him. 'Not to mention the Abwehr. They're the army, but they're not exactly gentlemen when it comes to women. You're not listening, are you? No, of course you're not. I've been a sod to you, and you wouldn't take in anything I said.'

For a moment they looked at each other. It was as if she was seeing him for the first time. There was no sarcasm, no arrogance about him; the professional mask was dropped and a man racked with some private anguish was pleading with her not to make it worse. She came and held out her hand to him.

'I have listened to you. And I understand the risks now. Maybe I didn't before, but you've made them a lot clearer to me. I will think about it, I promise you. And I'm sorry you feel like this. It must be awful for you, doing this job.'

He took her hand and turned it over, studying the palm for a moment.

'You have a long life-line, anyway,' he said. 'That's something. My mother believed in it. One other thing.' He let her hand go.

'Yes?'

'Have a drink with me tonight. Because tomorrow, I'm going to make sure Finch gives you hell all over again.'

Kate smiled. 'I'll meet you in the hall then. Half an hour? I'll look forward to it.'

She went out and he sighed. Then he clenched his fist and banged it down hard on the top of the desk. He had told himself he hated her before. Now that he liked her, it was even worse.

The evening drink with Michaelson became a joke among the group. At the end of a gruelling day, nursing their bumps and bruises, cursing the insufferable Finch who was obviously enjoying their humiliation, they waited for Captain Michaelson to go up to Kate and single her out.

'He fancies you,' Fred insisted. 'I've heard the gossip from the lads in the ranks here. He never bought a drink for

49

anyone except some French girl, and now you. They said he was cracked on her, too.'

Kate nudged him lightly in his sore ribs and he groaned. 'Shut up,' she said. 'Or I'll tell Finch you want to be guinea pig tomorrow!' Then later, when they were drinking coffee in the hall after dinner, 'What French girl?'

'Don't listen to him,' Gerard interrupted. 'He has a dirty little English mind. There was someone he liked; I've heard talk, but that's all.'

'What happened to her?' Kate asked. Nobody knew. Nothing changed during the day. Michaelson encouraged Finch to drive his pupils harder every session. Kate knew what was coming, and got her share of lumps and bumps, but she was a quick pupil and she wasn't frightened. It was obvious that Judy was. Whenever possible she made an excuse not to try and exercise with Finch. Finally one day, with Michaelson in the background watching, he cornered her.

'Now Miss,' he said, 'we're going to have a special demonstration for the class. You're a young lady doing something naughty with a suitcase. Taking something somewhere which the Huns mustn't find, right? Right. I'm a nasty Nazi and I stop you and pull a gun. Right? Now here's the case, all ready for you. Good weight inside it. You take it, Miss, right-handed aren't you – right? Carry it in your right then.'

'Why right?' someone called out. 'If you were right-handed you'd carry a bag in the other hand.'

Finch grimaced, pretending to smile. 'Now why don't you wait and see, right? There's method in my madness, ladies and gents. Always a reason. Take the case, Miss.'

Judy was very pale. She moved forward, lifted the heavy suitcase and stood awkwardly.

'You're walking out of a railway station,' Finch announced. 'You're clear so far. Then up comes the nasty Nazi, which is me. So start walking towards me, if you please, right? Right!' It was obvious that Judy was uneasy. Finch sprang in front of her, pulled a dummy gun out of his pocket and yelled at her in German. Judy froze. He yelled again. She swung the suitcase, but the move was hesitant. Instead of knocking the gun out of Finch's hand, he side-stepped her easily. She dropped the case and backed away from him. She shouted, 'No, you keep off! You're not going to hurt me like that again!' It was such a shock that nobody moved or spoke. They faced each other, Judy glaring at him, the instructor grinning as if he had proved a point.

Michaelson called out, 'Try someone else, Finch. Judy's a bit sore after last time.'

Kate waited, knowing he was going to pick her. And he did. She knocked the gun out of his hand before he'd finished shouting and heaved the case at his legs. He didn't fall because he knew the movement, but an ordinary soldier would have been disarmed and knocked off his feet, while she escaped.

There was a little burst of clapping from the class. She went back, scarlet-faced, and put her arm round Judy.

'Kick him in the balls next time,' she whispered.

After the session Finch made his report. Michaelson listened, made notes, added his own assessment and paused before leaving.

'You didn't let Fitzgerald catch you out, by any chance? I've known you play tricks like that to make them over-confident.'

Finch said, 'No, Sir. She got the timing right. She's not bad, that girl. Very quick reactions and she's not scared of a rough and tumble. Whereas the other one . . .'

'Yes,' Michaelson said. 'There is a problem there. See you tomorrow. Good night.'

'What does he talk about?' They all asked her the same question. Half an hour spent with Michaelson before dinner, sitting apart from the rest. What did he say? What did they have in common? Not shop. That was the unwritten rule among the staff. Off duty they never discussed the day's events with their pupils.

51

Kate shrugged. 'Nothing special. He likes cricket.'

They all laughed. 'Come on, Kate, don't give us that!'

The French were scathing. 'Cricket! Only an Englishman would talk about a cricket game to a pretty girl.'

It was true, though they didn't believe her. He talked about the cricket matches played on the village green in his Hampshire home. He talked about his parents, and a younger sister who was getting married to the son of family friends. He talked endlessly about civilian life and his memories of growing up in a secure and peaceful countryside. And Kate listened. He wasn't in love with her, or emotionally involved as her friends supposed. He wanted someone he could talk to and she had shown him friendship that night in his office. He was a sadly isolated man, doing a job he hated and didn't believe was worthwhile. He took refuge from it for half an hour each night with Kate Fitzgerald for the price of two gin and tonics.

Nobody would believe that explanation, so she joked about it and let them think what they liked. Judy was on the defensive for some days after the incident with Finch. She brushed Kate's sympathy aside.

'I don't care what they put in the report,' Judy declared. 'I'm not going to be knocked about by that little beast. He likes it; he likes showing off at a woman's expense, especially if he thinks she's from a different class! I had it before and I'm not standing for it again!'

Kate said, 'Oh come on, Judy, that's a bit far-fetched. He's a little bully, but you're reading too much into it. All right, you're not going to let him hurt you. That's fair enough. Tell him you're not going to work with him.'

'And I'm not,' Judy blazed. 'I won't have a dirty little man like that putting his hands on me.'

Afterwards Philippe said, 'She thinks Michaelson couldn't fail her, but that's not so. He could send a very damaging report to Baker Street if he thinks she's afraid of physical pain. She must realize that.'

'I will support her,' Gerard spoke up sharply in Judy's

defence. 'She's right. Right, right – Bah! That little pig with his gramophone record – he goes too far. It isn't necessary.'

Philippe turned away. He never argued when he had made a point. If it wasn't accepted, that was that. So nothing was said, but Finch never asked Judy to demonstrate with him again.

The last part of the course was teaching them how to kill without weapons. And Kate did not come out of it well. She was excellent at defensive work, but unable to approach an unsuspecting victim and break his neck with a trained blow. Finch shouted at her, lost his temper, knocked her flying on two occasions as a lesson not to pull back at the crucial moment, but she didn't do well.

'You wait, Miss,' Finch threatened her. 'You wait till they've got your best friend by the short and curlies, and you see one of 'em. You'll use what I've taught you and be glad of it!'

It was Christmas week when they ended the course at Loch Gary. Gerard opted out. He had thought very carefully and decided that he was not the right type to work underground in Europe. He didn't trust himself to withstand physical torture and for religious reasons he would not agree to take the famous L pill and commit suicide if arrested. This made him a danger to others and he had decided to return to his RAF base. He said goodbye and wished them all luck. Everyone else in Kate's group passed and there was no query about Judy. Everyone, staff, instructors and McKay and Taft, joined in the party the night before they left for a brief Christmas leave. Michaelson didn't stay long. He congratulated them in turn and she noticed he was especially nice to Judy. He said goodbye to Kate last.

'Well done,' he said. 'You really did well. But it doesn't alter what I told you. You will think about it, won't you?'

'I will,' she promised. 'Have a nice Christmas; are you going home?'

'Yes,' he answered. 'Thank God. Are you?'

She nodded, happy at the prospect. 'I can't wait,' she said. 'I must remember not to swear when I get home. My family'd have a fit if they heard me.'

He smiled too, the wintry smile that had no joy in it. 'I'll see you in Hampshire,' he said. But it was over forty years before they met again.

'I remember my Christmas leave,' Katharine said. It was darkening outside, the sun had set and there was a faint chill in the garden that sent them indoors. Paul Roulier poured them both a drink. The terrier jumped on her knee and made itself comfortable. It watched the Frenchman with bright, inquisitive eyes, and then went to sleep.

'It was a lovely leave,' she went on. 'I told my father and mother a pack of lies about my job as a translator. Funnily enough I felt my brother didn't quite believe it. He looked at me in an odd way and I was terrified he'd say something when we were alone. But he didn't and I never knew if he suspected the truth because he was killed in Normandy. Only twenty-three. What a bloody waste.' She lit a cigarette. 'Anyway we had a marvellous Christmas and I talked French non-stop, which made Maman very happy. And then I packed up and went to Hampshire. Beaulieu – you wouldn't know it, but it's a beautiful place in the heart of the New Forest. We stayed at a very grand manor house, and that was the second stage in the training. It was very varied, and much more technical than Loch Gary. They taught us simple coding and wireless transmission, how to leave messages – Don't they call it dead-letter boxes now? – German aircraft recognition, and a sight recognition of all the German ranks and uniforms. I remember I found that bit very confusing, but I liked using the radio. They said I had a flair for transmitting.'

'You didn't find it exciting?' Roulier questioned.

She said, 'No, more interesting than exciting. I had to exercise my soft little brain instead of my body. But we had a devil of a PT instructor who made us work out for an hour a day, to keep our fitness up. What was nice about it was Judy being there, and Fred. Fred made us all laugh and drove the technical instructors up the wall. I said to him one night when we were playing cards after dinner, "How the hell do you know so much about blowing open doors and picking locks?" I'll never forget the way he said it. Solemn as a judge. "It's my living, Katie. I'm a burglar in civilian life."

'And he was. We were a nice group, but Judy and Fred and I stuck together. I never saw any of the others afterwards so I won't bother you with them. They were all decent types, several girls this time. Couriers, wireless operators, a couple of real French tarts dressed up in uniform. We had fun guessing what they were going to do when they got there.'

'So you passed out of the course, all three of you? What about Philippe? Did you see him again?'

'Oh yes,' Katharine said. 'I did indeed. I'll tell you about the final assessment. I was so thrilled at getting through I didn't think about it at the time, but afterwards, going over it in my mind, there was something wrong from start to finish.'

She was surprised to see Captain Alfurd among the panel of officers. Each candidate came in alone and was asked a set of questions, followed by a brief conversation in their special language. The senior officer was a brigadier, a most un-soldierly type, with thick glasses and a donnish way of speaking. He praised her work at Loch Gary and at Beaulieu. She had impressed her instructors and the conducting officer with her determination and courage. It had been decided to pair her with an experienced woman agent.

Kate said, 'Is it Judy, Sir?'

The Brigadier smiled. 'You're not supposed to ask, but you're quite right. She will complement you. A little tougher and bolder, but then she is older and has been overseas before. You'll make a good team.'

'Thank you, Sir,' Kate answered.

Robert Alfurd nodded at her, smiling encouragement. She felt elated and proud. She had done well; they said so.

Determined and brave. Who would have imagined that the over-eager girl who maddened Michaelson at first sight should end up with a report from him like that. Philippe had been wrong about Judy. There was no mark against her because she was frightened of unarmed combat. A little tougher and bolder! Well done, Judy. She saluted, shook hands with everyone, and felt a warm squeeze from the young Captain. Outside the door she found Philippe waiting.

'You passed? Of course. Congratulations.' He put his arms round her and kissed her cheek. The hold was a little too tight and the kiss lasted too long. She broke away.

'Where's Judy? She's going too.'

'Well, that's wonderful,' he said. 'She will be pleased.'

'What about you?' Kate asked him. 'Are you next?'

He shook his head. 'No. I am already chosen. I was waiting for you. It's a pity we're not allowed out. I could have taken you to dinner to celebrate.'

'What a pity,' Kate agreed. I wouldn't have gone, she thought, wondering what it was about him that disturbed her. She didn't like that kiss and the firm hold on her body.

'I have a lot of things to do,' she excused herself. 'Packing and tidying up. We're going straight on tomorrow for our final briefing and embarkation. I was hoping to see my family before I went.'

Philippe said, 'Your first trip won't be a long one. You'll be working with me. I asked for you especially.'

'Oh?' She managed to sound pleased. 'That *is* flattering. Did you ask for Judy too?'

He didn't hesitate. 'No. Only for you. I'd better get packed too. See you before dinner. If I remember, they give us champagne tonight.'

It was a haze in her memory, that last evening at Beaulieu. The successful candidates were noisy and elated. There was an upright piano in the room where they served coffee; one of the girls sat down and began to play popular songs. Everyone joined in, clapping and banging table tops. She ended with the sentimental hit of the year, 'We'll Meet Again'. Vera Lynn's poignant love song of two lovers parted by the war brought tears to Kate's eyes. She had teamed up with Judy and Fred. He was brimming with wine and emotion, singing at the top of his voice.

Judy nudged her. 'He's got more to be happy about than most of us. If he hadn't passed, he'd have gone back to jail!' Her laugh was full of affection. Kate saw Fred grin and reach out to her. For a moment they held hands. Kate thought in amazement, Good Lord, they're fond of each other. And I never noticed it before. She thought wistfully, I wish I had someone, instead of Philippe following me with those chilly cat's eyes. I wish I had a man to sing to tonight. Maybe she had let her imagination run away, thinking there was anything but shipboard friendship between Fred and Judy. The professional safe-breaker and the daughter of a London surgeon, who was known to be a snob. Kate dismissed the idea as fancy. Later, Captain Alfurd came and joined her.

'I must say, you came through with flying colours,' he said. The pianist was playing dance tunes and some couples were inching their way round a corner of the room where there was a little space.

'I didn't expect to,' she said. 'My conducting officer in Scotland did his best to get me chucked out.' And to persuade me not to go at all, she remembered suddenly, but she didn't say it.

'That's his job,' Alfurd countered. 'You'd be surprised how many people give up under pressure.'

'I suppose so,' Kate agreed. 'It only made me more determined.'

'So we noticed,' he said, and laughed. 'Come and dance.'

He's very nice, she thought, drifting in his arms to the piano music. I don't mind him holding me at all. She settled her cheek against his and gave in to the subtle pressure in the small of her back to bend closer in to him still.

When she went upstairs he came with her. She turned at the door and said, 'Good night.'

'Does it have to be?' He bent and kissed her on the mouth. Kate was tempted. So tempted that she was surprised at herself. She kissed him, liking the probing intimacy. Then she pushed him away.

'Good night,' she said. 'I've got an early start in the morning.'

He didn't try to argue. 'I'll get in touch when you come back. Will you have dinner with me?'

'I'd love to.'

'Take care,' he told her.

'I will,' Kate promised and went inside. She fell asleep immediately. The next morning they were taken by motor-bus to a house three miles from Lineham airport. There, under the strictest security, they were given their assign-ments. Their destination was the South of France. There they would join the famous Dulac network. Judy was to act as courier and liaise between Dulac and the neighbour-ing network south of Nice. Kate was to be the wireless operator and Fred was to hold himself in reserve for a specific task at Dulac's command. The purpose of the two major networks in the South of France was to prepare the local French Resistance and the civilian sympathizers for the coming Invasion of Europe.

Paul Roulier hadn't interrupted her; memory, especially when long suppressed, can easily be sidetracked. She was talking fluently, once or twice correcting herself. Under the lamplight in the sitting room, Katharine Alfurd seemed to be shedding the years. The past was overtaking her; her voice belonged to the young girl sitting it out in Wimborne Manor, waiting for the flight to Gibraltar and the start of her dangerous enterprise. To prepare the French people for the Invasion. What a word-picture she painted of the excitement and the comradeship between the little group, mewed up in their last stopping place in England.

'We were there for a week,' she said. 'The weather closed in and there was no flying. We were completely cut off from the outside. Once you knew your assignment and your team, you weren't allowed to telephone, write a letter or leave the grounds. It was a bit like a prison, with soldiers patrolling, and no communication. We heard that someone broke out once before leaving on a mission, just for the hell of it, and they caught him and put him in Parkhurst prison till the war was over. He knew too much to be let out. There was a separate group from the Free French. We palled up with them, and it made the time pass. They had their conducting officer with them. He'd been right through their courses and he was holding their hands up to the last minute. I remember them commenting on the fact that ours hadn't come with us. It was unheard of to separate the trainees from their conducting officer half-way through the course. They couldn't understand it.'

'Naturally *you* wouldn't see anything sinister in it,' Roulier remarked. 'You weren't experienced. But what about Philippe and Judy? Didn't they think it peculiar?'

'Philippe brushed it aside,' Kate answered. 'You couldn't tell what he was thinking anyway. Judy just complained to the French; she was in a funny sort of mood those last few days. Everything SOE did was wrong and the Gaullists had it right. Fred was like a lost soul when he wasn't with her. He didn't speak a word of any language and that was where Michaelson would have been a godsend. I thought to myself, how on earth are we going to keep him hidden when we get over. If he opens his mouth to sneeze, he'll be caught. But you put those thoughts away damned quickly when you're waiting to go. If you start worrying, it's hopeless. We'd been taught to be positive, aggressive. I said to myself, Fred'll be all right. They know what they're doing. And of course I was thrilled to be working in the Dulac network. It really was an SOE legend. Again and again they'd made fools of the Germans. There were several hundred of them in that area and they'd done marvellous work in collecting information and sabotaging communications throughout the Midi. I kept wondering, what is Jean Dulac going to be like? Philippe wouldn't be drawn. "You'll meet him and you can judge for yourself," was all he'd say. It could have meant anything.'

She paused to light a cigarette. 'I've smoked like a chimney,' she said. 'Good Lord, look at the time. You must be starving. I forgot about food.'

Roulier said, 'This has been quite an ordeal for you, Madame. Let me go into your kitchen and see what I can find. I would be happy with a sandwich.'

'Oh, there's plenty to eat, I was expecting my grandsons for lunch yesterday. There's some Sauternes in the fridge. Are you sure you don't mind?'

He smiled. 'You know Frenchmen are quite at home in a kitchen. We're not like the English. I'm sorry about your grandsons. But then we wouldn't have been able to talk, would we?'

He had to admire the organization. He wondered how they'd managed to re-arrange the plan and get her family out of the way. Katharine Alfurd heard him moving round the small kitchen. He was right, of course. In all the years they'd been married, Robert had never cooked a meal. It was clever of the young man not to break her concentration. A very quiet, professional sort of person. He knew when to prompt, and when to stay silent. There was a sympathy between them, in spite of the age difference.

It was all becoming so real; memories were becoming thoughts and feelings, projecting her out of the present into the past. She had her dates right; the distant past was clearer than the events of a week ago. When he came into the room with a tray she said suddenly, 'Do you realize, the very time we were at Wimborne Manor, Christian Eilenburg was on his way to take up his post at Gestapo Headquarters in Nice?'

3

He had travelled by train overnight from Paris. He had a
slight headache after the party given at the Petite Étoile
restaurant. It was a happy evening, surrounded by his
colleagues. They'd provided some French girls, and he'd
spent a couple of hours with a redhead before catching the
train at the Gare du Nord. Promotion suited him. He was
proud of the Standartenführer flashes on his black uniform.
The silver thread was new and it shone. He had proved
himself at the Avenue Foch, showing that a young officer
could see problems with a fresh eye. SS General Knocken
had recommended Eilenburg for Standartenführer's rank
and a letter signed by Heinrich Himmler himself required
him to take charge of Gestapo operations in Nice. A strong
Resistance had been flourishing in the Midi, run by the
Communist-controlled Maquis and British agents. There
had been sabotage, serious acts of terrorism against German
personnel off duty, and evidence that information was being
gathered and passed to the Allies. A very strong hand was
needed, the letter said. The zeal and enterprise of Standartenführer Eilenburg had earned him this posting. The first
thing he did was to select a team of twenty men from the SD
section go to to the South with him. And one expert from the
French arm of the Gestapo, the Milice. Eilenburg had seen

him at work in Paris. A Frenchman more terrible to his compatriots than any German. And for motives that made Eilenburg disgusted and contemptuous. A sadist and a pervert, but a useful tool just the same. Better for him to sink to the lowest depths than for one of Eilenburg's own men. He was met by a big Mercedes at Nice station. There was a chronic shortage of petrol; many of the army officers had to share transport. But there was no limit on resources for the Gestapo. People made way for him as he walked out into the April sunshine. He saw the fear in the faces of the French, some sitting on their cases after waiting all night in the hope of a ticket. But there was open hostility too. That indicated how far German authority had deteriorated. He got into the back of the Mercedes and was driven along the promenade to his quarters at the Hôtel Negresco.

It was cold and windy, the slate-grey sea slapping angrily along the beach. There was nothing more desolate, Eilenburg felt, than a resort in the off-season. He had never been to the South of France before. He had arrived in Paris as a lieutenant, on his first tour of duty a year ago. He spoke very good French and was a talented police investigator. Hardworking and ambitious, he caught his superior's attention. He knew instinctively how to manipulate people without always using brute force. He was a clever, ruthless psychologist who understood how to turn weakness and veniality to his advantage. His first work in Paris was mostly routine check-ups on suspected persons on the Left Bank. Small, unimportant quarries. Petty thieves robbing drunken soldiers in the street. Prostitutes who sold bits of trivial information to third-rate Intelligence touts who would just as easily have worked for the Germans and often did. It was too easy to be a challenge, but he became known and feared among the Parisian half-world of crime, masquerading as Resistance. From there he moved to rapid promotion and to investigations on a more sophisticated level. When given a test case by his senior officer he proved himself a skilled and merciless interrogator.

A well-known architect, a respected member of the intelligentsia in pre-war Paris, was arrested after his telephone had been tapped. Reference had been made to Fresnes prison. A number of important Resistance workers were being held there from cities like Chartres and Bordeaux, waiting to be interrogated and then shot. A savage beating had failed to make the Frenchman give the name of the man who had telephoned him, or any explanation for what had been said. Eilenburg had sent a doctor to his cell. He came in person to apologize for the ill treatment and assured the prisoner that he would have the SS men responsible punished. He behaved very correctly, without being too friendly. He created the impression of a civilized young German officer who deplored brutality and was embarrassed by what had happened. He let two days pass. No more questions were asked; the Frenchman was left to torture himself with anticipation. On the third day, he was brought out, taken in a van to the rue des Saussaies and brought to the fourth floor. There were four men in civilian clothes. Three of them were Germans, but he didn't know that because they never spoke. The fourth was the celebrated sadist, borrowed for the occasion from the Milice. The shock of what a fellow countryman did to him, broke the victim. He confessed to a plot to rescue the prisoners in Fresnes, implicated everyone, and died of his injuries two days later. That was the beginning of Christian Eilenburg's spectacular rise in the Gestapo hierarchy. At twenty-six, he was promoted above men much older and with long experience. He was talked of as the successor to the great Reinhardt Heydrich, the 'Butcher of Prague'. Not unlike in looks either. The same striking Nordic type, almost white blond, with blue eyes and a fine athletic body.

The car drew up outside the Hôtel Negresco. A wedding-cake in plaster, he thought. All architectural icing, designed to sparkle white in the sunshine. On that chilly day it looked drab and grey, the palm trees huddled in the wind. But it was the most luxurious hotel on the playground coast of France, and he, from his modest background in Hamburg, would live in one of its finest private suites. He went inside. He ordered breakfast, had a hot bath. His personal servant had laid out a fresh uniform. He wandered into the sitting room, still in his dressing-gown. He tried the sofa and the two armchairs. Very comfortable. A small cabinet for drinks. He would send for a stock of spirits and cocktail mixes. He had grown to like cocktails in Paris, and was good at making them. Off duty he was gregarious, liked parties and pretty women. He did his job and then he felt justified in thoroughly enjoying life. There was a handsome writing desk by the window; he opened the drawers and found headed paper and envelopes. There was ink in the little bronze pot. While he was standing there, his breakfast arrived on a trolley. When he first came to Paris, the standard of living in good hotels and restaurants had intimidated him. His family were solid middle-class Germans, who never went to such places. Now, he had become quite at ease. He ate the food, grimaced at the coffee, which was made of acorns and tasted bitter, and decided he would write to his family before he went to his new head-quarters. He had an elder brother, posted missing on the Russian front. His mother had become an old woman when she heard the news. They were a united family, and the loss of Ernst brought them even closer. He was their only son now, and he became immediately responsible for them and three elderly grandparents. He wrote to them regularly, and looked forward to their letters. The Allied bombing had reduced Hamburg to a blasted ruin, but the Eilenburgs were moved to a little house on the edge of the suburbs. It had been requisitioned by the Gestapo when the air raids started. They had a store of such properties, ranging from large mansions in private grounds to modest bungalows. The previous owners had gone to concentration camps. His family were as safe as privilege could make them. The girl he was engaged to marry was a nurse. They had been at school together, and members of the Hitler Youth. Sweethearts from childhood, Christian knew he was going to marry

Minna. She was a gentle girl, devoutly patriotic. To her, even more than him, Germany and the Führer were one and the same. She had firmly refused to go to a hospital out of bomber range. Twice the hospital in Hamburg had been hit, with many casualties among the patients and the staff. On his last leave he had begged her to move to a safe place. The haunted face, the big brown eyes red-rimmed with sleeplessness and strain, tortured him and at the same time made him proud. Her place was with her people. She refused his help.

He wrote to her first. 'My darling Minna, I'm writing from Nice, having just arrived. A very luxurious hotel; my God, how I wish you could be here with me. I think of what you and all our people at home are suffering and I feel guilty because I have everything I want. I don't know how to live with my own safety, when I think of Ernst and you and so many of our friends. But this is a very important job. A big promotion. Can I boast a little bit to you? I've done so well in Paris, that General Knocken sent me here to clear up a bad mess. They've been killing our troops, damaging German property and spying on us. I haven't met the fool who was in charge, but I'll see him this morning. I'm going to teach these people a lesson. I'm going to make this a safe place for our troops to walk at night. They won't get on a train or travel in a truck convoy and wonder if they're going to be blown up. And anyone I catch endangering our security will pay a price, I promise you. For you, and for Ernst and for all our people and the Führer, I'm going to play my part in winning this war and saving Germany. I promise you.'

He wrote tenderly, reminding her of the last time they made love. She was so weary and nerve-racked it had taken a long time to reassure her and achieve climax. But it had been the best of all for him. He had felt so much a part of her that he could well have left a child behind. He hoped so. He longed for her and read her letters again and again. She must know by now that he wasn't good at expressing himself on paper. When he came on leave he would bring her back to France with him. He wouldn't listen to her a second time.

They'd marry and she'd come with him. He urged her to visit his mother and father. She was like a daughter to them. Ernst's girlfriend had married someone else. His parents didn't talk about her any more. He ended with their erotic nicknames for each other's bodies, wanting her as he wrote. Sighing, he closed up the letter. No German censor would read his love talk. The Gestapo were above the law. Then he began a long letter to his parents, describing the journey and the hotel and the weather, asking anxious questions about their health and welfare, offering whatever they needed. His father was a proud man, who had accepted the safe accommodation because of his wife and their respective parents. He refused to touch extra rations.

Eilenburg sealed that too. He looked at his watch. It was time to go down to the Headquarters at the Villa Trianon. If they thought they could over-ride the new man because he was young and Knocken's protégé from Paris, they would soon realize they were mistaken. Dressed, he paused for a moment to check himself in the mirror. He'd heard the references to Heydrich. Very flattering, he thought, except that he was ambushed by Czech agents and shot. By the time I've finished here, he said to his reflection, there won't be any agents left alive to shoot me if I walk unprotected down the Promenade and back.

He picked up the telephone. There were no preliminaries, just the order. 'Standartenführer Eilenburg – I want my car at the entrance immediately.'

Within twenty-four hours of his arrival at the Villa Trianon the people of Nice knew they had a new Gestapo chief.

They had two days' rest in Gibraltar after the long flight from England. Kate and Judy sunned themselves on the balcony of the private house where they were staying. It was surprisingly warm for those two days. Fred, who had suffered miserably from air sickness on the bumpy flight, amused himself playing cards with their hosts, and stayed indoors. They were Anglo-Spaniards, and they were known only as Maria and José. They were charming, generous people, engaged in several anti-Nazi networks that operated on the Rock. Theirs was one of several houses where SOE agents waited for the boat to smuggle them across to France.

Philippe disappeared the second day. He didn't say where he was going and towards mid-afternoon Judy asked Maria. They were forbidden to roam round Gibraltar.

'He's gone over the border into Spain.'

Kate stared at her. 'But it's full of Germans! Supposing he was recognized?'

The woman shrugged. 'He knows what he's doing,' she answered. 'He must have business with someone in Valerez. Don't worry about him.'

'I'm not.' Kate spoke sharply. 'I'm worrying about us. We're not allowed to go out in the street in case someone sees us in France and remembers. Why should it be safe for him?'

'Safe for who?' Philippe said behind her. There was a quick exchange in Spanish between him and Maria. Then he said to Kate, 'I'm sorry you were worried. What I did was perfectly discreet. You'll have to learn to trust me, Cecilie. From now on, we use our code names at all times. Cecilie, Julie and you, Fred, will be Pandora.'

Fred protested. 'That's a bloody girl's name.'

'She opened a famous box,' the Frenchman said, and smiled. 'I am Pierrot. The tide is right and we leave at midnight tonight.' He went out of the room. Kate frowned. 'I think it's a bit silly making us use our code names to each other.'

'It's standard practice when you leave on a mission,' Judy said. 'Cecilie's rather nice, it suits you.' She saw the look of disgust on Fred's face. 'Pandora's not too bad.'

She's very protective towards him, Kate noticed. She was really worried because he was feeling sick on that awful flight over. Cecilie, Julie, Pandora, Pierrot. What a strange name for him to choose; the faceless clown forever darting to and fro across the stage, a man hidden behind a painted mask.

And by this time tomorrow they would be in France. Every muscle in her stomach knotted.

'I'm scared,' she said out loud. 'I'm really scared. Isn't that awful?'

Maria laughed. 'Everyone is a little scared when they're waiting to sail,' she said. 'It's a very good sign. It will make you cautious. And that helps to bring you home. Who would like some wine?'

She spoke to Judy, who looked up quickly and said, 'What – Oh, yes, thank you.'

I wonder if she feels like I do, Kate thought. She's been very quiet about it. She's the experienced one. I think she's frightened for Pandora.

'Let's get our stuff together, Julie,' she suggested.

The other girl nodded. 'Good idea. Then we'll come down and have some wine.'

When they were in their room she said, 'Don't worry, it'll be all right. I didn't want to say much because poor Pandora has butterflies in the stomach ever since we took off. It's bloody awful for him, not speaking a word and having to lie up somewhere till he's needed. I'll be happy when I see him set up safely.' She put her arm round Kate's shoulders. 'It's the waiting that's difficult. The moment you land and make contact, you'll feel quite different.'

'I never asked you,' Kate said. 'Did you come this way before?'

'I parachuted in,' she answered. 'Into Brittany. That was pretty scary, but at least it was quick. I hate the sea crossing, I'm always as sick as a cat in a boat.'

And she was, right up to the moment when she was lifted ashore on a deserted beach just before dawn. Two men and a woman met them. They spoke in loud voices, laughing, offering cigarettes. Pierrot was known to them; she had begun to think of him by the code name. She wondered why they made so much noise. It seemed careless, when somebody, anybody, might have been walking out of sight but close enough to hear. She took a cigarette and found that she was so cold she couldn't light it. The trip had been rough and freezing. The cigarette made her feel queasy. She wished they'd stop talking at the top of their voices and get them off the beach. The felucca had turned about and was sailing away. For a moment they all joined in waving goodbye, then one of the men said to her,

'This way. We've got some hot coffee and some cognac. Take my jacket, you're shivering.'

They crowded into an ancient van, with a gas bag tied to its roof. There was no petrol for French civilians. They put brandy into the mugs of filthy ersatz coffee, offered more cigarettes. Two young men, one with a consumptive cough; he'd given her his jacket: a middle-aged woman with wiry hair touched grey in places. Julie had some colour in her cheeks. Pandora was silent and withdrawn, nursing the hot drink. They were talking eagerly to Pierrot. He didn't seem affected by the journey across; in the feeble torchlight he could have been wearing some kind of mask, with the pale eyes glittering through the slits. Kate shivered, still cold, but it was the goose across the grave shiver that she remembered from her childhood when she was frightened of something unknown that was about to happen.

The Frenchwoman announced, 'We're taking you through Nice and to your first safe house just outside. We'll have to pass the German checkpoint on the road because the curfew hasn't lifted.' She grinned at them. 'Don't worry, we're the van that brings the milk to the Hôtel Mondiale for the Boche officers' breakfasts. They always let us through and they never look inside. You just lie on the floor and we'll stack the crates in front of you.'

They passed through the checkpoint; Kate heard the guttural German voices and held her breath, waiting for the van doors to be flung open. The milk crates were wedged in front of them. They were bent double hiding behind them. They were in darkness and the stop seemed to go on for ever. Someone laughed; it was followed by a brisk order.

'*Machen Sie, dass Sie fortkommen.*'

They began bumping along and slowly Julie raised herself. 'You all right, Pandora?'

The reply from the far side was cheerful. 'Fine. How about you, love?'

He mustn't call her that, Kate thought in alarm. She ought to tell him.

She had lost the sense of time; in fact the last part of their journey was less than twenty minutes. When the back doors opened, the woman was smiling at them. The sun was fully up and the air smelt fresh after the stuffy atmosphere inside.

'We leave you here,' she said. 'Hurry, I'll introduce you, then we must get on or those swine won't have milk for their coffee. Or their slops emptied. I work there, you see. Useful, cleaning out their bedrooms.' She laughed, shaking her head.

They were in a quiet side road, surrounded by pine trees. The van had stopped in front of a pink-washed house, low-built and shuttered. The front door opened and a man and a woman came out. They were both elderly, the man limped as he came towards them. They embraced the woman and shook hands with Kate, Julie and the silent Pandora, who only grinned and nodded. The Provençal accent was very strong. Kate looked round, wishing they would go inside, out of sight. Nobody seemed concerned with security. And there was no sign of Pierrot.

She said, 'I think we'd be better in the house', and led the way.

'I am Marcel,' the old man said. 'And my wife, Jeanne. You will stay here with us until Dulac comes. You must be tired and hungry after the journey. My wife will make something to eat and I'll show you where you can sleep.'

'Marcel,' Kate said. 'Another comrade came with us. Pierrot, do you know him?' When he nodded, she said, 'He didn't come in the van – where is he?'

Marcel shrugged. 'He goes his own way,' he said. 'He must have other business. Don't worry about him.'

She and Julie were given a tiny attic room which smelt of must and had a window which wouldn't open. There were two small iron bedsteads with blankets and hard mattresses. It was swept clean, but airless as a tomb. Kate sat on the bed; she felt numb with tiredness.

'Julie,' she began, 'why didn't Pierrot come with us? I didn't even realize he had left the van.'

The other girl said hurriedly, 'Oh, God knows. He's a law unto himself. Look, I want to see where poor Pandora is – if he wants to pee he can't even ask where to go. I shan't be long.'

Kate sat for some minutes, waiting for her to come back. The time passed.

'She's not thinking of anything but him,' Kate said out loud. 'They've probably gone down to eat. I wish I felt hungry. Maybe I would if I wasn't so uneasy.'

She got up, stretched and rebuked herself. 'Stop talking to yourself, you idiot. You'll go round the bend.'

There was soup and coarse home-made bread. Wine was offered. Marcel and his wife were talking excitedly, asking questions about England. Kate liked them both and wondered how they had become involved in such dangerous work. Simple, honest people; living the frugal lives of the French under Occupation. She was sure that what they were eating was the old couple's ration for the day.

Julie said, 'When is Dulac coming?'

Their faces glowed with enthusiasm. 'Tonight. There'll be a meeting here. It's so wonderful when he comes. He brings such hope to us all.' They looked at each other and Jeanne said, 'He's a great man. You'll love him, just like all of us.'

Kate translated. 'Must be a bloody marvel,' Pandora muttered. He looked bewildered and disconsolate. He couldn't understand a word and kept watching Julie.

'Do you always meet here?' she asked.

Marcel nodded. 'We are the reception house. Dulac will decide what he wants you to do and where you are to go. Sometimes people stay here with us. We like it. Our sons are

71

gone and it gets lonely. There are no houses near, only the woods. It makes this a good place for people to stay. The Germans never come this way. We're left in peace.'

His wife said, 'We've talked enough; let the poor children sleep. They're always so tired when they first come.'

'Julie,' Kate said when they were upstairs, 'why didn't Pierrot come with us? He's our senior officer till we meet Dulac. Surely it's most irregular to disappear like that and leave us to it?'

Julie sounded sleepy. 'He knows this place backwards. He knew who was meeting us and that we'd be all right. I don't know why you get so hot and bothered about him.'

'I don't know either,' Kate answered. 'There's just something about him.'

The other girl laughed. 'He's keen on you, that's what it is,' she said. 'And you don't like him. It's a creepy feeling. I noticed him watching you the whole time at Loch Gary. He was so jealous of Michaelson, having a drink with you every evening. We all thought it was quite funny. But don't worry about it. He'll be too busy to be a nuisance. God, I'm exhausted!'

Kate said, 'It isn't that. He's so detached, so secretive. He's not a leader and walking off this morning proves it. He's out on his own, Julie, and that's not what he's supposed to be.'

Julie raised herself briefly from the pillow.

'My dear Cecilie, the first thing you've got to learn is that all that stuff they teach you at home has nothing whatever to do with the facts of life when you're over here. Why don't you go to sleep? I've had it, I can't talk any more.'

Moments later her breathing was deep and regular. Kate lay and stared at the ceiling. There were cracks in the plaster; a spider crawled out of one, froze at some sense of human presence and then retreated. She closed her eyes and slept.

*　　*　　*

It was dark when he came. They had been gathered in the kitchen for an hour. There were five members of the network, including the woman who worked as a chambermaid at the Hôtel Mondiale. When there was a knock at the back door, there was a movement of excitement among them. Pierrot came into the kitchen. Kate watched him. He was dressed in a formal suit and tie, and carried a shabby leather briefcase. He looked completely different; the cat-like face and eyes were merely nondescript. He had shed his personality and taken on a new one. A small-town businessman, provincial, badly dressed in ill-cut clothes. A man nobody would look at twice. He greeted everyone. They seemed pleased to see him. There was a friendly atmosphere. This was an old and trusted comrade. He made room for himself beside Kate.

'You seem rested,' he said quietly.

'Why did you leave us?' she demanded.

'I had work to do,' he answered. 'I knew you would be in good hands. And you were, weren't you?'

'Yes,' she admitted. 'But if we'd been stopped. . . .'

'Then I would have been captured as well,' he said coolly. 'And what good would that do anyone? The first rule over here is to survive. Remember that.' He put his hand on her arm and let it rest for a moment. 'I'm sorry if you were frightened. You'll get used to it. Dulac will inspire you.'

Even though she was looking up at him, Kate couldn't tell whether he was mocking or serious. She helped herself to a glass of wine. He had to take his hand away. When the knock came it was different. Bold and insistent, and Marcel jumped up and stumbled in his eagerness to open it.

'Dulac!' he cried out, and everyone got to their feet.

'He was not at all what I expected,' Katharine Alfurd said. 'I'd imagined some Hollywood film-star type, winning the war single-handed. He wasn't that sort of man at all.'

'I've seen photographs of him,' Paul Roulier said. 'And the statue. Maybe they flattered him.'

'Maybe,' she smiled slightly. 'He was so dark, that sur-

73

prised me. Very dark, with black eyes. And slight. Beautifully made, like a dancer. Not the beefy hero type at all. I remember thinking, good Lord, you could be an artist or a musician.'

'But he made an impact on you?' he asked. He felt her withdraw from him, from her surroundings. She was looking through him and beyond as she answered.

'Oh yes,' Katharine Alfurd said. 'From the first moment he came into that room I fell in love with him. The *coup de foudre*, it really can happen. Just like it says: you're struck by lightning and you're in love before you've even spoken. That was the impact on me. Afterwards, he told me he'd felt the same happen to him too.'

'I'm sorry,' Roulier said, 'if it distresses you to talk about him. But I have to know.'

She came back to him in her mind. 'Of course you do,' she said. 'It doesn't distress me; it's so long ago and some of it was so marvellous and so happy. I always try to think about that part, if I can. The other part – well, everyone knows about that.'

He didn't hurry her. He let a pause develop. Then: 'That was your first meeting – please tell me about it.'

Magnetism, Kate thought; even the lights seem to be brighter. The way he embraces Jeanne, kisses her and hugs her as if he were her son. The same with Marcel; he doesn't shake hands, he clasps them, as if that contact was the most important to him in the world. And the confident, brilliant smile that makes you want to smile back, as if he'd brought you good news. Yes, he would inspire me, she thought, feeling her rapid heartbeat. He was clapping Pierrot on the back, saying over and over how glad he was to see him, warming even that cold man into enthusiasm. And then he came to her, and they touched hands. Maybe nobody else round them noticed anything.

'You're Cecilie,' he said. 'Welcome to France. With your help she will soon be free again.'

Tears came into her eyes. She had to blink hard to force them back. He saw them and lifting her hand to his lips he kissed it. Then he turned away and took his place at the table and the meeting began.

Perhaps it was the voice she fell in love with. It wasn't mellifluous, or stagey like the Colonel in Baker Street who talked as if he were playing a musical instrument. It was a baritone in musical terms, clear and pleasing; he had a gift for words that caught the imagination, and the content was fiery with patriotism. And with humour. He radiated confidence and optimism. Everything was going well. France's ordeal would soon be over. Kate heard the theme of Europe's Liberation for the first time that night, but he never spoke as leader without making it a focal point. He introduced the new comrades. Each was asked to stand up and each was given a toast. Pandora, silent as usual, was nudged to his feet. He grinned awkwardly.

'Our friend from England,' Dulac said. 'Braver than most, because he doesn't speak our language and has to stay hidden until his moment comes. A very important moment,' he looked round the table, 'I want everyone to remember that, because it may be hard for some of you who have to take risks in the open, to think of our friend staying low in safety. But he has come here for a purpose and when we know what that is, he'll play his part as bravely as any one of us. Pandora, Dulac welcomes you!'

Julie translated; Pandora reddened and sat down as quickly as possible.

'Now,' Dulac sipped his wine. 'We'll make our reports. Gaston, you begin.'

There was a convoy of German troops expected to relieve part of the garrison at Antibes. Among them would be several senior officers wounded in Italy. Their destination was the Hôtel du Cap, now taken over by the German army as a convalescent home. Gaston had the information from a girl who was friendly with one of the staff working at the hotel. The officers were expected in the next month and the garrison in the area was preparing to be part-relieved. So, Gaston concluded, what plans should be made to attack the convoy and kill the senior officers?

'How senior are they?' Pierrot asked.

Gaston didn't know in detail, but nobody under the rank of colonel was sent to that hotel.

The woman who worked at the Hôtel Mondiale was called Marie. She took up the point.

'Colonels and upwards are worth killing,' she said flatly. 'But isn't it more important to wipe out these relief troops if we can? The others are targets, true, but they're not combatants at this moment. I say we should concentrate on the troops, and if we get the officers as well – eh, that's a bonus!'

There was a mutter of agreement. Gaston looked sullen. One forgets the human element, Kate thought. He's angry that Marie's pushed him into the background. He's glaring at her as if she was an enemy. Then Dulac interrupted, averting trouble between them.

'Gaston, this is very important information. Just the kind of exercise we need. And Marie, you have made a valuable comment. Ideally we should kill as many Germans, whatever their rank or condition, as we can, as often as we can. But first we need to know approximately how many relief troops will be coming. That will determine the method of attack; whether it is trucks, with armoured escorts or scout cars, and what time these officers are expected at Antibes, also how many. That will indicate the time the troops will come into Nice.' He paused and said to Pierrot, 'Can you get this information for us?'

Beside Kate, the Frenchman shifted slightly. She felt the movement and it signalled his surprise.

'I should be able to,' he answered. 'If you think it's worth the risk.'

Dulac smiled, as if he had said something rather foolish.

'It's not like you to talk about risks, my friend. You've been in England too long. Everything we do is a risk. Every time we go on to the streets, speak to each other, send a message, it's a risk. Yes, Pierrot, I want the information and you will take the risk. Jacques, how much ammunition and explosives have we at Saint Paul?'

Jacques was a squat, ugly man, with the grimy hands of a mechanic.

'Forty sticks of gelignite, a case of grenades, a thousand rounds of ammunition for the submachine guns. Enough to do a lot of damage, if we stop everything else. We have to choose between the power plant and this convoy. We can't attack both.'

Julie spoke up. 'What is the power plant?'

'Our next scheduled target,' Dulac told her. 'It supplies two factories making spare parts for the railway; also, the town of Nice. Destroying it would cause a lot of inconvenience and confusion to our own people, but it would be a blow at the German supply lines by rail. And its propaganda value would be high.'

'People here have a bad enough time,' Marie said. 'Taking their light and heat away wouldn't make them love us. What about the hospital?'

'It has its own generator,' Jacques answered. 'I service it; nobody would suffer more than a few minutes' darkness. I say we should blow the power station and maybe mount a small attack on the ambulances going to Antibes. Leave the main troops alone.'

'I agree,' Gaston said. He took out a pipe and filled it with a coarse tobacco. The smell was choking in the crowded kitchen.

Julie said coldly, 'Put that out, will you, please. I can't breathe.'

'Then take a walk outside,' he snapped.

'No, Gaston.' Dulac was pleasant. 'If you want to suffocate yourself you'll be the one to take the walk. I think you can wait till later for your smoke. Put it out, my friend. We have to come to a decision. When that decision is reached, we'll know whether to call on Jacques's people or not.'

Kate whispered to Pierrot, 'What people?'

His lips hardly moved. 'Maquis. Communists. He's their leader in this area.'

'Now.' Dulac had risen to his feet. Immediately he was in full command of them all. 'Normally we would vote. But there is a chance to do both, as I see it. What we have is enough explosive and ammunition to attack the troop convoy, provided it is not bigger than usual or specially protected. Pierrot will find that out. After that, we lie very quiet and ask London for a drop of more supplies for the power station. That gives us time. What do you say?'

'I say we put the plan to London,' Pierrot said. Nobody else had time to speak. 'I say we send a radio message and wait for their reaction. It may not be possible for them to make a drop for some long time. In which case we must choose one target and let the other one go – if it's the power station, the factories will have supplied the spares to the railways before we get a chance to strike. Let London decide.'

Kate had never heard him assert himself before. The change from cold detachment to hard opposition was remarkable. There was silence. The others were all watching Dulac. Whatever Pierrot said, they would follow their leader's decision. As I would, Kate decided. I'd like to say something, but it wouldn't be right. I'd like to support him because I think this is an attempt to challenge his authority. But I've only just arrived . . . it would be resented.

As if he knew her thoughts, Dulac turned and looked at her. 'Here we have Cecilie; a very good radio operator, I'm told. It's time she went to work. We'll send a message to London and she will transmit it for us this evening. My friends, let's have some wine and then go on our way. We meet when we have an answer. You'll be contacted in the usual way.'

She knew he was going to come over to her. Seeing him fill a glass, pause for a word with Gaston and the dour mechanic Jacques, who controlled the Maquis, nobody would have guessed that Kate was his objective. But she knew, and she

78

sat still until he took the vacant seat beside her. She hadn't noticed Pierrot leave. He hadn't won, but she didn't know why not.

'You look a little worried,' he said. 'It's all very new and confusing, isn't it?'

'Yes, a little,' she admitted.

'I am glad you came,' he said. 'London says you're very talented. Our last operator wasn't as efficient as I hoped.'

'Oh.'

The very dark eyes gleamed for a moment and Kate felt herself flushing red.

'Nothing happened to them,' Dulac answered the unspoken question. 'It was a man and he had a heavy hand. I sent him to another network. I don't mind if he makes a mess of their messages. You're not staying here, they have a detector van that sometimes trundles up and down. Not very often. They're not as dangerous in the Midi as they are in the North. If you get your things and your set, I'll take you to the place where you'll be living from now on. In ten minutes? That gives us plenty of time before the curfew.'

Kate got up. 'I'll be ready,' she said.

'Good.'

She ran up the stairs to the stuffy little room. Her suitcase with the hidden transmitter was under the iron bedstead. She folded her clothes and packed them in the body of the case. It was heavy, but not heavy enough to be suspicious if anyone else picked it up. The weight was adjusted to the sex and strength of the operative. Julie came into the room.

'You're leaving,' she said. 'God, that's quick. He doesn't waste time, does he? You'll send your first message tonight. You're not scared, are you? You needn't be. You're in a marvellous safe place, miles away from anything.' She came up to Kate and kissed her. 'Good luck,' she said. 'We'll meet in a few days. Poor Pandora's down there looking like a lost soul. I'll go and find him.'

She was gone, as Kate heaved the suitcase up and started

down the narrow stairs. Marcel and Jeanne were waiting for her in the little dingy hall. Each embraced her.

'You'll be safe with him,' they told her. 'He has a charmed life. It's an honour, my child, for him to take you to your safe house himself. Good night, God go with you.'

He was waiting for her outside. He took the suitcase from her and she followed him without speaking a word.

They travelled by bicycle, her case strapped to the back of her machine.

'I can't take it,' he explained. 'If we're stopped, Cecilie, they might wonder why I was carrying a case full of women's clothes. That would mean questions and we can't afford them. It's flat for most of the way into Nice.'

'We're going to Nice? I thought this house was in the hills.'

'It is,' he spoke over his shoulder. 'But we can't get there by bicycle. It would take too long and sometimes they have patrols on the roads up there. We have another method of travel.' He grinned at her; he looked much younger, almost boyish. 'You'll see. Just leave everything to me.'

They came into the town by the back roads. A few shops were open and some of the cafés were brightly lit. Kate realized that she was terribly hungry. There were bicycles everywhere, and a number of people strolled along the handsome Promenade des Anglais: groups of German soldiers, some with girls on their arms.

Most of the hotels were open; the Negresco and the Étoile d'Or were full of Germans. The lights were sparkling in the evening sunlight; sleek staff cars flying the swastika pennant crowded the forecourts. As they passed, Kate heard the hum of music coming from the Étoile restaurant.

'They eat,' he said, 'while we half-starve. They bring their fat wives and daughters down here and gorge themselves on French food and wine. They go back to Germany loaded with luxuries, half of it stolen from the Jews who've been arrested. And there are Frenchmen and women as guilty as

80

they are. Filling their pockets out of the misery of France. Those are the ones I want to see punished when this war is over. I have a list of my own. Turn right down here.'

They stopped at a little grocer's shop. The window was half-empty. Dulac looked round.

'Bring the machine inside,' he said.

A young woman came to meet them. She looked thin and hollow-eyed, and from a room in the rear a baby cried fretfully. Dulac placed a hand on her shoulder. Kate saw the look of devotion she gave him.

'I've brought a friend,' he said. 'We need to go out to Valbonne tonight.'

She said, 'I'll close up.'

Dulac went through to the back of the shop, Kate following. They found themselves in a kitchen, stone-floored and lit by one ceiling light that cast a modest glow over the old-fashioned scrubbed table. A baby whimpered in a cot in the corner, and something cooked on the big iron stove. Nappies dried by the side of it and a basket full of clothes waited to be ironed. Kate had left her bicycle in the narrow passageway. She went to the baby. It was small, and hiccuped from crying. She began to rock the cot. Dulac watched her and lit a cigarette. He felt suddenly very tired. He sat down at the table and smoked, watching Kate soothe the baby until it fell asleep. It was so long since he had seen a woman who moved him to anything but simple sexual appetite. She had beautiful eyes. Green and blue that changed in the light until they looked like a summer seascape. Dark hair with flecks of red in it. She left the child asleep and came to sit beside him. He felt exhausted but peaceful, not saying anything while he finished his cigarette. The young woman came in and he looked up.

'You'll need some food,' she said. 'I'll make something. There's wine on the shelf there.'

'I'll get it,' Kate said. She filled three glasses.

'Not for me.' The girl shook her head. 'I'm feeding and it doesn't agree with Louise.' She nodded towards the cot.

'Thank God she's asleep now. She cries all night sometimes.'

Kate said, 'How old is she?'

'Four months.' There was a flat despair in the voice. 'They took my husband away last August. Some labour camp in Germany. I've only had one letter since. He didn't mention Louise, so I don't know when it was written. He may be dead.'

She was putting out sausage and bread and a slab of home-made cheese on the table. Her movements were listless. As she leaned over him, Dulac put an arm round her.

'You mustn't say that, Beatrice,' he said. 'Pierre isn't dead. They're losing the war and they know it; they won't bother with letters. He'll come back to you and Louise when it's all over. You must believe that.'

She managed a thin smile. 'I believe it when you're here,' she said simply. 'But not when I'm alone. I think, he's dead and I'll never know how or where. Louise will grow up without a father. The Germans will close down the shop, or the van will get stopped on the way to Valbonne and they'll come breaking the door down in the middle of the night. I'm such a coward, Jean, when you're not here, you wouldn't believe it.'

She brushed a tear off her face, and turned back to the stove. 'I have some sort of coffee, if you can drink it,' she said. 'The wine is better. I wish it didn't give her so much wind.'

'One glass won't hurt her,' Jean Dulac said gently: 'and it will do you good. Come and eat with us.'

Without him, Kate thought, that poor girl would have probably killed herself by now. He's actually keeping her and that pathetic little child alive, by giving her hope. No Hollywood hero-type indeed, with grenades at his belt and rifle raised on high. The kind of man that really wins guerrilla wars, because he cares for his people and they'd follow him anywhere.

When they had finished, she got up and cleared the plates. 'You sit down, Madame,' she said. 'I will do the washing-up.'

She was quiet and efficient in a strange kitchen, he thought, remembering his mother's dictum about girls. You don't marry the face and the body, my son, you marry the cook, the mother and mathematician who knows how to run a house. He had never married. He practised law in his tiny office in the centre of Nice and he ran the most successful Resistance network in the Midi. He had women, but nobody he loved. And no woman for a long time. It was too dangerous.

He said, 'What time does the van leave tonight?'

Beatrice looked at the clock on the dresser. 'In half an hour. Always the same time, just before curfew. They've got so used to it, they don't bother about it now.'

'Is it yours?' Kate asked.

The girl laughed bitterly. 'Mine? I don't own luxuries like vans. I couldn't drive it anyway. My husband drove our van. When he went a friend bought it. The friend lives in Valbonne and brings his produce down to sell. I buy from him sometimes. He goes back every evening and comes in after curfew in the morning. He'll be here soon.'

They put Kate's machine in the back of the rickety old lorry that stood outside. The suitcase was hidden with it and lastly Kate climbed in and was concealed behind a wall of empty crates and boxes. The inside smelled pleasantly of vegetables and fruit.

Dulac said, 'I'll travel with our friend. Try and sleep a little; it'll take us a while to get there. Don't worry; if we stop, just stay perfectly quiet.'

She didn't mean to fall asleep. She was cramped and uncomfortable on the floor, and the old van bumped and jolted when they left the good road surfaces. She wedged herself into a corner and immediately slept. She woke when they pulled the barricade away and shook her.

'We're here,' Jean Dulac said. 'Come and meet Ma Mère. This will be your home while you're with us.'

It was a moonlit night and she could see the outline of the low Provençal farmhouse and smell the scented pines all round them. The driver guided them along a narrow path, more like a track, until they reached the back door. When it opened there was a gleaming light that framed a small round female figure. Kate felt herself drawn forward and embraced and then the door shut and they were all inside, crowded into a narrow hallway lit by oil lamps. A woman was smiling up at her, a white-haired, withered little grandmother of a woman, with bright dark eyes.

'Welcome,' she said. 'This is your new home. Come inside. Janot, bring the case and bicycle. I will show you where you sleep, my child. How young you are!' She clicked her tongue in disapproval, but the smile belied it. 'So young and so pretty. And so tired! You'll find the bed is good. We've been expecting you, you see – what is your name? Cecilie? Very good. Very good indeed. Come with me. Janot, be careful of that case. He's clumsy, my son, but he's a good boy. You'll like him. Jean, there is food and wine for you in the kitchen.'

'I've eaten, Ma Mère,' he called after her.

'With poor Beatrice? Pig-swill is all she has – go and eat and don't argue. I'll bring Cecilie down in a minute.'

The room was in the attic, but unlike the last one the windows were open and the night air was sweet. There were sheets on the small bed and they smelt of dried lavender. Kate had never seen anything more tempting in her life. There was an oil lamp on the table and a washstand with a jug and basin. Janot came in with the suitcase and lifted it on to the bed.

'I am Ma Mère,' the old lady said. 'Everyone calls me that, so you must do the same. You will find that this room is very good for your transmissions. We are well clear of the trees and quite high up. When you have arranged yourself, come down. Janot, don't stand there with your mouth open. Leave Cecilie to herself.'

The door closed and Kate was alone. She went to the window and looked out. Never mind the view down to the coast, she told herself. Never mind the clean, pungent smell of pines and wild thyme. It's a perfect location for an illegal transmitter. Hidden and high up. Open the case and get to work setting it up. Then go downstairs and remember that you have to make your first contact with London. And you can't afford mistakes, however tired you are. She turned back to the suitcase and unlocked it.

Colonel Reed was drinking coffee and reading the evening newspapers when the call came through from the radio room at Baker Street. He spent most nights in the building when an important mission was in train. His father lived in Montpelier Square, but the Colonel had persuaded him to store the furniture and close up the house during the air raids. He was comfortably settled in an old friend's house in Surrey. All they saw of the war were the vapour trails of fighting aircraft during daylight attempts on London. Now those had stopped. The Luftwaffe were shot out of the skies; when they came now, it was by night.

He sprang up and hurried down in the lift. The duty officer met him at the door. 'There's a message come in from Cecilie, Sir. It's being decoded now. I thought you'd like to see it.'

'I would indeed.' He spoke to the radio officer who had taken the signal. 'You recognize the sender?'

'Yes, Sir. It's Cecilie. No doubt; she's got a very distinctive touch.'

For weeks during her training at Beaulieu Kate had been transmitting to the operators at Baker Street. After a time the style developed and became so distinctive that the receiver could identify who was transmitting. Not all were proficient or even good; some were known by a pattern of mistakes. Kate by a combination of speed and lightness on the keys.

'Here's the decoded signal, Sir.'

Colonel Reed took the paper. He sat down and studied it for a time.

'Thank you, Banks,' he said, folding it and slipping it into his pocket. He said to the duty officer, 'See if Major

Wheeler's in the building, will you? If he is, ask him to come up to my room.'

Eric Wheeler was his assistant and friend of long standing. They had both joined the army at the same time, the Colonel leaving a City merchant bank and Wheeler a university career.

While he waited, Reed studied the message again. There was a knock on his door and Eric Wheeler came in.

'I was on my way home,' he said. 'What's up, Sir?'

'Cecilie's made contact from Dulac,' he answered. 'Here, see what you think.'

After a pause Eric Wheeler said, 'A bit ambitious, isn't it? A convoy of fresh troops, heavily protected, no doubt, and escorting some senior officers from the Italian front? Why not stick to the power station; it's more their line.'

'He likes taking risks,' Reed remarked. 'And so far he's got away with them. The drop is the decider, I think. We'd better send a message back telling them to wait till we hear from supplies and the Air Ministry. You know how beggarly they can be with their aircraft.' He yawned. 'And we'd better put a call through to the General's aide. They'll want to know about this. It's right in their man's territory.'

Wheeler hesitated. 'I don't see why they don't do their own bloody dirty work,' he said. 'And let us get on with ours.'

Reed said quietly, 'My dear Eric, so long as we tell them some things, that keeps them happy. This isn't important; but it makes it easier to keep other activities over there to ourselves. Get hold of that chinless idiot and tell him we want the General's opinion.'

Standartenführer Albert Stohler had entertained his successor to lunch.

They drank a fine Sancerre with some freshly caught *loup de mer* baked to perfection by the Standartenführer's French chef. A dish of potatoes, stewed in butter and herbs, melted in the mouth. Fine white bread and creamy butter tempted the appetite, normally starved of both. A vintage champagne was served with the lightest lemon sorbet. Though his guest refused, Stohler ordered a rare Armagnac with the coffee – which was real. Stohler had grown heavy during the year he had been at his post in Nice. His belly bulged under the black tunic, and there were veins on the surface of his cheeks. He had lived very well, as he explained to the young officer sitting opposite to him. Bled the French and the Jews milk-white. Fattened the SS funds. Kept the Maquis out of Nice, holed up in the mountains. And earned the civilian population's cooperation. He laughed contentedly.

'They knew what would happen if they didn't,' he said, swilling the Armagnac round and round in the balloon glass, sniffing it as it warmed between his hands. 'Forty hostages were shot in my first six months, after they blew up a train carrying ammunition to Marseilles. That took the stuffing out of them!'

'I'm sure it did,' Christian said. 'General Knocken thinks it is one of the best means of combating acts of terror.'

'Of course.' Stohler drank and savoured for a moment. 'Of course, but then Paris and all that part is a hotbed of trouble. We're comparatively quiet here.'

He eyed his replacement cunningly and smiled. 'You'll be wasted in this lazy part of the world. The weather's too hot for mischief. And most of them have Italian blood. All they want to do is eat and fuck and sleep in the afternoons. I don't know why you've been sent here. You'll be bored to death. Unless you like women a lot. I do. I can recommend several. You do like women?'

Eilenburg went slightly red. There was no deadlier insult to the SS than a suggestion of homosexuality. Although there were many in its ranks. He said calmly, 'I like women enough to marry one on my next leave.'

'I don't mind going,' Stohler said. 'I need a new challenge. This has been too easy. I suggest we work together for the first few weeks so that my staff get accustomed to you, and you can familiarize yourself with the problems we have here and our methods of dealing with them. You'll find the

Abwehr are a pain in the ass, but that's true everywhere, I suppose.'

'Perhaps,' Eilenburg said. 'I never worked with them.' He looked at his watch. It was nearly half past three.

'I think I should do as you say,' he said quietly. 'I think I should make myself known to my staff and familiarize myself with our problems. I have a letter for you, Herr Standartenführer. I thought it best to wait until after lunch. It is from General Knocken. I gave it to your secretary. Will you excuse me? And thank you for the excellent lunch. We don't live so handsomely even in the Avenue Foch.'

He had been assigned an office near to Stohler's. He went there and saluted the young SS secretary who was waiting in a cubicle outside. The response was a little slow.

'Heil Hitler!' Eilenburg didn't speak, he shouted. He shouted so loudly that the girl blanched and stiffened as if she'd been struck. 'Stand to attention at the salute! Attention, do you hear? Again, Heil Hitler!'

The reaction was instant. 'Heil Hitler,' she snapped back. Eilenburg came close to her. 'That is better,' he said slowly. 'Come into the office and close the door.'

A handsome desk, two telephones, filing cabinets, a large portrait of Adolf Hitler on the wall facing them. A vase of flowers on a side table. Cigars and cigarettes and a decanter and glass on a silver salver. He walked over, took out the stopper and sniffed. It was brandy. He said over his shoulder, 'Whose office is this?'

'SS Hauptmann Koenig, Standartenführer!'

'Did he drink brandy when he was working? Who puts flowers in an office? Cigars? Expensive ciagrettes like these?'

Eilenburg swung round on the girl. He was ashen with rage and the pale blue eyes were murderous.

'Clean this place out! This is an office where work is to be done, not a brothel! And send Hauptmann Koenig to me. At once!'

The secretary saluted, shrilled out, 'Heil Hitler!' and sped out to obey his orders. Half an hour later SS Hauptmann Koenig had been reduced to the ranks and Albert Stohler was sitting in impotent fury in his own office, reading Knocken's stinging letter of dismissal. It took effect from the moment Christian Eilenburg arrived in Nice. His next posting had not been decided. He was to leave for Germany and the SS HQ in Berlin immediately, to account for his failure as head of the Führer's Gestapo.

Kate couldn't sleep. Physically she was exhausted, but at a pitch of nervous tension; Dulac had stood beside her while she coded his message and transmitted it to London. She finished with her call sign and turned to look up at him.

'No problem,' she said. 'Everything clearly received, they said.'

'When will we get an answer?'

'Hopefully by the end of the week at this time. I was so scared I'd make a mistake – my hands were shaking!'

'I saw them,' he remarked. 'But not when you used your machine. That's the mark of a good operator.'

She felt his hand lightly rest on her shoulder. My God, she thought, I never knew a man could make me feel like this, just by touching me.

'I'll put the baby to bed,' she said, trying to sound casual. She put the transmitter back into the suitcase, locked it and pushed it out of sight.

'Ma Mère has gone to bed,' he said. 'Come downstairs and have a glass of wine. I don't fancy poor Janot for company tonight. Unless you're too tired?'

'Well, I am,' Kate admitted, knowing it was only half-true. But anything was safer than being alone with him so close, feeling as she did. The bed made her self-conscious. 'I am tired, but I'd love a cigarette.'

'I have plenty of those,' Dulac said, and opened the door for her.

It was very warm in the kitchen; everything shone in the

light of three oil lamps; there was a smell of smoke and cooking and wine which Kate found soothing.

Janot poured them all a glass of the dark red wine; she smoked Jean Dulac's cigarettes. The two men talked about local topics for a few minutes and then the young man heaved himself up from the chair by the stove and said good night. His mother was right; he was clumsy. He banged into the table as he moved, mumbled something and rubbed his thigh, grinning apologetically at them.

'He's the last son she's got left,' Dulac said. 'She had three killed in 1940 and she was widowed then. He helps her run this place; she rules him with a rod of iron, but she loves him and he's a good fellow. Absolutely loyal. But not very easy to talk to. Thank you for keeping me company tonight. I needed it.' He sighed. 'It's very lonely, being responsible for so many people. And now for you and your two friends. I made a brave show for the Englishman today, but how long can we keep him hidden, when he doesn't speak a word of French? London tells me he's a man who can open any safe or strong-room and there'll be a job for him, but when? I send them an urgent message tonight and they don't reply for five days – maybe even longer! I know, I've had experience of London.' He scowled, clenching and opening his hands. 'I want to take that convoy,' he said, almost speaking to himself. 'I want to show them that they're *never* going to be safe from Frenchmen.'

Kate said slowly, 'What about the wounded officers, travelling by ambulance?'

He glanced at her, his eyes black and cold.

'You don't like the idea of attacking helpless men? The Red Cross, is that it? Wait, my dear Cecilie, wait till you've been here a little longer. I'll take you to the place where they shot forty innocent men, some of them so old they had to be supported by the other victims, as a reprisal for us blowing up a goods train. There are no wounded men, only Germans. And Germans have got to be exterminated. Think what a blow it would be to them, if their relief troops were ambushed

90

and we killed some of their best senior officers, just when they thought they were going to sun themselves at Antibes! What a blow to the new man they've sent us!'

Kate said, 'What new man?'

Dulac shrugged. 'A new Gestapo chief. He took over from Stohler. Stohler's been here a year. He's a pig; he takes bribes, especially from the rich Jews here, and then sends them to the camps anyway. He ordered the hostages to be shot, but he's lazy and crooked and he spends his time lining his pockets and sleeping with any woman he fancies. Those women – wait, their turn will come! So they've replaced him. We've been too successful, that's the reason!'

His mood had swung from anger to excitement. 'We've hammered the swine for nearly a year now and they've kicked out the pig Stohler and sent some young thug from Paris down here to teach us all a lesson. But I'll be the teacher, Cecilie, if only those fools in London will support me!'

'I'm sure they will,' Kate said. He hardly heard her.

'First the convoy and then, while they're still reeling, the power station! One after the other, that's the way to strike at them. Not giving them time to recover and start arresting people. I'll light a firecracker under this swine Eilenburg. He'll wish he was back in Paris!' He got up, stood over her. 'I've held this network together, Cecilie, and believe me, it hasn't been easy. We've lost people. Good friends.' He chewed his lip at the memory. 'But nobody faltered. Whatever happened, they didn't betray us.' She knew that he meant 'me'.

'I rebuilt and repaired the damage to our organization and our morale. We lost a safe house, I found another one, better than the other. I gave my people success and victory over their enemies. They learned to trust each other again. Have you any idea what it's like to fear the neighbour you've known all your life? Not to trust your own family, even? That's what the Germans and their collaborators have done to French people. They have traded on the worst in human nature and made it work for them: suspicion, fear and greed.

91

It took a long time to convince friends I'd grown up with that they could trust me and we had the same goal. It wasn't done except with patience and caution and I'm not a cautious man.' He smiled at her. 'I like to act and if it means a risk, that doesn't worry me. But I'm responsible for so many others, as I said to you. It's a burden. You're a burden too.'

There was nothing else that she could say. 'I'm sorry. I thought I'd be a help.'

He gestured impatiently. 'Of course you will. You're a good wireless operator and you can keep your head. But you're you, a human being to me. I have to think of you like that, worry about you – try to keep you safe! That's what I meant.'

Kate got up. He looked feverish, his eyes too bright and his energy too febrile. 'I think,' she said quietly, 'that you should go to bed and get some rest yourself. Otherwise you'll be sick and the burdens will have to take care of themselves.'

Suddenly he laughed. He shook his head and looked at her. 'You're angry,' he said. 'You don't like what I said.'

'Not much,' she admitted. 'Please don't worry about me. I came because I wanted to and actually I've been very well trained at looking after myself. This is one responsibility you can forget about. I'm going to bed now. Will Ma Mère tell me what I do tomorrow?'

'You stay here,' he said, 'and wait for London's answer. When it comes, Janot will contact me. Until then, you keep out of sight.'

'Good night then,' Kate said and moved away.

'You're right,' he called out as she reached the door. 'I have a fever. But I'm never ill. I can't afford to be.'

Kate went upstairs and left him. No, she couldn't sleep. The outburst had shaken her; under the calm, reassuring public image, there was a highly emotional man, at odds with himself and with his English allies. And sick, too. He held so many lives in his hands. Fine, slim hands, the hands of an artist. She thought of them and the longing to be touched swept over her again. If he had opened the door at that moment, she would have welcomed him without a second thought.

Love? The idea terrified her. Was that what this meant, this electric charge that flowed between them? So different from the tempting sensuality of dancing with an attractive man, of being kissed and allowing small liberties. There would be no holding back with this man, if he wanted her. And he did. She sensed it in him as strongly as in herself. He would be gone by the morning. But when at last she woke and came downstairs, he wasn't. Ma Mère had found him collapsed on the kitchen floor and put him to bed.

4

By Thursday evening, eighteen people had been arrested. The orders had been specific.

'Half a dozen from the professional classes, school teachers excepted, the rest working people with some shop-keepers and the owner of some well-known café. That makes sure the news will spread. Bring them all here and lock them up. I'll see them in the morning.' Then the new Gestapo chief went back to his hotel to relax for the evening. The day had gone too quickly; he hadn't noticed how late it was when he finally left his office. Cleaning out the Augean mess left by Stohler's greedy regime would take some time. But the seizure of those eighteen French people would start the rats running, he thought. They'd no connection with each other, so far as the Gestapo knew. That would baffle the Resistance. Unless of course they'd drawn one genuine card from the pack without knowing it. He smiled and dismissed the idea. He didn't believe in miracles, only hard work and determination. For the moment he had cracked the whip as a warning. That would do for now. He ordered brandy in his room and drank it while soaking in a hot bath. He had a team working on the police records of every convicted criminal and others sifting through the families and contacts of anyone caught in anti-German activities. Particular attention was being paid to the friends and relatives of the hostages shot by Stohler eight months ago. Anyone taken in on suspicion and later released was to be placed on a separate file. Check and cross-check; that was the method used in Paris. Always, something came into the net as a result. He stretched in the hot water, finished the brandy. He wasn't tired; his brain was over-active, and so was his body. He needed a girl. Before dinner or after – he dried himself and decided that he didn't want to eat first. He telephoned and asked for the manager. The manager had gone home, he was told. The reception then. After quite an interval a man answered.

Eilenburg said, 'This is Standartenführer Eilenburg. I want a prostitute; young and clean. I like –' and he described it. 'And don't pretend you don't supply them!' The mumble at the other end infuriated him. From sexual excitement he passed to rage. 'Get someone here,' he shouted, 'or you'll find yourself in the Villa Trianon.'

He rammed the phone back on the hook, took a deep breath and threw the towel into a corner. Minna, he thought, why wouldn't you marry me and come here. I wouldn't need a dirty little French tart if I had you to love me. I only do the things I do because I don't want to think of you when I'm with them. Remembering that last night, and how tender they had been, he wondered again if she was pregnant. His desire had drained away, leaving him angry and depressed. He put on some clothes and decided to cancel the girl. If there even was a girl.

There was a knock. He called out, 'Come in,' and the door opened. She was a chambermaid, still wearing the drab uniform, with a creased white apron. She had taken off the ugly little cap and stood shuffling her feet, looking at him like a rabbit confronted by a stoat. She had dark hair and large brown eyes in a pinched, white little face. She reminded him of Minna.

'What do you want?' Eilenburg asked, although he knew.

She answered in a low voice, just above a whisper. 'Claude said you wanted someone, Monsieur. He sent me.'

'I asked for a prostitute,' Christian Eilenburg said. 'Not a human sacrifice. Go away.'

The big brown eyes looked sadly at him. 'He will sack me, Monsieur. Please.'

Suddenly he was dead tired. The anti-climax was complete, and with it came a terrible thought: if we lose the war, this could be Minna. He sat down, reached out for a cigarette.

The girl said desperately, 'Monsieur, I am a prostitute. I do that in my time off.'

He glanced at her briefly. 'Don't lie,' he said. 'Never lie to the Gestapo. That's something to remember. You needn't worry about Claude. Now get out.'

The door closed very quietly behind her. He could have touched the silence. The girl went back down the corridor. There was nobody in the laundry room at that hour. Claude would think she was upstairs. She sat down and stared at her clenched hands. They opened and lay quietly in her lap. The young German was the most beautiful-looking man she had seen in her life.

Jean Dulac had congestion of the lungs. Ma Mère came downstairs and told Kate, shaking her head.

'I've put a steam kettle in the room,' she said, 'and made him sit up, but his fever's high and you can hear the phlegm rattling when he breathes. Janot will bring the doctor. When he comes, you stay in the back. If he sees you, you're Janot's friend, you understand. Staying for a night on your way to Marseilles. But with luck you can stay out of sight.'

'Why don't I hide?' Kate asked. 'Isn't that the easiest?'

Ma Mère looked impatient. 'You're not hiding here,' she said. 'Behave normally. And don't ever try to "hide" on the spur of the moment, unless it's an emergency. People always leave things around when they stay in a house. Like that extra coffee cup for instance. Three cups on a table and only two people? Nobody's blind in France these days. We are all suspicious, especially the bad ones!'

She busied herself while she talked, a little woman with rapid movements and a sharp intelligence.

'He's quite ill,' she said. 'He mustn't try to get up. He hasn't a woman to take care of him.' She shook her head and clicked her tongue. It would madden Kate after a time. Not long afterwards the old van bumped up the road, and an elderly man followed Janot into the house. Kate effaced herself as they hurried upstairs. Afterwards the doctor came down and sat at the kitchen table. Ma Mère offered him some wine. She introduced Kate. 'Mademoiselle Latour, from Marseilles,' she said, and winked. 'Janot's girlfriend. Run out and see what he's doing. He has to take the doctor back to town.'

The doctor said, 'Keep him in bed for a few days if you can. I've left you some inhalant to clear the congestion and he has to sleep sitting up. Watch the fever and if it gets higher than this morning, call me. He may have to go to hospital.'

'Not while I can nurse him,' the old woman declared. 'He's never charged me a penny for all that work after my sons died. And what a mess it was – sorting out the boundaries between everybody – any other notary would have beggared me with the cost. No, he stays here and I'll get him on his feet. I can persuade Janot's girl to stay on and help me.'

The doctor wasn't really listening. He knew Dulac's reputation for helping poor people with legal problems. He had heard whispers of other activities but closed his mind to them. He didn't want to know. He had his family to consider and a large practice in the town where his father had been a doctor. He lowered his voice and said anxiously,

'You haven't heard what happened in town yesterday?'

Ma Mère shook her head. She poked it forward like a turtle ready to snap. Her eyes were sharp, watching him. Whatever it was, it wasn't good news.

'The Gestapo arrested about thirty people. Just picked

them up and took them to the Villa Trianon. There's a new man sent down from Paris,' he muttered. 'They say Stohler has been sacked. Thirty people, Madame! What does it mean?' He looked grey and anguished. 'There's been no sabotage or murders lately. Everyone is stunned!'

The turtle head drew back; cunning veiled the eyes. She said, 'Doctor, this is terrible. I knew nothing, how could I? We stay so quietly up here, my son only goes down to the town to sell his vegetables. Thirty people you say?'

'I've heard it was more,' he said gloomily. 'I know one of them, he's my patient. His wife came to me last night, weeping and in such a state, poor soul. He's a consumptive. He's only a street cleaner, what would the Gestapo want with him?'

'God knows,' Ma Mère answered. There was a knot in her chest that was tightening as he spoke. She knew a consumptive who cleaned the streets for the municipality. And he was a patient of the man sitting at the table. She pushed back her chair and said, 'I'll go and call my son. He'll take you back. What terrible times we live in. Those poor people!'

She found Janot outside. He was loading the back of the van with empty boxes. Kate was helping him. The old woman came up to him.

'Thirty people were arrested last night. I think Louis Cabrot was one of them. Pass the word, and then come straight back here. Take the doctor home now. Cecilie, you come into the house with me. Say you'll stay and help me nurse the notary and make it convincing. He's seen you and he's so frightened he'd betray anyone if he was asked a question. Hurry, Janot.'

She sped back inside the house and Kate followed, her heart thumping with alarm. If she couldn't act the part for a simple country doctor, what chance would she have with the Gestapo?

It wasn't difficult. He didn't want to linger and talk; he said he was glad she would stay because the old lady would get over-tired, shook hands briefly and hurried out to the van.

Ma Mère said, 'You were good, but not good enough. We're peasants; you're too middle class to be interested in my son. Next time don't be so ladylike. Now run upstairs and see if he wants anything. And don't tell him anything about the arrests.'

He was propped up high on pillows; there were red patches on both his cheeks. Kate stood by the bed and said, 'The doctor says you'll be fine if you rest and let us take care of you. Just for a few days.'

He held out his hand. She took it and felt how dry and hot it was. 'I think Louis Cabrot was one of them', wasn't that what Ma Mère had whispered to her son? Thirty people! She smiled down at him.

'Would you like anything?'

'I'd like you to sit down and talk to me,' Jean said. He turned aside and coughed. 'Damn this stupid illness! But it won't take me long. I get over things very quickly.' He coughed again, longer and harder.

'I'll get some water,' Kate said.

Thirty people and a new man sent down from Paris. The man Jean Dulac wanted to challenge by a double assault on the convoy and the power station. He had struck the first blow instead. A hammer blow. She poured water and held the glass for him. Who was Louis Cabrot, and how much did he know?

'I'm better now,' he said. 'Don't look so anxious. I've always had weak lungs. But I'm strong, I'll be up by tomorrow.'

Kate sat on the edge of the bed. 'No, you won't,' she said quietly. 'You'll stay and rest till you're fully better. You talked last night about being responsible for people. And it's true. You can't afford to be obstinate and put them at risk.'

'You're very serious,' he said. 'Are you still angry with me?'

'Of course not,' she said. 'I was over-sensitive; it was silly of me.'

Suddenly it was difficult to talk to him. The danger hung in the air, unknown to him, and Kate couldn't stop thinking about it. Last night, while she was transmitting to London, the man called Louis Cabrot was being interrogated. After a few minutes of awkward silence, she got up.

'I'll go and see if I can help Ma Mère,' she said. 'Why don't you sleep?'

The very dark eyes watched her to the door.

'Come back in an hour. I want you to do something for me.'

'All right. But only if you've been sensible and gone to sleep.'

She closed the door and hurried down the narrow stairs. Ma Mère was outside, stacking seed boxes. It was unusually warm. The sun beat down upon them. On any other day the backdrop of the mountains against the brilliant sky would have been idyllic. The scent of pine strees and wild herbs, wafted by a light breeze, teased the senses. They could see the rooftops of the town below them.

Kate said, 'Who is Louis Cabrot, and how much does he know?'

The old woman paused in her work. 'He was one of the committee who brought you off the beach,' she said. 'He knows you and the others who came with you.'

'The man with the cough,' Kate said. 'I remember him.'

'Janot has gone down to pass the news and see what he can find out.' Ma Mère went back to work. 'If they've arrested them to frighten people, Louis will be all right. They won't question him too hard. If there's a connection between the arrests,' she shrugged, 'we're all finished.'

'We can run for it,' Kate countered. 'We'll have a start on them.'

'You can run,' was the answer. 'But I can't. And he can't upstairs.' She looked at Kate. 'There's nothing we can do till

Janot gets back,' she said. 'Help me put these in the shed there.'

Janot drove down the twisting roads and on to the main road into Nice. The doctor lived in a fashionable suburb, in a large nineteenth-century house with tall palm trees and a fine garden, now sadly neglected. He got out and hastened inside. Janot waved, rammed the gear lever into position and with much rattling and protest from the engine, coaxed the old van through the last part of the journey. He stopped outside the grocer's shop where he had collected Dulac and Kate the night before. Two old women were inside, picking over the vegetables. Beatrice waited for them to make up their minds. She looked so pale and hollow-eyed that Janot hesitated. She saw him and said,

'I've got some of that cheese you asked for – bring your ration card, it's in the kitchen.'

He followed her. The baby slept; a large tabby cat un-curled from in front of the stove, stretched its legs and wandered out.

'Thirty people taken? Louis Cabrot?' Janot whispered.

Beatrice watched the women through the doorway. 'Not thirty. That's rumour. More like eighteen or twenty. And they've got Cabrot. Nobody knows why or what they're accused of. Relatives are down at the Villa waiting for news.'

'Anyone else from the network?' Janot demanded. Beatrice was the cover house for Dulac's couriers. News was brought to her and collected from her.

'No. It's more of a random pick-up. They took people from several districts. There's no connection. I can't stay any longer. I've got to serve the customers and get them out.'

Janot waited. He was not as slow-witted as his movements suggested. A quiet man, barred from the army by a heart murmur and so far not netted for the German labour camps. A taciturn man, who was content to say very little. He had learned to watch and remember. When the women had gone he went back to the front of the shop.

'Jean is sick,' he said. 'We're keeping him with us. But if there's trouble we should move him. I must get my mother away. How soon can you get any news?'

Beatrice hesitated. Then she made up her mind. 'I can go and see Cabrot's wife. She may know something. Get rid of your van round the back and stay with Louise. There's some juice in the bottle there if she wakes. I'll be as quick as I can, but I can't say how long.'

She closed the shop door and locked it, twisted a fly-blown sign that said in home-made letters, *Fermé jusqu'à trois heures*. She changed into her only pair of street shoes, kicking the slippers into the corner, and went out by the back door. Janot drove the van round to the narrow alley at the rear and came back into the kitchen. The cat had reappeared. It looked at him with indifferent, yellow eyes and went under the kitchen table. The baby stirred and mewed in its sleep, but didn't wake. Janot sat down to wait.

While the hours passed in agonized uncertainty for Kate in the house in the hills at Valbonne, and for Janot in the stifling kitchen; while the relatives of the men and women in custody begged for news from the Gestapo officials at the Villa Trianon, Christian Eilenburg was collecting information in his office.

At the opposite end of Nice, on the way to the tiny fishing village of Villefranche, the man known as Pierrot came out of his apartment in a small block of flats near the harbour at Beaulieu. He looked back before he shut the front door and called out.

'I shan't be long, my darling. Eat your lunch and I'll be back as soon as I can.'

He didn't have far to go. One flight down to the second floor and he knocked at another front door. It was opened and a man said, 'You're late. Come in – we've got some coffee left.'

He and his companion were in civilian clothes. They were

relaxed and friendly. Pierrot joined them, accepted coffee and a cigarette.

'I've just come from Nice,' he said. 'Your friends have made many arrests all of a sudden. What's behind it?'

The older of the two men scowled. 'The new man,' he said. 'Eilenburg, from Paris. Fancies himself another Heydrich, so we hear. But he's good, don't underestimate him. He has a reputation. I think your people are going to find it getting hot for them from now on.'

'Hot for you too,' Pierrot remarked. 'Stohler was easy; so long as he got money and women he didn't care too much. How do you feel about this development? It's going to make our arrangement more difficult.' He drew calmly on his cigarette, a professional among other professionals.

'I don't see why,' his companion said. 'We've worked together for some time without the Gestapo interfering. So long as you have our protection, they won't touch you. But about these arrests – well, if they've got anyone who knows something and they put pressure on them. . . .'

'They won't interrogate unless they suspect a Resistance member,' Pierrot said. 'And none of these people are connected. Labourers, artisans, shopkeepers and the proprietor of Le Chat d'Or, for God's sake! That place caters for your people, he's a well-known pro-German! It doesn't make sense.'

'Terror makes sense,' was the answer. 'And that's what Eilenburg understands. We in the Abwehr are gentlemen, on the whole – but they don't play by Intelligence rules. They set their own, and frightening the innocent is one of them. You have a special interest, haven't you?'

'Perhaps.' Pierrot was cool, facing both men.

'What have you got for us?' the senior asked him, cool and casual in his turn.

'Nothing yet,' Pierrot answered. 'But I soon will have. We've got a new wireless operator. Find out what's behind this business in Nice and I'll show you the transcripts as soon as I get them.'

'Good enough,' came the reply. 'I'll make enquiries. Will you be in your apartment tonight?'

'Yes. I am always at home on the weekends whenever possible. I'll hear from you then?'

'If we have anything to tell you, yes. Is there a name you're interested in?'

Pierrot hesitated for a second. 'Cabrot,' he said. 'I want to know if he's being questioned, that's all.'

He went slowly up the single flight of stairs and paused outside his own door. He unlocked it and went inside. The sound of a gramophone stopped him in the hallway. Popular dance music. Music that meant France before the war, when life was full of promise, and treachery unknown. He went into the sitting room and the music engulfed him.

The SS Hauptmann in charge of the prisoners made his report to Eilenburg that afternoon. Preliminary questions had been asked, but nobody had been interrogated. The information given tallied with the records kept by the municipality. The proprietor of Le Chat d'Or was demanding to see the Standartenführer. Eilenburg looked up briefly.

'Take him downstairs,' he said. 'Beat him and then bring him back. There won't be any more complaints after that.'

One of the men, the SS Hauptman continued, was chronically sick and coughing blood. Eilenburg didn't even glance at him; he went on making notes in the margin of the report.

'He was examined by the SS doctor, who recommended we release him. There is a risk he might collapse and die, Herr Standartenführer. The doctor said he was in an advanced stage of consumption and this had been accelerated by shock.'

The papers were lowered and Christian Eilenburg put down his pen.

'Shock? Has he been treated differently from the rest?'

'No, Standartenführer. Just asked simple questions like the rest and kept in a cell with three other men. One of them called the guard when he started spewing up blood.'

Eilenburg pushed back his chair. The Hauptmann stiffened, getting ready to salute on dismissal. But Eilenburg didn't tell him to go. He got up and balanced on the edge of his desk; he had the pen in his hand and tapped it against his polished boot.

'He must be very frightened,' he remarked. 'More than the others. Now why? Why should one man have more to fear from us than any of the others? They've all been breaking the law in one way or another. Nice is rotten with corruption. Who is this man and what is his work?'

'A street cleaner, named Louis Cabrot.' The Hauptmann consulted his list. 'Aged twenty-seven, married, two children. Lives in the rue Livry. His papers are all in order. Exemption from the army because of his health. No criminal record. Family French peasants, living up near Antibes.'

Eilenburg said quietly, 'I'll see him. Put him in an interrogation room.'

Jean Dulac was awake when Kate came in. He watched her put down a tray with some soup, tidy the cover of his bed.

'Where's Janot?'

'He took the doctor home,' she answered.

'That was hours ago. He never stays in town. Why isn't he back?'

She turned away to open the window wider. She didn't want to look at him when she lied.

'I don't know. Do you want me to call Ma Mère?'

'No. Come here, Cecilie. Tell me what's wrong.'

'Nothing. You're feverish; I'm not surprised, it's so hot in here.'

'I knew by the doctor,' he said. 'He was nervous, agitated. Answer me, or I'll get up and go downstairs to find Ma Mère. She won't lie to me. That's why she hasn't been up here, isn't it? She thought you might get away with it?'

Kate came to the bedside. 'Yes, there is trouble,' she said flatly. 'The doctor said thirty people had been arrested in raids all over Nice yesterday. Janot went to find out whether one of our people was among them.'

He pulled himself up on the pillows. 'Who was it?'

'Louis Cabrot. Something the doctor said about a patient of his with TB. Cabrot has it and he's a patient. We've been waiting for Janot, but Ma Mère says there's no need to worry if he's a long time. He's got to see people and try to find out.'

'Why the arrests?' Dulac demanded. He moved his head to one side and coughed savagely. 'Thirty! That's hostages. Why?'

'The doctor didn't know,' Kate said. 'He was frightened to death by the whole business. Ma Mère doesn't trust him.'

'Ma Mère's right,' he answered. 'If they question Cabrot, they'll find out about Marie and the pick-up. He doesn't know Pierrot, or me. He's only a little man in the network, who knows the beaches and where it's safe to land. But Marie knows more, if he leads them to her. And once the Gestapo hear that agents have been landed, they'll start tearing the town to pieces to find them. I must get up!'

'No!' Kate caught hold of him as he moved to throw the bedclothes back. 'Don't be stupid – what can you do? You wouldn't last five minutes if you tried to go down there in this state. You want them to catch you and destroy us all?'

To her surprise he didn't resist. He was gasping for breath. He swore angrily at his own weakness. She took her hands away.

'If anyone goes down,' she said, 'it'll be me. I've got a bicycle. If Janot isn't back in the next hour, I'm going to Nice to contact Julie and Pandora. They've got to join us up here before the Gestapo finds them. Will you promise me to be sensible? Stay where you are and get this damned infection under control. The doctor said a couple of days would make all the difference.'

He waited for a moment, trying not to cough.

'Give him two hours,' he said at last, 'then go down. Tell

Ma Mère I want to see her. And be careful. You know what to say if you're stopped, and your papers are foolproof. Just keep your nerve.'

'Don't worry,' Kate said quietly. 'I've practised that story till I could say it in my sleep. And I'm not frightened. They won't catch me out.'

He smiled a little. 'I think London has sent me someone very special.'

They didn't need to wait for two hours. By later afternoon the van rattled up the road and both women ran out to meet it. One look at her son's face told Ma Mère that it was the worst possible news. He climbed down and they went into the kitchen together. He slumped in a chair.

'It's Cabrot,' he said. 'His wife was waiting at the Villa. Beatrice was with her. They said he'd been taken in for special questioning by the new chief himself. The poor girl was crying and begging, telling them he was consumptive. One of them said, "We know. He's coughing blood all over the floor at this moment!" Beatrice took her away. She's staying at the shop with the children. I came home as soon as they told me. What are we to do?'

'I've got my orders,' Kate said. 'I'm to go down and contact two friends. If this poor devil gives way, they'll be in danger. Ma Mère, I've got to bring them here. I'm sorry, but there's nowhere else.'

'We've plenty of room.' The old woman didn't hesitate. 'Why do you have to go alone? Janot makes the evening run as usual. He can pick them up.'

'I'll bring them to the shop.' Kate dismissed the objection. 'They don't know Janot, they mightn't trust him.'

'There's a curfew from eight o'clock,' Janot said slowly.

'If the SS are on duty they'll search everything. Normally the army knows us and doesn't bother. How long will it take you to find them, Cecilie? And how will you get them to the shop in time?'

'I'll get them there,' she said. 'It's four o'clock now. It'll take me an hour to get into Nice, but it's downhill all the way, thank God. Can you make your evening delivery by seven? That gives us time to get out before the curfew.'

'I can do that,' he nodded. 'But if you're not there I can't wait. You'll understand?'

'I'll be there,' she promised. 'If I'm not, don't take any risks. Get out, and we'll wait till your evening trip next day.'

'Be careful,' the old woman said. 'For the sake of us all. You know so much, my child.'

Kate didn't listen. She ran up to her room, collected her identity papers, a little money and the lipstick she'd brought out with her from England. The top of the crimson stick concealed a suicide pill. Ma Mère needn't worry about her giving the Gestapo any information if she was arrested.

There had been a certain amount of cooperation between German military Intelligence and the Gestapo in the Midi. Stohler took a tolerant view of his Abwehr rivals, and exchanged information with the accredited agents living at Beaulieu. They even dined together and were on easy social terms. When Pierrot's contact telephoned the Villa Trianon and asked if they were detaining a Louis Cabrot, the SS officer on the desk obliged as usual.

'Yes, he was one of those arrested yesterday. He is being interrogated by the Standartenführer.'

Pierrot's contact put the phone down. It was a meagre favour in exchange for seeing the transcript of messages passed between London and the Resistance. But the real bargaining counter was one flight of steps above. Pierrot would continue to sell his soul to the devil and his countrymen to the Germans. The money was just enough. Pierrot got the answer that evening. Louis Cabrot was suspected and being questioned. When would they have the transcripts?

He sounded worried. Not for some time, he said. The group would disperse and lie low on the assumption that Cabrot had been forced to give information. He would be in touch with them but not for a while. He rang off. One

German said to the other, using Eilenburg's imagery without knowing it.

'The rats'll be on the run by now. I think we should pay a courtesy call on the new Standartenführer. Keep the relationship sweet.'

His companion agreed. They had shared the same flat in Beaulieu for the past year. Neither was homosexual: the elder was a married man with three young children. Both had been policemen in civilian life, one in Divisional Headquarters in Berlin, the other a talented provincial from the force at Stettin. They were keen, experienced investigators, who brought their skill in catching criminals to catching spies and collating information. Their hands were not bloody; they despised and disliked the savagery of the SS and the Gestapo, but they had to live with both. Recruiting the Frenchman known as Pierrot was one of their major Intelligence coups since they came to work in Occupied France. They left the apartment and went into Beaulieu to have dinner. Both men had acquired French girlfriends and the four of them had a very jolly evening.

Christian Eilenburg went upstairs to his office. He used the private lavatory reserved for his predecessor, washed his hands and brushed the white dust of the basement cell off his uniform. He shut his office door, opened the window wide and lit a cigarette. He had ordered Cabrot to be released. He had questioned the man for twenty minutes and knew from experience that he would not survive even limited torture. It was doubtful if he would recover from the collapse and haemorrhage from the lungs. Eilenburg didn't believe in brutality for its own sake. He took no sadistic pleasure in watching or inflicting pain. To him it was an instrument to be used for a necessary end. It was pointless to assault a man in Cabrot's condition. There was a better way of getting information. He relaxed for a few minutes, thinking. They had gathered a lot of data from the frightened prisoners. On the first examination it appeared useless and unconnected with anything subversive. But analysis might prove otherwise. And reports of public reaction were very satisfactory. The complacent citizens of Nice were in a fine state of alarm. An earlier curfew, taking effect after forty-eight hours and enforced by his own SS troops, would hem the people in their homes and close the cafés and shops. The French hated losing money. Quite soon there would be a deputation at the Villa Trianon. He would wait for the leaders of business and the professions to come and soften him as they had done Stohler. He spoke into the internal telephone.

'Has Cabrot gone yet?'

'They're sending an ambulance, Herr Standartenführer.'

'He's to go home, not the hospital. That's the condition of release. And you know what to do.'

'Yes, Herr Standartenführer. The whole family will be watched.'

Cabrot was a member of the Resistance. Eilenburg knew it as soon as he walked into the cell. The smell of the man's fear was as pungent as the blood he coughed up on to the dusty floor. Everyone who came to see him would be watched. Free, he'd lead the Gestapo to more conspirators than he could have named.

He gave a second order. All the prisoners were to be held overnight, and the relatives sent home immediately. No questions were to be answered about their welfare. And that was when he heard of the Abwehr interest in Louis Cabrot.

Kate cycled past the pink-washed house. She didn't look at the windows or show any interest in it. She went on to a bend in the road and then jumped off and pushed the machine behind a tree. She waited, but nobody was following her. It was just before five o'clock. Her legs ached from furious pedalling to make up time on the way down from Valbonne. She made her way carefully to the side of the house, checking that the road was empty, and slipped in through the front gate and round to the back door. It was closed and there was no sign of anyone moving inside. She knocked, tried the handle. She was sure a curtain moved in an upper window. She knocked again, more urgently. At last the door opened. It was Pandora, looking anxiously at her from inside. Kate didn't speak. She pushed her way past him and slammed the door shut. Suddenly her heart was racing and she was out of breath.

'My God,' she said, 'where's Julie? Where are the others?'

'The old lady's gone into town for something,' he mumbled. 'Julie got a message. She's out on a job. Am I glad to see you, Katie. Here, come in and have a drink.'

So friendly and relieved; didn't he know there was a Gestapo hunt going on and the whole town was in a state of alert. . . .

'Oh, Pandora,' she said. 'For Christ's sake!'

He stared at her. 'What? What's up?'

'Nothing.' Kate moved past him. 'I'll have a glass of wine. Come on, let's keep in the back. No, *don't* pull the curtains. It's quite light with the door open!'

'What's up?' he asked again.

Kate said, 'Didn't Julie tell you?'

He pulled a face. 'She just said there was a spot of trouble and she had to take a few messages. She said to stay quiet in here and not go out. They were all jabbering together and I didn't understand a bloody word as usual. What is it? You look done in, Katie.'

'I'm all right,' she said. The wine was acid. 'There's more than a spot of trouble, Pandora. A lot of people have been arrested, one of them was that poor fellow with the cough who brought us ashore. If they question him he'll tell them about us. So you and Julie've got to get out of here and come back into the hills with me. And we've got under three hours to make it before the eight o'clock curfew! Did she say where she'd gone? Or when she'd be back?'

He said, 'No. She did look pretty scared.' He caught hold of Kate's arm. 'She'll be okay, won't she? I mean, I'll go out and look for her with you.'

'And be picked up by an SS patrol? No thanks, Pandora.

Julie's experienced; she'll take care of herself. Don't worry about that. It's not getting to the pick-up place in time that's worrying me – we'll have to stay here another night and I don't fancy that if they're pulling the poor devil to pieces.'

They were silent after that. Pandora got up and moved round the back room restlessly, hovering near the window. Kate bit her lips not to snap at him to sit down. He was worrying about Julie. Not about himself or Kate or the others. She looked at her watch. It was past six. Pandora saw her do it and said,

'Look, you go on. Just tell me where we've got to get to and as soon as she comes back we'll follow on. There's no use you hanging around here, Katie, if there's going to be trouble. Push off, will you?'

She shook her head. 'Ten more minutes. Then we both go.'

He stared at her. 'Leave without Julie? You must be joking.'

She got up and stood facing him. She was so frightened that she became furiously angry with him. He was so emotionally tied up that he'd lost all sense of security.

'Listen to me,' she said. 'You can't speak French; if any German comes up here, you'll blow the whole mission wide open with your first word. Julie could bluff it out, so could I or any of the others. But not you, Pandora. You're the death of the lot of us. If she's not back in the next seven minutes we're going and you're coming with me. I hate to say this, but I'll report you if you refuse. Dulac could have you shot.'

He looked at her with disgust. 'Here she comes,' he said, and turned his back. Kate didn't waste time; she let Julie in, explained that they were in danger of arrest and bundled them both out of the house.

'I've got a bicycle,' she told them. 'Pandora, you'd better take it. Here's where you go to.' She gave brief directions. The way was straightforward: once out of the back roads he would reach the outskirts and turn on to the Promenade. He had to take the fourth turning to the right up to the top of a short hill. Beatrice's grocery shop was half-way down on the right-hand side, on a corner.

'If she's alone, just say one word: "Dulac". If she's not, don't speak at all, just wait.'

He tried to argue. Kate felt she could hit him. Julie intervened.

'Fred, do as she says. Two girls can maybe get a lift. I know another place we can stay if we don't get to the shop on time. But you've *got* to get into the hills. Please, Fred. Please, darling.'

There was no pretence about them now. They embraced and kissed each other, oblivious of Kate.

'You take care now,' he told her. He set off pedalling strongly; once he looked back.

'Come on,' Kate said. 'I don't think we'll get there, but we've got to try.'

On the Promenade there was little or no traffic. Two cars, gas bags wobbling on their roofs, passed them, ignoring the signals to stop. They didn't dare to attract attention by running.

Julie said, 'We'd better give up; it's twenty to seven. You told Janot not to wait.'

'I know I did,' Kate answered. 'But I think he will. Pandora'll see to that! Come on, there's nobody about, let's run from here.'

They had come to the right-hand turning and the street was empty. They ran. Some of the shops had already closed. There was a strange silence; shocked, the people had retreated into their houses. Memories of the arrest and execution of the hostages nearly a year ago drove out the false sense of security. For a long time the conqueror had been lax, the Resistance flourishing in defiance. Now they were afraid again and the windows were shuttered and the doors locked against the unknown. At the top of the hill the girls slowed and began to walk. A few cycled past them, grim-faced; a German staff car, army pennants flying, sped ahead. They reached the corner shop. It was locked and the blinds drawn.

Julie swore in French. She went up and rattled the door handle. Nobody came.

Kate said suddenly, 'Round the back! That's where Janot parks the van!' And that was where it waited, Janot anxiously tapping both hands on the wheel. The two girls scrambled into the back. Pandora grinned at them in the corner. Janot switched on and the engine croaked and coughed into life and they were on their way. Exhausted, Kate squatted on the bare boards behind the wooden crates. Julie and Pandora were holding hands and murmuring. They were moving slowly, too slowly, she thought in panic. Eight o'clock was the curfew. The patrols would be out and road blocks set up to catch the transgressor. If they stop and search us, that's the end, she decided. All this for nothing. We'll be taken or shot. She opened her bag and slipped the lipstick case into her pocket. She wondered whether Julie and Pandora were also prepared. Without realizing the significance for her, Kate decided that she would ask to be issued with a gun. The sense of being caught unarmed and helpless, with no alternative but suicide, swept all scruples aside. She didn't remember her question to Captain Alfurd when he took her to lunch in London all those months ago. 'I wouldn't have to kill anybody?' She thought of Louis Cabrot at Gestapo Headquarters and for the first time in her life she began to hate.

'We got through,' Katharine Alfurd said. 'When I thought about it afterwards, it was the most rickety, bumbling operation imaginable. Maybe that's why we weren't stopped. Nobody would have dreamed that three Allied agents were hiding behind a few fruit boxes in a van so old it was practically falling to pieces. And luck was with us. No doubt about that.'

'One always needs luck,' Paul Roulier said. He knew the places she described. He knew the turning off the Promenade that led up a short hill and then down towards a small square. She wouldn't recognize it now. There were smart apartment blocks and fashionable shops. And Germans strolling along the pavements, innocent of old crimes. The new generation in a world that was beginning to forget. Until they brought Christian Eilenburg back to France. 'The man you call Pierrot,' he said. 'Where was he while all this was happening?'

The look on her face surprised him. 'Holed up with his friends in the Abwehr,' she said bitterly. 'As we afterwards discovered. He wasn't on the run for his life or sweating it out in the Villa Trianon.'

'You still hate him?'

'You think I shouldn't? Just because he's dead?'

'That's not for me to judge, Madame,' Roulier answered. 'He lived a lot longer than the people he betrayed.'

She got up. 'I won't be a moment. Please help yourself to a drink.' She went upstairs to her bathroom, Polly, the terrier, trotting after her. She felt overcome with feelings of pain and anger. She looked at herself in the mirror. A woman in her late fifties, younger-looking than her years; the respectable widow of the late Colonel Robert Alfurd, who'd been active in charities and served on the Council.

'You had the chance once,' she said to the woman in the mirror, 'you didn't take it. And he got away with it all. You thought he'd be tried and punished and you didn't pull the bloody trigger.' She turned away, snapped out the light and killed her accusing reflection. She was calm when she came back into the sitting room. She smiled at Roulier, saw he had a drink and helped herself. He noticed the composure, he admired the self-control. He couldn't help seeing that her legs were beautiful. Odd how the remains of sex-appeal lingered, like scent on a handkerchief left forgotten in a drawer. She must have been powerfully attractive. A challenge to a man. A challenge that Dulac, the great hero of the Resistance, hadn't been able to resist. And nor had his compatriot, the traitor Pierrot.

'When did you get an answer from London?' She had slipped away in those few moments. He recalled her gently.

115

'Whether to attack the convoy and the power station,' he prompted.

Kate frowned. 'We didn't get an answer,' she said. 'We got an instruction. A flat order. The convoy of troops and the German officers it was escorting were not to be touched.'

'And the power station? That was a very important target, surely?'

'That was being favourably considered,' she said. 'You've never seen anyone so furious as Dulac when I passed him that message and he read those exact words.'

He was well enough to get up and come downstairs. His temperature had been normal for twenty-four hours and he was restless and irritable. Ma Mère said that he was doing himself more harm than good by staying in bed. They were gathered in the kitchen when Kate came down with the decoded message from London. Three days of staying inside the house, relying on Janot's daily trips to Nice for news of what was happening.

Louis Cabrot had been sent home. He was seriously ill and his wife didn't know if he would recover. That was good news; Kate and Julie were delighted, Pandora too, when they explained it to him. Only Ma Mère and Dulac were silent; Janot spoke so little he wasn't noticed.

The immediate danger was over. But it was wiser to stay where they were until Dulac was well enough to take control and go back to the town. Eilenburg's new curfew would make movement round Nice more difficult.

Dulac threw the message down. 'Not to be touched?' He glared at them, not seeing them in his anger. 'A convoy of German troops and some very senior staff officers and London says they're not to be touched!' He swung round on Kate. 'You're sure you haven't bungled this?' he demanded. 'You must have misread them – they wouldn't dare send an answer like this!'

'I'm afraid they have,' she said. 'I checked twice. You've

116

asked for their advice and they've given it. If you don't like it, it's not my fault.'

He ignored that. 'It's not advice,' he said. 'It's orders. Orders to us, to Frenchmen! You take this down, Cecilie. Take this message and send it off tonight!'

She didn't argue. He wasn't a man to contradict in such a mood. She sat down with pad and pencil. He spoke rapidly, snapping off the words. ' "Dulac acknowledges London's message. In reprisal for the arrest of eighteen French civilians, the convoy of replacement troops will be engaged. No assistance from London will be needed." Send that, Cecilie.' He made an effort and added, 'Please. Ma Mère, I'd like to talk to Janot alone.'

The old woman said, 'We'll go to the parlour.'

Kate took the pad and went out with them. Julie stopped her. 'You're not going to send it like that, are you? They'll be furious.'

'I'm working for Dulac while I'm here,' Kate replied. 'Not for Baker Street. That's his message and that's what I'm sending. I don't blame him either.' She went on up the stairs to her room.

Alone with Janot, Dulac sat down. His fine hands were clasped together, as if he were a priest hearing confession.

'What's the word on Cabrot?'

Janot said, 'He's very sick.'

'But not beaten, not tortured?'

The young man shook his head. 'His wife said not. They asked a few questions. The new chief came himself. Then he was released. Just like that. But nobody knows why.'

'I know why,' Dulac said sadly. 'And so do you. Something has to be done.'

'No one has been arrested,' Janot mumbled.

Dulac looked up at him. There was no anger left, only a drained, unhappy man forced to pronounce sentence.

'They've released him because he's promised to work for them,' he said. 'They never let anyone go because they're sick. They question them until they die. I don't judge him,

117

Janot. None of us must judge him. But you must do it tomorrow. That is an order.'

The young man nodded. 'I'll go there tomorrow,' he said.

'You're a patriot,' Dulac told him quietly. 'Remember that and it will give you courage. Now call Ma Mère, will you? I'm going up to speak to Cecilie.' He paused and put his arm round Janot's shoulders. 'You shall come with me when we attack the convoy,' he promised. 'After tomorrow, you will do more for France than carry messages.'

Kate had transmitted the message. She packed the set away and hid it as usual. He didn't knock, he just opened the door and stood looking at her.

'Did you send it? Exactly as I gave it to you?'

'Yes. Word for word.'

'Can I come in?'

Kate said, 'Of course.'

I can still remember that feeling, Katharine Alfurd thought, leaving the silence to lengthen. All the old clichés, the pounding heart and the trembling, when he put his arms round me. The kiss that was more sexually exciting than anything I'd imagined, or ever experienced with anyone before or since. I never shared it with a man again. And I'm not going to share it with you, sitting there, waiting. I'm not going to tell you what he said or I said, or what happened between us. You're being quiet and tactful, not trying to pry. You're a good operator.

'I need you tonight, Cecilie,' he said. 'I need you very much. Are you a virgin?'

'Yes,' she whispered. 'That doesn't matter.' She reached up and kissed him as passionately as he had kissed her.

As he undressed her he said, 'I love you.'

'I sent his message to London,' Katharine Alfurd said. 'And afterwards we became lovers. Would you pass me that ashtray, please?'

He got up and put it beside her. She had made the statement and closed it off. He wouldn't ask a personal question; that was understood.

'The next day Janot went down to the town as usual. Dulac said he was completely recovered and was going back. Ma Mère tried to argue with him, but he wouldn't listen. Julie and Pandora were to follow the next day, using Janot as transport.'

'What about you?' Roulier asked.

She said, 'He took me with him. And that's how it was from then on. He kept me with him as much as possible.'

'Even when it was dangerous?'

'Yes. I didn't care. In a way I felt he took less risks if I was there.'

'You didn't stay at the safe house then?'

'No. I took the transmitter and went with him to Nice. I used his flat.'

Roulier said quietly, 'Wasn't that very careless?'

'It was criminal,' Katharine Alfurd admitted. 'But that was how it was. He wanted me with him, and I went.' I would have done anything, gone anywhere, she thought. I didn't even think about danger. All I wanted was to make love. To touch him, to feel him holding me. Even when I discovered why he'd come to my room and gone to bed with me that first night, even then I couldn't help myself.

He had slipped through the back door, avoiding the Gestapo watcher in a parked car up the road. Louis Cabrot was asleep. Janot moved very silently. The big clumsy man was like a stealthy cat as he approached the bed. There was a chipped enamel basin by the bedside, with bloodstained cotton swabs in it. Cabrot looked sunken and grey, his mouth ajar, the rasping breath indicating that he was sleeping and alive. Janot didn't look directly at him. He had seen Cabrot's wife in the yard at the side, hanging out washing. The back door was open and he sneaked inside. He had a cushion in his hand, picked up from a chair in the kitchen. He still didn't look directly at Louis Cabrot when he held it over his face. Cabrot's wife finished putting out the washing. There was a lot to do with all the stained pillowslips and his clothes and the children's. She paused, stretched her aching spine with one hand on her hip, shouldered the empty basket and went back into the house. Five minutes later she went into the bedroom to look at her husband, and began to scream.

Christian Eilenburg heard of Cabrot's death by midday. The deputation of citizens waited on him at three o'clock. He kept them waiting for half an hour and then saw them in his office. The Mayor was a respectable middle-aged hotelier, who had lived on terms with Stohler and protected his town and his people out of his own pocket. Eilenburg knew all about him, and about the others who came with him, to plead for the release of the hostages and the lifting of the punitive curfew. He stayed behind his desk and looked at them one after the other, like a snake confronted by a row of rabbits.

'I have very little time,' he announced. 'Monsieur le Maire, state your business please.'

He saw the hatred in the man's eyes and the fear. This was not Stohler, greedy and merciless but open to offer. This prototype of Hitler's nightmare ruling race made them feel already dead men, mouthing their pleas and protests without sound.

'This has been a peaceful and cooperative town,' the Mayor insisted. 'In spite of the incident eight months ago, the people of Nice are anxious to maintain good relations with you and the army, Herr Standartenführer. Arresting these innocent people and confining everyone to their homes under this new curfew doesn't make sense to any of us. If it is a demonstration of authority, I assure you, it's unnecessary, and could have unfortunate consequences.'

Quite a brave speech, Eilenburg decided. It wouldn't make any difference to his response but at least the Mayor had earned his respect.

'The only unfortunate consequences could be for the

people of Nice,' Eilenburg said. 'This is not a demonstration of authority. I have authority. I have it from Reichsführer Himmler himself. You mention an incident eight months ago. Forty people were shot in reprisal for an act of terrorism. The criminals were never caught. You say your town has been peaceful and cooperative. Let me remind you of the sabotage and murder that has gone unpunished under Standartenführer Stohler.' He pushed his chair away and stood up, overshadowing them all from his height. 'For every German soldier murdered, there will be twenty Frenchmen shot. For every act of sabotage or destruction aimed at German property or the German war effort, there will be fifty Frenchmen shot. You complain about the present curfew? Unless you can deal with the terrorist elements in your town, there will be no need for a curfew, because I shall recommend that the population be transported to labour camps at the rate of ten per cent per month!' There was total silence. He said, 'I will release the people arrested as a token gesture. I will also amend the curfew back to its original times. For two weeks only. And during that time, I want hard evidence of your cooperation. I want information which will help me to capture the Communists and terrorists who have operated so freely in this area for the last two years. If I don't get it, Monsieur le Maire, you and your deputation will be among the first deported to the East. Good afternoon!'

Cabrot was dead. Conveniently dead, before the Gestapo could compile a list of suspects. Eilenburg dismissed the deputation from his mind. They had gone away cowed; the Mayor was a man of courage and principle, and if his judgement was right, wouldn't sacrifice the people of Nice. Or himself, and leave the town without a leader. Before long, someone would begin betraying the Resistance.

He concentrated on the death of the humble street cleaner, who had interested the military Intelligence. He had released him for nothing. He used the telephone.

'I want a post mortem carried out on Louis Cabrot. I'm not interested in the widow's objections. See to it!'

At the end of the day he called for his car and went back to the hotel. He had dinner in the restaurant with two of his Paris subordinates. One of them suggested a visit to a nightclub. There was a good floor show and a discreet brothel upstairs. He had been told that the Gestapo went in free of charge. Christian Eilenburg refused. He had work to do, he said. Another time, perhaps. They thanked him for dinner and left.

He sat on in the lounge, drinking coffee, reading the French newspapers. He was expecting letters from home, but none had come. He felt restless and lonely, sitting there. He regretted not going with the others to the nightclub and maybe taking a look at the brothel. Abstinence wasn't healthy. It made a man brood and think too much. But it was late and he felt depressed. A waiter came and asked if there was anything he wanted.

'No,' Eilenburg said. 'Nothing,' and then added, 'thank you.' He watched the old man move away. They were all so polite; he could feel their hatred and fear and ignore it. It had been worse when he first went to Paris. The sensation of being loathed was new to him. Some men reacted very badly to living in a miasma of hostility. It made them savage. It impaired their efficiency because all they wanted to do was strike back. Eilenburg had resisted that temptation. He refused to diminish himself by being cruel or brutal to the people who hated him, because of that hatred. He stood above them. When it was necessary he unleashed the sadist from the Milice and the thugs in his own organization. He had learned to live with the feeling of isolation outside the company of his fellow Germans. To take women when he needed them and never look at their faces, because of what he would see there.

That night he felt acutely alone. He threw the papers aside and went out to the lift. When he opened the door of his suite, he saw a quick movement from the bedroom. Gun in his hand, Eilenburg moved to the doorway. The chambermaid with the haunted look of Minna was turning down his bed.

* * *

'Sit down, Colonel Reed. The General asked me to apologize for not seeing you himself, but he's very tied up at the moment.' The speaker was Lord Wroxham, a man in his mid-thirties. Reed knew his background better than he knew the man. Born in the purple of the British Establishment; too tall and too thin, as if the inbreeding of centuries had produced what the racing world dismissed as a 'thorough-bred weed'. He had beautiful manners, marred by a subtle hint of condescension. Reed detested him. He had been telephoned late at night and asked to come to the War Office for consultations. He used the word in inverted commas. Consultations my foot, he told Wheeler as he got ready to leave Baker Street. Bloody interference in our operations. He was in an aggressive mood, ready to confront the General himself. But the General was tied up, and only his aristocratic front man was waiting.

'Can I get you some tea or coffee? A drink perhaps?' The charming smile was like bullet-proof glass. 'I'm sure we can run to a whisky and soda.'

'Nothing, thank you,' Reed snapped. 'I've interrupted a lot of work, so if you can come to the point, I'd be grateful.'

Lord Wroxham unfolded his long body into a chair. He said quietly, 'It's about your Dulac network, Colonel.'

'What about it, exactly? You've had the information the General asked for; there's nothing new to add.'

'The reply sent to your message was a flat refusal to obey instructions, as we understood it.'

Reed said, 'Not for the first time. You people aren't used to dealing direct with agents in the field. They get very touchy at times. It'll be sorted out.'

'Can you guarantee that?'

Reed lost his temper. 'No, of course I can't bloody well guarantee what somebody in France is going to do! What I can guarantee is that we have experience in dealing with men under these conditions and we know best how to handle them. I wish the General would let us get on with it!'

'Colonel Reed.' There was an edge to the voice now and a very hard stare went with it. 'Colonel Reed, this man Dulac is going to attack a convoy of German troops and a group of senior army officers travelling with them. It is absolutely imperative that he doesn't go ahead with this plan. And it's your responsibility to make sure of it.'

Reed got up. 'What's so special about this convoy and these officers? If you're taking this attitude, you've got to explain why. It's possible that an explanation conveyed to Dulac may be enough.'

'The last person to know is anyone the Germans may capture,' Wroxham said. 'The General authorized me to answer your question, Colonel, on the understanding that you treated it as top secret. We have information that one of the most important anti-Nazi generals in the German army is travelling with the group of officers. This man is vital to Allied plans, and mustn't be put at risk. That's the reason why your people have got to leave that convoy alone.'

After a pause Reed said, 'This information comes through your own channels. And you're sure it's reliable?'

'Unquestionably. It should be reliable to you too. The General has authorized me to give you the contact's name.'

He took a slip of paper out of his breast pocket and handed it to Reed. Reed looked at it. He reddened slowly. 'I shall make the strongest possible protest about this,' he said. 'At the highest level.'

'It's already known at the highest level,' was the answer. 'This and other deceptions have been authorized. It's vital that we mislead the enemy, no matter what the cost.' Suddenly he spoke as one man to another. 'It can't be easy for you having us poach on your ground, but there are enormous issues at stake. If you can't stop Dulac from making a balls-up, then we'll have to deal with it ourselves.'

Reed choked on a furious reply. Then, typically, he crushed his temper down. The shock of the name on that paper had shaken him for a moment. But not for long. He realized that if he started an internal war, he wouldn't win.

124

The guns were too heavy on the other side. By cooperating, he would keep control.

'I'd like to take up that offer of a whisky, if I may,' he said suddenly. 'And I hope you'll join me.'

The polished manners reappeared. 'That's a splendid idea. I know the General hoped we'd be able to have a chat and exchange views. What would you like, soda or water?'

'Water,' Reed said. He sat down again and relaxed with an effort.

The younger son of a duke, whose great-grandfather had been prime minister, ordered drinks and then pulled up a chair close to Colonel James Reed.

'I do sympathize with your difficulties,' he said. 'I was operational in North Africa for a time. That's where I learned the value of what we're doing. I had a CO who was as cunning a devil as you'd ever meet. "You can kill as many men with lies as you can with bullets, laddie," he used to say. That "laddie" used to drive me mad, but the rest of it was good sense. You know the value of misinformation, Colonel; your people have used it very effectively.'

'Not as effectively as sabotage and gathering real information,' Reed countered. He recognized the offer of a truce and his instincts sensed advantage. He could bury the hatchet when he had to.

'Misleading the enemy is going to be more important in winning the war than blowing up trains and ammunition dumps,' was the reply.

Reed sipped his whisky. 'And where does this anti-Nazi general fit in with misinformation? Is he supposed to pass it on?'

Before the answer came he knew it would be a lie.

'He will provide a vital outlet, feeding the High Command exactly what we want them to hear.'

'The landing in France, for instance,' Reed murmured.

The response was enthusiastic. 'Precisely. And that's where your people can be invaluable, Colonel.'

'They can organize uprisings all over France to coincide,'

Reed said. 'We have an extensive programme of sabotage of vital rail links and bridges which can impede the movement of German troops. Our operatives are specially trained to coordinate French Resistance and the Maquis when the time comes.' He noticed the bland expression on the other man's face. He's heard it all before, he thought, and it doesn't mean a damn. None of it is what he's really talking about. And suddenly he saw the scale in perspective himself. A few thousand men and women, widely scattered throughout a large country, throwing their lives in the balance to dynamite a bridge or a rail terminal, imagining that they could really make any difference to the mighty army of Nazi Germany gathered to repel the greatest invasion fleet in history.

'Can I get you another, Colonel Reed?'

'No, thank you. Let's get back to Dulac. You're insisting that he leaves the convoy alone because of your man; and I can't give that reason, obviously. So what happens if he won't listen?'

Lord Wroxham studied his hands for a moment and then looked up. 'Our friend Pierrot will have to deal with it.'

'How, deal with it?'

'That will be up to him. We never ask for details, only results.'

'I see,' Reed said. 'We'll make radio contact tomorrow. I'll let you know what happens.' He got up. He looked very tired, the younger man thought. As if he had heard news of a personal loss.

'Colonel Reed,' Wroxham said. 'I know our departments haven't exactly seen eye to eye over a lot of things. Speaking personally, I've been in the position of whipping boy as far as you're concerned and I haven't enjoyed it. I think the time has come when we should work in full confidence together.'

He was lying before, Reed decided, but he means this. 'Is that the General's view?'

It was a slight smile, but slyly humorous. 'I was speaking

for myself,' he said. 'I don't worry the General with every little detail.'

Reed considered for a moment. He felt his antagonism to the man draining away.

'Why are you suggesting this?' he asked quietly. 'I don't see any advantage in it for you.'

'In the next few months,' he answered, 'you may have to sacrifice a number of your people and I'm going to have to ask you to do it. It will help us both to live with ourselves afterwards if we act together.'

They walked down the narrow passage and took the lift up to ground level.

'I'll phone through for your car, Colonel.'

Reed said, 'I didn't bring one. I'll walk. Good night, Major.'

He held out his hand. 'Why don't you lunch with me on Thursday?' he said. 'We'll have been in contact with France by then.'

It was the beginning of a friendship that was to last for forty years.

It was dangerous to call a meeting; but it was absolutely necessary to get the group leaders together and formulate their plan of attack. The Gestapo had released their prisoners and the curfew was put back to its old times. News of Eilenburg's ultimatum was all over Nice. Fear and suspicion were poisoning old friendships within a few hours of the terms being known. Families were under threat. Ten per cent of the populace a month, unless the Resistance was sacrificed.

Jacques from the Maquis in the hills was there when they met that evening; Dulac and Kate, with Julie and Pandora sitting in shadow at the back; Janot and the widowed Beatrice from the grocery shop, Marie who worked at the Mondiale and the surly Gaston. The last to come into the smoky kitchen was Pierrot. He went up to Kate. The cat's eyes were red-rimmed, as if he hadn't been sleeping.

'How are you?'

'Fine,' she said.

'I have been worried about you.' His voice was low. 'Things have taken a turn for the bad here. I'm glad you're all right.' He took a seat beside her.

'Don't worry about me,' Kate murmured. 'I've been out of it.'

'Except for cycling into Nice and picking us up.' Julie leaned across to them. 'And getting Pandora and me up to Valbonne one jump ahead of the bloody SS patrols!'

He turned to look at Kate. 'You were sent to do that?' He seemed to have lost colour. It's anger, she realized, pure, blazing anger. And then he glanced at Dulac. It was only for a few seconds, but Kate saw something that horrified her: hatred. Real hatred for the man who was leading them – for the man she loved with total passion and commitment.

Dulac got up. He said simply, 'Thank you, my friends, for coming to this meeting. I know it means risks for many of you. I wouldn't have called it unless it was vital. The Gestapo have begun a campaign of terror and intimidation and we've got to respond to it. You've all heard what they've threatened to do unless our fellow Frenchmen betray us. And there are too many who know or suspect just a little, for any one of us to feel secure. One word is all they want, one arrest. Like Louis Cabrot, picked up at random.'

Beatrice said in her flat voice, 'He's dead. His wife found him.'

'I know,' Dulac said.

'They've taken him away for a post mortem,' Beatrice went on.

Kate saw Dulac start in surprise. 'Who's taken him?'

'The Gestapo. Louise couldn't stop them. They haven't given the body back yet.'

'Why should the swine do that?' Gaston demanded. 'They killed him!'

'He wasn't beaten,' Beatrice volunteered. 'Louise told me.'

'Post mortem?' Marie shook her head. 'I don't understand.'

'I do.' The Maquis leader, Jacques, spoke up. 'I think we all do. Cabrot agreed to work for them. That's why he was released. Dulac?'

Kate shivered. It was stuffy and hot, with them crowded into the small kitchen, but she still shivered.

'I dealt with it,' Dulac said. 'I don't pass judgement on any man, but we couldn't take the chance.'

There was complete silence, after one gasp from Beatrice. Kate saw her eyes fill with tears, before she turned away.

'Will the post mortem show anything?' Pierrot asked the question.

'I don't know,' Dulac answered.

Kate's hands were clenched until they ached.

'And you were sure Cabrot was guilty?' It was Pierrot again.

Dulac accepted the challenge. 'The evidence spoke for itself. He wasn't interrogated, he was released ahead of the others. The new man at the Villa Trianon is no humanitarian. We know that. He sent Cabrot home for other reasons. We couldn't take a chance. I accept the responsibility for what was done. Outside this room, Cabrot was a hero of the Resistance and that's how he'll be remembered.'

'I think we've wasted enough time.' Jacques voice rose angrily. 'If Cabrot was a traitor he got what he deserved; if he wasn't, he was a hero who died for France! Now, comrades, what about the living? What are we to do to protect ourselves?' He too was on his feet; an ugly, powerful man with a raucous voice. 'You people talked about attacking a convoy of Germans. And then blowing the power station. We were supposed to wait for London to tell us what to do.' He snorted with contempt. 'Have they answered?'

Kate watched her lover. Louis Cabrot, the consumptive, was dead. She forced her hands apart and gripped the sides of the wooden chair. The brute force of one personality against the charm and magnetism of a man different in all

129

aspects. The natural leaders of the community had always been the lawyers, doctors, teachers. But no longer. The symbol of the French Communist Party stood across the table from the man of the middle classes and metaphorically clenched a fist in his face.

'They've answered,' Dulac said. 'We attack the convoy. That, my friends, is why I've called this meeting. Jacques, I'll deal with your point first. How do we protect ourselves? You must make your own arrangements. You operate in the hills and you can fight from there. We are from the town. We have nowhere to run. We stay and we fight here and we die if it's necessary. You're afraid of betrayal, aren't you? So am I. More afraid of Frenchmen being forced to betray Frenchmen than of anything the Gestapo can do. So I say our answer to the ultimatum is to strike back. We have two weeks' grace. It's not enough.'

'It's enough for the power station,' Jacques retorted. 'I say we hit that for a start.'

Pierrot said coldly, 'You realize that fifty hostages will be shot?' Jacques gathered phlegm in his mouth and deliberately spat on the floor.

'This is a war,' he said. 'We can't afford sentiment. All right, we can try and rescue them, but I say we blow up the power station as an answer to the threats. And we kill as many soldiers as we can pick off. You talk about two weeks! Two weeks or two months, it's not going to make any difference. Either we fight these bastards to a standstill or we give ourselves up!'

They waited for Dulac then. He looked drawn and as he started to speak he began coughing. Kate moved to the sink and brought him a glass of water.

'The convoy is the more important target of the two. There are a number of senior army officers on their way to Antibes. If the Gestapo takes hostages, so will we.'

There was a murmur of excitement among them then. Kate felt Pierrot stiffen, because they were close enough to touch elbows on the table. There was no room for her to move away. She saw the scowl on Jacques's face and realized that for his own reasons he wanted the other target. Dulac knew it too.

'You'll have the big bang, my friend,' he said gently. 'I promise you that. But you must help us first. Help us to destroy that convoy and capture some of the officers. Then we can bargain with Eilenburg on our own terms. I put it to the vote.'

Only Pierrot and the sad-eyed Beatrice abstained. There was a low cheer from everyone else. Jacques, who had been openly aggressive, now embraced Dulac, invigorated by the prospect of action.

'Afterwards the power station, eh?' He nodded and grinned.

Marie clapped her hands, Gaston rubbed his; Julie translated excitedly for Pandora. Dulac looked across at Kate.

'Thank you for the water,' he said. He sat down and banged on the table. 'Now we've made our decision. So let's start on the plan of action. Pierrot, you said you could find out exactly when the convoy arrives. Have you any news?'

'No,' he said. 'I've had to lie low like everyone else. While the truce lasts I can try to find out.' He lit a cigarette. Kate noticed that his hand was shaking. He passed one to her and slid the matches over as well. He kept his eyes on Dulac. 'I didn't vote for it because I don't see how you can do it in the time,' he added.

'Unless you use your contacts, we can't,' Dulac retorted. 'So it's up to you. Get me the dates, that's all we need. After we know that, we can finalize the plans. Jacques, we'll need every man you can muster, with small arms, grenades and that bazooka.'

'What about supplies from London?' the Maquis leader demanded. The bazooka, dropped by one of SOE's precious supply planes, was the treasure of his arsenal.

'They'll be coming,' Dulac promised. 'We have their full support.'

She had never imagined that he would lie. It was so

unexpected that she nearly said something. Pierrot's hand gripped her arm and she was silent. A calculated lie, not just a sidestep from the truth. London had refused help and ordered the convoy to be left alone. She lost the next few minutes of discussion; the voices rose and fell without her taking in what they said. When it was over they split up into tiny groups. Gaston and Marie were arguing as usual; Jacques was in close conversation with Dulac. Strange, she thought, how the prospect of fighting drew such natural enemies together.

Pierrot said, 'Are you going back to Valbonne?'

'I'm staying here now,' she answered. She tried to move away before he could ask the next question.

'Where's here?'

She said coolly, 'With Dulac. That's my base now.'

There wasn't a flicker in the eyes when he heard it. 'Meet me at the Café de l'Europe on the Place de La Liberté. I'll be there from seven o'clock onwards. Unless he forbids you.'

She faced him, their voices low. 'Why should he?'

He shrugged. 'Why should he, you're right. He wouldn't be jealous of me. So I'll wait for you, Cecilie. I've had word from London. Something special they want you to do.' He moved away, someone blocked her view for a moment and when it was clear he'd gone.

She went up to Dulac, touched his arm. 'I'll make my own way,' she said. 'I want to do some shopping. Don't worry if I'm late.' She hadn't imagined she would lie to him either.

One by one they dispersed; on foot, by bicycle, Janot making a long detour to where his van was parked. Beatrice was beside him. She was silent while they walked and during the drive back to her shop. He made up a load of empty boxes and set off for Valbonne as usual. Beatrice watched him go through the back window. It was grey with dirt and her face was a dim shadow behind it.

A neighbour's daughter was sitting with the baby. She was a pleasant, slightly retarded child of fourteen. Simple, but reliable. Beatrice gave her a bag of fresh vegetables as

132

payment. Louis Cabrot. She said the name to herself as she lifted the baby and it began to whimper and then cry at full strength. 'Cabrot agreed to work for them.' The smelly brute with his black hands, spitting on the floor by her feet! Poor Louis, whom she'd known since they were at convent school together. He and her dead husband had been boyhood friends. A poor man with terrible health; a wretched job that scraped a little money together for his wife and the two children he adored. He had worked for the Resistance without a thought for his own safety. 'If Cabrot was a traitor he got what he deserved; if he wasn't, he was a hero who died for France.' She was concentrating on the words of the Maquis leader because she hated him. She had slammed the door of memory on what Dulac had said. But little by little it was coming open. She gave the baby its bottle and settled down to feed it. She thought of the lawyer who had helped her and so many like her. Janot's mother was only one of many widows who were in his debt. Such a kind, gentle man: strong and wise and dedicated to the cause of French liberty. She had often thought she would have died for him, if the test came. Believing in him and working for him had kept her from ending a life that had no meaning. The child was not enough. Sometimes her crying was a torture that she could barely stand. What had he said about Cabrot? 'I dealt with it.' She put the baby down hurriedly and ran to the sink. She had eaten so little that it was impossible to be sick.

'And what was the message from London?' Paul Roulier asked her.

'There wasn't one,' Katharine Alfurd answered. 'He wanted to be sure I'd go. I nearly got up and walked off, but the place was full of people, lots of German soldiers drinking beer and picking up girls. I didn't want to draw attention to myself, so I did nothing. I let the swine talk. I let him buy me some coffee and pretend it was a normal conversation. I'll never forget that evening.'

'Why, what was so special about it?'

She gestured with one hand, impatient at the question. 'I'd come up against reality for the first time,' she said. 'A poor devil with consumption hauls me through a bloody minefield on a beach and gets me safe ashore and the next thing I know he's been "dealt with" because he's under suspicion. I couldn't believe it; I didn't want to accept it. I didn't, now that I think about it. I deliberately shut it out of my mind and if I hadn't met Pierrot at that café, I might have kept it out.'

'A lot of people had to make decisions like that,' Roulier suggested. 'Dulac was no exception. He was a sensitive man, it must have been terrible for him. But you realized that later, didn't you, Madame?'

She sighed. 'Of course I did. I learned quickly not to judge. Not to ask too many questions. I was in love, you see. But not blind. I knew when Dulac was wrong, and I tried to tell him.'

'But he wouldn't listen,' Roulier prompted.

'Why should he?' Katharine countered. 'What did I know, fresh out from England? Anyway, that was what Pierrot wanted. He wanted me to use my influence and stop Dulac from attacking the convoy. Do you mind, Monsieur Roulier, I'm terribly tired and I'm not thinking as clearly as I should.'

'Of course, I'm so sorry.' He got up. 'I can come back tomorrow?'

'Why don't you stay the night? I always keep the spare bedroom ready.'

He didn't undress at once. He heard her come upstairs, calling the terrier. The English were so unhygienic. No animal would have been allowed into his bedroom at home.

It was a very still night; he opened the window wide and leaned out. The scent of the garden drifted up to him: the cottage lily, named after the Madonna, with its sickly perfume that reminded him of funerals; the musical chime of the church clock. He could see the spire silhouetted against the sky in the moonlight. Such peace and timelessness: so much passion and turmoil inside the little cottage, locked into the memory of one woman. She had a gift for making the past real and the dead alive. He could see them as she talked, caught up in the re-enactment of her own life. She had made him smell the places she described: the stuffy French kitchens, their walls impregnated with the smell of food; the body smells of working people, of frightened people who didn't know they sweated; attic rooms, where the pine trees whispered outside the window in the light breeze after a hot spring day; the grocer's shop and the sad little baby whimpering in her cot. He undressed and lay on the bed smoking. Katharine Alfurd's spare room was typical. Rather spartan, faded chintzes, a watercolour hung far too high on one wall, an old-fashioned double bed with the luxury of down pillows and linen sheets. So very English. How had 'Cecilie' endured it for so long – it wasn't her true setting, this cosy cottage in the over-pretty village. How she must have suffocated at times, playing the role of the Colonel's wife. Living with a man who had buried his own past and forced her to do the same. Roulier wasn't tired. He lay and finished his cigarette and thought about Katharine Alfurd. He wished he had been born when she was young.

How well she remembered that meeting in the café – better than she would ever tell the Frenchman. For the first time she saw the other side of Occupied France.

There was a three-piece band playing popular dance music inside the restaurant; the tables were full of people drinking and talking at the top of their voices. The punitive curfew had been lifted and the town was reprieved. The German soldiers and the girls were what surprised her most. Not the jackbooted thugs of the SS, but young men enjoying themselves, playing the eternal sex game with girls of their own generation as if there were no war at all. She had been shocked and Pierrot said,

'This is part of life too, you know. It isn't all secret meetings and terror. Life has to go on, and for most people it's trying to be normal. I know what you're thinking. Look at them. Fraternizing with the enemy . . . after what happened the other day, how could they?'

She said in a low voice, 'That's exactly what I'm thinking.'

'Then you shouldn't,' he said. 'Don't judge; that's the first thing to learn here. Don't judge them and don't judge Dulac for having Cabrot murdered. He had to do it.'

She turned away. 'I don't want to talk about it. I didn't want to come here in the first place. Now you tell me it was just an excuse. No message from London, just a lie. Why did you bring me here?'

He moved his coffee cup aside. 'You've got to stop him attacking the convoy and kidnapping the German officers. It's obvious there's something between you – so put it to good use, Cecilie. This plan is a disaster. London knows it and said so. But he's determined. Talk to him, try and get him to see that it can't possibly succeed.'

'Why can't it?' she demanded. 'He's got the Maquis to back him up, plenty of ammunition, and if you can get him the timing, it should succeed. And how else is he going to stop the Gestapo carrying out their threats to shoot people and deport them unless he has something to bargain with?'

Pierrot said quietly, 'All he will do is play into Eilenburg's hands. The Gestapo won't care if German staff officers are killed. Especially some of these officers. It will give them the excuse to treat Nice as they treated Lidice after Heydrich was murdered. They'll lay waste here and all over the Midi. That's what this man wants. He's set out to provoke the Resistance and divide them from the civilian population by reprisals. Cecilie, Dulac's a great man in his way and a patriot. But he's a fool to be led into this. For God's sake try and make him see sense. Otherwise the whole thing will end in tragedy.'

She looked at him in silence for a moment. So difficult to see the real man and the real motive. The low monotonous voice threatening disaster could have been telling the truth or, just as easily, lying.

'Why are you so sure it'll go wrong?'

'Because it will be betrayed,' he answered. 'That is what Eilenburg is waiting for; that's the reason behind the ultimatum to the Mayor. Someone will come forward to save themselves and the town. Now, I think we should go. Will you meet me here the day after tomorrow at the same time and tell me if you've had any success? I beg of you, try!'

That night, lying in Dulac's arms, Kate tried.

'You're influenced by London,' he accused.

'That's not fair,' she countered. 'I sent the message and I backed you all the way. Darling, what if Pierrot is right? Supposing someone cracks and tells the Gestapo?'

'Who?' he countered. He pulled her closer to him. 'The Maquis is solid. Jacques knows how to cope with anyone unreliable. And apart from his people there's our own council. Beatrice and Janot and Ma Mère, Gaston and Marie.'

Lying in the shelter of his arm, Kate said, 'And there was Louis Cabrot.'

He said gently, 'My darling, nobody can be blamed for what happens when they're arrested. But you're talking about deliberate betrayal. Cabrot didn't go to the Gestapo. Nor will anyone else.'

'Did he have to be killed?'

'Yes.' The answer came without hesitation. 'Too many lives were at risk. The agony for me was making that decision and sending someone else to do it. It's not the first time, either, but that was the worst. Poor devil, he didn't even know me, but I knew him. That was the night I came to you. I needed you so badly . . . you'd no idea.'

No, Kate thought, I hadn't. I made love to you and you were the first lover in my life and you'd just sentenced one of your own men to death.

'They won't be able to find out in the post mortem, will they?'

'No.' He sounded low. 'Do you still love me?'

Kate turned and took him into her arms. In the light that

137

burned beside the bed she saw how tired and drawn he looked and burdened by what he had done.

'I shall always love you,' she said. 'And you mustn't think about it any more. Come to me, my love, and let me show you.'

They fell asleep at last.

In the apartment at Beaulieu, Pierrot was dressing, careful not to make a noise. He paused to make sure his wife was resting peacefully and then slipped out and down the stairs. The more senior of the Abwehr officers let him in.

'Sorry I'm so late,' he said. 'I couldn't get away before now.'

'So what's the news?'

'Not good, I'm afraid. I could do with a drink.'

In the luxurious bedroom at the Negresco, Eilenburg was the first to wake. He pressed the light switch. She lay curled up beside him, one arm above her head. She looked very young and vulnerable, the brown hair damp and curling, and dark shadows under the eyes that were so like Minna's. He could look into her face, sleeping or awake, because he wasn't afraid of what he'd see. It was a very odd sensation for him, this feeling of pity, even tenderness for a girl who wasn't Minna. Only a resemblance, he insisted, covering her naked breasts with the sheet. A trick of the imagination that turned the blaze of sexual encounter into something more significant. He got up, moving carefully so she wouldn't wake. He went into the bathroom, got under the shower. It was cold and he grimaced. What was he washing off, he thought in surprise? The sweat of a fierce lovemaking, or the guilt of his emotional betrayal? He wouldn't see her again, he decided. He'd give her some money, issue a permit for extra rations – she was far too thin and delicate from overwork and poor food – and tell her to keep away. Move to another hotel. That was the best. Quite a sum of money, so she would be well set up if she didn't find work straight away. He came back into the room and she was sitting up. She smiled at him and the big brown eyes were soft and shining.

She didn't say anything but just held out her arms. He came to her.

5

The Mayor held a conference; he called in the prominent businessmen, the parish priests and the owner and editor of the local newspaper. They gathered at the Town Hall at eleven o'clock on the following morning. He spoke to them briefly. Nice and its inhabitants were under a suspended sentence. They were all faced with an impossible dilemma. He paused and looked at certain people. The Resistance had been very active in the last two years and the Gestapo had been unusually lenient in its attitude towards the town. Albert Stohler had been approachable. He coughed at the word that meant bribeable and hurried on. His successor seemed determined to provoke a violent confrontation. His threats were compatible with his reputation. He also had his name to make in that part of France. Questions were asked then. What was the alternative? Had anyone approached the military authorities? What about representations to the Vichy Government?

The Mayor shook his head. The power of the Gestapo was greater than the army or the French Government. General Knocken, head of the Gestapo in France, was their only hope of appeal. There was a long silence. Finally the Mayor said, 'I am the one who should go. It is my responsibility.'

The meeting ended. As the Mayor anticipated, some,

whose business interests were protected by Gestapo influence, sent in a report to Eilenburg. The summons to the Villa Trianon came that evening.

Eilenburg was friendly. He treated the Mayor with respect, invited him to sit down, offered him a drink. Then he handed him the report of the meeting. The Mayor didn't read it.

'I can think of several people who could have sent you this, Standartenführer,' he said. 'It doesn't surprise me.'

'And do you really imagine General Knocken will see you?' Eilenburg enquired. 'Do you know how many other people wait for days on end, hoping to get a hearing from him?'

'I have no doubt there are many,' was the calm response. 'But I am the Mayor of one of the most important towns on the Midi. I think he would see me eventually.'

'And what would you hope to achieve?' Eilenburg asked him.

'Some measure of restraint on the reprisals you threaten to take here. I would try and convince him that if you carry them out, a comparatively peaceful and cooperative section of Southern France would rise up *en masse* against the German Occupation forces. He might not want that to happen.'

Eilenburg laughed. He shook his head.

'No civilian population has risen up, *en masse* or otherwise, against the German forces since France was defeated. How many active members do you think the Resistance can call up in the whole of the country?' He leaned towards him. 'Less than two thousand. They're scattered through the countryside, the mountains, the industrial areas and they're regularly wiped out. Most of the activists are Communists, Monsieur le Maire. We know about the so-called secret armies, waiting for the Allied Invasion to rise up and come out in support. In reality they don't exist. A few bands of murderers waiting on word from Moscow; that's the core of the Resistance here. And of course the Allied agents they send in from London: amateurs, women. We've picked them up as they landed and shot them before they had a chance even to send a message. But go to Paris by all means, and try.' He leaned back. The Mayor pushed back his chair. Eilenburg waited till he was standing and then said, 'One moment. I can save you the journey.'

The Mayor looked at him and wet his lips. At last, the price would be named. No different to Stohler in principle, but greedier. . . .

'I would hope so, Standartenführer.'

'Then sit down and we'll talk,' he was told. It made him feel foolish to take the chair again.

The Mayor said, 'What do you want from us?'

Eilenburg said quietly, 'I want the leaders of the Resistance. Whoever they are. Give me the men who've killed German soldiers and destroyed German property over the last two years. I want the men and the women too. You call them patriots; I call them murderers, cowards who let the innocent die for them. Forty citizens was the last tally, wasn't it? The last time Stohler decided to make an example? Until you bought him off. I am not to be bought. Understand that.'

The Mayor said, 'I understand that.'

'Good. Now, let me show you something. It may help you to make up your mind.'

He pulled a report out of a folder on his desk and pushed it across to the Mayor.

'That is the post mortem our doctor carried out on a local man who died a few days ago. A man I questioned here myself and released because he was too ill to keep in jail. I thought he was innocent of any connection with the Resistance. Just a poor devil in the last stages of consumption who cleaned the streets for a living. Read it.'

The Mayor did so. The name meant nothing. He looked up. 'Asphyxia? He choked to death?'

'Suffocated,' Eilenburg said. 'Probably with a pillow. I was wrong, Monsieur le Maire; he had helped these Resistance heroes. And in return they murdered him because I let him go free. You may keep that report.'

'Why should I want it?' the old man asked slowly.

'It will help you to see where your real responsibility lies,' Eilenburg answered. 'Show it to others. Ask yourselves whether it's worth protecting people who would do that to one of their own.'

'It wouldn't be any use,' the Mayor said. 'Nobody would believe a report that came from here.'

'They'd believe it if it was printed in the *Nice Matin*,' he countered. 'Give it to the editor. He was among you this morning. Good night.'

The Mayor was shown out of the office. When he was alone, Eilenburg scowled. A clever man, the Mayor. Brave and cunning. It wouldn't do to leave him free for long. Unless he damned his soul and collaborated with the Gestapo to save the town. That was Eilenburg's gamble. He dismissed his staff and went back to the hotel.

The girl was waiting for him. Her name was Antoinette. She smiled and hurried to meet him. He slipped his arm round her.

'You bought that dress today?'

'Yes. From a shop on the Promenade. Do you like it?'

'Very much. And the shoes. They're pretty.'

She nestled into him like a kitten. She held out one small foot in the neat little red shoe.

'I love my new clothes,' she said. 'I've never had anything like them before.'

Eilenburg kissed the top of her head. 'You shall have lots of clothes and shoes. And maybe a nice fur to keep you warm in the winter. How would that be?'

She wrapped one thin arm round his waist. 'I wish I could give you something.'

He smiled. 'You can. But we'll have dinner first. I'm going to take you down to the restaurant tonight.'

She drew back from him. 'Oh no. I'd feel so awkward.'

For a second he doubted her. Nothing showed on his face.

'Awkward to be with me, Antoinette – yes, I suppose that's right.'

Her vehemence surprised him. 'That's not the reason. I'd be proud to be with you, anywhere. I just meant that I've never been in a place like this except to clean the slops and change the beds. Will you tell me what to do? What to eat with?'

He felt so relieved he hugged her.

'We'll have dinner up here for the first time, then,' he promised. 'When you come to the restaurant you won't feel shy.'

The girl sighed. 'I wonder what Claude will say,' she murmured.

'Claude?'

'The receptionist. He sent me up here the other night. You sent me away.'

'So I did,' Eilenburg admitted. He stroked the soft curly hair and lifted her face up to kiss her. 'I'd forgotten about Claude. He was a pig to you, wasn't he?'

'He is a pig to everybody,' she said. 'It doesn't matter. If he asks me for money I won't give it.'

She didn't see the look in his eyes, because hers were closed as she reached up for his lips.

'He won't ask you for anything,' Eilenburg said.

The next morning, while they ate breakfast, Paul Roulier said, 'I have been thinking, Madame Alfurd. How would you like to go back to Nice?'

She was taken by surprise. 'What for?'

'A short holiday. You'd be my guest. I can promise you, you'd be very comfortable and you could revisit some of the places. Wouldn't it help?'

She hesitated. Go back to France. Her husband would never go. He'd made excuses every time. He didn't want to waken old memories; she had been content to let them sleep in her mind until he died. Go back and see it all again. It had hardly changed in 1947. The marks of the war were still

144

there. She remembered seeing Pierrot in court that autumn afternoon. Philippe Derain, on trial for his life as a traitor in the pay of the Germans.

'You say I'd be your guest,' she said after a time. 'Monsieur Roulier, if I accept this invitation, you've got to answer me a question that I've deliberately not asked you. You spoke of finding the people who betrayed us in the war. "Will you help *us*," isn't that what you said?'

'Yes,' he agreed. 'Obviously I am not investigating this alone.'

'Then who are you representing?' Katharine demanded. 'Whose guest will I be if I go to France?'

'I can't tell you that,' he answered. 'Not until we have all the evidence we need. But I can give you my word that we are Frenchmen and our motive is the same as yours. To find out the truth and flush out the guilty. If we don't I can promise you something else. Christian Eilenburg will never be brought to trial and the real traitors will be safe for ever.'

Katharine Alfurd said, 'How can you be sure of this?'

'Because already efforts are being made to do a deal,' he replied, 'on your side and in France. Public opinion wants to see Eilenburg punished. But very powerful people are determined to prevent it. As they prevented Pierrot from being convicted. We want to expose them. It would suit their purpose if Eilenburg dies in prison and what he knows is buried with him.'

'I see,' she said. 'Eilenburg won't be allowed to defend himself. I see how it follows. But I don't see what difference I can make.'

'All the difference in the world,' was the reply. 'If you can persuade Eilenburg to talk to you. If you trust me and come back to France, I'll guarantee you get to see him.'

She began to stack the crockery; he could see she was agitated and he didn't offer to help. She went out to the kitchen and he stayed at the table, listening to the sounds of plates clattering and an exclamation as she dropped something. When she came back he got up and waited.

'I can leave Polly with my daughter,' she said.

He didn't understand what she meant. 'Polly?'

'My dog. I can't take her with me.'

'Oh, no, of course not. What about a kennel?'

'Certainly not.' Her tone was sharp. 'I'll ring up my daughter and ask her.'

Roulier said, 'Don't tell her where you're going.'

Katharine stared at him. 'Why on earth not?'

He frowned. The truth or a half-truth – she wasn't a woman who would forgive a lie. 'Because it could be dangerous for you, if it was known that you had gone to Nice,' he said. 'Surely you can see why?'

Katharine sat down. She had forgotten to remove the marmalade jar. It was a present from her grandchildren for her last birthday. White pottery with a bright orange lid.

'I'm the last one left,' she said. 'That's right. All the others are dead. Just me and Eilenburg.'

Roulier nodded. 'Are you still prepared to go?'

She smiled slightly, which surprised him. 'Why not? I'm not leaving very much behind. So long as Polly doesn't fret. I'll ring my daughter now.'

'Cecilie.' He got up as soon as she approached the table. The café was as full as before; the band was strumming away the same selection of popular tunes from inside. A German NCO looked up at Kate as she passed and grinned at her. She ignored him and sat opposite Pierrot.

'He won't listen,' she said in reply to his whispered question. 'He's not frightened of being betrayed either. I did my best.' She ordered coffee and took one of Pierrot's rank cigarettes.

He said, 'Did you bring me the transcripts?'

'Yes, they're in the newspaper.'

'I'll take them to the lavatory, read them and then bring the paper back. I won't be long.' He picked up the folded copy of the *Nice Matin*, excused himself and disappeared into the main building. In less than five minutes he was back, the newspaper laid on the chair beside her.

'He lied when he said London was giving us full backing,' he muttered. 'I suspected it because of the messages I was getting. He's crazy to do it, Cecilie. Did you read your newspaper by any chance?'

'No.' She shook her head.

He was taut and angry. 'Then look at the fourth page, second row down. A little piece about someone we both know. Don't worry, I've taken the transcripts out. I'll destroy them when I get home. Go on, read it.'

It was a short paragraph. It reported that Louis Pierre Cabrot, having been released from Gestapo custody, had been found murdered at his home two days later. Post mortem examination showed he had been suffocated while asleep.

Kate folded the newspaper. 'Oh my God.'

'Yes,' Pierrot said grimly. 'You can see what it means. Murdered. And not by the SS. It's been very cleverly done. Cecilie, I'm coming to the apartment tomorrow to see him. Tell him I'll be there just after six. I'll pay the bill. Say goodbye now and we'd better make it look natural.'

He got up and before she could stop him, he bent over and kissed her hard on the mouth.

'Don't!' she hissed at him.

'We're being watched,' he murmured. 'Your NCO hasn't taken his eyes off us. Kiss me back, Cecilie.'

She did, and she saw the desire in his eyes as he held her.

'I won't let him sacrifice you,' he whispered, and she turned and hurried away.

Pierrot had been telling the truth about the German. He got up and tried to block her way. He followed her out and Kate pedalled hard away from the café to escape him. At a safe distance she stopped, and began to wheel her bicycle along the Promenade. There was a slight swelling on her lip where Pierrot had kissed her. She had never been afraid of a man in her life. There was something so strong and insistent

147

about the desire he felt for her, and which seemed to escape his control whenever he touched her. His tongue had stabbed at her lips like a weapon. She had felt no excitement, only anger and resentment. In some way he and the grinning German lumbering after her were identified in her mind. She rubbed her sore mouth with the back of her hand. Next time, she said to herself, I'll slap his face if he tries to take advantage like he did today.

She walked on slowly. There was no breeze and it was hot, the sun glancing back off the streets. The giant palms stood motionless along the sea front, giving no shade. As a child she had spent the summer holidays in Normandy, where the sea was cold and bracing, unlike the milk-warm Mediterranean. Taking her time that afternoon, Kate remembered those easy days with longing, when she and her brother played racing games against the surf and their father taught them both to swim. Happy family holidays that seemed so far away. Beautiful peaceful France where she had grown up in the carefree years when nobody imagined there could be such a thing as war and Occupation.

When she reached Jean's flat she ran up the stairs in her eagerness to see him. She threw her arms round his neck and clung and he said gently,

'What is it, my darling? What's the matter?'

'Nothing,' Kate said, holding tight to him. 'I've been feeling very homesick suddenly.'

'Well, you're home now,' he told her. He kissed her with tenderness.

'I've got things to tell you,' she said at last. 'And this newspaper.'

He sat with his arm round her while she described her meeting with Pierrot. She didn't mention the kiss. He read the item in the *Nice Matin*, frowned and put it down.

'You don't think it matters?' Kate asked him.

'No,' he answered, 'I don't. I don't think anything Pierrot said matters either. He's over-cautious, pessimistic. He's that type; he's a little jealous of me. He thinks a professional should run the network. I don't take him seriously, sweetheart, and you mustn't either. I know what I am doing. Now come here; I've missed you.'

He was a skilful lover and every nerve-ending in her body responded to his touch. The revulsion she felt for Pierrot became a blazing desire for sexual fulfilment when she was in Jean Dulac's arms. Passion engulfed them both. The newspaper with the little item about a poor man's death was tossed aside and forgotten and they lay at last exhausted in each other's arms. But the niggle of doubt and fear was with her when she woke.

'Lord Wroxham is in the coffee room, Sir. Up the stairs and on your right.'

Colonel Reed said, 'Thank you,' briskly and followed the directions. How did club servants know if someone had never been there before? It didn't put him in a good mood to be classified as an outsider. It was a magnificent staircase, floored in mahogany with a wide sweep of faded green carpet, held at each step by a gleaming stair-rod of polished brass. He ran his hand up the massive balustrade. No dust. The portraits of great statesmen of the Tory Party glowered at him from the walls. A bust of his host's great-grandfather sneered at him from the top of the stairs.

The tall figure sunk in an armchair seemed to be dozing. He proved himself wide awake by leaping up as soon as Reed appeared in the doorway. The smile was no longer bullet-proof. It transformed his rather canine face; he looked deceptively handsome for a moment.

'Hello, Colonel,' he said, shaking hands.

'Morning, Wroxham.'

Reed's irritation disappeared. After the last lunch spent in Reed's favourite Soho restaurant, both men were surprised how much they liked each other. Wroxham admired the older man's insight and daring; Reed was fascinated by the complex intelligence of the aristocratic fop he had made fun of for so long. They found a common sense of humour. More ironic than ridiculous. Banana-skins didn't appeal to either. They had begun to work very closely together. There were times when Reed's SOE associates weren't consulted until he'd talked to Major Lord Wroxham on the General's private line. They drank sherry before lunch.

Reed decided to get the bad news over. He scowled, and his fine voice came down a register.

'We've got trouble with Dulac, I'm afraid. He's gone out of control.'

'How, exactly?'

Reed's frown deepened. 'Taken the bit between his teeth. Refused to listen to instructions and is planning to go ahead with his attack on the convoy. In fact,' he glanced up at the attentive face of his host, 'in fact he's planning to take some of the officers hostage against Gestapo reprisals.'

'Oh, for Christ's sake,' Wroxham sighed. 'That's the last straw!'

'Ironic, wouldn't it be, if he picks up your tame general,' Reed suggested.

'Ironic isn't the word I'd use, Colonel. Well, I'm afraid we'll have to do as I mentioned that day at the War Office. Take things into our own hands. Let Pierrot deal with him.'

'You said you weren't interested in methods,' Reed reminded him. 'Only results. Dulac is one of the best network leaders in France. He's highly regarded by de Gaulle's lot and frankly, he's given wonderful service to us in the last two years. I'd have to know more before I'd agree to any steps being taken against him.'

'How much more?' The question was asked softly.

'All of it,' Reed said flatly. 'And I didn't believe a word of that cock-and-bull story about misinformation. I want the truth, Richard.' He used the Christian name like a password.

'The truth,' Richard Wroxham said at last, 'will be in the safe at the Hôtel du Cap at Cap d'Antibes. Which explains why Fred the burglar was foisted on to your training scheme.'

He finished his sherry. Reed did the same. Wroxham went

on slowly talking. A waiter appeared to say that their table in the club dining room was waiting, but Wroxham sent him away. At one point Reed said,

'So that's why Michaelson was sent on sick leave in the middle of the training schedule.'

'He'd begun to undermine morale,' Wroxham said. 'And he was sniffing around too much. He had a love affair with a girl who got caught and executed at Ravensbrück. That was the start of his trouble. He'd damned that operator Julie in his report. We had to get him out of the way. He's in Washington, wasting his time as an attaché at the Embassy. We can finish this over lunch if you're ready.'

'I'm always hungry,' Reed said. 'I hope the food in this Tory stronghold is good. I'd better confess I lean to the Liberal Party.' They laughed together.

'The food is terrible,' Wroxham said. 'But the cellar is the best in London. As I shall take pleasure in proving to you. Let's go down before the cold meat's gone. It's the best thing on the menu.'

It was a long lunch. Reed had a car to collect him this time and after the vintage port he needed it. He had a slight headache and he ordered the driver to stop in Green Park so he could walk it off. He set off across the grass, an energetic army officer in his late forties, swinging his arms and striding out, watched by odd courting couples sitting under the trees and children playing on the pathways.

The truth at last. The truth of a ruthless manœuvre to strike at Nazi Germany that made the sabotage and Intelligence work of the Resistance look as puny as children playing nursery war games. But those children would be sacrificed and their death sentences pronounced in England. One mission must succeed and to make sure of its success, another must fail. He swung round and strode back to the waiting car. Wroxham was right when he said they needed to be friends if they wanted to live in peace afterwards with what they had to do.

He worked on at his top-floor office until late that night.

151

Part of that work was to liaise officially with Wroxham and his section at the War Office, to stop Jean Dulac from ruining the plan.

'My daughter said she'd drive over and collect Polly this afternoon,' Katharine Alfurd said. 'I told her I was going to spend a few days with an old school friend who'd suddenly surfaced. I made up the name – she didn't even hear it, I don't think.'

Roulier asked, 'Didn't she wonder why you couldn't take the dog with you?'

'Because my friend has cats,' she said promptly. 'And you know what cat-killers Jack Russells are!'

He smiled. 'I didn't know. Let me take you out to lunch somewhere and then I'll keep out of the way till your daughter comes. Isn't there somewhere nice near here?'

Kate thought for a moment. 'Yes, there is. There's a very good restaurant at Littlewick, about six miles away. Robert used to take me there on special occasions. I'm afraid it's very expensive.'

'Then we'll go,' he said. For a moment she felt quite young again. Excited at the prospect of a special lunch.

'It's called the Old House,' she explained. 'We don't need to book on a weekday, but you can't get a table at weekends. I'll go and put on something smart!' She gave him a brilliant smile and hurried upstairs.

It was so long since she had been taken out. Robert had been meticulous about birthdays and anniversaries, but he never did anything extravagant on the spur of the moment. And why should he, she defended him. He was contented and liked his routine. How could he have known that sometimes she longed to break the monotony. . . .

She found a silk dress she hadn't worn for a long time. Later that evening they were flying to the South of France. Extraordinary, she thought, turning to look at herself in the mirror. Lying to Dorothy, who didn't even listen to the details because nothing interesting could possibly happen to her mother. Going out to lunch with a man who didn't treat her as if she were boring and old. For a moment she had a very odd sensation. The woman in the looking glass was shedding her personality. Mrs Alfurd, the Colonel's widow who lived in Nut Tree Cottage with her little terrier, was blurring at the edges, like a watercolour left out in the rain.

'Maybe,' she said out loud, 'I'm becoming myself again.' She went down the stairs and he opened the front door for her. 'You look charming. That's a lovely dress.'

He was French and they always noticed how women looked. But it was nice to be told so, all the same.

'Thank you,' Katharine said.

It was a very special lunch. She was anxious at first, knowing the importance of good food to a Frenchman. There was no attempt at cuisine, nouvelle or otherwise. Simple English food, beautifully cooked meat and fresh vegetables, old fashioned puddings and cream so thick it clung to the spoon. And they talked of other things. He had been married, he told her. Divorced for five years. One girl who was at school in Switzerland. He didn't see her very often. The marriage had been happy but it had no real roots. Time proved an enemy. They were both bored and he was involved with another woman when his wife decided she wanted to marry her lover. He shrugged and smiled, dismissing the episode.

'We're not bad friends; I don't follow the modern custom of playing golf with my ex-wife's husband and being very civilized about it. Frankly, I hate golf and he's rather boring. So I live alone and I am quite content. Tell me about your daughter. Why didn't she listen when you told her you were going away this morning?'

'Because she hasn't listened for years to anything I say,' Katharine answered. 'It's a strange thing, but she's not a bit like her father or me. To be honest, she's a bossy, bustling woman, and if it wasn't for my grandsons, I wouldn't mind not seeing her at all. They're great fun; dear little boys and I love them. But I've embarrassed Dorothy talking about the war and the things we've been discussing. She makes me feel ashamed, as if I were making it up and anyway nobody wants to know. I don't like being dismissed like that. It hurts to be told you're a bore to people. Even if it's true.'

Paul Roulier said, 'You could never be a bore. May I ask you something very personal?'

Katharine answered, 'Yes, I think so.'

'Were you happy with your husband?'

She said, 'That *is* personal.'

'I apologize. But I'm curious about you, Madame Alfurd.'

Kate lit a cigarette.

'Don't you think you'd better call me Kate?' she suggested. 'And why curious?'

'Because you don't seem to fit in,' he said after a moment. 'Maybe I'm not expressing myself too well – my English isn't good enough.'

'Your English is as good as mine,' she retorted. 'All right, perhaps I don't really fit in with Amdale and the twilight of my life. I think that sounds so dreary, don't you, as if everything was fading away just because one gets older. But I've lived a certain kind of life for forty years. I didn't have to, I chose it. Does that answer your original question, Paul?'

He had a trick of half-closing his eyes before he answered a question that needed some thought. Cat-like, she thought suddenly. That's what he is. A feline man. Soft-footed and powerful, like a tiger.

'No, it doesn't,' he said. 'Perhaps you didn't choose it. I think it was chosen for you.'

She stared at him. 'Chosen? What on earth do you mean?'

He signalled for the bill. 'He married you to keep you quiet,' he said softly. 'And in your heart you've known it for all these years. In the last two days we've started to unpick a conspiracy that has stretched like a spider's web, catching people, tying them up in silence. I believe your marriage to Colonel Alfurd was part of that conspiracy.'

She picked up her handbag, put her cigarettes and lighter away.

'Maybe it was,' she said. 'But he did love me.'

He stooped, picked up the gloves she'd dropped and handed them to her.

'I've never doubted that,' he said.

Katharine saw her daughter's Ford Cortina pull up outside the gate. She moved away from the window. Paul had driven away, leaving her at the cottage.

'I'll telephone in one hour to make sure your daughter's gone,' he said. 'Our flight is at seven.' He lifted her hand and kissed it. She blushed. She hadn't blushed for years. '*Au revoir*, Kate.'

Dorothy came up the path, opened the front door and called out, 'Mother?'

'In here, darling.'

She got up and kissed her daughter. It was a mutual peck, a habit that had little meaning. In her teens Dorothy had chided Katharine once with 'Mummy, don't *hug* me all over the place, it's so embarrassing.' So un-English was what she meant. Rebuffed, Katharine didn't try to show affection.

'You're looking well,' Dorothy said briskly. And then, frowning slightly, 'I haven't seen you all dressed up like that for ages. Is it new?'

'No, quite old in fact. How are the boys?' Katharine changed the subject and her daughter explained what a nice time they'd had sailing. Great fun for them and such a coincidence, meeting a couple who had a boat and offered to take them out for the day – of course, she added, they were so disappointed not to come down, but she'd promised on their next half-term. . . .

Katharine offered her a cup of tea. Dorothy said, no, she'd make it. She treated her mother as if she were always tired and did things for her that made Katharine feel incapable. It was such a pity, she thought, sipping tea she didn't want, wishing she was closer to her only child. What a shame to sit here and make up a pack of lies about a non-existent friend, instead of telling her the truth. But Dorothy would have been horrified, rushing to the phone to speak to her husband, convinced that her mother was either inventing the whole story or about to be kidnapped and murdered by some confidence tricksters. The little terrier, sensing upheaval, retreated under the table. No use regretting an intimacy which had never existed, Katharine realized. She was light years away from the matter-of-fact woman sitting opposite, already making excuses about having to get back early. Dorothy took the packet of dog biscuits and a couple of tins for the reluctant Polly, who had to be caught and put on the lead. At the door, she pecked her mother's cheek again and then said,

'By the way, hadn't I better have a telephone number?'

Katharine said lightly, 'I'm sorry, dear, I can't remember it exactly, you know how vague I am, but I'll ring in a day or so and give it to you. Thank you so much for taking Polly. She'll be very good.'

'Of course she will. We'll go for nice long walks. Have a nice time, Mother. It'll do you good to have a break.'

'I think so,' Katharine said, and stood waving as they got into the car and drove away.

By ten o'clock that night she was driving with Paul Roulier along the wide coast road from Nice airport. It was dark and warm as velvet; the windows were all open wide and a breeze fanned them as they drove. He had ordered champagne on the flight over and raised his glass in a silent toast. They hardly spoke after he collected her from the cottage. Perhaps we've said too much, she thought, watching the descent over the sea to Nice, seeing the kaleidoscope of lights on the coast. He made me see something I've been shutting out for all these years, and he's leaving me time to get used to it. But his silence is companionable. He understands and I know it. I know what that raised glass of champagne means, without the need for words. We're allies, he and I, and if the enemy thought they were safe at last, they will soon find out there's no such thing as safety.

They continued on the coast road. She said, 'Why are we going out of Nice?'

He glanced at her for a moment. 'We're not staying in Nice. We are going to the Hôtel du Cap, at Antibes. Nobody will think of looking for you there.'

There was nobody at home. Colonel Reed walked round the garden to the back and peered in through the kitchen window. He went back down the path, noting the neat flower beds and well-kept lawn. The last time he came was for Robert's funeral, two years ago, at the parish church at Amdale. A sad day for him, Colonel Reed thought, remembering the service in the Norman church, a trusted colleague and friend. The friendship had lapsed after he married Kate Fitzgerald; lunch in London twice a year, when they had an unofficial reunion of the old Baker Street Boys, as they called themselves. His wife, Kate, didn't know about it. Alfurd had buried the past for them both. Firmly and effectively. Reed came back from a holiday in Spain to attend his funeral. Tea and drinks at the little cottage afterwards, with the widow looking stunned and lost and the sensible daughter and son-in-law taking care of the guests. He sat in his car for a moment, thinking. Then he called at the village pub, ordered himself a drink at the bar and asked where he could find Mrs Alfurd.

'She was here three days ago,' the barman remembered. 'Always pops in for a drink and a bite to eat on a Saturday. She's lonely, I think, and likes to talk to people. Sad, being a widow.'

'Indeed it is,' Reed agreed. 'That's why I thought I'd drop in on her and see how she was. The Colonel and I were old friends. And you haven't seen her since Saturday?'

'No, Sir, but then I wouldn't. She only comes in at a weekend when there's people about. There was a fellow came in that lunchtime – they were chatting away in French in no time.'

Reed raised his eyebrows and smiled encouragingly.

'Really? I didn't know foreigners came here.'

'They don't normally, Sir. We get a lot of ramblers and people sightseeing, but not foreigners as a rule. They got on very well; had lunch together and I think she must have invited him back. She does talk to strangers a bit. Goes on about the war. Nobody minds, she's such a nice lady. By the way, was that little Russell of hers in the house? Barks like mad if anyone comes near.'

'No,' Colonel Reed said, 'I don't think it was.' He finished his drink.

'Then she must be away,' the barman said. 'Always takes it with her.'

He watched the distinguished gentleman go out. Went a funny colour when he mentioned the Frenchman and Mrs Alfurd. He dodged round the bar and peered through the window. He saw the stranger get into an old Daimler. He didn't drive away for quite some minutes.

Dorothy was watching television with her husband. The little dog was sulking behind the sofa. She sighed and he looked up and said,

'What's the matter, love? You've been very down all evening. Mother again?'

'Yes,' she said. 'As usual. Peter, I don't know what's the matter with me, but she makes me feel so guilty whenever I see her. Why do I always feel on the defensive, as if I were being mean and neglectful? Don't I do my best?'

He reached over and took her hand. He loved her, or he would have grown impatient with the endless repetition over the years of her problems with her mother; worse when that cold fish of a father had been alive.

'Of course you do,' he said. 'She's very independent, you know that. We've asked her to come and stay and she gets out of it every time. She likes to live her own life and if she knew you were sitting here making yourself miserable she'd think you were mad. Now come on, darling, you've taken that bloody dog for her and what more can you do?'

'She was upset because the boys didn't come,' Dorothy went on. 'I knew as soon as I walked in. I said how sorry they were and we'd bring them next half-term, but she just looked at me and asked if I wanted tea. She looked odd today: all dressed up and made up to the nines. I felt she was dying to get rid of me.'

'And weren't you dying to go?' her husband asked.

She squeezed his hand. 'Yes, I was. Peter, you're a saint. You see everything in perspective; I just get fussed and start waking up in the night worrying.'

He slipped his arm round her. 'Watch the programme,' he admonished gently. 'We've missed half of it talking about your mother.'

She had been an awkward, introverted girl when they first met; not even pretty, rather sharp-tongued. He couldn't understand why she had attracted him, but on impulse he asked her out. It was a slow courtship; neither was inclined to rush into a relationship. When they did sleep together it was understood that they would get married as soon as he had been promoted and could afford a house. He met the parents in due course. The Colonel and his lady. Living in a charming cottage, with expensive little antiques and remnants of their life in the big house in the village. He didn't like Dorothy's father and the reason was quite simple. He didn't like the way he treated Dorothy. He showed his indifference and that turned only too easily into impatience. And then there was her mother. He could see why the girl he loved was shy and stiff with people. How difficult to have a mother so obviously beautiful even in middle age, with that combination of sex-appeal and charm. How frustrating to be in competition with her for the attention of a father who adored his wife and clearly didn't like his daughter. He and Dorothy had been married for fourteen years, were comfortable financially and loved their two sons, but Dorothy still suffered the effects of that lonely childhood and he still resented how she had been rejected.

When the telephone rang he swore and cut off the sound of the television. He said irritably,

'Dot, it's for you. A Colonel Reed, friend of your parents.' He held out the phone and she took it from him, making a grimace. Reed – she mimed ignorance and then said in her bright voice,

'Hello, this is Dorothy Miller speaking.'

It was quite late when Colonel Reed got back to Montpelier Square. The telephone call to Katharine Alfurd's daughter had confirmed his suspicions of the Frenchman in the pub who joined her for lunch. He lifted the telephone and dialled Richard Wroxham's Wiltshire home. There was a pause, then the familiar voice said,

'Jim? How are you, nice to hear from you. There's a note thanking you for our splendid dinner in the post.'

Reed didn't waste time. 'Kate Alfurd,' he said. 'Cecilie. Don't you realize we forgot about her? I've just been down to Amdale. No, I don't know why, just instinct I suppose.'

Wroxham said slowly, 'It's never been wrong yet. Go on.' He listened for the next few minutes.

'I checked up in case she was with her daughter,' Reed concluded. 'She'd left her the dog to look after. Some cock-and-bull story about going to stay with a friend who had cats. Oh, for God's sake, Richard, isn't it obvious? She left the bloody animal behind because she's gone to *France*! Yes, with whoever this Frenchman happens to be. What a coincidence, finding the last surviving member of the Dulac network in a village pub on a Saturday morning!'

'What are we going to do?' Wroxham's voice was calm; he never showed his feelings in a crisis. Once, Reed had seen him cry. Just a glimpse of tears in the eyes before he turned away and talked of something else. His mother had been killed in a car crash.

'You've got contacts in France,' Reed said. 'I suggest you tell them to look out for her. Remind them how much trouble she caused in the past. And according to the man behind the bar in that pub, she's been talking about the war!'

'We can't have that,' Wroxham said. 'Not now, not after all these years. I'll phone a friend of mine, put him in the picture. Good God, Jim, just think we were talking about it a couple of nights ago.'

'Bloody woman,' Reed muttered and hung up. He didn't speak his thoughts out loud even to Wroxham. What a pity Eilenburg let her get away.

'There are the transcripts.' Pierrot dropped them on the table. 'They confirm everything I've told you.'

The Major in the Abwehr nodded, started reading through them. Kate's messages to London, their replies; the angry exchanges between Baker Street and Dulac. Pierrot waited, looking out of the window with his back to the Major. The meeting with Dulac had ended in a furious row between them. He had put London's view in terse and brutal language. Dulac had retaliated with accusations of English deceit and self-interest. They didn't care what became of French civilians so long as they could select the targets that suited *them*. He wasn't going to listen to any argument against killing the German troops replacing the garrison and taking hostages against Gestapo reprisals.

'It's pride!' Pierrot accused. 'You've decided to take on this German and you don't care who suffers in consequence! Dulac has to win, Dulac has to cover himself with glory!' For a moment it seemed as if they might come to blows.

The Major had finished reading. Pierrot turned away from the window.

'There's only one way to stop this man,' the German officer said, 'and you must realize it. He can't lay hands on that convoy because of the General and his staff officers. Will you see to this, or shall I?'

Pierrot said, 'Leave it to me. You've finished with those?'

'Yes. You can destroy them now.' The Major smiled unkindly. 'By the way, your money has arrived. Here.' He opened a desk drawer and took out an envelope. 'I asked for a bonus for you; you'll be pleased, I think.'

'Thanks,' Pierrot said. He put the envelope in his inner pocket. 'Everything is expensive; this will be very useful.'

The Major looked up at him. 'Are you going to tell me what you plan to do, or is it better not to know?'

'Better not to know,' Pierrot answered. He left the flat and went down into the street. He bought a bottle of good wine and some cheese at black-market prices and, on impulse, some flowers from a stall at the end of the square.

From the window of his flat the Abwehr Major watched him come back and into the building. He noticed the flowers. Strange, he thought, remembering his old career as a policeman, how the most contemptible beings can have a human side. He turned away. His friend was in Nice at an army meeting. He would take his French girlfriend out to dinner and they could spend the night at the flat afterwards. He was going to miss her when his tour was up. And if all went well, it might end much sooner than anyone expected.

In the flat above, Pierrot became Philippe Derain, coming home after a day in his bookshop, having made a little profit. His wife looked up fondly at him, and propelled the wheelchair across the room. He bent and kissed her and placed the flowers in her lap. Six years ago polio had struck; she was paralysed from the waist down and unable to do anything for herself but move the chair from room to room. He loved her as he would have loved his child, because the wasted body didn't belong to a woman any more. The pinched face, the sad eyes and trusting look were childlike. The poor slack body lay inert beside him in the bed and a thin hand would creep into his at night, as if to apologize for the end of their married life. He loved her tenderly and cared for her as only a man can, when he loves with such a depth of pity. Taking German money to make her comfortable didn't worry him at all. Later he played the dance music she loved and they listened to it together, winding the gramophone and changing the records, till she was tired and he wheeled her into the bedroom and got her ready for bed. A nurse looked after her when he had to go on business. Sometimes he was away for weeks on end. She never complained.

He didn't sleep until long after they were both in bed. The church clock in the square chimed one, then two, and at last three o'clock. In the morning, he got up early, made breakfast and then kissed his wife goodbye. She wished him a good day at the shop. He turned at the door and waved and she blew him a kiss. He had an old car with a gas bag on the roof. By mid-morning he knocked at the door of the Cabrots' little house in Nice and Louis Cabrot's widow let him in.

Eilenburg had spent a profitable day. He could see how Stohler had amassed money merely by sitting still. The first response to his bargain with the Mayor was an anonymous tip to the Gestapo that a family of rich Jews were hiding in a villa on the Cap. Eilenburg decided to lead the raid himself. They arrived just before daybreak. Ten men fully armed in two scout cars, with a closed lorry following behind. The road led down past Cap d'Antibes towards Juan les Pins. The sunrise was glorious, bathing the unruffled sea in a flood of pink and gold. The villa was set back in a huge walled garden a quarter of a mile inland, approached by a narrow track with splendid ornamental gates. The gates were padlocked, the approach untended. The upper windows of the villa were visible from the road and they were shuttered. Empty, it proclaimed, abandoned and shut up since the German occupation of the coast.

Eilenburg's men broke the padlock, swung the gates back, and the cars raced up the weedy drive. Inside, they found three families, numbering twenty-four adults and children, including one baby a few weeks old. The mother had died soon after giving birth, because no one had dared to get a doctor for her. They found her grave in a flower bed at the back. The lorry was filled with the weeping human cargo, the doors bolted and the procession started back to Nice. Eilenburg wandered through the villa, taking stock of the fine

163

rooms and the elegant furniture under dust sheets. The Jews had lived on the ground floor at the back. He looked at the squalor engendered by secrecy. Camp beds, rubbish, the boxes of possessions heaped on top of each other. Rooms that smelt airless in the heat, because they had been too frightened to open the shutters fully. They had confessed to living there for over a year. They wouldn't say whether the villas belonged to any of them. Eilenburg thought probably not. All Jewish property was confiscated automatically and ransacked. This was owned by absentee French, who had let the Jews hide there. It could be a beautiful place to live, he thought. The upstairs bedrooms had a magnificent view over the sea. There were grandiose trees and palms in the garden. Cleaned up and the garden put right, it would make an ideal retreat for him and Antoinette to share until he married Minna and brought her back. She would enjoy living there. He went back to Nice and during the afternoon he sat in on the interrogation of the Jewish males. They offered no resistance to the questions. No violence was necessary. They offered money and jewellery for their lives. He listened quietly, thinking of Stohler. The baby was a problem. He decided not to waste time. The money and the jewellery, including wedding rings and watches, were collected and he signed a receipt. The lorry came to the rear of the Villa Trianon and the people were herded into it. Eilenburg's deputy told them they were being taken to a transit camp and from there they would proceed by rail to a labour camp. The lorry drove off. The money and valuables were duly assigned to the SS central fund and sent off to Paris.

He got back late to the hotel. It was a promising start. But not enough. Throwing him a handful of helpless Jews as a sop wasn't good enough. He wanted Frenchmen. Men and women from the Resistance. That was the price the people of Nice had to pay and nothing less would satisfy him. But he was in a good mood when he joined Antoinette. She wasn't shy about the restaurant any more. He was proud of the way she looked when she walked in with him. Smartly dressed now, with her hair done and a nice string of pearls. Given by a local jeweller when they admired them in his shop. He thought how very pretty she looked, as she sat opposite him, smiling and talking about her day. She didn't work any more, of course. She spent time with her family; he'd been so good to them, she murmured. All that food – she shopped for little luxuries on the black market and she sunbathed and swam. Like a child, he thought indulgently. Innocent and carefree, as he hoped Minna would be one day, when the war was won and they could settle down. She did remind him of Minna so much. He kept telling himself that. And of course, she loved him; she told him so often and without any guile. She told him how beautiful he was and how she worshipped him. No regrets, he asked her once. No fear of what other people would call her for being his mistress? The answer haunted him, 'How can I regret falling in love?' Just that. He told her about the villa over dinner. He didn't go into details, or mention the Jewish families. He asked her if she would like to move there with him when it was ready. 'I don't mind. I'll go there if you want me to.'

He promised to take her there the next day. They were asleep in each other's arms when the telephone rang. He woke slowly and irritably. It was dawn, much the same time as when he drove through the gates of the villa at Antibes. She stirred and murmured. It amused him how deeply she slept. He used to tease her about it. Grumbling, Eilenburg got up and picked the receiver off the hook. They had to repeat the message twice. The hospital where Minna worked had been bombed the night before. She was one of sixty staff and patients killed.

The relief garrison and the officers on leave from the Italian front were due to arrive by train at Menton and then to proceed by lorry and motor transport along the coast road through Nice to Antibes. The garrison at Antibes numbered some three thousand men. It was a closely guarded area because of the hotel where senior officers spent convalescence, and the coves and inlets which might have given access to foreign agents. As a precaution the beach was heavily mined and it was impossible for a Frenchman to go through to the Cap without a special pass or a work permit. It seemed as if Pierrot had given up trying to dissuade Dulac from the planned attack. In the course of that week there were three clandestine meetings between the network leaders and Jacques's Maquis. It seemed that, having accepted defeat, Pierrot was devoting himself to making the venture a success. He brought the date and a rough timetable of the Germans' schedule to the first meeting. Kate sat in, but didn't enter the discussion. She was the radio operator and only there because she was Dulac's mistress. She remained in the background and this gave her an opportunity to watch and listen. Dulac was enthusiastic, optimistic as always. He inspired them all, and Kate recognized that magic quality in him which she had seen the first time. He was a leader who didn't dominate by force of character. He drew people to him. He generated a kind of love and trust from men and women as different from each other as the surly Gaston and his arch-enemy, Marie, who worked at the Mondiale. They believed in him. Jacques, the dedicated Communist, believed in him too, when the decision had been taken. It was Pierrot who worried her. He had produced the timetable, the date, some quite remarkable details as to where the German officers would be in the convoy. She longed to ask how he knew and who had supplied information as confidential as this, but nobody else questioned it. His source must be known to Dulac and the others. They trusted him; Kate didn't. He stayed outside the magic circle of Dulac's charisma. There was no glow upon his face as he listened. She had seen the hatred in him and it was unabated.

'I won't let him sacrifice you.' She couldn't get that remark out of her mind. He had fought against the plan to the last. Now, suddenly, he was in favour of it. 'You don't care who suffers . . . Dulac has to win.' His feelings hadn't changed, only his obstruction. Premonition, her Irish grandmother called it. The foreknowledge of disaster. It came over her that night, sitting in the shadows of the kitchen, while they sat in the circle of the overhead light around the table. Their faces seemed to fade and the excited voices with them. They're going to die. It's like a play, knowing what happens in the last act. She felt a sense of panic and then anger at herself for being superstitious. She heard her name and said, 'Yes, I'm here,' in a voice that sounded shrill and uneasy.

'We want you to send a message to London one last time,' Jean Dulac was saying. 'Telling them what we're going to do and suggesting that a drop of weapons would be the reward for our success.' He looked briefly at the Maquis leader. 'I know you want this, Jacques, and I agree, we'll need London's help. We've won our way so we can be generous. Even to our English Allies!'

There was a laugh when he said this. Pierrot pushed back his chair. There was silence as he spoke directly to Jean.

'If Cecilie is going to contact London tonight, she should not transmit from the centre of the town. I've protested about this several times. Before Eilenburg came there was one detector van operating in the area. Now there are three. It will be a long message and may require her to wait for a reply. On grounds of all our safety, I insist that she sends the message from a new locality. I can accommodate her and the radio set in my own apartment at Beaulieu. There's no activity there at the moment and it would be completely safe.'

He glanced round at the circle of faces; there was a murmur of agreement.

Dulac said, 'Since when have three detector vans been on the streets here?'

'Since last night,' Pierrot retorted. 'All counter-activity has been stepped up by the Gestapo. They know radio operators are working here and in Cannes, apart from Jacques's people in the hills. Cecilie, we are all at risk if you use that set in Nice again!'

Attention had moved to her and slowly she got up and faced them.

'This is such a vital message,' she said, 'I'd rather not send it from my base. If I leave now, I should be in plenty of time.'

'Good.' Several voices spoke up. There was a sense of relief. She saw Pierrot's smile of encouragement and thought, I'm not spending the night in your flat, my friend.

He came to her and whispered, 'My address is 23 rue de Tivoli, top floor flat, apartment C. Someone will let you in if you say you are a friend come to spend the night.' For a moment he touched her hand under the table. 'I'm glad,' he murmured, 'you've been in danger too long,' then he turned away.

Dulac followed her out into the hallway. He bent and kissed her on the lips.

'Come back in the morning,' he said. 'I shall think of you all night.' He kissed her again. It needed all Kate's self-control to resist the invitation of that second, searching kiss.

'Take care,' she said and hurried out.

She cycled back to Jean's apartment, collected the transmitter in its suitcase and strapped it securely to the pannier at the back. Her papers were in the bag slung over her shoulder and the lipstick to hand in her pocket. She began the long ride up into the hills to Valbonne. Ma Mère was mending on the back porch when Kate arrived. She exclaimed in pleasure.

'Cecilie! Come in, my dear child. Look at you, melting in the heat. I'll get you something cold to drink.' She clicked her tongue against her teeth. 'Then you can tell me why you've come. Janot should be back soon. Sit in the shade, silly child. You're likely to get sunstroke taking all that exercise in this heat.' She bustled away and Kate leaned back against the step and closed her eyes.

'I've brought my radio,' she said later. 'I want to stay the night and send from here. I got worried about using the transmitter in the town. I've got away with it so far, but I didn't want to push my luck.'

'Very wise,' the old woman said. She glanced slyly at her. 'He shouldn't have taken you in to live with him. He's never done that before. He must be very fond of you. But he shouldn't take risks.'

Kate didn't answer. She drank the cold lemonade. The sun was going down.

Ma Mère said, 'It'll be curfew time soon. I wonder where my son has got to?'

'I'd better set up the machine,' Kate said. 'In my old room, if that's all right.'

'Yes, yes. I'd better put the supper in the oven. He's always hungry when he gets home.' She disappeared into the house.

Kate sent out her call sign half an hour later. It was a beautiful twilight, with the first stars coming out. She composed her own message, coded and transmitted. She requested an immediate acknowledgement. Then she lay back on the bed, lit a cigarette and nearly fell asleep until the signal came through on the earphones. Message received. Instructions would follow in the next four hours. She went downstairs to keep herself awake. The old woman was sitting at the kitchen table, doing more mending. She looked up and said, 'He's not back. Something must have happened.' The hands holding the sock in its wooden darner were trembling and she let the mending fall. Kate came to her quickly. She saw a streak on the withered cheek, where Ma Mère had been crying.

'Hasn't he been late before?'

'Not on a routine run,' was the answer. 'He was delivering vegetables as usual. Picking up the boxes. He should have been home hours ago.'

Kate suggested gently, 'The van could have broken down. I often thought it wouldn't make the journey.'

Ma Mère got up slowly; swept the socks and the darning into a canvas bag. 'Maybe,' she said. 'It could be that. Did you send your message?'

'Yes, I'm waiting for the reply. Sit down and I'll get the food. And don't worry. He'll be here in a minute.'

'You eat,' the old woman said. 'I'm not hungry.'

It was well past midnight when London sent their answer. Kate asked them to repeat it. A message of the utmost urgency and importance would be relayed to Cecilie fifteen days from now. She was to hold herself in readiness and Jean Dulac and the principals in the network, including the Maquis, should be present. The London operator signed off.

When Kate came downstairs she found Ma Mère fully dressed, with a canvas grip in her hand. She looked very old, and grey-faced.

'You must go at once,' she said. 'Remove all traces from that room, cigarette ends, anything to show you were there. Get your bicycle and go.'

Kate said, 'What are you talking about? It's two in the morning! Where are you going?'

'Away from here,' Ma Mère answered. 'I have a feeling they've caught my son. If I'm wrong, there's no harm sp in a night in the countryside. I've done it before. But you must get right away. Hide till it's past the morning curfew, then go into the town. Be very careful before you approach your apartment or anywhere Janot knows about. I'm going to lock up now and walk.' She turned away, the old bag over her left shoulder. Kate came to her. She started to protest.

'Let me come with you, then,' she said.

'No. That way they'll catch us both. Hurry up, for God's sake.' For the last time she clicked her tongue. Kate ran upstairs. She glanced quickly round the bedroom. She straightened the bedcovers, thumped the pillow, pulled the chair away from the table where she set up her radio. She found two spent matches and threw them out of the window. She'd brought the little tin ashtray with its squashed butts down to the kitchen with her. In a few minutes she had strapped the suitcase back on to her bicycle. The moon shone brightly overhead. The dumpy little figure was in the doorway as she wheeled it out. She waved silently, then turned and Kate heard her locking the back door.

'Ma Mère,' she called out. 'He'll be back in the morning. . . .'

'Pray God,' was the reply.

Kate mounted and started off down the narrow road. She was the other side of a hedgerow some half an hour later, coasting on the downward slope, when she saw the gleam of headlights approaching. She jammed on the brake and jumped off. There was no ditch, only a large tree up a slight bank. The light of the oncoming car cut through the darkness at the end of the corner. Fear gave her the strength needed to haul the cycle with its burden up the bank and lay it flat behind the tree trunk. Then she flattened herself to the ground. Instinctively she shut her eyes as the car passed her. When she opened them it had gone out of sight round another bend. She had no proof that it was German and on its way to the farm. But nobody else would be driving at that hour and at that speed. She dragged the bicycle upright, steered it down the little bank and on to the road. She jumped up and began pedalling as fast as she could. She didn't even know that she was crying.

Shops were opening and people were on their way to work. Another cloudless brilliant day, the sea sparkling blue like a sheet of ruffled silk. Window-boxes and hotel gardens were vivid with geraniums; lines of washing were strung from working-class flats like bunting on a festive day. Kate was so tired she wheeled the bicycle up the hill towards the little square where Dulac lived. There was a telephone booth on the corner. She parked the cycle and went inside.

She couldn't find the few centimes needed to make the call. No change. She could have beaten her fist against the metal box in frustration. She couldn't see his apartment from the kiosk. 'Be very careful before you approach your apartment or anywhere Janot knows about,' Ma Mère had warned. He knew about Dulac, about her, about Beatrice in the grocer's shop. Kate felt sick. She left the kiosk and stood supporting herself on the bicycle for a moment. There was a pâtisserie doing a thriving trade on the other side of the road. She thought helplessly, I must do something. I can't stand the suspense of not knowing what's happened to him another moment. I'll go to the shop and ask to use their telephone. Otherwise I'll go to the apartment and to hell with the danger. . . . The proprietor of the baker's was a surly man.

'Try the kiosk over the road,' he said and turned back to his customers. His wife saw the tired girl with despair on her face. She heard the lie. 'Monsieur, it's out of order.' It wasn't because she had seen someone use it not ten minutes before and talk for quite a time. She beckoned to Kate.

'Through the back here,' she said. 'I'll show you.'

Kate followed, started to say that her father was ill and then stopped when the woman held up her hand.

'Use the telephone,' she said. 'I don't want to know anything about it. Leave the money on the table when you've finished.'

It rang for an eternity. When the maddening burr burr burr was cut off Kate held her breath. Dulac said, 'Hello?' He sounded out of breath.

'It's Cecilie,' she said. There was a pre-arranged signal if the Gestapo were there. All the agents had a code word to warn others not to come near. He didn't use it.

He said, 'Darling, where are you? I was in the bath . . . you sound strange.'

'I've just come down from Ma Mère,' Kate said, lowering her voice. 'I'll go to the café the other side of the square. Come there and don't waste any time.'

She hung up. He was safe. He hadn't been traced, if Janot had indeed been arrested. From feeling sick, she felt dizzy with relief. She left ten francs on the table and slipped out, pushing her way through the queue of people wanting to buy bread. She found a table towards the back of the pavement, sank down into the chair and tried to stop shaking. An old man wiping his hands on a greasy apron shuffled over to her.

'Coffee, please.'

'You'd do better with hot water,' he mumbled. 'Filthy muck, that's what it is these days.'

He went off and Kate fumbled in her bag for a cigarette. It

172

was a test to hold the match steady. She saw Dulac cross the square. He hurried to her and before he could say anything she whispered, 'Just sit down and listen. I didn't go to Beaulieu. I went to Valbonne. Janot didn't come back last night. Ma Mère thinks he's been arrested. She took off into the hills and I hid till the curfew was over and came down here.'

The old man brought a cup of dirty brown ersatz coffee and a little jug with some milk. When he had moved away Jean Dulac said to Kate,

'Ma Mère did the right thing. So did you, my darling.' He rubbed his hand over his forehead. There was a sheen of sweat on it; he turned aside and choked back a cough. Kate reached out and caught hold of his hand.

'It's probably a false alarm,' she said. 'I think we both panicked. I expect that old rattletrap broke down and he'll be home as soon as it's mended.'

He wasn't listening; he was staring past her, to the square behind. She felt his hand grip hers till it hurt.

'I don't think so,' he said. 'Don't look round. The Gestapo have just driven past. They've turned up the street to my flat.'

He insisted that they separate. He gave her an address and made her memorize it as they hastened away from the square.

'It's empty,' he told her. 'There's a key under the oleander bush on the left of the back door. In a little flower pot. Let yourself in and wait for me.'

She held on to him for a moment.

'Why don't you come with me? Darling, for God's sake, they're after you. You'll be picked up!'

'No, I won't,' he said. 'I have to warn Beatrice; if it's not too late.'

Kate remembered then. 'Julie and Pandora,' she cried out, 'they've got to be hidden. Let me get them.'

'No,' he said again. He pulled her close to him, people

173

passing glanced at them and then went on their way. Lovers saying goodbye. It was a common sight.

'I love you, Cecilie. If I have to worry about you, I won't be able to do my duty for the others. I want to know you're safe and you will be if you go where I told you. Nobody knows of the place except me. I'll get to Julie and Pandora. Janot knew nothing about them. The link breaks with Beatrice. Kiss me.' She did and it seemed like the end of her life as they held each other. She could feel the tears spilling out and running down her face. He broke away from her, pushed her to the bicycle and turning, hurried in the opposite direction. Kate watched him go. She saw several people looking curiously at her. She found a handkerchief, wiped her eyes and jumped on the machine. Forty minutes later she was down a cul-de-sac ten miles from the centre of Nice. It had been a good residential area before the war. Most of the houses were windowless and overgrown with weeds that choked the entrances. There was a silent, desolate air about the place. She found the house, with its battered name on the gate: La Rosée. The key to the back door was in the pot, lying carelessly on its side under the oleander. She opened the door, heaved her cycle in after her and shut and locked it. Silence; heavy, stale air. Cobwebs, a buzz of flies in a corner. Dust floating in the shaft of sunlight through a damaged shutter. Slowly Kate walked from the back to the front. The carpets had been taken up. Patches on the polished floorboards showed where they had been. The same for pictures on the walls. Chairs and a sofa remained. The upholstery had been slashed. Beds on the upper floor, mattresses cut open. No ornaments, pictures; mirrors starred and broken. The place had been robbed of everything portable and what was left wilfully damaged. She sat down on the edge of a big mahogany double bed, its mattress protruding stuffing like entrails, and found herself curling up and closing her eyes. Exhaustion, mental and physical, overwhelmed her. In the stifling semi-darkness of the unknown bedroom, she fell asleep.

*   *   *

Dulac was too late for Beatrice. He saw the crowd gathered outside the grocery shop on the other side of the road. He kept in the rear and asked a woman what everyone was gaping at.

'There's been an arrest,' she muttered. 'I didn't see it myself. It's a poor widow, they say.' She glanced sideways round her. The word was a whisper. 'Gestapo.' Dulac mumbled something and moved away. Beatrice and the baby. Oh, God, God, where are you? He didn't dare take the bus. He walked, keeping to the inner side of the pavements, stopping to look in shop windows, making sure he wasn't being followed. By the afternoon he reached the house where Julie and Pandora were living. He knocked and Julie opened it. He saw by her face that she had heard the news. She looked hollow-eyed and ghastly.

'Marcel was in the town this morning. He heard there'd been a raid on your apartment.' She leant against the wall and gave a long sigh of relief. 'He didn't know whether you'd been picked up. My God, I've never spent such a day!'

He didn't waste time. 'Get ready and make sure you clean out your rooms. We're joining Cecilie. I can't travel by public transport because they'll be looking for me and checking buses. You can, so long as Pandora keeps his mouth shut.'

She looked defensive. 'He's got his deaf-mute card,' she snapped. 'He knows what to do. We've travelled before now. Come on, let's throw our stuff into a bag. Where do we go?'

Dulac didn't hesitate. Julie was experienced and convincing with a first-rate cover story and papers. But Pandora, with no protection but the forged deaf-mute card? No, they couldn't be trusted with the address of the safe house where Cecilie was hiding.

'Wait for me outside the cinema in the rue de la Révolution,' he said. 'Give me an hour's start. I'll walk there.'

She looked as if she was going to argue, but decided not to. 'We'll be there,' she said.

Kate woke to find Jean sitting on the bed beside her.

'Oh, thank God,' she said and threw both arms round him. He held her tightly, kissing her feverishly.

'I need you,' he said again and again, as they made love. When they were quiet she remembered he'd said the same thing the first time, the night he sentenced Louis Cabrot to death. He didn't sleep; he lay beside her and stared at the cracked plaster ceiling overhead. The sadness that follows fulfilment. There was a Latin tag for it, she couldn't remember how it went. At last Kate said, 'Did you find the others?'

'Yes. They're here. They'd already taken Beatrice away. I can't bear to think of it.' He jerked away from her, sat up and covered his face with his hands. 'When they took her husband she tried to kill herself. She was pregnant. I went to see her in hospital. I'd done a small conveyancing on the shop when they got married. I tried to give her a reason for living. She still had the child; she didn't seem to care. So I asked her to work with us. I said she was needed. I could justify what happened to Cabrot – I couldn't risk the network – but how do I live with what is happening to Beatrice? Tell me, my darling, how do I stop myself from going mad?'

Kate came to him, drew him back to the bed. She put his shirt on and buttoned it. He was shivering.

'You mind so much,' she whispered, seeing the agony and unable to soothe it. 'You can't torture yourself.'

'They'll torture Beatrice,' he said. 'Why didn't I let her die in peace and the poor little child with her? Why did I try to play God and have this happen to her?'

'Because she *was* needed,' Kate answered. 'She saved other people's lives and everything she did had one end. To win the war and avenge her husband. She knew that, my love, she wasn't stupid or blind. She knew the risks. They may not hurt her; you can't be sure.'

He didn't seem to hear. 'Someone betrayed her,' he muttered. 'Someone betrayed Janot. And knew that both of them would lead to me. Who did it? Who would do such a thing?'

Kate put her arms round him. 'We'll find out in time. Are you calmer now? Please, darling, try to be calm.'

He looked at her. 'I have blood on my hands,' he said. 'Not even loving you makes them clean.'

Kate said slowly, 'If you feel like this, perhaps you should give up.'

'I've thought about it,' he answered. 'When things went wrong and we lost people . . . forty were shot because I organized an attack on a train. It was a great night, Cecilie, we blew up the track and the train was derailed. It was full of German troops. Hundreds were injured and killed. We celebrated when we got back. We sang songs and got a little bit drunk. But forty men were shot as a reprisal. I knew many of them. I lived with that. I lived with it because I went on striking at the Germans. I gave myself no rest, I risked my life a dozen times to make sense of those French dead. How do I make sense of Beatrice? And poor Janot – with his simple trust in me. And what will happen to Ma Mère? How long can she hide?' He swung round on Kate in rage and despair. 'We can't touch that convoy – we can't even come out of hiding to hear London's message, until we know who has betrayed us. We're shut up here, helpless, immobilized. I shall go mad unless I can take action. . . .'

Kate said gently, 'It won't bring back the dead. Risking yourself won't help either of them. You've got to be patient. Think, Jean, try and think who it could be.'

He was dressed, pacing restlessly up and down the bedroom.

'I've got to find the traitor,' he went on, not listening. 'While I sit here the Gestapo murders my friends. How many more, Cecilie? How am I to know who else has been betrayed to them?'

She said, 'Who else knows about this house?'

'No one,' he retorted. 'This is the last resort and nobody knows except me. We're safe enough.' He sounded bitter. 'Let's talk to Julie. Let's go through everyone who could be suspect. I can't sit in idleness. Can't you understand that?'

'Of course I can,' she answered. 'I do love you, if that helps at all.'

'It helps more than you'll ever know,' Jean Dulac said. 'Kiss me.'

She held out her arms. It was a long kiss, empty of passion. When they separated, Kate slipped her hand into his. All her love for him was in that tender, comforting embrace, and that was what he'd wanted from her. They went downstairs together.

'Christ,' Pandora muttered. 'That poor sod and the girl with the baby.' He kept repeating it until Julie lost her temper. She was visibly on edge, unable to sit still for more than a few minutes, chain-smoking.

'Oh why don't you shut up?' she rounded on him. 'What's the good of thinking about them? They're gone and that's the end of it – we've got ourselves to worry about!'

They'd gone round in circles, mentioning one name after another, discarding them in turn. At last Dulac said, 'Julie, you'll have to go to Nice.' Kate saw her face turn white.

'Me? What for?'

He didn't notice her reaction. 'I want you to find out if anyone else has been arrested. You're perfectly safe. Poor Janot didn't even know a name for you. In any case you're the only person who can go. They're looking for me, and Cecilie has no contacts. We'll sleep on it for tonight. Tomorrow, you can make a start.' Kate thought in alarm, she's terrified. She shouldn't be sent anywhere if she's that frightened.

She woke in the early hours, shocked and panicking, dreaming she'd had a fall and was still spiralling into the void. And the reason was suddenly clear. The words were a whisper in her mind, becoming a cry of warning. 'I won't let him sacrifice you. . . .' Pierrot had got her out of Jean's apartment the very night that Janot was arrested. His determination at the meeting: 'On grounds of all our safety, I insist that she sends the message from a new locality . . . I

178

won't let him sacrifice you.' Someone inside the network had betrayed them. Then she checked herself. Pierrot had always objected to her transmitting from the centre of Nice. It was only coincidence again that he suggested she came to Beaulieu with him. Unless he knew that Ma Mère's son would be arrested and the Gestapo would have Jean's name by morning. I should go, she thought. I should go to Beaulieu and face him. Not Julie. Julie's scared to death of doing anything. And Jean mustn't know or he'll stop me. . . . It was daylight and the curfew would be lifted in an hour. She eased out of the bed, took her clothes and slipped away. The bathroom worked, although water ran red from disuse. Kate washed and dressed, combed her hair and found the deadly lipstick that concealed her safeguard against capture. She used it lightly, tied a scarf over her hair. She left a note on the table downstairs. 'Don't send J. till I get back. It may take some hours. Cecilie.' And then added, 'Don't worry.' She collected her bicycle and left the house by the back door. It took three hours hard cycling to get to Beaulieu.

Eilenburg hadn't come back to the hotel for two days. He had slept in his office on a camp bed, and followed the interrogation of the man Janot, and then of the woman who kept the grocer's store. The man resisted stubbornly, until the ingenuity of the Frenchman from the Milice reduced him to such agony that he began screaming information. Eilenburg left at this point. He went up to his office and issued orders. Notes of the man's admissions were sent up to him at intervals. He studied them carefully. A regular pick-up of agents from a grocery in the Place de la Cour; his home in Valbonne was a clearing house. He took orders from the local leader. The name followed. Eilenburg read that item several times.

The leader. The leader of the local Resistance. Delivered in one coup. He lit a cigarette, inhaled deeply. He must go on concentrating, working without pause. That kept the pain at a tolerable level. Like an anaesthetic. So long as he stayed at the Villa Trianon and immersed himself, he could cope with Minna's death.

There was a knock at the door. A junior officer came in, looking hesitant. Eilenburg snapped at him. 'What is it?'

'The suspect is dead, Herr Standartenführer.'

Eilenburg didn't say anything for some moments. He got up from his desk. 'Send Melier up here.'

When the Frenchman came in he brought the stench of his work with him. Eilenburg came up to him. He looked into the pallid face, lightly oiled with the sweat of his labours and his own excitement. 'You've killed him,' Eilenburg said quietly.

'He must have had a weak heart,' was the reply.

Eilenburg clenched his fist and slammed it into the man's face. He was a small man and the blow sent him crashing back against the wall. Blood welled from his nose. It gave Eilenburg real satisfaction to see him bleed. 'You incompetent pig,' he said. 'He had more names to give. You went too far!' The man struggled to his feet; he jammed a dirty handkerchief against his face. Eilenburg said, 'Make a mistake like that again and I'll have you shot. Now get out of here before you stain the carpet!'

He had sent a car to Valbonne, ordered the arrest of anyone found there, and planned the arrest of the lawyer Jean Dulac. He would be taken at his apartment that morning. Eilenburg drew a deep breath of satisfaction. The woman at the shop in the Place de la Cour was brought in while he was shaving. He told them to keep her in a cell till he was ready to see her. He let her wait for two hours and then one of his junior officers asked her some preliminary questions. Eilenburg went down and took his place at the back of the room. She was a wretched creature, he thought; red-eyed with weeping, skinny as a starving cat. Why did women have to involve themselves? He had no mercy for those who enticed soldiers into back streets so they could be murdered, or fed them poison in a glass of wine. He let Melier have those. But not this pathetic little peasant, wringing her hands and begging them to let her go because she had a baby at home. She was a Resistance worker, an enemy of Germany. A liar and an accomplice to men who blew up supplies and killed Germans. He leaned forward and interrupted, 'Do you know who betrayed you?'

She shook her head. Naked fear gaped at him. And hiding in its shadow, hatred. He gave a name, and she gasped, and stuffed her fingers in her mouth. It wasn't the name of the man lying dead two doors away. She began to cry all over again.

'I'm not going to let anyone hurt you,' Eilenburg said. 'If you help me I'll let you go home to your child. And we already know about Jean Dulac. All I want is one more contact. Just for confirmation.'

When he came upstairs to his office again, Beatrice was on her way to the women's prison in Marseilles. There she would be shot. She hadn't said anything. He hadn't allowed his men even to slap her face. She was lucky to be out of reach when he heard that Dulac had been warned, and fled before the SS arrived. All he had netted was one dead man and a woman who wasn't worth questioning. He fell asleep at his desk, and finally gave in and went back to his hotel.

There was nobody there. Antoinette had gone. She had left the clothes and the pearl necklace behind. He collapsed on the bed, tearing at his tie and shirt collar, ripping at his uniform in a paroxysm of grief. Minna was dead. Crushed, mutilated, buried, under heaps of rubble. He cried out, defenceless against the loss. When he recovered himself he supposed he'd slept because it was dark.

He called her name. 'Antoinette?' Then he remembered she had gone. He'd sent her away. The night he heard the news of Minna's death. He'd struck her and screamed at her, and told her to get out. . . . He telephoned.

They brought her back. He had bathed and changed his clothes. He had a large cognac by his side and he was calm. She came into the room and stood silently, looking at him.

181

Her eyes filled with tears. 'Will you forgive me?' he asked her.

'Yes,' she said. He got up and stood, holding out his hand. She came towards him hesitantly, and then put her hand into his. He looked down at her.

'Minna isn't dead so long as I have you,' he murmured.

'Who is Minna?'

'The girl I was going to marry. She was killed in an air raid that night. I went mad when I heard it. I'm sorry. I hope I didn't hurt you.' She shook her head.

'Will you come back to me, Antoinette?'

She put her arms round his waist and rested her head against his chest. He gripped her close and sighed a deep sigh of relief. 'Poor Christian,' she said. 'Poor darling love. I weep for you.'

'Don't,' he told her. 'Help me to forget. Stay with me.'

'I'll never leave you,' she promised. 'I'll stay with you always.'

The next morning he drove to the villa at Cap d'Antibes; she went with him, and they walked through the rooms together. She said, looking at the ground floor, 'Who lived here before?'

'Just vagrants,' he answered. 'Do you like it?'

'Yes.' Antoinette had never seen a private house like it before. More like the hotels where she'd worked since she was fourteen. So big, with lovely ceilings and the view over the sea. 'Yes, I'd like to live here with you,' she said, and squeezed his hand. 'And I'll make you happy here.'

'I know you will,' he said. 'Choose what you want for furniture and curtains, anything that pleases you. Tell them it's got to be ready by the end of the month.'

He went back to the Villa Trianon and she began a tour of the best shops in Nice.

Kate passed the block of flats; she cycled on, round the corner and then stopped. He had whispered the address. Apartment C, 23 rue de Tivoli. She walked back slowly, glancing up at the windows. It was a modest pre-war building. It was already dated, and the façade was peeling. But bright windowboxes made the shabbiness cheerful. She pushed the front door open and went inside. It was a small, dark hallway with a single chair, as dated in style as the architecture. A stair with a chromium handrail wound upwards, a tongue of yellow carpet spanned the steps and looked new. Kate started to go up. She heard the voices below her. One French, one German. She stiffened, not sure whether to go on or turn round and pass them quickly.

She went on. They followed. The woman was French; she was laughing and talking about a trip to Cannes they were planning that night. 'If you can get away from your duties, darling.'

'The Gestapo are busy doing the dirty work for us.' His guttural French was very good. 'We won't be on duty tonight. Karl's senior officer – he always gives the late shift in the office to a wet-nose from Berlin.' They were close behind her.

There was a landing on each floor. Kate went up past it and then turned and looked quickly. She didn't even notice the woman. All she saw was the man who came out of the flat door as the German Major stopped in front of it. She heard him say,

'Good morning. You're early. Been to see Karl?'

She didn't hear Pierrot's reply. Shock paralyses some. It galvanized Kate. She didn't need to see or hear any more. All she knew was that apartment C was above, and he might be coming up the stairs after her. She ran up and reached the landing. There was the front door marked C. In panic, she swung round the narrow landing, and then saw the door that opened on to the fire-escape. It was locked. No key. But a bolt, half-way up from the floor. It was stiff, but she levered it, and then the door was open and she was outside, perched on the rickety stairway, high above the ground. She looked down, and almost cried out. The old fear of heights hit her like a blow in the face. She reeled and clutched at the railing. Then she remembered Corrib's Peak. She took a very deep breath and looked away from the ground. It took five minutes of slow descent, avoiding the lure of the pavement below, to get her down to street level. Then Kate looked up. The roof was ridiculously low. The fire-escape stair was less than fifty feet above the ground.

She turned and ran back to where her bicycle was waiting. That pre-dawn premonition had been right. The traitor was Dulac's deputy, the man who had gone back to England specially to pick out his team for work in France. A double-agent, working for the Germans. 'Good morning. You're early. Been to see Karl?' A friendly greeting to someone they knew well. No doubt was possible after that. She felt sick with anger. Janot and Beatrice. If she had gone to Beaulieu to transmit, she would have been safe and Jean Dulac arrested. He had tried to *save* her. She felt sickened, remembering how he had touched her that last night at the end of their training in England; the 'friendly' kiss that was full of desire. The kiss he forced on her in the café, while the German NCO looked on, titillated.

She thrust the machine into the bushes, letting it fall, and burst into the house. Julie was in the kitchen. Julie said, 'For Christ's sake, where have you been? He's been going crazy!' Kate didn't answer. She went out and into the hall. She shouted for him. A door opened and banged upstairs and he came running down. He was relieved and furious at the same time. 'Where have you been? How dare you go off like that!'

'I've found your traitor,' she said. 'You're hurting me.'

He stepped back from her. 'What are you saying? How have you found him?'

Kate sat on the bottom step; she felt suddenly so exhausted she couldn't stand any longer. 'I went to Beaulieu,' she said slowly. She told him what she had seen.

'That's who betrayed us,' she went on. 'He's working with the Germans.'

Jean reached down and helped her up. 'I know he is,' he

said. 'My poor Cecilie, Pierrot's been paid by the Abwehr since they occupied the coast. We know that; he's a double-agent, giving them information with London's blessing.' He shook his head at her. 'Sweetheart, he has a crippled wife. German money keeps her in comfort. I've known all about it.'

Kate stared at him. 'You mean you knew he was passing information to the Abwehr and was taking money? And you trusted him?'

'Of course,' he said calmly. 'London trusts him. He's their man; long before he made contact with us he was working for the English, moving backwards and forwards through Spain. He's a professional spy, my darling. That bookshop has been a cover for years.' He put his arm round her. 'What a shock it was for you – of course you thought he was betraying us.'

Kate didn't move. 'He tried to save my life,' she said. 'He tried to get me to go to Beaulieu the very night they arrested Janot. Jean, you must listen to me! He knew the Gestapo were coming for you because Janot wouldn't be able to hold out, and he wanted to get me to safety – Oh God, you're not listening, are you?'

He said firmly, 'No, I'm not. You're jumping to conclusions because you don't like him; you never have. But that doesn't make him a traitor. Yes, he did insist that you transmitted from a safer place than my apartment. He'd been arguing that point ever since you came to live with me. Not just that night, but many nights – every time we met. So that explains the coincidence. Darling, he was right. It was an extra risk. I was being selfish because I love you and I wanted you with me all the time.' He said quietly, 'You are never to take things into your own hands like that again. You could have been picked up and destroyed us all. Do you understand that? Never again.'

Kate moved away from him. 'I understand. But I'm right about Pierrot and you're wrong.'

She stayed away from Jean that day, deliberately avoiding

him. She sat in the wilderness of a garden under a shady tree and went over the arguments in her mind, over and over again, playing the devil's advocate against her own suspicions. Nothing quelled her instinct that the real traitor was Phillipe, code name Pierrot, who lived behind a painted mask, enigma to friends and enemies alike.

'It was Cabrot's wife,' Jean Dulac announced. He addressed himself specifically to Kate and explained what Julie had discovered. He had sent her to Nice to buy food and make discreet enquiries, and one of the places she visited was Louis Cabrot's house. Neighbours had told her that Madame Cabrot had gone, taking her children with her, on the same afternoon that Janot was arrested. She had said she was going to stay with her parents. They were intrigued to see a taxi come and collect the family and their luggage. It appeared they meant to stay away for some time, taking so many parcels and boxes with them. It wasn't difficult to track down the taxi; there were very few and mostly used by the military. The driver who took the Cabrots to Nice station was happy to talk about it, for a small tip. The children were whining and miserable, the woman was apprehensive; she seemed to have plenty of money when she opened her purse to pay the fare. He had helped her with the luggage and put them on the train. The train for Paris, he confirmed.

Julie said, 'Her parents live in Saint Jean de Luz. Just to make certain I asked him how he came to fetch her. He said he was called from the rank outside the Negresco, given the address and told to go there. He didn't want to say any more than that, but he let me draw my own conclusion.'

Jean said, 'The Gestapo sent her to safety after she'd betrayed Janot. It's the usual reward for giving information. As soon as I thought it out, I knew it must be her. It was the item in the *Nice Matin*; it was my fault, I didn't see the danger. I didn't think anyone would believe it.'

'But it happened to be true,' Kate interrupted. 'Cabrot

was murdered. Only why did it take his wife so long to go to the Gestapo? That was printed nearly two weeks ago.'

Julie countered impatiently, 'I don't see what you're arguing about. I know you made up your mind it's Pierrot, but this proves he had nothing to do with it. That bitch betrayed us and ran away. Plenty of money, the driver said she had – they paid her, and fixed her up in Paris so we couldn't take revenge.'

Jean said, 'We've nothing more to fear. At least we know who did it, and now we can start to rebuild.'

Kate asked one more question. 'Do people like the Cabrots read the *Nice Matin*?'

He showed his anger. 'Leave it alone, Cecilie. It's finished. Now, Julie, we must get organized. I want Jacques and Gaston to meet at the factory in twelve days to hear London's message. Whatever it is.' He paused, his own excitement rising. 'It isn't any ordinary message if we're all to hear it together. Afterwards, we go ahead and carry out the attack against the convoy!'

The news of the arrests of Resistance members was heard with a mixture of feelings: anger and sorrow; relief, secretly expressed, that the threat of deportation had been allayed, if not lifted. The Mayor, torn between patriotic loathing for the man and the need to find out whether he was satisfied, called on Eilenburg.

It was a short meeting, at which he was kept standing. The leaders of the Resistance and of the local Maquis had not been captured. The town was granted a further stay of execution for one month. If there was any act of terrorism in that time, reprisals would begin at once. If no one had come forward with information when the four weeks were up, the deportations would start. Eilenburg turned his back on the Mayor. He ordered house-to-house searches for Jean Dulac. A large reward of twenty thousand francs was offered, posters giving details and with a crude enlarged photograph of the wanted man were posted all over Nice, and as regularly defaced and torn down. Nobody came forward, and the atmosphere was heavy with apprehension. Two men were shot while caught on the streets after curfew by one of the SS patrols. Investigating them yielded nothing. They were criminals with a long record for burglary and had no Resistance connections.

Eilenburg took Antoinette out to the villa at Cap d'Antibes, to see how the work was progressing. The painting was finished; Eilenburg had used his own men to speed up the work and they were in charge of the French who laid carpets and did interior repairs.

It was becoming a luxurious retreat; he wandered round the gardens with her hand in hand, astonishing the few SS who glimpsed him through the trees. Nobody imagined the Standartenführer to have a sentimental side. The girl had only to express a wish and it was granted.

They soon learned to do exactly what she told them. She seemed oblivious of the hatred of the French people who were pressed into service. Their looks and muttered insults were ignored. She seemed to move in a world inhabited only by her lover, and to have no interest in anything or anyone outside.

Once, one of the women sewing curtains came up to her and said, 'Mademoiselle, couldn't you use your influence to help poor Beatrice Druet?' hoping to arouse some sign of shame.

Antoinette's big eyes were innocent and clear. She shook her head and an expensive scent floated into the other woman's nostrils. 'I know nothing about things like that, I'm sorry,' she said, and moved away.

It was a strange interlude at La Rosée. Two sets of lovers, different in all respects from each other, passing the few remaining days in isolation from the world. Julie had become suddenly withdrawn and she avoided Jean and Kate, forcing her lover into seclusion with her. It was as if that final exposure to danger when she went into Nice had drained her.

They stayed aloof, whispering and holding hands, the woman sulky and suspicious as if she were anticipating yet another order to put herself at risk. It was a time of mingled happiness and misery for Kate. The man she loved was volatile, subject to swings of mood from despair to over-confidence. The danger was past, he repeated, the traitor exposed and harmless. No more arrests had taken place. And the time was precious to them, before they gathered in the disused factory three streets away to hear what London had to say of such importance. They must be happy, he insisted, and because she loved him so desperately, Kate tried. At times it was easy, when they lay together in the secluded garden under the shelter of the trees, and he talked about the future when the war was over.

He had a dreamer's love of painting word-pictures, and, lying with her hand in his, Kate listened and followed along the path of fantasy. He asked her to marry him. 'We'd be so happy here, my darling. You love France as much as I do. We'd have a good life together, bring up our children. You will marry me, won't you?'

And she said, 'Yes, you know I will,' and knew in her heart that it would never happen. He talked about his family, and his childhood, and she saw them all quite clearly, the mother and the father who had died just before the war. The younger sister who had gone to Canada and married there. Two little girls, he said, but not as pretty as our children will be. They kissed and made love as if they had a whole lifetime before them. He talked constantly of the message that was coming. He speculated and she listened, not offering an opinion because the last thing she wanted to think about was the reality ahead. She didn't believe that they were safe. She didn't believe that the danger had gone with Louis Cabrot's widow and children on the train to Paris. But she said nothing, because there was nobody to listen, and she couldn't bear to quarrel with him. As if, she felt sometimes, she had to make their last days happy.

And then it was their last day, and at six o'clock that

evening they would leave the safety of La Rosée and gather in the empty factory to hear what London had to tell them. It was 13 May. A Thursday. A bright, hot early summer's day, and the four of them came together in anticipation.

'Thank God it isn't Friday,' Julie remarked. 'That'd be a nice omen for whatever it is!'

'For Christ's sake,' Pandora erupted suddenly, 'take a hold on yourself –' She glared at him, knocked her chair over and rushed out.

Kate found her in the garden after the brief quarrel. She was sitting under a tree, both arms round her knees like a very young girl, and she was crying. Kate sat beside her. 'What's the matter, Julie? Come on, don't cry, it wasn't a big thing, you know.'

'I know it wasn't,' she said. 'It's amazing, but it's the first cross word we've had! Cooped up day and night for weeks with nothing for the poor pet to do but sit and worry about me. . . . I'm not crying because he told me off, Cecilie. You know it isn't that.'

Kate said gently, 'What is it then?' Julie swallowed; she had lost a lot of weight, Kate noticed suddenly, seeing the Adam's apple move in her throat.

'I'm scared,' she said in a low voice. 'I'm scared to death, and I'd like to go home now and take Fred with me. I've been scared for ages, if you want to know. I wake up at nights thinking I hear them breaking down the door. I'm terrified every time I have to go out into the bloody streets and carry some damned message.'

She wiped her eyes with the back of her hand. It was trembling. 'Fred knows,' she said. 'I was all right to start with, I'd done it before and got back, but this time – I've lost my nerve, that's the truth. I can't stop thinking about what happened to that girl Beatrice, wondering what they did to her. . . .'

Kate put her arm round her. Not only her hands but her whole body was shivering.

'Julie, I'm so sorry. It must be hell for you. Look here, let me talk to Jean, let me suggest you and Pandora stay right out of anything and just lie quiet here till we can arrange a pick-up for both of you. Why don't I do that?'

Julie turned to her. 'Would you, Cecilie? I don't mind what anybody thinks of me, but I'm not going to be any use to anyone if I stay much longer. . . . I just can't stand up to it any more.'

'I'll speak to him today,' Kate promised. 'Don't worry about it. You've been very brave to face it.' Julie blinked and swallowed hard again.

'I've been such a bitch lately,' she said. 'Snapping at you and at Freddie. I didn't mean it. I've felt so awful.' The tears came again. 'Will he send us back, Kate?' she asked. 'I've got to get out – I can't bear the not sleeping, and jumping at every sound.'

'Of course you'll go home, and remember to call me Cecilie. We don't want to make Jean angry and he would be if you let that slip.'

'I won't,' Julie promised. 'But it's all part of the silly charade, isn't it? Code names for people you've known for months on end by their real names. Every time he calls Freddie Pandora I could scream! When will you talk to him?'

'Today,' said Kate. 'I promise. Come on, let's go back and find Fred. Kiss and make up, eh?'

The other girl managed a smile. 'He's so sweet,' she said. 'I've never met anyone like him. So funny too, and so gentle. Thanks.'

She gave Kate a quick embrace, looked embarrassed and then hurried back into the house.

They were gathered on the top floor of the factory an hour before the time for London's message. Dulac, Julie and Pandora, who refused to be left behind, Kate and Jacques, with Gaston muttering as usual. They didn't smoke and talked in whispers. Jacques produced a bottle of wine, and they drank from it, Julie excepted. She gave a little grimace of disgust at the idea of sharing the bottle with the two men.

191

As they made their way in couples to the factory she had asked Kate, 'Did you say anything to him?'

'Yes,' Kate said. 'He understands. But after today, you're not operational unless there's an emergency. I'm to ask London to recall you as soon as possible.'

'And Pandora too?' The pretty face was strained and eager.

'Yes, of course,' Kate answered. She wasn't going to tell her that Jean had been bitter and contemptuous when she told him.

'She's frightened,' he had exploded. 'What about all the rest of us? What about Ma Mère, hiding out in the hills, Beatrice standing in front of a firing-squad? Can't stand up to it, is that what she said? What a selfish little brat she is – I'll send her back, don't worry, and the sooner the better!'

'He'll look after you and Pandora,' Kate assured her, and they went into the empty, dusty building and up the stairs, carrying the receiver between them this time.

'We're ready for the convoy,' Jacques said in his hoarse whisper. 'I'm getting a hundred men from Vercours. They're bringing their own arms.'

'Good.' Jean Dulac pressed his arm. 'Good. One more week, that's all.'

'What about the supplies?' Jacques queried. 'They're guaranteed,' was the answer. At 1900 hours Kate switched the set to receive, and adjusted her earphones. There was static for some minutes. Everyone was silent; the tension was prolonged as they crouched by the radio set, waiting, watching the still figure of the girl with the earphones, adjusting the set to cut out the interference. Suddenly she jerked her head up. It was a moment that Kate was to live over and over again in her memory. It would be clear in every detail like a photograph, with the yellowed figures fading with the years.

The message was clear at last. It wasn't coded. 'The candle of the wicked shall be put out.' Kate repeated it in a voice that trembled. She passed the receiver to Jean Dulac.

He repeated it, thrust it at Jacques, who couldn't understand.

'The candle of the wicked shall be put out!' He forgot to whisper. His voice rose in a cry of triumph. 'Invasion,' he shouted. 'The Invasion has begun!' Remembering it afterwards Kate saw the figures in the frame leap into life, throwing their arms round each other, kissing, some in tears. She was hugged and held by Jacques and Gaston and then she was in Jean's arms, holding on to him and laughing with excitement. She could never forget their joy. The joy of a long hope realized, the hope of Liberation after years of despair. Invasion. The Allied Invasion of Europe had come.

They forgot about caution. Jacques stood and roared, 'Vive la France! Death to the Boche!' Gaston was hopping from one foot to another, shaking his fist. And Jean Dulac, his face ablaze with emotion, caught hold of Julie's hand and forgave her everything in that supremely happy moment.

'My friends,' he said, 'we all know what to do! We've waited and planned for this moment. And at *last*, the time has come!'

In the upper room of the factory the leaders of the Resistance movement made their joint plans that night. Euphoria swept them all along on the same high tide of daring. Jacques promised the destruction of the rail link to Marseilles. German supplies would be halted, troop movements forced to take to the roads where they were vulnerable to ambush. The contingency plan for disrupting this vital line of communication was agreed as part of the Allied Invasion. Echoing Jean Dulac, he exulted, 'At last, our time has come. And I swear to you, comrades, we won't fail you. After tomorrow there won't be a train leaving the area!'

Jean Dulac proposed an immediate attack on the power station, bringing all local factory production to a stop, and plunging the Germans into darkness. It would be a signal for a general revolt of the civilian population. And he ended by saying, 'We fight to our last bullet! Long live France and Liberty,' in a voice that brought tears to their eyes.

Once more they embraced, the ill-assorted bedfellows of French Resistance, with wet cheeks and joyful laughter.

One by one they slipped out into the street and went their separate ways to gather their comrades together for the opening stages of the final battle. It was accepted that many would die without seeing the Liberation. They would be the heroes of tomorrow. Gaston and Marie would act as couriers for Dulac. There was a total radio silence from the BBC French Service that night. No coded messages were broadcast. This confirmed the news sent direct by radio to Cecilie. They didn't go to bed that night; there was nothing to do but listen to Dulac's excited explanations of the attack prepared against the power station. And after that, he went on, they would attack the convoy, with what men he had left, and undoubted help from people only waiting for the Allies to invade. He would leave as soon as the curfew was lifted the next morning.

Pandora stood up and said to Julie, 'I'm going with him. You tell him for me.' There was nothing she could say to stop him, and the two men clasped each other's hands in token of their mission.

Jean said goodbye to Kate in the room they had shared upstairs.

'I love you,' he said. 'If I don't come back, you must never forget that. But I will come back, and we'll have our life together when the war's been won. No goodbyes, my darling, just kiss me.'

For a long moment they embraced and she didn't say the word that was forbidden. Not 'goodbye'. Just 'God be with you. Be careful if you can,' then he was gone.

Julie was crying. She had tried to be calm, to be brave and confident for Pandora's sake, but it crumbled away when he took her in his arms and she held tight to him and wept. 'You shouldn't go,' she said, over and over. 'You didn't come out for this. . . . Oh Freddie, Freddie, I can't bear it.'

'I came out here to give those buggers a kick in the teeth,' he said. 'And I'm going to do it, any way I can. Just for poor little Beatrice, remember? Don't worry, love, I'll be all right. I'll be back and we'll be dancing in the streets. Chin up now, just to please me?'

For a long moment they looked at each other. 'There's my sweetheart,' he said gently. 'Good girl. Any idea how much I love you?'

'As much as I love you,' Julie said. 'I'll die if anything happens to you.'

'Then you're going to be a very old lady,' he smiled at her. Then he too was gone, and both women came downstairs and took each other by the hand without saying anything. It would be forty-eight hours before the power station was attacked.

There were twenty men converging on the main electricity supply centre for Nice and the surrounding countryside. They were armed with sten guns and grenades, and a supply of dynamite. They moved in the darkness, sheltered by a clouded sky which hid the moon. They had blacked their faces with soot, and were dressed in rough camouflage. They came on foot and by bicycle, their weapons packed on their backs. Dulac had given orders that anyone intercepted by the German patrols was to kill as many as possible before turning their guns upon themselves. The heroism of their Maquis comrades, wiped out in their magnificent sabotaging of the railway link, inspired them with selfless courage.

The Allies had landed in Europe; rumours flew and were readily believed. A massive airborne army had dropped at Dunkirk, revenging the defeat of four bitter years ago. Liberation was a reality at last. The time had come to drive the enemy from the blessed soil of France. There were no women among them. Wives and daughters waited at home, and prayed. Kate and Julie were part of that sisterhood that night. They had left the kitchen windows unshuttered; the lights of Nice flickered in the distance through the trees. They were too far away to hear the noise of battle or the detonation of the charges that would black out the countryside for miles around. They didn't talk; Julie was tense and silent. Once or twice Kate heard her clear her throat and guessed that she was fighting down tears.

The time didn't pass, it crept; every moment lengthened into one hour, then two, three. Kate went to the window. Nothing had changed. The lights glimmered in the distance; the night was quiet. 'Something's gone wrong,' she said at last. 'They were due an hour ago.'

Julie came and stood beside her. 'I knew it,' she whispered. 'I knew it when I said goodbye to him. . . . Oh look, Cecilie, look!'

Every light was snuffed out. Julie burst out laughing; it had an hysterical note in it. 'They've done it . . . they've done it, they're all right!'

Kate sank down on a chair. 'Thank God,' she said. 'Close the shutters, I'll light the candles and we'd better get the fire going in the stove. They'll want something to eat when they get back.'

Julie did everything with feverish cheerfulness. She chattered nervously, talking about Pandora, laughing at her own fears, and Kate didn't dare think what would happen if he wasn't one of the survivors. The power station was heavily guarded. Sentries and patrols had been increased since the attack on the railway terminal; Dulac expected casualties. The stove was hot enough to boil water and they drank tea while they waited. Kate almost fell asleep; even Julie had calmed down and was dozing. She woke and looked at her watch. 'It's three in the morning,' she exclaimed. Kate wasn't in her chair. She was out of the room, and for a moment Julie panicked. She called out, and opened the door into the passageway.

Kate came towards her. 'The lights are on,' she said. 'They didn't blow it up.'

'Where are you going?' Antoinette asked him. He dressed quickly. She sat up in the handsome new bed in their bedroom at the villa, her head a little on one side, a worried

196

frown on her face. The telephone call had wakened them and he sprang up after only a few words. Eilenburg said, 'There's been an attempt to blow up the power station. I must go, sweetheart. Don't worry, go back to sleep.'

'You won't be in any danger, will you?'

'No,' he promised. 'There was a skirmish with our troops but it's all over. They've got some of the people and they're bringing them in to Nice.' He crossed to the bed and kissed her. He stroked the top of her head. 'Be a good girl and lie down,' he said. 'If I'm not back for breakfast don't worry. I'll telephone you when I can.'

He dressed in civilian clothes, and left the bedroom quietly. She was a nervous girl, tension and disturbance troubled her. If she became anxious about him she had bad dreams. Once outside, he brought the villa to life. Lights flooded the ground floor: his driver was roused and the car skidded round to the front, scattering gravel. He arrived at the Villa Trianon as the lorry with the prisoners was pulling up outside. He went upstairs to his office and called for reports. The army had sent a young Captain to give the up-to-date account of what had happened. Eilenburg told him to sit down, sent for coffee and cigarettes and listened.

Just before midnight one of the patrols had seen a movement at the perimeter of the wall surrounding the main generator building. The men had acted intelligently; instead of investigating and declaring themselves, they radioed for help and kept watch. A group of men broke cover and scaled the wall: the officer in charge ordered his men to stay quiet and allow the enemy to approach and signal others to follow. In all, three groups got into the outer perimeter and the first group penetrated close to the main generator building. That was when the German forces came into the open. The intruders had fought back, killing four men and wounding a dozen. All but six of them were killed and of those six, two were seriously wounded and one had shot himself at the moment of capture. One charge of dynamite had been thrown through the ground-floor window in the generator

room and had caused a temporary blackout which was
restored within two hours. Eilenburg congratulated the
Captain, said good night, and sat alone in his office thinking.
Two major outbreaks of sabotage in forty-eight hours, one of
them seriously disruptive. The latest had failed, but only
because luck had sent the patrol an intelligent NCO. Why?
Eilenburg asked that question and could not imagine the
answer. Why should a highly organized and clever Resistance suddenly launch itself into suicide attacks? He rang on
the internal phone, and ten minutes later he went down into
the basement to find out for himself.

It was daylight at last. Julie said, 'I can't stand sitting here.
I'm going to find out what happened.'

Kate tried to bar her way. 'They could be hiding somewhere, they could be lying low till tonight. For God's sake
don't lose your head and go into Nice!'

'Lose my head?' The words were shrill and angry. 'Don't
you care what's happened to Jean? Don't you even want
to know whether he's alive or dead? My Christ, you're
a cold-blooded –' She turned and ran out of the room.
Moments later she came down. She was dressed, and incon-
gruously made-up for the early hour. Under the powder and
scarlet lipstick, she was haggard and sallow. 'I'm going,' she
said. 'I'm sorry I said that about being cold-blooded. I know
you love him, but it's different for Fred. Don't you see how
helpless he is? Not speaking the language, if he's lost or
hurt. . . .' Tears welled up and she brushed them away. 'I've
got to go, Kate. Don't worry. I've got my bloody pill if
anything goes wrong. Wish me luck; I'll be back as soon as
I've got any news.' She shut the door before Kate could say
anything to stop her, and seconds later Kate saw her walking
down the little pathway. That image stayed imprinted on her
memory for all the years ahead. Julie, in a bright cotton dress
and sandals, swinging a bag in her left hand, walking down
the path to the gate.

* * *

'You're Jean Dulac,' Eilenburg repeated. The man didn't answer. Eilenburg said, 'You are the lawyer, Jean Dulac. I know all about you. You are just making things unpleasant for yourself by refusing to answer.' According to the army report, he had tried to put something into his mouth when he was taken, and one of the soldiers had bayoneted him through the upper arm. The wound had bled copiously through the field-dressing. He was too weak from blood loss to stand for much longer without fainting, and the pain would be severe. Even more severe when the initial shock wore off, which was happening at the moment. Eilenburg looked at him for a time, asking the question that would condemn him to death with stolid patience. 'You are Jean Dulac, aren't you?' No reply. Just the eyes, dilated with pain, looking steadfastly into his.

Eilenburg knew the meaning of that message of defiance. He pushed back his chair. 'I will have your wound properly dressed,' he said. 'And then I shall put you in the hands of a fellow Frenchman, André Melier of the Milice. I think you know what to expect from him.' He got up and said, 'Take him upstairs and let the doctor look at him. Give him some coffee and a cigarette. Time enough to think, and if he still won't answer, bring him back down here. I'm going home; you can get me there.'

Jean Dulac's mind was perfectly clear. His arm was properly bound up and in a sling. The pain was a separate entity with a fearful intensity of its own. He drew on the cigarette they had given him; it was possible to feel pleasure in such a small thing at such a time. Jean Dulac. He spoke his own name in the secrecy of his thoughts. Jean François Marie Dulac, aged thirty-six and four months, unmarried. Able to smoke a cigarette and enjoy it. He was sitting down, watched by the two impassive SS guards who had stood silently while their SS doctor patched him up for the French-man Melier to tear to pieces. Yes, he said in his inner conversation, I know who he is, and what will happen in the hours ahead. And I know what I carry inside me; the one secret that he must never know. Not my name. Not the name of my dead comrades, or even the safe houses, because I could tell him those. The dead are out of reach and the safe houses will be empty by now. No, my beloved Cecilie, they won't find out through me where you are hiding. He said, 'I feel dizzy. Can I have some air?' He let them support him the few steps to the window. When they opened it, he breathed in deeply and closed his eyes. He said, 'That's better,' and stepped back. For a split second he sent his mind in search of God, and on that prayer he flung himself forward and through the window. He fell from three floors on to the paved patio where the old owners used to sip their cocktails before dinner, and died instantly.

People whispered about what had happened. A terrible business, they said, watching their companions' reaction. Dozens killed and others captured and sent to the Villa Trianon for questioning . . . some wounded, too. There were casualties among the staff on night-duty at the power station . . . some of the wounded were in the hospital here in Nice. Julie listened; bought the newspapers, read the headlines condemning the outrage, realized that no editor dare call it anything else, noted the casualties in hospital, some hadn't been identified. And the murmur that was spreading through the shops and cafés, fuelled by the official radio and press, that there was no Allied Invasion, and the whole thing had been a rumour started by the Resistance to bring the people out into civil conflict with the police and the German authorities. . . . She spent a long time sitting with a cup of coffee, and longer still going from one kiosk to another, trying the two telephone numbers she knew of her old safe house and one of her contacts in Cannes. Neither answered. They'd packed up and fled, she thought. Nobody can tell me whether Fred is alive and in that hell hole of a villa – Oh God, don't let me think of that – or one of the men in hospital that they haven't identified, or among the dead . . . most were killed, the papers said, calling them terrorists and

Communists. The time passed. She sat on in another café, lighting cigarettes with a hand that wouldn't stop shaking, and thinking over and over again that Fred might well be in Nice hospital, and couldn't say a word to help himself.

The day became evening. Kate sat under the tree in the villa garden and pulled up blades of grass, one by one, and split them and threw them away. She didn't eat; she felt suspended in time, breathing and aware, but without hope. Here they had talked of marriage; she could remember that and think about it. He seemed very close at times, as if she might turn and see him sitting there beside her. 'We'd be so happy here, my darling. . . . You will marry me, won't you?' And her own answer, 'yes', knowing it would never happen because the course was set for tragedy and nemesis was called after a clown. Birds sang in the garden and a large bright butterfly settled close at hand on a flowering bush and opened and closed its wings in ecstasy. It was sundown when she went back inside. The house echoed, smelt empty and disused again. And she walked upstairs to the room they had shared and lay on the bed where they had slept in each other's arms after their supremely happy lovemaking. She realized by the time it was past curfew that something must have happened to Julie.

There was nothing she could do but wait. Wait for some-one to come who was a friend, if there were any left. Or take her transmitter and go to the factory and send them one last message.

There was no one in the street; she walked slowly, carrying the suitcase, pushed the broken door and slipped inside. Up the stairs, finding the case so much heavier than usual, into the room where they had embraced and cried out in joy because they believed they would soon be free. The marks of their feet were still in the dust. Kate sat down, opened the case, set up the radio and began to transmit.

* * *

Eilenburg was having lunch when he was given the message that his prime prisoner had committed suicide by throwing himself out of the window. He didn't speak for so long his frightened assistant thought he had hung up. He gave a brief order and then replaced the receiver on its hook. The guards who had permitted him to escape interrogation were to be held in close arrest before a court martial for negligence. He went back and finished lunch with Antoinette. It was a glorious day and the garden was shady and delightful. She loved the flowers and spent hours arranging them in the house. He said, 'I can spend the rest of the day with you, darling. What would you like to do?'

They returned later from a two-hour drive round the coast, stopping at the Hôtel du Cap where German officers rested after combat, where they drank English tea, and he allowed her to amuse and enchant him so that he forgot what had happened that morning at the Villa Trianon. Thrown himself out of the window. How disappointed that little pig Melier would be – he held Antoinette's hand and thought how happy she made him. The message was there when they came home. A woman had been arrested at Nice hospital, where she'd been caught enquiring after the casualties brought in from the power station. She was waiting at Gestapo Headquarters.

Richard Wroxham was working late that evening when his friend Colonel Reed was shown into the office. 'I've brought this,' Reed said. 'You can doctor it up for your General.' He sat down and sighed. 'Before you read it,' he said, 'it's as well to remember what was at stake. Sometime in the next three weeks we launch Overlord. After all the years of planning and the bloody mess-ups like Dieppe, it'll be the real thing. Have you been down to the South Coast?'

'Yes,' Wroxham answered. 'I went last Thursday. It's building up every day. What's happened, Jim?'

'Read it for yourself.'

The radio operator known as Cecilie had told of disaster

with economy of words. The Maquis and the Dulac network had responded to London's last message. They had been wiped out as a result.

Wroxham said, 'What message did you send?'

Reed stood up. 'The candle of the wicked shall be put out,' he said. 'It was the only way to stop that hothead from attacking the troops going to Antibes. You know what it would have meant if he'd captured or killed your German General and his friends. Hundreds of thousands of men will be fighting in a short time. If we've reduced those casualties, then it's justified. It's no good thinking about it, Richard, the man got out of control. I had to take drastic action. Can you come out tonight? I think I'd like someone to get drunk with.'

'Sorry,' Wroxham answered after a moment. 'I'm going out to dinner. I wish I could get drunk with you. Thanks for coming over yourself, Jim.' He came to the door and laid a hand on the Colonel's shoulder. 'You were right to do it,' he said. 'We both know that. Good night.' Wroxham went back to his desk and sat down. He read the brief, sickening message once more, and then folded it and put it in a drawer. He phoned his wife and told her to go on to their friends and he'd join her later.

Then Wroxham drafted a report for his General, assuring him that SOE had put its house in order and prevented a serious setback to Allied plans by a piece of adroit deception. He didn't say against whom. The General wouldn't ask. He wasn't concerned with details, only the success of the tremendous strike against German-occupied France. Wroxham sat on alone and did the one thing he had always advised others not to do, when engaged in similar work. He thought about the men and women in the field. He phoned his wife again and made an excuse not to join the party at all that evening. He cleared his desk, locked up and left the massive bomb-proof building, coming up into the clear air of Whitehall. He set out to walk towards his London house in Kensington. It would take time, and he wasn't in a hurry to get back there and be alone. He was at the Knightsbridge end of Piccadilly when the girl stepped out of a doorway and accosted him.

He was so startled he stopped, and she stood cheekily in front of him, smiling and asking if he'd like to go home with her. Home. No thank you. He was very polite. She looked disappointed, and shrugged. She'd make it nice for him, she said hopefully. Ten quid, and anything he liked. Wroxham said suddenly, 'No thank you, but I'd be glad if we could go and have a drink and a chat somewhere.' That would earn her the ten quid. She knew just the place. They went off in a taxi that was lurking nearby. She wasn't surprised. A lot of men settled for that and paid for it too. They stopped in Wardour Street, and the girl led the way into a club that was so dark and smoky Wroxham could hardly see where he was going. A three-piece band played dance music at the far end and a few couples circled round a tiny square of dance floor, clutching tightly at each other. The girl was well known. She was given a corner table, and a surly waiter asked what they would like to drink.

Wroxham said to her, 'You order what you like.' She had a pretty face, coated with unnecessary make-up. There was a small lamp on the table with a red shade which gave a flattering light.

'Champagne?' she asked.

Wroxham said, 'Champagne, and make sure it is.' The waiter moved away.

She giggled. 'He didn't like that,' she said. 'If a client's drunk they bring any old cat's pee and charge double. Got a cigarette?' Wroxham gave her one. She watched him in silence for a moment, puffing greedily. 'You look as if you've had a bad day,' she said suddenly. 'Cheer up – here comes the shampoo!'

She was very young, he thought, seeing the childish mouth widen in a delighted grin when the cork popped. Eighteen at most. Younger than the girl who had sent the tragic message from France, but not much younger. . . .

'What's your name, darling? I won't tell.'

'My name is Richard,' he answered.

'What's yours?'

'May. Like it?'

'It's very pretty. Like you.'

She laughed and sipped the champagne. It was very poor quality. 'That's better,' she said. 'Now, tell me about the bad day.' She settled back with professional interest.

He said quietly, 'If I could tell you about it I wouldn't be here. So let's say it was bad, shall we?'

'Okay,' she agreed. Then with a slight tilt of the head which made him immediately think of a curious sparrow, she said, 'Somebody got killed? I met a man once who'd lost his wife and two kids in an air raid. . . . Sat with me all night getting drunk as a skunk, and crying. . . . Not that bad for you, eh?'

'No,' he said. 'Not a wife and children; not even people I knew. Knew personally I mean. But very dead all the same. Give me that bottle, will you?'

The girl poured for him. She bit her lip, and then said brightly, 'Look, worrying won't do any good. If you didn't know them it can't be so bad. People get killed in wars.'

'They do indeed. And a lot more will be killed before it's over. And because of these people who've died, a lot of others could be saved.'

'Then that's how you've got to look at it,' she said firmly. 'Think of the ones who'll be okay. Come and have a dance?'

'No thanks,' he said. 'You're a nice girl; where do you come from?'

'Leicester,' she answered. 'Bloody awful place to be; I left home and came up here to have a bit of fun.'

She had small hands, rather red and with bitten nails. They were twisting in and out when she talked about her home town. On an impulse he reached out and took hold of one. I can't do anything for Cecilie, facing the end in France, but at least I can be kind to you, you funny little thing . . .

poor little devil. *Fun.* 'May,' he said gently, 'let's order another bottle of that stuff, shall we? And then we'll talk about something cheerful. . . .'

He got mildly drunk that night; she persuaded him to dance, and was surprised to find she liked him holding her. He didn't paw or nuzzle. He held her hand on the way to their table and said 'thank you', which was so quaint she laughed. They came out into the street and the inevitable taxi slid up to the kerb. There was a regular trade outside the club and few people bothered to look at the meter. She lived in the Edgware Road; Wroxham got out and came to the door with her. It was a dingy building, composed of little flatlets. He opened his wallet and counted out ten pounds. The girl hesitated.

'You can come in if you like,' she said. 'I'd like it if you did, and that's straight.'

'Not tonight, May,' he said. She looked disappointed, and suddenly he said, 'When can I see you again?'

Within a month he had installed her in a flat of her own; it was a relationship that lasted for nearly twenty years, and he was with her when she died tragically young of cancer. She never knew, and he had forgotten, that it all began because she had helped him get through the worst night of his life.

Kate decided to leave the radio in the factory, hidden under a heap of mouse-infested sacking. She was safer without it; she could come back next day and radio in for instructions. Maybe she was frightening herself for nothing. Julie could have stayed overnight in one of the safe houses, caught by the curfew. She could come back in the morning. Maybe Jean was alive and in hiding. . . . Maybe. She didn't believe it for a moment. Instinctively she knew she was truly alone.

And her fate depended upon the girl whose nerve had broken before it was even tested. If Julie had been arrested, the next visitors to La Rosée would be the Gestapo. She couldn't go back to the villa and risk being caught in the middle of the night. Jean knew where she was, but he would die before he told them. Not so Julie. She closed her eyes to shut out the agonizing mental picture of the man she loved in Gestapo hands.

'Please God,' she prayed, 'let him be killed . . . let him be dead rather than that. . . .' She began to weep, sobbing as she hadn't done since childhood. 'Oh God, God, what's happened to him . . . what's happened to all of them? She sat crouched in the darkness, so torn with grief that suddenly she crumpled up and slept from sheer exhaustion.

When she woke it was raining. There was a leak in the roof and she was wet and cold from lying under it. Shivering, Kate brushed the dirt off her clothes and began the climb down the staircase. Her plan was to move cautiously in the direction of La Rosée. She had been trained in the procedure for approaching a house suspected of being staked out by the Gestapo. German cars parked within two streets' vicinity were a warning, so too was any sign of disturbance since she had left last night. Deliberately she had left the gate unlatched. If it was closed, then someone had come in. The rain was slackening, and a piercing shaft of blue sky appeared through a rift in the clouds.

Mediterranean storms were swift and violent but they didn't last. The streets were washed silver grey by the rain and the air smelt cool and fresh. She saw no cars parked anywhere near and began to feel confident. She walked past La Rosée first time, on the opposite side of the road. Nothing moved inside the garden, and the gate was not latched. Wet and hungry, Kate decided it was safe to go back. She slipped across the road, pushed the gate open and ran up the little pathway to the back door. Inside the hallway she heard a movement coming from the kitchen. Hope soared for a moment and she called, 'Jean? Julie?' The door slammed open and she was seized, pinned against the wall by a man in civilian clothes, and with both arms wrenched behind her back propelled into the kitchen.

'Well, Mademoiselle.' Another man with fair cropped hair

was sitting at the table. 'You've taken a long time to come home, haven't you? Where have you been?'

She asked for her jacket. It was hanging over the back of the kitchen chair. The fair-haired man picked it up, searched the pockets and found the lipstick.

'You won't be needing this where you're going,' he said. He dropped it on the ground and deliberately smashed it with his heel. There was a red smear on the stone floor like blood. The man holding Kate handcuffed her hands behind her back.

The car was outside in the street; she was pushed along the path and shoved into the rear seat, with her captors on either side. They smoked and talked in German and she felt the fair one glance at her from time to time. She looked ahead and kept her knees together to stop them shaking. Cold with fear was not a cliché. She was chilled and trembling, sitting between them, their elbows in her sides, their thighs pressed against hers. Especially the man with fair hair. Julie, she thought, Julie told them. Oh God, why didn't I take the jacket with me . . . hopeless to blame herself. She hadn't a chance when she was seized. Julie hadn't taken her L pill in time either. They must be able to feel her trembling. They must know how terrified she was. Multiple rape was one method the Gestapo used on women who refused to cooperate. God help me, Kate prayed as the car came to a stop outside a handsome pink-washed building. God, please help me to be brave because I can't die and escape what's coming.

They took off the handcuffs and left her in a cell. The floor was bare, and there were empty wooden wine racks along one wall. A single naked light burned high overhead in an arched ceiling. There was nothing to do but sit on the floor, or stand, while she waited. She rubbed her bare arms against the dank, cold air, and then she prepared herself as she had done in childhood before going to bed. She knelt down, and began to pray.

Eilenburg congratulated his two men. Skilled policemen

who had joined the Gestapo and distinguished themselves in Paris. He heard the brief account of the girl's arrest. The military had already been informed that the last suspect had been captured, and the Dulac network had ceased to exist. With the exception of their own agent, who remained to monitor any attempts to replace the casualties by SOE. Eilenburg had a headache, and it was increasing. He thought about leaving early and spending a quiet evening with Antoinette. The peace of the villa was soothing to his spirit. He already loved the place. He had no need to see the girl or involve himself further with the process of interrogation. His assistant said, 'She's been here two hours. How do you want her questioned, Standartenführer?'

He looked down at the report on his desk. The other woman had said she was the radio operator. She would know the codes for transmission to London. She could be made to send a message asking for reinforcements. Psychological pressure, not physical duress, was the best way to achieve that. Perhaps a glimpse of her colleague might persuade her to cooperate. He phoned down to the basement and gave an order. He decided that in spite of his headache he had better see her for a brief interview afterwards.

A uniformed SS guard took Kate along the passageway. It had been the old wine cellar of the Villa Trianon, but each cave had been fitted with rough wooden doors. Each had a sliding peephole. They stopped and the guard pushed Kate up against the gap in the door. She couldn't see anything at first except the bright overhead bulb, the stone walls and floor, then Julie lying under a blanket, a naked foot protruding. There was a vile smell. The guard said, 'She's sleeping. Tonight, she'll be shot.' He dragged Kate away and slammed the peephole shut. 'Upstairs for you,' he said in his thick French. As she walked up the steps into the daylight, tears welled up and trickled down her face. He thought she was crying for herself.

'Sit down,' Eilenburg said. She started to say no, but was pushed into a chair. Her eyes were blurred, she couldn't see him clearly. Just a man behind a desk in a black uniform, with white-blond hair. He had just ended an angry telephone conversation before she was brought in.

'Would you like a cigarette?' This was the soft approach; she'd been warned about that in training. First they're rough and threatening, and then a new man comes in who seems decent, even sympathetic. He'll persuade you to see sense for your own sake. If you resist, he'll call in the others. Probably be the one who watches and directs them. Don't take cigarettes, coffee or any other favours.

There was no point in dissembling. Julie, she thought, and suddenly her fear became a blinding hate and anger.

'I want nothing from you, you filthy bastard.'

The shock made him look at her properly. The men sometimes abused and defied, but it was very rare indeed from a woman. White as death, face wet with tears, spitting at him like a wildcat. Courageous, he thought. Brave and foolhardy. Very young. He felt contempt for the people who had sent her and the miserable broken woman who had tried to resist and failed so pathetically.

'You saw your companion? Yes, obviously you're upset. If I send my man out, will you behave yourself or shall I have you restrained?'

'I've got nothing to say, so you might as well get on with your interrogation,' Kate said. 'You're wasting your time trying to fool me. Go to hell!'

Eilenburg made a judgement. He said to the guard, 'Get out. Stay in the corridor. I can deal with her if she's troublesome.' Kate saw him leave, and the man got up from behind his desk and sat on the edge of it facing her. Slowly he lit a cigarette. 'I'm sorry about what happened to your friend,' he said. 'I gave her the same chance as I'm giving you. She wouldn't take it. She had a bad time and she will be executed this evening. Your name is Cecilie and you are a radio operator who landed here to work with Jean Dulac and his network. I know everything about you. You were Dulac's mistress. He's dead, did you know that?'

She didn't answer; if possible she lost more colour but that was all. 'He was very brave,' Eilenburg remarked. 'I admire courage, even though I have to break it. He'd given us a lot of trouble for a long time and we had to catch him. Of course, having a traitor among you helped us.' He didn't even look at her when he said it. After a moment he observed her with an expression of interest. 'You loved him, didn't you, Mademoiselle? Do you know how he died?'

'No,' the voice quivered this time. 'I don't want to know. You said he was brave. That's good enough.' Her head lowered slightly.

'He wasn't tortured,' Eilenburg went on. 'He would have been, unfortunately, because he had no intention of betraying anything or anyone to us. Especially where you were hiding, I can see that now. So he threw himself out of the window. Just down the passage there, in the room at the end. He didn't suffer, it was instant.'

She mumbled something; he thought it was 'Thank God.' She covered her face with her hands and stayed very still. He waited. Then he said, 'Where's your radio?'

Kate raised her head. 'I destroyed it,' she said.

'Without asking for help?'

'I sent a message. I told them I wouldn't transmit again. Then I smashed up the set.'

He put out his cigarette. 'I don't believe you. You don't expect me to believe you either. Do you want to be hurt? Do you want to end up like your friend? Why did they send her in the first place? She was quite unsuited to this sort of work.' He seemed almost to be talking to himself. She wanted to get up and scream at him to stop, stop telling her, stop pitying his own victim. 'She lied so badly, it was pathetic. She didn't even have a proper story prepared. I have an interrogator who loves nothing better than a really brave man or woman so he can reduce them to a gibbering wreck. She broke very easily. Just a few slaps and some sex with my men. That's what she feared more than pain. Did you know that about her?'

211

Kate said nothing. Hot and then cold in turn, and the floor was fuzzing into a blur. Finch, she thought, fighting the faintness, 'I won't have a dirty little man like that putting his hands on me. . . .' They'd beaten and degraded her and thrown what was left into that cell, covered with a dirty blanket. His voice seemed to fade and then come back louder than before.

'I did my best to persuade her,' Eilenburg went on, the quiet voice patiently explaining. 'I appealed to her to save herself just as I am doing to you, Cecilie. I admire courage, believe me. I don't like having to hurt women. I don't want to send you down to that Frenchman. You won't be able to hold out, any more than your friend.'

Kate looked at him. 'Don't be too sure,' she said. For a moment they stared at each other. He had the palest eyes she'd ever seen, with tiny pupils. He locked his hands and stared over the tips of his fingers. He shook his head slightly.

'All you have to do is give me your call sign to London. Without suffering a lot of pain and indignity first. Because you'll give it to us in the end. You could save your life, do you realize that? A lot of your people have collaborated with us and are living as free men and women. You'd be surprised how many. Suffering and death are not inevitable.' He paused, lit a cigarette, watched her without seeming to pay her any more attention. Everything he did was a silent message. I am about to lose interest in you. And when that happens, you're lost. . . .

Kate cleared her throat. You're not going to give in so get it over with. Cut off the escape route before you have another moment to be tempted. . . . The words sounded hoarse and faint.

'I told you, go to hell, you bastard.'

He stretched out his hand to a buzzer when the telephone rang. He picked it up, spoke in rapid German. Kate closed her eyes. She began to shiver.

Some moments passed, he was still talking. She opened her eyes, focussed on him. He was looking at her, holding the receiver. He put it back on the telephone. His voice seemed to fade and then come back louder than before.

'It seems you have a powerful friend, Cecilie. How lucky for you. But then you're an attractive girl. He's bought and paid for you. Get up; you're free to go.'

She didn't know how she got to the street outside. She had no possessions, nothing to sign for when she was released. They steered her to the front door and let her stumble down the steps. She had to lean against the wall to steady herself. For the first few moments she panicked. It was a trick. Next minute someone would come up behind and seize her and take her back. But no one came near. A car chugged along from the top of the road; Kate started walking, trying not to run. When it pulled up beside her she did run and then suddenly she stopped and turned. 'Cecilie – here, get in quickly.' She struck out at him blindly, seeing the cat's eyes narrowed in concern and feeling his hand reaching out to take her arm. She hit him several times, and then everything darkened and faded, and she was unable to fight any more. On the way to Beaulieu she had to get out because she was going to be sick. He supported her while she retched on an empty stomach, and then sank back shivering for the rest of the journey. 'It's shock,' he said, 'you'll be all right. They didn't hurt you –'

'I saw Julie,' she whispered. He put his arm round her. She wrenched away from him. 'Don't touch me! Don't come near me!' When the car stopped, she tried to open the door and jump out. Pierrot reached across and held the handle shut.

'Let me go,' she shouted at him. 'I'm not going with you anywhere. . . .'

'I got you released,' he said. 'You're coming with me and you're going to do as I tell you. Resistance in Nice is finished. Except for me. And my work isn't over. Now get out and come with me.'

She saw the woman sitting in her wheelchair. She glanced up and smiled at Kate, and then went on reading. He showed her a bathroom and said he'd have some food and coffee ready when she came out. She couldn't bear to look at herself in the mirror. She was alive and safe. Bought and paid for, that monstrous man had said. Free to go. Jean was dead. She wept, her tears falling freely. Julie, broken in body and spirit, waiting to be shot. . . . She washed her face and, trembling, came out into the flat to find him in the kitchen, with hot coffee and bread and cheese laid out for both of them.

She wanted to say, 'I'm not going to eat with you,' but didn't. Now was not the time. She was in his hands. Bought and paid for, the Gestapo murderer had said.

'I'll kill you when the time comes,' she said silently.

'Sit down,' Pierrot invited. 'Eat and try to be calm. You're safe now. Afterwards I'll take you in to meet my wife. You saw her, didn't you?'

'Yes,' Kate said. 'She's crippled. That's why you did it.'

'Did what?' he asked softly.

'Took money from the Germans. Sold us out.'

'Yes, I take money from them, I work for them. Otherwise you wouldn't be here now. But I am not what you think.'

'Did you go on the raid with Jean?' she asked him.

He nodded. 'Yes. Unfortunately I couldn't protect Pandora. He was killed in the first exchange with the Germans.' He looked coldly into the distance. 'It was a disaster. Dulac was told not to expose him. He didn't listen. The poor devil died for nothing. They are all dead now.'

'Yes,' Kate said. 'Except for us.'

She stayed in the flat in Beaulieu for a week. She didn't go out, even for a walk. It seemed as if her will had been broken. Shock, Pierrot insisted. It takes some people like this. You'll get over it. Eat and rest while you can. And he said it again, 'I have work to do.' His wife was very gentle; she chatted to her silent visitor, as if she knew that inconsequence was what she needed. She embroidered beautiful linen squares. She was making a tablecloth, she explained, and offered to show Kate how to do some simple background work. Kate shook her head. She enjoyed watching, she said; she didn't want to sew herself. She watched more than the skilful needlework. She watched the man who she knew had betrayed them, the survivor of the massacre at the power station who had been able to get her released from the Gestapo. She saw his tenderness to his crippled wife, and the desire in his eyes when he looked at her, thinking himself unobserved. She noticed his absences and once or twice slipped out and opened the front door, hearing him stop at the flat below and be let in by his German paymasters. Once when he was out and she had seen him go from the sitting room window, she went into their bedroom and found a gun in the chest of drawers. It was a German Luger pistol, and it was loaded. Under the bed she found what she was looking for; a portable transmitter in a standard SOE case. Working for both sides. Radioing London and selling the information to the Germans. Slowly Kate took the gun in her hands, turned it over, checking the safety catch. So many dead looking over her shoulder, asking the same question that was in her mind. 'He killed us, can you kill him – can you face him and pull the trigger?'

'Put that away,' he said from the doorway. Kate turned and raised both hands as she had been taught, and brought the gun level with his chest. He stood quite still for a moment, and then quietly closed the door and came towards her.

She said, 'Stop. No nearer.'

He obeyed, but he didn't seem to be afraid. 'You won't shoot me,' he said. 'You wouldn't do anything so foolish. I saved your life, remember? You won't kill me, Cecilie.'

'Just tell me something,' she spoke very softly. The gun was steady in her hands. 'How can you sleep at night?'

The pale eyes blinked and then stared fixedly as before. 'I don't,' he answered. 'But not because I am a traitor. Will you listen to me?'

She shook her head. 'No. There's nothing you can say. I followed you here, and I saw you with the Germans downstairs. I heard them talking to you. I tried to warn Jean but

215

he wouldn't listen. You can't tell any lies to me. I know what you are and what you've done.'

He said gently, 'Then shoot me. Pull the trigger and have done.'

'Philippe?' The voice came from the sitting room and the woman immobilized in her chair. 'Philippe, can you help me – I've dropped everything on the floor. . . .'

He looked at Kate and said, 'My wife needs me. You can shoot me in the back if it's easier.' He turned and moved towards the door.

Kate lowered the gun and slipped the safety-catch to 'on'. 'After the war,' she said, 'you'll be tried and punished. And I'll be the one that gets you hanged.'

'Maybe.' She saw his crooked smile appear and disappear, and then he left the room.

When he told her he'd arranged her escape through to Spain, she said, 'You're a fool, don't you realize that as soon as I get back, I'm going to report you? Don't you care?'

'Not much,' was his answer. 'I have one more thing to do here and then I shall be taking my wife to a safe place. I don't care what you say to those murderers in Baker Street.'

'You call *them* murderers?' She rounded on him in amazement.

'Think about it,' he said. 'Thanks to Jean Dulac they had no other choice, I suppose. But it was murder just the same.'

'I shall tell them what you've said,' she declared, passionate with anger. 'I'll point you out as the filthiest traitor there's ever been!'

He shrugged. 'I'm sure you will. You are a woman of great determination. But not very clever when you fall in love. You didn't see how vain he was, and how arrogant. He destroyed himself and all the others. At least he had the decency to commit suicide.' She slapped him hard across the face. He rubbed his cheek and smiled. It was a bitter grimace.

'My thanks for saving you from Eilenburg,' he said softly. 'I've loved you for a long time, but I shall be glad to see you go tomorrow.'

6

As the car approached the Hôtel du Cap, Katharine leaned forward. The magnificent façade was floodlit. The building was pearl-white in the arc lamplight, roofed in grey, with the grandeur of the classic French château. On the sweep of gravel in front the most expensive cars in the world waited for their owners to go inside, and the attendants to drive them to their garages. Crimson geraniums were banked on either side of the steps leading to a huge entrance, glass-plated and combining the best of modern design with the classicism of the architecture. She turned to Roulier as the car stopped and said, 'My God! I've never seen anything like it –' She saw him look at her and smile.

'The most expensive hotel in the world and the most luxurious. Pretend you are a millionairess, Kate.'

The door was opened and she got out. An exceptionally handsome young man hurried to Paul Roulier. The baggage would be sent up and the car put away. Paul gently took her arm as they walked up the steps to the splendid entrance. She gazed round her while he went to reception and registered. Enormous custom-built sofas with handsome glass-topped tables, a spiral staircase in the centre, built round an old-fashioned type of cage lift that whispered up and down behind its gilded gates. Flowers everywhere, superbly arranged. A chatter of American voices, some guttural German that made her jump.

A good-looking man in a cream suit approached her, followed by Paul Roulier. He introduced himself as the manager, shook hands, and hoped she would like her suite. Roulier said, 'I have the keys. I'll take you upstairs first, they'll bring your bags. The lift?' Her amazement was amusing him and he didn't try to hide it.

She gave him a challenging smile. 'Why not? Millionaires don't walk.'

'Round here they do,' he said as they glided up one flight. 'And they play tennis. You'll see more well-preserved seventy-year-olds here than anywhere else. With occasionally a very beautiful wife.'

The room was exceptionally decorated, by any standard, and a lovely arrangement of roses and carnations was on the writing table. The page appeared with her suitcase. It looked so shabby that she laughed. Paul tipped him, and they were alone. Katharine said, 'You're not paying for all this, are you?'

'No,' he replied. 'Only for myself. I have a room down the corridor. It's a very agreeable place to stay. And I want you to enjoy it. Shall I come back in twenty minutes and we can have a drink in the bar?'

Don't bother to bring many clothes, he had told her. Now she understood why. Nothing Colonel Alfurd's widow possessed would be suitable. When she opened the wardrobe door to hang up the summer dresses and casual shirts and trousers she had brought, she found half a dozen brand-new outfits with her name on a card pinned to each. The size was right. The shoes fitted perfectly. When she saw the handbags in their cellophane wrappings, she slammed the cupboard door.

When he came back as he'd arranged, he found her wearing one of her own dresses. She saw the quick glance, and the slight frown. She walked past him and towards the

218

stairs. 'Let's walk down, shall we?' She didn't wait but let him follow.

In the main hall she hesitated. He came beside her, and said gently, 'The bar is through that archway to the right. I've ordered champagne.'

Beautiful, Katharine thought. More grand flower pieces, glittering glass and buttercup yellow and white. The first actual bar I've ever seen that didn't look vulgar. The carpet was a museum piece. He led her to a table in the corner. All the others were occupied. When they sat down he offered her a cigarette.

'I'm sorry about the clothes,' he said. 'That was a mistake. They can be sent back.'

'I'm glad to hear it. What a waste of money otherwise.'

'Please don't be angry.'

'I'm not angry. I'm sure you meant well, or whoever is footing the bill, but I prefer my own clothes. If they're not up to standard for a hotel like this, you shouldn't have brought me.' She tapped the cigarette end and knocked ash into the ashtray. 'I can't offer to pay my own bill, but I don't want to feel any more beholden than I have to. That made me very uncomfortable indeed.'

He bowed his head a little in apology. 'Will you forgive me? A Frenchwoman wouldn't have minded. She'd have looked at the labels first.'

'Maybe I've lived too long in England. What are the labels, by the way?'

'I thought Lanvin would suit you,' he answered. 'Here's our champagne. Tell me something, Kate?'

'What? Thank you,' she said to the waiter, 'that's lovely.'

'Why do you trust me?' She sipped the drink. It was perfect. A middle-aged woman at the table called the waiter. She gave her order in German. The head barman answered in the same language. She was smart and very handsome, with a burly husband, burnt cork-brown by the sun. 'I didn't expect they'd come here,' Kate said. 'It's a very odd feeling, hearing them talk, and seeing how natural everyone is. So friendly. She's just looked over and smiled at me and I've smiled back. It's the same hotel in the same place, but they've done more than gut it and bring everything up to date. They've wiped out the past.' She held the chilled glass in both hands. 'You wouldn't understand what I mean. You're too young.'

'I understand very well,' Paul Roulier answered quietly. 'I'm glad you've noticed it. I think it's very important. When you're ready, we can go down to the restaurant and have dinner. And you haven't answered my question.'

'No,' Katharine admitted, 'I haven't. Because I don't know the answer yet. I just followed my instinct when I met you. I trusted you then and I trust you now. I can't give you any reasons.' He got up and held his hand out to help her up.

'I don't want any reasons,' he said. 'Just reassurance. You can be very formidable when you're angry. For a moment I was afraid I'd lost your confidence.'

'I was afraid I'd lost my independence,' she retorted. 'So we're quits. I'm hungry, aren't you?' They went down a wide flight of steps into the moonlit garden, along a gravelled pathway to the restaurant built overlooking the sea.

They didn't talk about the war. They discussed the menu, the other diners; they relaxed very quickly and conversation was surprisingly easy. She wasn't smartly dressed, but somehow it didn't matter. People looked at her anyway. She was a fascinating woman, Roulier admitted, with a vivacious personality that commanded attention. In the soft lighting of one of the most flattering settings in the world for any woman, she looked deceptively young. Beautiful wasn't too strong a word, even at her age. The fine features were as clear-cut as ever, and she had eyes that sparkled. . . . He stopped himself thinking any further because there were twenty-odd years between them, and in the morning it would all be different. The new wardrobe hadn't been his idea. No more mistakes like that; he'd make that very plain. He'd agreed against his own judgement, treating an exceptional woman like an ordinary vain and greedy one.

They walked back up the long slope, with its discreet lighting all along the route, and the majestic hotel blazing like a palace ahead of them. This time he didn't take her arm. It was very odd, the desire to go to bed with a woman so much older. He'd never experienced it before. By the morning, he told himself again, it would be different. Katharine stopped outside her bedroom door.

'What a wonderful dinner,' she said. 'I haven't enjoyed myself so much for many years. Thank you, Paul.'

'Thank you,' he said, and left her quickly. She sat by the window looking out over the gardens towards the distant sea. A soft breeze carried the familiar scents of pine trees and thyme and the faint tang of salt in the air. So very different from the last time she had come to the coast. 1947, when the scars of war were still bleeding in so many parts of France. But the beautiful coast had escaped. The thrust of the Allied armies hadn't penetrated there. The retreating Germans had left it as they came, with minimum destruction. But the bitterness and the denunciations were as lethal as bombs and battles were fought from street to street. The prisons were full; men and women accused of collaborating were being tried and punished, and each village held its own court martial and condemned the guilty. Those who had supported the Nazis were driven out; women who consorted with them weren't shaved and publicly exhibited any more. At least that horror had stopped, but the denunciations flowed into the police. Old spites were settled, and many suffered who were innocent. Katharine had come back to give evidence at the trial of one of the worst traitors in the war.

He had walked out of the court a free man. She left the window and began to undress. Tomorrow she would make the first of several pilgrimages. To the house where she and Dulac had spent the last weeks of their lives together. The empty house which had belonged to a family of murdered

Jews. Their last act had been to give their friend Dulac the key.

'If you don't mind,' Katharine Alfurd said, 'I'd rather go there alone. I only want to see if it's still there.'

Paul Roulier said, 'Of course. You take the car; I have some things to do this morning, and I hope to have a very important appointment set up for tomorrow.'

'What sort of appointment? For me?'

'For both of us,' he said quietly. 'I'll be able to tell you about it when you get back.' He took her hand and kissed it. It was a lovely drive along the old coast road to Nice. Antibes itself was small and picturesque, an ancient coastal port with its fortress jutting out over the sea, and yachts at rest in the marina, flying every nation's flag in a light breeze.

The broad sweep of the beaches, flanked by hotels and the handsome private villas set back behind trees and hedges. The palms, majestic and timeless as ever, symbols of the sun, and a benevolent climate where the rich could escape winter's cold. Children bobbing in the sea, shouting in the distance and laughing. Sunbathers stretched out in sleepy worship, fleets of cars jamming the roads at traffic lights, the yachts in the blue distance and a cruise ship on the horizon. She noticed the changes, the splendid new hotels, sheeted in glass that caught fire from the sun, the shopping centres on the front with magic names like Dior and St Laurent, ogled by women tourists window-shopping. The beach shops with their colourful goods spilling out on to the pavements, proprietors sunning themselves and chatting. The old railway line running parallel, unchanged from forty years ago. People drinking coffee at tables under bright umbrellas.

It was so long since Kate had driven on the right-hand side of the road. Nice was beautiful in the daylight. Handsome shops and hotel buildings, the white wedding-cake Negresco, with its distinctive awning and the brilliant flowers and shrubs flanking the entrance. Wealth and security were as obvious as the flags flying from the hotel roofs. France was rich and living well, enjoying the present and confident about the future. The past was a small black cloud that nobody wanted to look at anymore. Until Christian Eilenburg was extradited from Chile. She could imagine how embarrassing that must have been, how a lot of people would resent the bloodied waters being stirred up when they had been calm for so long. She turned into the town centre, climbing up the hill, stalling the car once at a traffic light. Up and then leftward, leaving the smart shopping centres behind, going into the sedate residential area of the prosperous middle classes who lived and worked in Nice. There was the street that she remembered; a pleasant tree-shaded road, with houses on either side. Nice houses, fresh with paint and colourful shutters. The house was the last on the left-hand side, set back a little from the road, not as far back as she thought, but then some of the sheltering trees had been cut down. She stopped, got out and walked to the gate. The name had not been changed. La Rosée. She pushed it open and walked up to the front door. It was different of course. It seemed much smaller, less overshadowed. The sun beat down on it, and the door was painted a bright yellow. Baskets of flowers hung on either side, and there was a child's tricycle parked up against the wall. She thought of the bicycle that had carried her so many miles all those years ago. There, to the rear of the house, was the thicket of bushes where she used to hide it. . . . She didn't ring the bell, because there was a dog barking inside, and a woman looked out of the window. 'Yes?' she called out.

Kate said, 'Excuse me, I used to live here. I was only having a look.'

The window shut and a moment later the door opened. The woman standing inside was quite young; she looked suspicious. 'I'm sorry, but we don't like people poking round. It upsets the dog.'

Kate came a little nearer. 'Have you lived here long?'

'Ten years. You say you used to live here?' Curiosity was

getting the better of her, but she still held the door and didn't ask Kate to come in.

'I stayed here,' Kate replied. 'During the war. I haven't been back since.'

'Oh, I don't know anything about that.' The reply was brisk, all interest gone. 'That's well before my time. You'll excuse me.' The door was firmly shut. She turned slowly and walked back down the short path, pushed the wrought iron gate open and latched it shut behind her. There was no atmosphere, no charging of the emotions. The house could have been any house in the street, impersonal, inhabited by strangers.

Kate got into the car, switched on and reversed out of the road. She felt overborne by sadness, and that sadness was turning into the pain of grief she had suppressed and denied for most of her life.

The factory had gone. Katharine Alfurd stood looking at the site. The two-storied building, painted an ugly grey, with blind windows and the side door which they had used to get inside, creaking on a broken hinge, was like a phantasm before her eyes. The reality of a modern supermarket took several seconds to break through the illusion. Nothing remained; the past was obliterated, like the old factory. There was no imprint of tragedy except what she carried on the negative of her memory. She put the car into gear and drove slowly back to Cap d'Antibes.

He was waiting for her when she walked into the hotel. That didn't seem real either, even when he came up and took her arm. A handsome American couple passed them on their way to play tennis. Young and vigorous, the golden rich of the new age.

'Come and have a drink,' Paul Roulier said quietly, 'and tell me about your morning.' She made an effort to smile. 'Not much to tell, I'm afraid. A drink would be nice. I found my trip down memory lane worse than I expected.'

She was silent for some time. He didn't press her. He

noticed a slight tremor when she lifted her glass of wine.

'Would you like some lunch?'

'I'm not hungry, thanks. Don't let me stop you.'

In the end he said, 'Tell me about it; it'll make it easier if you can share it.'

'Share it?' she asked him. 'I can't share it with anyone. I'm the only one left. I went back to the house we hid in at the end. The woman wouldn't let me in. It looked different, but I should have expected that. The factory was pulled down, of course. There was a huge supermarket instead. Nothing left, Paul. Nothing to show what happened. May 13th, it was. A Thursday, not Friday. That would have been too ironic, wouldn't it? That was when we got the message. Just after seven o'clock in the evening, and the radio was crackling and I couldn't hear properly for ages. It seemed like ages anyway. You don't know about that, do you?'

Roulier shook his head. 'No.' She stared past him to the view down the splendid steps, flanked by banked geraniums of luscious pink. The sea shimmered in the distance. 'The candle of the wicked,' she said slowly. 'That was the signal sent that night. The candle of the wicked shall be put out. It was the code for the Invasion of Europe. Every network knew it, and knew what to do when it came. And we did it, Paul. Without pausing to think. At dawn the next morning the Maquis blew up the section of railway line connecting with the main terminal at Marseilles; it was heavily guarded and they were caught in a gun battle with German troops. Most of them were killed. And Jean mounted an attack on the power station.' He wanted to reach out and take her hand, but he didn't move. 'We never questioned. The rumours spread of course, and everyone believed there'd been a landing and the Germans were censoring it. But no one heard it on the wireless. Only me, transmitted direct from London.'

'It would have been broadcast on the BBC French Service,' Roulier said. 'If it had been genuine.'

'Yes,' Katharine Alfurd said. 'If it had been genuine. I

have never known what made them do it, I only know they did.'

He made up his mind. The timing was right. 'That's what we are going to find out,' he said. 'Why did the British send the local Resistance and the Maquis to their deaths? Christian Eilenburg is going to be tried for killing your comrades, for driving the hero Jean Dulac to commit suicide. But it was your own people who betrayed them. And you're the only one who escaped and knows what they did.'

Kate said quietly, 'Are you working for the Germans?'

'No.' She believed him. 'I've got permission for us to visit Eilenburg in Marseilles prison. Tomorrow morning. Will you see him?'

'That's the appointment?' He nodded; he felt very tense, waiting for her reaction. Everything, months of preparation, the time spent gaining her confidence, the money involved, all depended upon her answer. Kate said, 'Who are you working for?'

He said, 'When you've seen Eilenburg I'll tell you.'

She got up. 'What time in the morning?'

He reached out and gripped her arm. 'Ten thirty. You are brave, Kate.'

'Not really,' she answered. 'An old man in a jail, forty years later. Would you mind if I spent the afternoon by myself?'

'If that's what you want,' he said. 'There's a beautiful private beach here, I can arrange. . . .'

She interrupted him. 'No thanks, I don't feel in the mood for lying in the sun. I'll just go and wander round.'

'Don't worry about tomorrow,' he said. 'I'll be with you.'

She smiled at him but didn't seem to hear. He watched her walk out of the bar, and when she was out of sight he called the head barman. 'I want to make a telephone call in private,' he said.

'Of course. This way, Monsieur.' He was shown into the games room at the back. He dialled a number, spoke a name, and then said, 'She's going to Marseilles to see him. I'm very confident. But she's insisting I tell her who my client is.' He listened for a moment and then said, 'Very well. I'll be in contact after the meeting. Yes, yes, he's had the message. Everything has been arranged. Until tomorrow.'

The police in Nice had no report of a Mrs Alfurd registering at any of the hotels or pensions. Immigration at the airport had no record of the name either, but that meant she had already arrived. The authorities at Cannes were notified and they included Juan les Pins and Antibes. It took time, and time was at a premium if Katharine Alfurd was to be reached and stopped. It was out of the hands of old warhorses like Colonel Reed and Lord Wroxham; the young hard-liners of modern Intelligence were given the scent and told to find the quarry. It didn't take them long.

Kate was sitting at a café on the quay at Antibes. It was hot and she was thirsty after the long walk down from the hotel. Sunglasses protected her eyes from the glare, and they gave her a brief respite from detection. There were a number of women her age wandering round Antibes, or sitting in cafés and bars. Women with dark hair slightly touched with grey, slim, medium height and possibly with a younger man who was French. For over thirty years Kate had lived in a country at peace, where the senses were asleep to danger. At home in Amdale she wouldn't have noticed the man, but unconsciously she was thinking as if the past were now, and the old responses woke and watched for danger. He was looking for someone. He was looking at faces as he sauntered past so casually, with a sweeping glance that only lingered on women. On one woman, who was middle-aged and American, with a camera slung round her neck and postcards on the table. And then passed on to her. And away, and then back again. He took a seat not far from her. Not sure, because of the sunglasses. Kate didn't argue with her instinct. She trusted it then as she had done so many years ago, when every

German soldier was an enemy and every glance a menace.

She signalled the waiter, and ordered a cup of coffee and an ice cream. The young man was looking at her without looking, as only a professional can. Kate picked up her bag, opened it, pretended to fiddle with a powder compact. Money, a handkerchief, make-up. No identification. She crumpled the few notes in her hand, shut the bag and left it on her chair. She got up and went inside to the lavatory. The man didn't follow or move. She had done what no woman ever does, leave her handbag behind. Not a newspaper or a book as a marker, but a careless hostage, guaranteeing she'd be back in a few minutes. She left the café by the kitchen entrance, and without knowing why or what was threatening her, she ran down to the main square. There were no taxis. Five minutes at the most, and whoever the man was he'd realize she'd tricked him and begin to look for her. She dared not try to get back to the hotel on foot; there was a bus stop, with a little group of people waiting. Kate hurried across the road, and as she did so, the bus to Cannes came round the corner. She pushed her way through and jumped inside. Ten minutes later it set her down a short walk from the Hôtel du Cap.

'Good afternoon, Madame,' the smiling doorman greeted her.

She didn't answer. She went up to Roulier's room. There was no answer. She shut herself in her own room, trembling and out of breath. She rang down to reception. Monsieur Roulier – no, he's not in his room, can you page him, please? 'He went out, Madame. Some time ago.'

Kate said, 'Ring me the moment he comes back,' and hung up. And then began to think she had imagined it, that the man in the café was perfectly innocent, and she'd behaved like a panic-stricken fool. There was one way to make sure, she thought. A good memory was a blessing. The name of the café at Antibes. She got the number through the switchboard. She'd left her bag behind and forgotten her bill. The reply was meant to be reassuring. A gentleman had collected Madame's bag and paid her bill. Kate said, 'Thank you.'

'It could be dangerous for you,' Roulier had said, and when she queried the choice of the Hôtel du Cap, 'Nobody will think of looking for you there.'

She had forgotten until that afternoon what it felt like to be afraid for her life.

He didn't waste time when she told him. His face closed up, as if a shutter had dropped. He didn't argue or ask more than one or two sharp questions. Then he nodded and said, 'I was afraid this might happen. But not so quickly.'

Kate said, 'Who's looking for me? Do you know?'

'The English, I suspect, backed by certain French interests. They've moved very fast.' He frowned, hesitated and then said, 'We must get to Marseilles tomorrow. That's the first consideration.'

'Not my safety?' Kate asked the question quietly.

He said, 'If you're afraid, you can go back to England tonight. But I don't think you will.'

'You said nobody would think of looking for me here. But this hotel has to submit a list of registered foreigners like any other place.'

He was thinking aloud. 'They'd try Nice first,' he said. 'They'd assume you'd stay there. But you were seen in Antibes, which means they've found nothing in Nice and are looking further afield. Now they know you're here, because you ran away. That was a stupid thing to do. Kate, you can't stay here now. But we won't check out. There's a private villa, very close; we can go there tonight and on to Marseilles tomorrow.'

'Why didn't we go there in the first place?' she demanded. 'Who owns this villa?'

'I can't tell you that until you've seen Eilenburg,' he said. 'You'll have to trust me. Don't take anything but what you need for tonight. We'll slip out after dinner and say nothing at the hotel. Excuse me; I'll meet you downstairs.'

*　　*　　*

The man who had taken her handbag made his report. No identification, but the photograph matched. The suspect had made a run for it and he'd lost contact. She was in the Antibes area and should be traced within the next twelve hours. He listened to his instructions; they came direct from Paris. Mrs Alfurd was to be persuaded to return to England. He queried the word persuaded. It had a wide interpretation. Eliminated? Eliminated if necessary but only as a last resort. Understood. What about the man with her? No action to be taken against a French national unless it was untraceable. The agent understood again. He had a wide brief. He started that same evening with the smaller pensions and hotels.

Roulier drove into the villa in darkness. Kate couldn't see much of it, because there were no lights outside, and they went in through what was obviously a back door and up a rear staircase. He guided her along a corridor that opened out into a handsome landing, and opened a door for her. 'You'll be comfortable for tonight,' he said. 'Don't worry, you're safe here. Sleep well, and I'll come for you in the morning. We'll leave at eight. Good night.' He kissed her quickly and unexpectedly on the cheek and then hurried away. There was nothing to identify the place. No books, or magazines; empty drawers and a vacant bathroom. It was as impersonal as an hotel room. She could have found a Gideon Bible on the bedside table. The window looked out on to darkness. The linen was starched and cold as if it had been waiting a long time for a guest. 'You'll be safe here.' She remembered the feeling, and knew what the room felt like. It was a safe house, like the other safe houses where she had hidden from the enemy. Only now the enemy was her own side, hunting her down because she was the only survivor of an old and shameful massacre. She and the Gestapo Standartenführer waiting in Marseilles prison. She thought of the young professional in the café. He was a familiar type; very fit, highly trained, blank-eyed. He'd know how to get a woman out of the way if she was being a nuisance to

someone. Then all they had to do was make certain Eilenburg didn't come to trial. At his age it wouldn't be too
difficult. The secret of what happened to the hero Jean Dulac
and his heroic network would stay in some government file,
and the guilty would die peacefully, old men full of honours.

Katharine Alfurd kicked off her shoes. 'Like hell they will,'
she said aloud to the bare walls. 'Like hell they'll shut me up
and get away with it.'

He tried to wait patiently. He measured the length of his cell
three times, and then sat down and read the Bible they'd
given him, glancing through the Gospels with indifference,
taking his mind off the coming visit. She was the difference
between life imprisonment and a short sentence, he'd been
told. You must think back and remember everything so that
you can convince her when you meet. You mustn't hesitate
or get confused. She can save your last years from ignominy.
She can give you an ironic victory over your judges. And
we've brought her here; there is her photograph so you can
search your memory and remember everything. As she was
when you last saw her, and as she is today.

He wished his hands would stop trembling. Weakness,
and age, he thought defensively. Not guilt. I've lived without
guilt for all these years and my conviction isn't shaken. I did
the right thing for my country and I am not ashamed. I've
marshalled all the facts and incidents and got my memory
into focus. Now I'd better concentrate on this Christian
nonsense, since it's all they'll let me read, and try to be quite
calm until I'm sent for. . . . No watch, no means of telling
the time. Ah, there, the door is opening.

Christian Eilenburg got up. The prison officer said coldly,
'You've got visitors. Come with me.' He followed with a firm
step, and his blue eyes were bright and piercing as they used
to be. He wondered if she would recognize him.

Katharine Alfurd stood up, and for a moment she felt Paul
Roulier's hand on her elbow, giving her support. She freed
herself firmly. He was so old. Old and white-haired and frail,

231

in the prison uniform. She would never have recognized him. There was a table between them, and a French prison officer who had to remain throughout the interview. He gave the old man a chair, and he sat down very slowly, stiff and uncertain in his movements. They put out chairs for her and for Paul Roulier. Roulier spoke first. 'How are you today?'

The voice was surprisingly strong. 'Better. I feel better every day. The doctors are pleased with me.' The mouth turned down in sarcasm. 'They don't want me to have another heart attack.'

'Nobody wants that,' Roulier said. 'This is Madame Alfurd.'

'I know it is,' Eilenburg said. There was an extraordinary moment when he looked at her, and for that moment, the years fell away. 'Cecilie,' he said. 'You called me a filthy bastard.'

'And so you were,' she heard her voice say. It wavered, and without warning her eyes filled and overflowed with tears.

'Don't cry,' Eilenburg said. 'There's no reason to cry now. You didn't cry then. I remember how brave you were.'

'Do you remember the others too? The ones you beat and crippled – the women you gave your men to torture –' Roulier had eased his chair back, leaving them facing each other. He saw the French gaoler standing impassive at the side, hearing everything and showing nothing.

'Yes,' Eilenburg answered. 'I can remember them if I want to. Some I respected, some I despised. Some of them, like your woman companion who was so terrified of rough handling, I pitied. I was sorry for them, sorry I had to treat them badly. But it was my duty. Was it your side's duty to betray them to me? Have you asked yourself that?'

'Yes, I have,' Katharine answered. 'That's the only reason I'm here. I wouldn't breathe the same air as you, if it wasn't for that question. We had a traitor, a man who was working for you. He was never punished after the war. I did my damnedest and so did a lot of people in France, but when he was tried, people behind the scenes made sure he was acquitted. Why? Do you know why?'

'Philippe Derain, the bookseller from Beaulieu,' Eilenburg said softly, leaning towards her. 'A double agent, working for both sides. Paid by us and paid by London. I read about that trial in Spain where I was hiding. You gave evidence against him; so did others. Nothing happened. He was set free. I remember thinking it was strange you should hate him so much when he saved your life. He got you released through the Abwehr. I was very angry at their interference. But perhaps a little relieved to see you go.'

She saw a smug little smile, proclaiming his softheartedness, and could have struck him. As she had struck Pierrot, the traitor. He leaned back in his chair.

'The Abwehr lived to regret that association,' he said. 'I never trusted him. I wouldn't have let him go on after we destroyed Dulac. But they insisted. He was their man. I had to cooperate at the time. Later, when I was in Marseilles in charge, I couldn't find him. He destroyed the evidence we wanted. So maybe that's why he was protected afterwards. Maître Roulier, do you have a cigarette?' He glanced at the prison officer. 'I'm permitted to smoke?' There was a brief nod.

'Thank you. Ah, this is good.'

Katharine said slowly, 'What evidence? What do you mean?'

'Germany was fighting for her life,' Eilenburg said. 'Your armies were pushing on to the Rhine. You were mounting an invasion on the coast here. And that was when the traitors at home decided to strike. Some of them were here, in France. I came close to catching them, but Philippe Derain was paid by them. I said he was an Abwehr agent, didn't I? He earned the blood-money they paid him for betraying Dulac and his people. Blood-money from both sides.' He sucked greedily at the cigarette. 'You accused him of that betrayal at his trial. It was fully reported in the Spanish papers. But you couldn't prove it, Cecilie. Nobody could, because he'd done it so cleverly. Saying he worked for the Abwehr wasn't enough. Saying he got you released wasn't evidence that he'd denounced his Resistance comrades to the Gestapo. It should have convicted him but it didn't because there was a piece of the puzzle missing.'

'What was it?'

'His instructions from London,' Eilenburg replied. The blue eyes glittered like sapphires in a skull. 'Instructions to hand over Jean Dulac to us, and destroy his network. He didn't succeed because Dulac was warned and got away. So your own people pronounced the death sentence. They sent that radio message, didn't they? Knowing what the results would be.'

He rubbed out the exhausted cigarette stub in a tin ashtray. 'I'll stand trial for what your people will call war crimes. I'll be abused and vilified and they'll drag out the old insults like the "Butcher of Marseilles". But you know that the men who sent Dulac and the Maquis out on to the streets to fight on a false message were the ones who are really guilty. I did my duty to my country and my Führer. I would do it all again. But they'll escape. Unless you stand up and tell the truth. This time, they won't be able to hide from it.'

'Your time is up,' the officer announced. The chairs scraped back, Eilenburg needed help to get to his feet. He held out his hand. 'Whatever you think of me,' he said to her, 'I was true to my beliefs and to my own people.' Katharine stared at the hand, skinny and wrinkled and not very steady.

She turned her back on him. They walked out into the brilliant sunshine, and she shivered. 'Do you believe in hell?' she asked Roulier suddenly.

He looked surprised. 'No. Why, do you?'

'There must be a place for people like him,' she said. 'There must be a hell. Did he expect me to shake his hand? To touch him?'

'Apparently. He doesn't see himself as guilty of anything.' He opened the car door for her. 'How do you see him?'

Katharine asked. 'He called you Maître – are you his lawyer?'

'I'm his lawyer's assistant,' Roulier admitted.

'You said you weren't working for the Germans,' she reminded him. 'That was a lie, then.' He started the car and they moved out into the traffic.

'It was true; my client isn't German. You're blaming me for taking the case, aren't you, Kate?' She shrugged, looked away from him out of the window.

'Lawyers can't take sides,' she said. 'I suppose the money's good. Where are we going now?'

'Back to the villa,' he answered. 'You wanted to meet my employer. They'll be there this morning.'

The man looking for Kate Alfurd had a French counterpart. They liaised in a café at Juan les Pins. It was full of young holidaymakers, a paradise for the jeans and pop brigade who swarmed over the town. The cafés and restaurants were full; the discos bulged and blared. There was an atmosphere of gaiety and exuberance that was infectious to the visitor whose youth was in the past. The two men blended well; if they were a little too well-built, thick-necked and muscled in their T-shirts and shorts, it wasn't noticed. They huddled in a corner drinking lager and talking quietly with the noise of a live group belting out over their heads.

'Bad news,' the Frenchman said. 'The lawyer brought a woman to see him this morning. The description fits. It's her, and she's vanished.'

'Shit,' the Englishman muttered. 'I thought I'd got her this morning. Guess where? The Hôtel du Cap! I got the name from the police. When I went there they stonewalled.'

'They would,' his companion scowled. 'Have to protect the millionaires. She'd left, then?'

'No; not checked out, I got that much from the reception. It was as easy as pulling teeth to get them to say anything. I hung around, and I didn't get the feeling I was exactly welcome. I bought a drink at the bar, and do you know how much it cost me?' He named an astronomical sum. The Frenchman whistled in sympathy. 'After a long wait, while they didn't see me on purpose,' he grumbled. 'No sign of her or the man. So I left. I staked out the entrance and the way down to the Eden Roc, but they weren't in the restaurant or on the beach. I didn't bloody know she was in Marseilles. All I can do is stick it out till she gets back. If I show up there again I'll get thrown out.'

His companion had a dour, ill-tempered face. 'I'll pay a visit,' he promised. 'They won't be funny with me. I'll get the information, and if she's there, I'll let you know. Then it's up to you.'

They paid for their drinks and left. That afternoon, when the patrons of the hotel were drifting down to take tea on the terrace, and coming up from the tennis court, the reception-ist was faced with a young man of hostile attitude who demanded to see the manager. Before the receptionist could say he wasn't available, the ID of the SEDEC was thrust in front of him. The French Secret Service was not impressed by wealth or privilege; the manager was found and came to the foyer in a hurry. After ten minutes spent in his private office, he escorted the young man upstairs and personally stood by while he went into Katharine Alfurd's room and checked her belongings. They came out together and down the handsome spiral stair, back into the private office at the rear. 'When the lady comes back,' the manager was told, 'you will immediately ring this number.' He was left with the card in his hand, and the slam of his own door echoing after his visitor.

They had left the villa by the same back stairs that morning. Kate had glimpsed a magnificent garden with lawns and flower beds through the trees as they sped down the back drive and out on the road to Marseilles. They returned and drove through the front gate. The façade was beautiful. White stucco, delicate wrought iron, a balustrade spilled over by geraniums, and a king palm standing at a majestic height in the centre of the gravelled sweep. A manservant opened the front door and they were in a cool, tall marble hall.

A massive flower arrangement of hothouse lilies and rare orchids stood on a scagliola centre table. 'In here, please.' The servant opened a door and stood aside for them. Roulier led the way. It was a soft green room, full of flowers, a refuge from the heat outside. Beautiful early French furniture, a pair of Regency lacquer commodes that belonged in a museum; over the fireplace a famous Renoir, discreetly lit.

Kate stood and looked round her. The safe house was safe no longer. She could feel the presence even before she saw the woman. She got up from a deep chair and came towards them. She was small and greyhound thin, with a face so perfectly made up that it was like a beautiful mask. A mask that showed no trace of age but wasn't young. Large brown eyes with a gentle expression in them, and a painted red mouth with tight lips that opened slowly in a smile. She moved with grace, like an actress crossing a stage, and a diamond flashed blue fire from the folds of her silk dress.

'Madame Vigier,' Paul Roulier said formally, 'may I present Madame Alfurd.'

'It is a pleasure to meet you.' The voice was light and sweet. 'I am so sorry we didn't meet last night, but I was dining with friends. I hope you were comfortable.'

'Very comfortable, thank you,' Kate replied.

'Please sit down. Has Paul told you about me?' She indicated a sofa, and Kate followed her and sat down. The woman moved beside her. Another diamond blazed from her hand as she settled the folds of her skirt.

'I am Antoinette Vigier, and you are my guest while you're in France. Paul, how did this morning go?' She had a smooth authority; more than authority, it was power. When she spoke people listened, and her questions would always be answered.

He said, 'Very well, Madame. Very satisfactory.'

'And how is he?' The voice was tender.

'Better; stronger.' A look passed between them, which Kate saw. Roulier said, 'Excuse me; I have some calls to make,' and left them alone as arranged.

'Madame Vigier,' Kate turned towards her, 'you say I'm your guest. Are you employing Paul Roulier? Are you the client he talks about?'

'Yes, I am.' The big brown eyes looked at her out of that ageless face, and they were old and sad.

'Why are you helping Christian Eilenburg?'

She gave a little smile. 'You're very direct, Madame. You don't waste time, do you?'

'No,' Kate answered. 'Nor do you, I think. I would like some kind of explanation before I commit myself any further.'

'Of course. It must have seemed strange to you, all the secrecy, Paul coming out of the blue to see you. But there was a need, you see. I had to be protected or I couldn't help my husband. That answers your question, Madame Alfurd. I am Christian's wife, not that woman he married in Chile. He married me in 1945, just before he had to flee to Spain.' She saw Kate glance at her jewelled hand and the wedding ring on it, and again she smiled.

'I always hoped to join him, but it wasn't possible. So I married again; twice, both of them very nice men, and as you can see, very very rich. I am a widow now, unfortunately. If I hadn't met Christian, I would still be scrubbing floors in some hotel round here.'

She reached for a silver box. 'Will you smoke? No – how wise. I can't give it up, I'm afraid. It makes my doctor very cross.'

'You married him,' Kate said slowly, staring at her. 'You married Eilenburg in 1945? You're French – you're from the Midi –' It was like a nightmare; the beautiful woman, smiling and talking in her soft voice, the Frenchwoman who had married the war criminal and was paying for his defence.

'I met him here,' Antoinette Vigier said. 'I was a little chambermaid at the Hôtel Negresco. The hotel receptionist was a pig; he sent me upstairs because the German officer wanted a girl, and he couldn't find one, so he told me to go. Or be sacked, of course. So I went. I was so terrified, Madame, I was a poor little virgin and I didn't know what the German beast was going to do with me. Do you know what he did? He sent me away. He said, "I asked for a prostitute, not a human sacrifice." I was so frightened, I said, "I am a prostitute." I can see it now, Madame, I can see this amazing man, so handsome, so proud, being kind to me in his own way. Nobody had ever been kind to me before! Nobody. But this young man, so beautiful – like a god.'

'I don't want to hear,' Kate said. 'What happened with you and him is nothing to do with me.' The hand on her arm was surprisingly strong.

'You don't want to listen because it's not a horror story. If I told you he had ill-treated me, threatened me, you'd sit still and say nothing. You asked for explanations, I didn't offer them. I became Christian's mistress. I fell in love with him and I am still in love with him. We lived together in this house. Twenty years ago I got my second husband to buy it for me. I didn't care how much it cost. I wanted to be here and remember my time with Christian.'

'Why didn't you go to him?' Kate asked. She felt numb and sick. 'Why didn't you join the other sadists and murderers hiding out there with him?'

Antoinette Vigier got up and stood facing her. Two red patches burnt on each cheek, like dabs of paint. 'What hypocrites you people are,' she said. 'Sadists and murderers because they were Germans. The Frenchmen who butchered young soldiers as they slept, the women who saw men die of strychnine poison that they'd given them, they were heroes and heroines of the Resistance!

'What did the torturers of the OAS do to their prisoners in the Algerian war? What did the Russians do when they marched into Berlin? What does every nation do to its enemies today, when we're supposed to be at peace? Christian was at war. I was with him the night his German fiancée was killed by English bombers, nursing the sick in hospital! How many children died in the fire storm at Cologne? Nagasaki, Hiroshima? Oh, you make me sick, Madame Alfurd, with your double standards. At least I am honest. I loved him and I didn't ask what he did in the course of his duty. And I'm not going to stand by and let them drag him out and put him on exhibition in a courtroom while the collaborators and the crooks who profited from what he did, here in Nice and Cannes, pass judgement on him! And I know them, believe me –' She began to pace up and down, twisting her hands together, working herself into a passion as she went on. 'How do you think I was provided for? How do you think I got away and made a new life for myself where I wasn't known? Men here who owed him favours and didn't want me talking about them – they paid to get me out. Otherwise I'd have been paraded with my head shaved, while the old bitches spat in my face and the men punched me in the breasts – and then sent to prison! No, Madame Alfurd, you were one of the heroines, and your lover has a statue to him in Nice, where every year people lay wreaths. He was a patriot. Christian, fighting for his cause and his country, is the "Butcher of Marseilles". Well,' she stopped, then swung round on Kate again, 'we shall see when the trial comes. Paul tells me your Intelligence people are hunting for you – they don't want you and Christian to exchange information. Naturally, they can't afford that. They have to protect their own heroes, don't they? And they will, my dear Madame, even if it means pushing you under a motorcar to stop you talking. Now.' She made a visible effort, drew a deep breath and composed herself. 'Now, let's have a drink and try to be calm. I apologize if I've been rude to you. But this has been a terrible ordeal for me, too.' She turned away and Kate saw her blink back tears.

Kate said, 'I won't help him. He killed my friends. There was a girl I worked with; she was caught and they raped her till she gave me away. Then she was shot. Don't ask me to excuse that. I don't know how any woman could excuse it to herself.'

'He told me about her,' Antoinette Vigier said. She had regained her composure. 'She was a victim of the war; and a victim of her own people who betrayed her to the Gestapo. What about that, Madame Alfurd? If I can make excuses for Christian, can you excuse them?'

Kate said very slowly, feeling as if she were choking with anger, 'No, I can't. And that's why I'm here.'

'Then I will call Paul back, and we shall have a drink and be friends,' Antoinette Vigier declared. 'If not friends, allies at least until the trial is over.' She rang a bell and the manservant appeared. 'Ask Maître Roulier to come in,' she said. 'You saw him today.' She turned back to Kate. 'I can't go, you understand. All I have is other people's reports – how did he look?'

'Old,' she answered coldly. 'White-haired and shaky. I wouldn't have recognized him in a million years.'

'But his spirits were high?' The question was asked anxiously.

'They seemed to be. He had a lot of facts to hand, he seemed to remember everything as if it were yesterday. I imagine,' she didn't hide her sarcasm, 'he's been briefed.'

Antoinette Vigier brushed that aside. 'Of course. He needs help if he's going to defend himself. Paul is very thorough; quite a number of people have been helpful, apart from you.'

'French people?' Kate asked.

'Yes, in fact we even found a little woman living in Paris whose husband had been in the Resistance, and your friend Jean Dulac had him murdered because he thought he'd agreed to work for the Gestapo. When she discovered that, *she* worked for the Gestapo. I went to see her; it was quite fascinating.'

'Her husband's name was Louis Cabrot,' Kate said quietly. 'I remember. She betrayed us.'

'Wouldn't you have done the same?' The soft voice asked the question, and Kate couldn't answer. 'It isn't all black

241

and white, is it? The poor devil hadn't done anything wrong; he was too ill to be questioned, and Christian sent him home. That will come out at the trial too.'

'She's agreed to give evidence?' Kate asked her.

'Yes; she feels very bitter even now. She has given a deposition and she has promised to come as a witness. What will interest you is that the poor woman would never have known what the Resistance did if one of its own members hadn't told her. She said he came and showed her a newspaper report. The German doctors had already told her her husband had been murdered. Naturally she didn't believe them. But she believed him. He had an odd code name. Harlequin –'

'Pierrot,' Kate corrected. 'My God, that's how he did it. Through Cabrot's widow.'

Roulier came in and she heard Madame Vigier ask if he would get them a drink. He spoke to Kate, 'There's champagne, whisky, gin, what would you like?'

'I don't care,' she said. 'Anything. But not champagne, thanks very much.'

'Now,' Antoinette Vigier announced, 'we will all feel better in a few minutes. More relaxed. Paul, will you explain our plan to Madame Alfurd?'

He cleared his throat. The intimacy that had grown up between them seemed no more than a pretence, a fiction he had created to gain her confidence. He was businesslike and cool, the front man for his rich employer.

'I am preparing the case for Standartenführer Eilenburg's defence,' he said. 'My colleague will lead.' He mentioned one of the most famous defence lawyers in France. 'Will you give a deposition stating everything that you have told me about the events in Nice at that time? Just facts, that's all. And will you be prepared to come to court and take the witness stand? That's really the most important part of all, if we're to present a true defence. And if you are to expose the people who have protected themselves for all these years. I believe that is what you really want, isn't it?'

Kate didn't answer. She put down her drink. 'I don't know,' she said. 'I need time to think about it.' For a moment the big dark eyes of Antoinette Vigier went black.

'Think about your lover,' she said. 'You mentioned that girl who was captured . . . think about the people in London who deliberately betrayed them. If Christian is on trial, they should be tried with him. And you, Madame Alfurd – what did they do to you?'

She didn't wait for Kate to answer, she ignored Roulier's signal to stop. 'To keep you quiet they ordered one of their own officers to marry you. To shut you up. They boxed you in without you even knowing it. Was it a happy marriage? A happy life? They're hunting you now, and I meant what I said. You won't be allowed to expose them if they find you. Believe me, a signed deposition is as much in your own interests as in ours. Once they know we have that, they won't dare to harm you. I am going upstairs to change; I will see you at dinner.'

She closed the door and immediately Paul Roulier came and sat beside Kate. He took her hand and held it. 'I'm sorry she said all that. I couldn't stop her.'

'It doesn't matter,' Kate answered. 'You've really caught me, haven't you, Paul? You've done a wonderful job for her. I hope she pays you a fat fee.' She pulled her hand away.

'Kate, listen to me. I know what I sounded like, but I had to satisfy her. If she thought I had any personal feelings she'd dismiss me right away.'

'Personal feelings?' she repeated. 'What kind of personal feelings can you have in a case like this – you're a professional, aren't you? You have a job to do and you do it. I am part of that job, that's all.'

'It isn't all,' he said. 'It was in the beginning, but it isn't now. Lawyers and doctors should never get involved with clients or patients. I set out to persuade you to come here and help in Eilenburg's defence. And it wasn't just for money, either. I don't like the English, I don't trust them and everything I discovered while I was investigating this made me more convinced than ever that they fought to the last Frenchman through the Resistance.

'I had no view either way when I met you. But it changed. It changed during the days we spent together and I began to see the past through your eyes. Kate, will you believe me when I say this? I admire you. I understand you and I love you for being the woman you are. If you want to get out of this now, I'll take you to Nice airport and put you on the plane. Without any deposition.' He got up, fumbled for a cigarette.

Kate said quietly, 'You'd be ruined. She'd see to that.'

'She won't be in a position to ruin anyone if she goes through with this,' he said. 'She's going into court to speak for him. She'll destroy herself to try and save him. And more than herself.'

'What do you mean?'

He sat opposite her this time, his head low. 'That's another thing you were never meant to know,' he said. 'Her last husband was Alfred Vigier, the socialist millionaire. Friend and adviser to President Mitterand. Just imagine what the scandal will do to the government when she announces that she was the mistress of the Gestapo chief who murdered French Resistance heroes and that she is paying for his defence!'

'The wife,' Kate corrected.

He shook his head. 'It wasn't legal. I didn't tell her that; they went through some ceremony with a man who wasn't accredited mayor. She got to Switzerland and married a Swiss after being his mistress for some years. Then when he died she came home and met Vigier and married him. When she goes to court she could bring down the government!'

'And that was another motive?' Kate said slowly. 'She's unbalanced, isn't she, and you knew if you encouraged her to do this, what it would mean in political terms.'

'Yes.' He looked directly at her. 'I did, and I wasn't alone. Mitterand is a disaster for France. If we can help to bring him down by means of this trial, then it's our duty to do it. And we will. But you don't have to be a part of it. I don't want that any more. I don't want you at risk, and that's what's happened. Kate, go upstairs and get your things. She takes hours to dress; I'll bring the car round.' She stood up, finished the drink. She hadn't even noticed what was in it.

'You're part of the Fascist Right,' she said.

'I'm a French patriot,' he countered. 'I shall come to England and see you. There's no reason why you should live alone.'

'I'm twenty years older than you are,' she said quietly. 'You could be my son.'

'I could be your lover,' he said. 'Think of that. I have; many times since we met.'

Kate went over to the table and said, 'I think I'll have another drink. It doesn't take me hours to dress before dinner. I'll see you later, Paul.'

He went upstairs and knocked on Antoinette Vigier's door. She was fully dressed, reading from a thick file. She took off her glasses and said, 'Well? Have you convinced her?'

'She was upset,' he said. 'For a moment I thought you had gone too far, Madame. Her private life is nothing to do with this.'

'Oh yes it is,' she countered. 'I saw her face; she hadn't been happy. She'd been cheated, and she knew it. Will she give the deposition? Will she give evidence?'

'I think so,' he answered. 'I'll try and get the deposition drawn up tonight and we can get it witnessed tomorrow. At least that will guarantee her safety.'

'I'm not interested in her safety,' Antoinette said coldly. 'She hates my husband. Only personal revenge will make her help him. I think she's influenced you, Paul. Has she?'

He said, 'No,' and it was convincing. 'She's a brave woman, and if you want her to help us, you mustn't antagonize her. That's my advice.'

She put on the glasses and picked up the papers. He was dismissed.

The evening was like a play; Kate felt as if she were on stage and an invisible audience was watching. Paul Roulier and Antoinette Vigier were fellow actors. The food was superb, the service silent and impeccable, there was candle-light and beautiful silver, with flowers on the table. The conversation was like dialogue written for the second act of a drama, before tragedy erupted. They talked about the weather, the garden, the shops in Antibes and the difficulty of getting well-trained servants; they discussed the merits of restaurants she'd never heard of, and Antoinette dismissed the Hôtel du Cap with a remark about it being full of Americans. Kate almost left the table when she said it. Oblivious, the other woman went on, 'Of course it's not what it used to be; my late husband knew it well before the war, his parents used to stay there. It was very select then. It was a convalescent home for wounded German soldiers during the war.'

The convoy that had challenged Jean Dulac, with its quota of senior Abwehr officers. . . . London's reluctance to let him attack it. And the bitter opposition of Pierrot to the plan, which only changed to support when he knew that Dulac had been betrayed to the Gestapo. How much did the woman know about that? How much had Eilenburg discus-sed with her? The phrase came floating back through the tinkling voice of Eilenburg's mistress, reminiscing about her last husband's views on the hotel.

'He destroyed the evidence we wanted . . . maybe that's why he was protected afterwards. . . .' In the turmoil she experienced at that meeting, she had heard something vital and overlooked it. What evidence had Pierrot, the traitor and double-agent, destroyed that so benefited the Allies that he was immune from justice? She leaned forward, and suddenly the air of play-acting disappeared. There was no stage, no artificial interlude. Everything was real again and charged with tension. 'Madame Vigier, about the time our network was broken in May 1944, there was a changeover of the garrison at Antibes; some German officers were due to arrive at the Hôtel du Cap. Do you remember anything about them?'

Antoinette Vigier didn't hesitate. 'Oh, yes. We were living here at the time; I remember Christian going up to the hotel to have dinner with some of them. There was a general he was interested in.'

'In what way interested?' Kate asked her. She saw Roulier lean forward and put down his wine glass. He was paying very close attention.

'He didn't believe he was reliable,' she said. 'A number of the old Junker families were anti-Hitler. When he began to look like losing, of course. Christian hated them; he used to say to me, "We are from the ordinary people. These aristocrats only think of themselves. The Führer can't rely on them as he can on the SS." He didn't trust the army, and of course he was right.'

She rang a bell and pushed her chair back. Kate noticed that Paul hadn't moved to help her. She could feel him watching her. 'Let's go into the salon,' Antoinette said. 'We can take our coffee there. And then,' she gave Kate a charming smile, 'Paul can draw up your deposition.' She swept past them out of the dining room. Kate followed quickly, avoiding Roulier.

They sat together and coffee was handed them by the same manservant who had served dinner. Antoinette Vigier gave a little yawn. 'I am tired,' she said. 'Will you excuse me if I go up early and leave you together?'

When they were alone, Paul said, 'You've decided to go through with this? Won't you think again?'

'I've come this far,' Kate said, 'and I'm not going back now. I'm not signing any deposition till I've seen Eilenburg again. When can you arrange it?'

'You've got to tell me why,' he insisted. 'Something she said about the German officers and the general – what did it mean to you?'

'Nothing that's going to help your client,' she said. 'But it might answer a very important question for me. I've got to see him again – God, I let it pass this morning without following it up. What a fool!'

'Why don't you tell me?' he demanded. 'We've worked together all the way on this – Kate, please trust me. What did Eilenburg say that you missed?'

She lifted the lid of the silver cigarette box. Gauloise. She lit one, and the strong tobacco smell evoked him instantly. The sensitive face with the very dark eyes, the lean body and the artist's hands. The pain of that memory brought a hand to her heart in the oldest reflex action of grief. How many times had he lit a cigarette and passed it to her, when they lay side by side?

And that other memory, jostling him out of the way, a man with bright blue eyes and white-blond hair, saying in his Germanic French, 'He had no intention of betraying anything or anyone . . . especially where you were hiding. . . . So he threw himself out of the window.' No, she couldn't trust Paul Roulier any more. His motives and hers were not the same. He wanted a scandal, seeing a political advantage. She wanted the truth about why the man she loved and all her friends had had to die. She got up. 'If you want me to sign a deposition, Paul, I'll do it after I've seen Eilenburg. Now I'm going up to bed. I'm tired too, as it happens. I'll see you in the morning. Good night.'

He stood in front of the door. 'I told you; I don't want you to stay. I don't want you to be involved. Go home; let your people know you've withdrawn from all this, and there won't be any trouble then.'

'I'm sure there won't,' she said quietly. 'But I'm near the answer to a question that's got to be answered. What use I'll make of it depends on what it is. Good night.'

There was no sign of Antoinette Vigier the next morning. When Kate came downstairs there was an empty feel about the house. She wandered through to the salon, and everything was cool and shuttered, as if nobody had been there for a long time. She felt someone behind her and swung round, startled. It was the smooth old manservant, asking if she would like to breakfast in the conservatory.

She said thank you, and followed him. There was no one else in the pretty glass-walled annexe. 'Where is Maître Roulier?' she asked.

'He left early, Madame.' And Madame Vigier herself – she did not come down till midday, was the answer. Kate poured coffee, and pushed the fruit and croissants aside. She didn't feel hungry or rested, in spite of a deep sleep that was near to exhaustion. The conservatory was full of houseplants and exotics. She felt claustrophobic, as if the green growing things that climbed the walls were moving towards her.

The atmosphere of the villa was like the woman who owned it. Beautiful, lavish and distorted, an island of fantasy in the sea of real life.

And then there was the man so much younger than she was, who had brought her here, and was trying to persuade her to leave before the end and abandon the quest. He had said he loved her. 'There's no reason why you should live alone. . . . I could be your lover.' It would be a poisoned love affair, as sick as the passion that motivated the woman in her room upstairs, who'd carried it with her through two marriages and forty years. As twisted as the love Pierrot felt for her, so that he rescued her from the fate he'd brought the others. And yet he'd also loved his crippled wife; she'd seen his tenderness towards her. Sexual desire for Kate hadn't altered his love for the other, helpless woman.

'I've one more thing to do here, and then I shall be taking my wife to a safe place.' His wife had been alive in 1947, but that was so long ago. She hadn't been in the court when Kate gave evidence and he watched her from the dock. He had walked out a free man. And then died in a car crash eight years later. He was alone. She got up hurriedly, and went out into the passage and the large entrance hall. Through into the salon again, searching for a telephone. There it was, discreetly hidden on a side table near the sofa – one of the latest designs, unobtrusive in the midst of bronzes and porcelain and enamelled boxes. She lifted it and dialled enquiries. It didn't take long. A Madame Derain was listed in apartment C, 23 rue de Tivoli in Beaulieu. Kate said thank you, and put the phone back. Apartment C, 23 rue de Tivoli. It had taken her three hours to bicycle there from Nice. So early in the morning, just after curfew was lifted, when there was no traffic on the roads. There was a bell by the fireplace. She pressed it, and the manservant came in, wearing an apron and carrying a cleaning cloth. She got the impression that he resented being rung for by her.

'I need a taxi,' she said. 'Is there a taxi you use nearby?'

'Madame uses her car,' he said. 'I'm afraid I can't help you, Madame.'

'Never mind,' Kate said briskly. 'I'll find one for myself.'

It was a glorious day. She walked quickly down the well-kept drive, anxious to be out of the grounds, as far away from the villa as possible. She wondered whether Antoinette Vigier knew she had left and was watching from behind a curtain in a window above. She didn't look back.

Philippe Derain's widow was sitting with her back to the window. The bright sunshine made a halo of her white hair. She stared at the woman who had announced herself as Madame Alfurd, from England. Her voice was sweet and clear.

'I don't think I know you, Madame,' she said. 'I don't recognize your name.'

'I married after the war,' Kate said.

Philippe's widow had aged very little except for the snow-white crown; her face was pale with the ethereal look of the sick, and her hand when Kate shook it was like a dried leaf. She moved the wheelchair with the touch of a button and it swivelled round. 'Please sit down,' she invited. 'Forgive me for not recognizing you. When did we meet?'

'In May 1944,' Kate answered. 'You and your husband sheltered me from the Gestapo.'

'We sheltered many people,' was the reply. 'What was your name then?'

Kate said, 'I didn't have a name, Madame. Only a code, it

wouldn't mean anything to you. I worked with your husband for a time. You know that Eilenburg is going to be tried for war crimes against the Resistance?'

'Yes.' The voice was unemotional. 'I've read about it and seen it on television. He looked such an old man. I wonder what good it does to bring up the past.'

'A lot of people feel like that,' Kate said. 'But I don't agree with them. He killed my friends, and one of them committed suicide rather than give way to torture. I think he should be punished.'

The lips turned upward in a sad smile. 'What a vengeful person you must be,' she said. 'Nothing can bring them back. Nothing can bring my husband back, and it wasn't the Germans who sabotaged his car. It wasn't a German who stood up in court and tried to get him hanged after the war. Why did you do it? Didn't you care that he saved your life?'

Kate said slowly, 'Why did you pretend not to know me, Madame Derain?'

The thin shoulders lifted slightly. 'I wondered what you wanted, coming here after what you did to Philippe, after all these years. Of course I recognized you. You haven't changed so much, and I had good reason to remember you. Philippe was in love with you, after all.'

'There was nothing between us,' Kate protested.

Again she smiled. 'And if there had been? Do you think I'd have grudged him a little happiness when I couldn't give it to him myself? That wasn't important to me. Why have you come here, Cecilie? I remember the name too; he used to talk about you. Even afterwards when you tried so hard to destroy him.'

'I want to find out the truth,' Kate said. 'Philippe betrayed the network. He worked for the Germans and for Britain. I was Jean Dulac's lover, and by chance I saved him from arrest. Why, Madame Derain? Why did your husband do it? Every word of my evidence was the truth. Who was he really working for?'

'Why didn't you ask London?' came the answer. 'Surely

you knew the answer was with your own people – they didn't let him be convicted because they dared not. So they arranged for a car crash later on.'

'That's impossible,' Kate said slowly. 'Nobody would murder him years later. Why?'

'Because he knew the truth you talk about,' she said. 'The real facts behind the lies and deceptions and betrayals. He was approached to write his memoirs of the war, did you know that? Some friend in the book trade thought it would make a lot of money. Philippe said no, but someone must have heard and been afraid he might be tempted. So the brakes on his car failed on the Grand Corniche, and he went over the edge. I had it investigated privately. The police were not concerned. After all, he was suspected of treason during the war, in spite of being acquitted. People prefer to believe the worst, don't they? His death didn't interest anyone except me. Probably they said, "Serve him right". So the truth died with him. Except that he had talked to me and I know what really happened.'

Kate said after some moments, 'I saw Eilenburg yesterday. He said Philippe destroyed evidence the Germans wanted. Madame Derain, do you know what he meant? It could change everything. It could clear Philippe's name! It could put the guilt where it belongs!'

'And where is that?' the woman asked gently. 'Are you still pursuing vengeance?'

'No. Not vengeance. Justice. I've lived with lies for all these years, because I was persuaded to accept them. I've been the guilty one. I want to make sense of Jean's death; I want to know why a girl I trained with was brutalized and degraded and then shot like a dog, why all those men were killed at the power station, and why an Englishman who couldn't speak a word of French was sent over here, for what? I beg you, tell me what really happened!'

'What will you do with it, if I tell you?'

Kate said, 'I don't know. Make it public if I can.'

Madame Derain examined her fragile hands, twisted the

wedding ring round and round and then said suddenly, 'If an accident was arranged for Philippe, they won't let you speak out.'

'You're the second person who's said that,' Kate said. 'And it's true. I came here and within a few days, I was being followed. But I got away and nobody knows where I am. If you'll give me the information I can protect myself, I promise you.'

She waited; the room was hot and silent and the woman in the wheelchair was very still. At last she spoke. 'Philippe was the real hero,' she said. 'They put up a statue to that foolish man you loved, while my husband's reward was suspicion and shame. You will find a bottle of wine through there, Madame. If we are going to talk about the past, we'll need something to give us courage.'

7

The receptionist said, 'I'm sorry, Madame Alfurd, but the manager is at his house. He won't be back at the hotel until after five o'clock.'

Kate said, 'It's very important; could you phone through and ask him to see me, please?'

The receptionist hesitated. He shrugged slightly. 'I can try him at home,' he said. 'One moment please.' He went into the back office and put through a call. The response amazed him. The manager never interrupted his afternoon with his family unless there was a crisis at the hotel.

He returned and said, 'He's coming, Madame. Please wait in his office here.'

It was a pleasant, businesslike room, in complete contrast to the luxurious foyer beyond. A plain desk, an elaborate telephone system for internal use, two large framed photographs of a pretty woman and two children. She sat down and waited, but not for long. The manager came in, shook hands, smiled with his usual courtesy and took his seat behind the desk.

'I'm sorry to disturb you like this,' she explained. 'It's kind of you to see me.'

'Not at all,' he disclaimed. ('When the lady comes back, you will immediately ring this number.' The lout from

254

SEDEC had slammed that office door till the walls shook.) She was leaning towards him expectantly. He had not made the telephone call. Yet.

'How can I help you? Is something wrong?'

'How much do you know about the hotel during the war? Towards the end, 1944.'

The question surprised him. 'Nothing from personal experience. I was only a child. But its history is well-documented. It was a convalescent home for senior German officers, right up until just before the Allied Invasion down here. It was heavily mined and guarded during the war – in fact one of our gardeners was killed years later when he set off one of the mines they'd buried in the grounds.'

Kate said, 'Was it ever attacked or damaged while they were using it?'

'Oh yes,' he answered. 'Soon after the Allies landed in Normandy some Resistance people broke in and blew up this part of the building. It all had to be rebuilt afterwards.'

'Why did they do that?' she asked. 'Was anyone killed?'

'I don't know for sure. I think it was an attempt to get at the German records which were kept in a safe near here. If so, they failed. Everything was destroyed, and there was a fire. Luckily it was put out in time or the hotel would have been gutted. That's one act of wartime heroism I don't like very much. Think, if that fire had spread!'

'Yes indeed,' Kate said quietly. 'How very lucky it didn't. The people who did it were never caught?'

'I don't believe so,' he answered. 'The hotel was cleared of Germans after that. Madame, may I ask you how long you're staying?'

He was so polite, but the eyes were shrewd. 'May I ask why you ask?' she countered.

He said calmly, 'Because we have a tradition of protecting our clients' privacy. Enquiries have been made about you, and I'm afraid they're too official for me to ignore. I would prefer to report that you had checked out, if you don't mind.'

'I don't mind at all,' she said after a moment. Inevitably

they had got to the hotel. 'But I think it would save everyone a lot of embarrassment if I made that report myself. Did they leave you a number to call?'

'I have it here,' he said, opening a drawer in his desk. 'First you must assure me that there will be no disturbance or scandal that could affect the hotel.'

'It's wonderful that it means so much to you,' she said.

'It is my whole life, Madame.'

'Don't worry. I shall ask the person who called on you to come and see me. Then we will leave together. I'll speak to them from my room.'

She went up in the lift, smiled at a young couple passing on their way to play tennis, and let herself into the room. Fresh flowers again, a shaft of sunlight playing through the blind, coolness and peace. But not for long. She lifted the telephone and asked for the number on the paper the manager had given her.

She waited for him in the bar. It was odd, Kate thought, how calm she felt, how self-confident. A quiet dinner alone in the restaurant, the food delicious, no sense of awkwardness at being without a man. She ordered a brandy, chatted to the head barman for a few minutes, and settled back to wait. She saw him pause in the doorway, and look quickly round for her. Then the glance of recognition and the quickened step as he approached.

For a moment he paused, looking at her. 'Mrs Alfurd? Kate?'

'Hello,' she said. 'Hello, Captain Michaelson. Sit down, won't you.' He had changed, but not so completely that she couldn't recognize him. With an effort. Her memories of him from all those years ago had grown dim. Not as tall as she thought, heavier of course, and with thin fair hair that was mostly white. Well-dressed; French casual clothes, expensive shoes, a very good wrist-watch.

'You haven't changed,' he said. 'It's amazing. When they showed me the photographs of you, I knew at once. Can I order a drink for you?'

'I haven't finished this,' she said. 'Pierre's coming over. Do you like brandy? It used to be gin and tonic, at Lossiemouth.'

He glanced at her. 'Fancy you remembering that,' he said.

'That's my trouble,' Kate answered. 'I've got such a damned good memory. It seems it's finally got me into trouble.'

'I don't see why you say that,' Michaelson said. 'You've been foolish, but there's no real harm done. Luckily they got in touch with me when this business blew up. So I came down from Paris. I've been waiting till you were found. It's good to see you after all this time.'

'It's good to see you too,' she agreed. 'I was expecting some strong-arm goon to turn up. Hardly my old instructor from forty years ago. Before we say anything, I'd like to know where you fit in.'

He smiled; she remembered that rare smile, always wintry even when it did appear.

'You're still as direct as ever, I see. Very well, I'll put myself in the picture for you. I work for my adopted country on a part-time basis now. It used to be full-time, but I'm rather old now, as you appreciate. So I help out, sit in on specialized problems like your appearance out here in connection with Eilenburg's defence lawyer. That upset a lot of people, in England and France. So they asked my advice on how to deal with it. I told them to find you but not to do you any harm.'

She said coldly, 'Were they intending to?'

He shrugged. He'd become very French. Adopted country, he'd said. 'Not any more.' He avoided the question neatly. 'I said they had nothing to fear from you and they believed me. I assured them that you would never lend yourself to anything that would discredit our efforts during the war, or harm Anglo-French relations.'

She actually laughed. 'How very presumptuous of you! Supposing I meant to blow the whole dirty business that happened here sky high, what would you say to that?'

He said, studying his hands and not looking at her, 'I'd be very disappointed that the girl I trained and got to know would stoop so low. Have you any idea how low it would be, Kate? And what real purpose it could serve? I don't think you have.'

'Why don't you tell me?' she suggested. 'Perhaps I know already, perhaps I don't. You were always a good lecturer. Explain it to me.'

'Only if you'll have an open mind. I know how you felt about Jean Dulac. I know how you moved heaven and earth to get Philippe Derain convicted as a traitor. Only someone very strongly motivated would have gone as far as you did. But you were wrong. Derain worked for us from the beginning. Everything he did was with London's knowledge and on their orders.'

'Including betraying his friends in the Resistance? Setting the Gestapo on us?'

He nodded. 'Including that. He had no choice. Jean Dulac brought it on himself, and on the others. He had to be stopped, Kate.'

'Because of the German General who was travelling in that convoy?' she interrupted. 'Because the life of an anti-Nazi German was more valuable than the lives of people who were fighting on our side and risking themselves every day? What was in the safe here, that was worth killing off the Maquis and the Dulac network? And you didn't get it after all, whatever it was, because Derain didn't know how to blow a safe properly, and he wrecked everything!'

'You have a lot of information,' he remarked. 'You've been very active. But it's not quite accurate. Derain didn't try to open the safe. He couldn't. The man sent out specifically from England had been killed, because Dulac disobeyed orders once again and took him on that raid. Poor chap, I remember him very well. A convicted burglar and expert safe-breaker. Killed for nothing. So Derain had to do the best he could, and if we couldn't get the information, he made sure the Gestapo didn't either. You don't know what it was, do you?'

Kate said flatly, 'No, but I shall soon. And that will answer the last question and the worst. The one I tried not to think about for all these years. Why did London send the code message for the Allied Invasion of Europe, knowing it was nearly three weeks premature? They finished Derain's work, and all those Frenchmen died. Are you telling me that those German records, whatever they were, were the reason for that?'

'Yes.' Michaelson answered without hesitation. 'None of this would have been necessary if Jean Dulac hadn't relied on his own vanity and love of glory beyond the broad strategy of winning the war. He is responsible for the tragedy, Kate. That statue in the Place de la Libération is a mockery.' She opened her bag, lit a cigarette. He saw that the lighter flame wavered. 'I'm sorry to say this,' he said. 'I know you loved him.'

She drew on the cigarette, deeper than she should, and the smoke caught her and brought tears to her eyes. Or so she pretended. 'I heard rumours about you,' she said at last. 'When we were training. You fell in love with one of the girls you sent to France; the Gestapo caught her. Was it true?'

'Her name was Lisette,' he said. 'She operated in Paris. Our friend Eilenburg was her interrogator. Are you going to give evidence in his defence?'

She didn't answer. He said, 'Have you given his lawyer a deposition?'

'Not yet. Do I need to, to be safe?'

'I've told you, no. Will you go back to England and forget about this?'

'I'm going to have another brandy. Do join me, Captain Michaelson.'

'My name is Robert; thanks, I will. Take my advice and go home. Leave the past buried.'

She smiled at him and said softly, 'What about the dead? They won't stay quiet; there're too many of them. I found out

259

about another only today. You said Philippe worked for London; he must have been very loyal to keep quiet when he was arrested and tried in a French court. Why did they have to murder him by fixing the brakes on his car? Now he's on my conscience too. Here's our brandy. Thank you, Pierre.' She gave the barman a brilliant smile. He winked to himself as he left the table. Very attractive woman; and another man eating out of her hand. Michaelson had turned red. She watched the embarrassment and wondered if it was shame. 'What was in that safe?'

'A list of the July conspirators. The German General was one of the organizers of the bomb plot to kill Hitler. He had a photocopy of the names and he was using it to recruit from the Staff officers at the hotel. If that plot had succeeded, the war would have been over a year earlier. We wanted that list. When Dulac ruined everything we had to make sure the Gestapo didn't find it.'

'The plot failed,' Kate said slowly. 'Hitler wasn't killed. So that was all for nothing too. They sacrificed all those people to save the General so he could murder Hitler. And it failed. Was he hung with piano wire like the others?'

'He shot himself,' Michaelson answered. Kate lifted her brandy.

'He was luckier than some. Do you know who's paying for Eilenburg's defence?'

'Not precisely. It's been kept very secret, but we believe it's a consortium of neo-Nazis.'

To his amazement she laughed out loud. 'Of course you would think that, wouldn't you? So did I at one time. A secret conspiracy working to undermine the unity of the Western Allies. It's a woman, can you believe it? A very rich woman, who was Eilenburg's mistress during the war. She wants to get him off because for forty years she's been in love with him. He was the only man who was kind to her, she said. She's the widow of a millionaire socialist, and the Fascist Right want to expose her connection with Eilenburg in court because it'll embarrass the government.' She laughed again, but it was bitter laughter. 'Nobody's interested in justice or telling the truth, are they? If I go home, as you suggest, there'll be a trial, and a scandal, and Eilenburg will be sentenced to life imprisonment. But nobody will know the truth. The heroes will stay heroes and the villains will be villains.'

Michaelson looked down at his hands again. The habit irritated her.

'It would be best,' he said.

'Tell me something,' Kate asked him. 'Why did you come to live in France? Why did you become French?'

'Because I felt close to Lisette. I was pushed out to America after training you. I'd gone soft, and it was noticed. I couldn't settle anywhere. So after the war I came here and made it my home. And I've been happy. It's my country now and I love it. That's another reason why I don't want to see the past raked up. There's no death penalty. Just prison, and he'll get that anyway. I've practically guaranteed to take you back to England.'

'I thought you had.' Kate shrugged. So much for all the talk about safety. Do what you're told or else. 'What happens if I won't go?'

He frowned impatiently. 'Nothing. I told you. Be reasonable for heaven's sake.'

'No car accident for me?' she asked softly. 'Did you know Derain was murdered?'

'Yes, we knew. And we knew who was responsible, but what was the point of trying to prove it. . . . You always assume the worst about your own side, don't you – well you're wrong. French interests here in the Midi got rid of him. They believed he might be tempted to write about the past, and too many people had something to hide. He was a good man, Kate, and he knew the risks. Very few career spies like him die in their beds. Incidentally, how do you think his widow lives so comfortably? There's not much money to be made in a bookshop. She's been handsomely looked after, though she doesn't know it.'

'Blood-money,' Kate said slowly. 'All those people who were sacrificed. It's easy for you to rationalize; you can accept the logic of sacrifice, the end justifies the means. I had to see it first hand. Why did they send Julie out? You knew she was a risk; the first time anyone roughed her up she was going to break. She should never have got through. You didn't pass her, did you?'

'No, I recommended she be sent back to the FANYs and told to forget SOE. I'm afraid she was the necessary weak link in the chain.'

'Oh God,' Kate whispered. 'Of course. The fail-safe if anything happened to Derain. Get her arrested and that was the end of the network.'

He said quietly, 'Kate, pause a minute. Julie is one of SOE's heroines. Any evidence you give will take that away from her. Jean Dulac is a hero, so are the Maquis leaders. People are proud of what they did and they believe they suffered and died for a great cause. I believe that too. I had to live with what happened to the girl I loved and she died just like they did. It's taken me a very long time to come to terms but I have, and I've gone on working for the things she died for, if you like. Nobody can stop you pursuing a private vendetta against Jim Reed and Dick Wroxham. You can throw mud at them and give Eilenburg's defence some powerful ammunition. He'll end up as quite a patriot, by the time they've finished. If that's what you want, then go ahead. Think it over. I'll phone you tomorrow morning.'

He got up and she faced him. 'The best possible solution would be no trial at all,' he said. 'Good night, Kate.'

She watched him walk out; he carried himself well.

'Can I get you anything, Madame?' Pierre came over, smiling.

'No thank you,' Kate answered. 'It's such a beautiful night I think I'll go for a walk in the grounds.'

The sea was like black silk, the white swathe of the moonlight made a pathway to oblivion that shimmered to a far horizon. The sound of a slight swell splashing against the walls below was soothing. The gardens behind were lit, and fairylike. The ocean held no menace; she thought, this is the peace that is eternity. No Christian heaven or hell, the conflict continuing into the after-life. Just a gentle sound that never ends and nothing to remember. Are you quiet now, my lover and my friends; are you still and serene, and I've agonized in vain for all these years. Is he right? What will you gain from my peace of mind? You won in the end because Eilenburg lost. And everything he stands for was defeated. That's what you risked your lives for; and so did I. Funny how I've forgotten that. . . . She turned away, leaving the dark sea at her back, and the lights in the trees leading to the hotel were warm and beckoning. She began to walk towards them.

'I'm so glad you decided to come back,' Antoinette Vigier declared. 'We were so worried when you disappeared like that! Weren't we, Paul?'

He said, looking hard at Kate, 'Yes. I imagined you'd thought better of it and gone back to England.'

'I did think about it,' Kate admitted. 'I wondered what my daughter would say, and my friends at home, when it all came out. Then I felt I couldn't run away from my responsibility. So I came back.'

She looked at both of them and smiled. 'We'll have champagne to celebrate,' Antoinette decided. 'Ring the bell, please, Paul. You'll join me, this time?' she asked Kate. She was exquisitely made up, but there were dark shadows under her eyes and her manner was too bright.

'Thank you, that would be lovely,' Kate answered. There was a pause while the champagne was brought in; Antoinette Vigier lit a cigarette, smoking it rapidly.

'What beautiful flowers,' Kate remarked, breaking the silence.

'How kind,' she answered. 'I arrange them myself. I remember when Christian brought me here, the garden was so overgrown, but I found some flowers and tried to make a pretty vase for our room. I'd never done such a thing before,

263

you know. I always threw the dead flowers away when I worked at the hotel. I remember so well thinking how lovely it was to cut them and choose the colours and put them in a vase. So I made a hobby of it. Christian loved flowers. He said a house wasn't a home without them!' She turned her attention suddenly to Paul Roulier. 'When can I see him? How much longer have I got to hide away?'

'Not too long,' he said. 'But you've got to be patient, Madame. First, we arrange a second meeting with Madame Alfurd. Then we have her deposition filed, and after that, you can come out into the open. It won't be too long.'

'It seems unbearably long to me,' she said. 'I try to imagine how he looks – those newspaper photographs were so awful. But they were taken so he'd look old and sinister on purpose. He was so handsome, Madame Alfurd. You wouldn't believe how beautiful he was! Of course, you met him, didn't you? How stupid of me, I forgot.' She gave a trilling laugh, as if she were talking about a social encounter at a party long ago.

'Yes I did,' Kate said quietly. 'But I'm afraid I didn't take much notice of his looks.'

The eyes darkened, and there was no smile any more. 'He didn't hurt you, did he? He was perfectly polite and let you go. Here's the champagne. My favourite drink. Whether it's to celebrate or to mourn. When my two husbands died, I drank it after their funerals. I'll drink to my real husband now. To Christian. And to justice!' She drained the glass and set it down. Kate left hers untouched.

She said, 'Madame Vigier, I want to make my position quite clear. I'm going to give evidence at the trial, but not because I want to help your husband. It'll save us both embarrassment if you stop talking about your private life. If you'll excuse me, I think I should go back to the hotel. Paul, would you be kind enough to give me a lift?' At the door she said, 'Good night, Madame Vigier.' Antoinette Vigier lifted her head and looked at her; then she turned away without answering. The door closed and she was alone. The glass of champagne was still on the table where the Englishwoman had left it. She got up, crossed over and picked up the glass. She used a foul epithet, dredged up from her gutter past, and then said softly, 'But she'll do what we want, my darling, so I'll drink it for her. To you, my love.'

'If you've finally made up your mind,' Roulier said as they drove, 'then I won't try and argue any more. Are you certain you can believe him?'

'Quite certain,' Kate said. 'I told you, he was my conducting officer, Robert Michaelson. There's nothing they can do to stop me. And don't argue, Paul, because I'm not going to change my mind. I shan't go back to the villa, there's no point; she and I will only fall out if I do. She's crazy, isn't she?'

'Only on this one subject,' he answered. 'On business, she's very sane indeed. That's why both husbands left her everything. They knew she'd manage her own affairs better than anyone. She's even richer since the last one died.'

'It hasn't made her very happy,' Kate said. The car drew up at the entrance. He turned to her, and said, 'I meant what I said the other night. When it's over, will you think about me?'

'No, Paul,' Kate answered. 'There's no future for a woman of my age with a man of yours. When it's over, I've got to make my own life. Look for someone younger, my dear. You'll find her. Good night.'

It was a short walk from his cell to the interview room. Eilenburg didn't try to hurry. 'Conserve your strength,' he told himself every day. 'Calm your mind and relax your body. Sleep as well and eat as well as you can. Your day is coming and you must be ready.' She had written to him, and the letter had been palmed to him, rolled into a tiny cylinder, the last time his lawyer came to visit. He read it over and over again. Forty years, and he could visualize her as if she were beside him. Slight and no higher than his shoulder, with those liquid brown eyes that gazed at him. A passionate child who never questioned but only gave, and gave again. As she was giving now, when life had parted them for so many years. She was rich and able to take care of him as he had taken care of her. She had never stopped loving him, and one day soon they would be together. She signed herself 'Toinette'. When he read it he cried. Flanked by a prison officer he shuffled along to the interview room. They were sitting there waiting. The lawyer and the woman. Cecilie. He smiled. How angry he had been when he was forced to release her. How fortunate, as it turned out, because what she would say in open court would make all the difference to his sentence. More than that, it would vindicate his life. By charging him with war crimes, the old enemy would condemn itself. He came forward and they stood up. The warder was beside him, stony-faced and sharp-eyed. The lawyer came towards him, held out his hand. This time there was no note. The woman Cecilie didn't move; last time she had ignored him, turned her back rather than touch him. Her hatred was there still, as strong as the day she defied him in his office at the Villa Trianon.

A strange ally for Antoinette, this woman who hated him so much. But hated the ruthless betrayal of her own side more. He sat down. The exchange began.

'How are you feeling?' from the lawyer.

'Quite well. I sleep a lot. I read the Bible.' A change of expression from the woman. Suspicious, contemptuous. He said, 'I'm not converted. It's all they allow me. To me it's still Jewish fairy tales.'

'Madame Alfurd has some more questions she would like to ask you.'

He gave her a twisted smile, sly and cynical. 'I'll do my best to answer. How are you, Cecilie? You look well today. What do you want to know?'

Kate could feel her heart beating faster and faster. The room was airless and smelt of prisons. The old man opposite watched her with the half-smile on his face and the vivid blue eyes probing into hers.

266

So beautiful, Antoinette Vigier had said, he loved flowers. A house wasn't a home without them. 'Tell me the truth,' Kate said at last. 'Do you regret anything you did?'

The head came up in pride. 'I regret nothing. I did my duty for my country. I would do the same again.'

She thought of Michaelson and looked down at her hands, imitating him. 'Why didn't you add Heil Hitler,' she said.

The voice was gently mocking. 'Because you've said it for me.'

She took a deep breath and steadied herself. She pushed back the chair, which scraped across the bare floor. 'That's all I wanted to know. At least you're honest. I shan't be seeing you again before your trial. Goodbye, Standartenführer.' He saw her hand stretch out to him across the table, and he was surprised. It was an unexpected victory for him. He clasped it. Her grip was firm and he winced. She turned away, speaking to the lawyer over her shoulder. 'I'm going outside. I'll wait in the car if you want to talk to him.'

The sunshine was bright and hot; she wanted to run but she was breathless and trembling. She walked away down the street. The car park was in the opposite direction. The hand that had shaken his was tightly clenched as if in protest. When she hailed a taxi cruising past, it was still a fist. She got inside and sank back against the seat. She felt dizzy and weak. The driver had to ask her twice before she answered.

'Nice airport.' She put her head back and closed her eyes.

In the mirror the driver saw his passenger sitting with her eyes shut and her lips moving. Maybe she was praying. The world was full of nutters, he decided, and thought about the very big fare he was going to charge for going all the way to Nice. He didn't see the slow tears that rolled down her face, and the names were soundless. 'Lisette,' she whispered last of all, 'I didn't know you, but it's for you too. Now you can all rest in peace.'

At the airport she was taken into a private lounge. He was waiting for her. He still held himself well, she thought. He led her to a sofa. 'Are you all right?'

267

'Yes, I'm all right.'

'Do you want anything? You look shocked.'

'Here, this belongs to you.'

He had a box ready, and he took the ring and shut it away quickly. 'Did you manage it? Are you sure?'

'I'm not sure,' Kate answered. 'But you'll know soon enough if I didn't. I'd like some coffee if that's possible.'

He hesitated, put a hand on her shoulder. 'I'll order some. You just relax. It's all over now. You'll be home in a few hours. I've arranged for a car to meet you at Gatwick and take you to Amdale.'

She turned her head and said wearily, 'I'd like to detour and pick up my dog, if that's not too much trouble.'

'No trouble at all,' Robert Michaelson said gently.

It was reported on the inside column of the fifth page of *The Times*, as part of Foreign News. Christian Eilenburg, the wartime 'Butcher of Marseilles', had died in his sleep in prison. It was a brief item, and it almost escaped Colonel Reed's notice. As soon as he read it, the telephone began to ring. 'Mental telepathy, old chap,' he said to Wroxham on the other end. 'I was just going to ring you. Thank God for that!'

'Yes, it's saved a lot of trouble,' Wroxham agreed. 'There's not much Mrs Alfurd can do about it now.'

There was a billboard up outside the cottage. For Sale, in bright red letters. Dorothy winced when she saw it, parked the car, and with a sigh opened the gate and went to the front door. Her mother opened it. 'Hello, Dorothy – you're looking very well. I've just made some tea.'

They sat together in the neat little sitting room. There was an air of impermanence about the place, Dorothy noticed. Pictures and ornaments were missing. There could have been suitcases in the hall. She nerved herself to bring up the subject once more. 'Mother, about this move to France, are you quite sure you know what you're doing?'

'Yes, quite sure,' Katharine Alfurd said. 'Contracts were signed for this place this afternoon, so there's nothing to keep me here any longer.'

'I don't know how you can just walk away from your home like this,' her daughter protested. 'You and Daddy lived here all your married life. Peter and I and the boys aren't that far away, and you've got friends and neighbours all round . . . what are you going to do living on your own in a village in the South of France . . . it's so expensive!'

'Not really,' her mother explained. 'One can live very simply – I've got a marvellous price for the cottage and there's no need to worry about money. It's a sweet little place, and you and the boys can come out and stay with me.' She smiled, and it was genuinely affectionate. 'I mean that, darling. I'd love to take the boys round the coast and show them some of the lovely fishing villages. We could have such fun!'

'Peter thinks it's crazy,' Dorothy said again.

'He'll get used to the idea,' Katharine Alfurd said. 'I'm lonely here, Dorothy. It's got too many memories of your father and I was getting a bit odd, talking to myself round the place. Making a clean break is what I need, if I'm going to have any kind of life now that he's dead. I won't be sorry to see the back of Amdale. Polly will love living in Valbonne. It's full of rabbit holes!' She laughed with pleasure at the idea. 'More tea?'

'No, thank you.' Her daughter glanced at her watch. Nearly an hour and a half and she ought to be getting home soon. I wish she wouldn't do this, she thought. It makes me feel so guilty, as if I've failed to look after her properly. But what else could I do? She's so independent. . . . Maybe in a way it'll be a relief, not having to come over and phone up all the time. . . . I shouldn't think like that. I really shouldn't. . . .

Katharine said, 'Now that the sale is definite, I want you to have the furniture.'

Dorothy went red. 'Oh, I couldn't – all your things. . . .'

'I don't want them,' she said. 'They wouldn't look right in my little house. I'm going to have a lot of fun finding the right pieces down there. Queen Anne would look ridiculous. I want you to take everything and what you don't want, sell and use the money. That would make me really happy. Darling, look at the time! Shouldn't you be getting back before Peter comes home?'

'Oh Lord, yes, I suppose so.' Dorothy picked up her bag, looked round, bit her lip and said, 'Mum, it was staying with that friend of yours that brought all this on, wasn't it? You've never been the same since.'

'No,' Katharine said gently, 'I think that's right. I seemed to get my life into perspective. All of a sudden the dead were buried and I was free.' She saw the confusion on her daughter's face and put her arm round her. 'Only a figure of speech. Come on, off you go. Give Peter my love, and lots of love to the boys. I've got a lot to do in the next week or so, but we'll keep in touch. Bye, darling.' She kissed her, and it wasn't a token any more. She came to the door, caught up the little terrier, and waved her daughter out of sight. Together they went through and out into the garden at the back. Soon the ordered beds and the neat lawn would be exchanged for a rocky hillside garden, heavy with the scent of pines and wild thyme. The mild English climate would be a memory, the scorching Mediterranean sun a loved companion through most of the year.

She held the little dog in her arms and watched the sun set red behind the English oak trees. 'He didn't die for three days,' she said. 'It could have been natural causes after all. I'll never know and it doesn't matter. All that matters is I'll never hear voices on the wind again. And you and I, Polly, are going to start a new life.'

She turned back to the cottage and went inside. Soon afterwards the sun went down.

EVELYN ANTHONY

Evelyn Anthony is one of Britain's bestselling thriller writers and her books are available from Arrow. You can buy them from your local bookshop or newsagent, or you can order them direct through the post. Just tick the titles you require and complete the form below.

☐	ALBATROSS	£1.75
☐	THE ASSASSIN	£1.95
☐	THE AVENUE OF THE DEAD	£1.75
☐	THE DEFECTOR	£1.75
☐	THE GRAVE OF TRUTH	£1.95
☐	THE LEGEND	£1.95
☐	THE MALASPIGA EXIT	£1.95
☐	THE OCCUPYING POWER	£1.95
☐	THE POELLENBERG INHERITANCE	£1.95
☐	THE RENDEZVOUS	£1.95
☐	THE RETURN	£1.95
☐	THE COMPANY OF SAINTS	£1.95
☐	VOICES ON THE WIND	£2.25

Postage _____

Total _____

ARROW BOOKS, BOOKSERVICE BY POST, PO BOX 29, DOUGLAS, ISLE OF MAN, BRITISH ISLES.

Please enclose a cheque or postal order made out to Arrow Books Limited for the amount due including 15p per book for postage and packing for orders within the UK and for overseas.

Please print clearly

NAME...

ADDRESS...

....

Whilst every effort is made to keep prices down and to keep popular books in print, Arrow Books cannot guarantee that prices will be the same as those advertised here or that the books will be available.